DESTITUTE

Doris trembled as she grabbed the sides of the luxurious leather chair in the Dunbar's stately library. The family's lawyer apologetically said, "Your father lost your home on a business deal before he died. You will have to move . . . with no money for the future."

How could these great trials be overwhelming her? Her nineteen-year-old brother had just married a wicked, street-wise dancer . . . her stepmother was determined to make her life miserable . . . her stern, unfeeling fiancé offered no sympathy and urged her to sever family ties and responsibilities . . . and the care of the younger children had fallen to her.

Could anyone offer any hope for Doris's endless troubles? Could there be an answer beyond the thunderstorms in her life?

Tyndale House books by Grace Livingston Hill.
Check with your area bookstore for these best-sellers.

LIVING BOOKS ®

JOB'S NIECE

LIVING BOOKS ®
Tyndale House Publishers, Inc.
Wheaton, Illinois

This Tyndale House book
by Grace Livingston Hill
contains the complete text
of the original hardcover edition.
NOT ONE WORD
HAS BEEN OMITTED.

Copyright © 1930 by J. B. Lippincott Company
Copyright © renewed 1958 by Mrs. Ruth H. Munce
All rights reserved

Living Books is a registered trademark of Tyndale
House Publishers, Inc.

J. B. Lippincott edition published 1930
Tyndale House edition/1993

Cover artwork copyright © 1993 by Bruce Emmett

Library of Congress Catalog Card Number 93-60011
ISBN 0-8423-1145-9

Printed in the United States of America

99 98 97 96 95 94 93
 8   7   6   5   4   3   2   1

AT half past midnight Doris Dunbar was still sitting at the desk in the library, her head bent over a paper on which were many columns of figures. She was surrounded by piles of bills in orderly rows, covering not only the top of the big old desk, but also several neighboring chairs; a regular blizzard of bills, long overdue, some of them many times duplicated, with little impertinent foot-notes of reminders. The lamp-light fell on the slender figure touching to bronze the hair that was folded in wide burnished bands about the symmetrical young head. That was the first thing that one noticed about Doris, her glorious uncut hair, that, nevertheless, did not give her an air of being out of date. When she lifted her head to reach a fat pile of bills from one of the large department stores, the light glanced sharply on the white oval of her cheek and brought out the blue shadows under her tired eyes, giving to her face a look of delicacy that was almost startling.

Doris found the amount of another bill and set it down in round clear figures below her last column, catching her breath and drawing her delicate brows with a troubled frown as she sent the forceful pencil through its calculations and set down the appalling result. She paused a moment dejectedly and glanced up at the remaining piles of bills on her left, shook her head sorrowfully, and then went at her task once more, her pencil flying rapidly, until the sharp click of the latch in the door as it was released made her start and look up.

In the doorway in her nightgown with a trifling pink kimono flung about her shoulders, stood Doris' sister, Rose. Her arms were outspread from frame to frame of the doorway as if she were half afraid and were clutching for support. There was a mingling of defiance and fright in the attitude of her dark bobbed head, shingled close in the back with one heavy wavy lock hanging over her left eye.

"Doris Dunbar, what on earth are you doing down here at this time of night?" she challenged excitedly. "And in *this room!* The very first night Daddy was taken away! I think you are *terrible!*"

Her voice broke in a sob and she tossed back the wavy lock of hair resentfully showing big frightened eyes.

Doris half rose, startled, and looked at her with troubled eyes.

"Why Rose, dear! I thought you were asleep!"

"Asleep! How could I sleep, with Florence carrying on in her room across the hall, moaning like a sick baby? And you, not coming to bed hour after hour! I don't believe I shall ever sleep again! I'm frightened! I don't see what life has to be this way for, anyway. It's *awful!* I wish we were *all* dead! I wish we'd *never been alive!*"

"Hush, dear! You're all excited! Come, I'll put these things away and turn out the light and we'll go upstairs."

"I don't want to go upstairs. I shall scream murder if I have to hear Florence moan once more! I know I shall.

I can't stand it!" And she suddenly slumped sobbing into a chair.

"I can't stay in this terrible room. I see Daddy's dead face all the time. Let's go, quick! What are you waiting for?"

"I must put these papers away, dear. It won't take but a minute. I can't leave them out. Hannah is so curious."

"What does it matter? What are they anyway?"

"They are bills, Rose, Daddy's bills. Awful bills!" she said with a long drawn sigh and a return of the trouble to her eyes. "But we don't want Hannah to see them. She talks so. She would tell everything she knew."

"Bills?" said Rose resentfully. "What are bills? What does anything matter now? Come, quick! I'm all trembling! This room is terrifying! Why should you care about bills? And *to-night!*"—reproachfully. "It doesn't seem respectful to Daddy."

"They've got to be paid," said Doris sorrowfully, "and Mr. Hamilton is coming to-morrow to go over everything with us."

"Well, let him pay them then, isn't that a lawyer's business? It certainly isn't yours."

"It's got to be somebody's business, Rose, and you know Florence isn't in any condition to look after business."

"Oh, Florence!" said Rose scornfully. "She isn't in any condition to look after anything and never was. I wonder why Daddy ever married her."

"Don't!" said Doris sharply. "This is no time to criticize our father. I know he thought he was doing it for our good. I remember he told me so when I was a child. He said he wanted me to know that he never would have brought another woman to take our mother's place if he had thought he could bring us up right without a mother."

Rose curled a trembling lip:

"Pretty mother she's been! She's nothing but a baby!"

Doris wheeled upon her sister:

"Rose, you must stop. It is not our place to go back into the past and criticize. We must see to it that we don't make any mistakes ourselves, and I guess we will have enough to do that way without trying to fix up mistakes of the past. We're going to have to face some pretty big problems the next few days, and the less bitterness we have in our hearts the better we can do it."

"What do you mean, problems?" asked Rose blinking out from under her lock of hair. "Is there anything I don't know about?"

"I am afraid there are a good many things we don't any of us know yet," sighed Doris, laying the neat piles of bills crosswise upon each other in the open desk drawer. "Here are all these first, and they're bad enough. Rose, there are over three thousand dollars worth of just *little* bills here, and some of them have been running for months, and as many as five or six notices have been sent begging for the money."

"But I don't understand! Why didn't Daddy pay them?"

"I'm afraid he didn't have the money, dear," Doris answered in a sad little voice.

"How ridiculous!" flamed Rose. "Daddy was rich! Why, look at the mink coat he bought Florence at Christmas! Look at the rock crystals he bought me,— and your little car."

Doris spread out her hands pathetically:

"The bills for them are all here, Rosie, every one! And your silver slippers, and the hats we got last Fall, and the new dining-room set, and Ned's radio—*all!* Everything that's been bought lately! And there's only *one payment* made on my car! It isn't mine at all! They have threatened to take it away! *Oh, Rose!*"

"I can't bear it!" screamed Rose. "Let's get out of this room! I don't believe it! Daddy wouldn't do a thing like that!"

"Daddy didn't mean to, I'm sure. Things got tangled up. He couldn't help it, I'm positive. There was some investment that failed—I've gone far enough to find that out. Come, I'm ready now."

"Well, why don't we pay them right away then?" asked Rose half angrily. "I'm sure I don't think it's nice toward Daddy not to get them paid up. Couldn't Mr. Hamilton sell something? Didn't Daddy have bonds and things?"

"I don't know yet," said Doris miserably. "I've only found debts."

"Doesn't Florence know?" asked Rose sharply. "It's her place to. She was his wife. Have you asked her?"

"She goes into hysterics whenever I speak of it. I tried twice yesterday. And she would order the most expensive things for the funeral. I couldn't seem to make her understand. You see, Mr. Hamilton had hinted to me that Daddy was in trouble financially, but that he would see us through till things were straightened out. It is awfully embarrassing."

"But what did Florence say when you told her?"

"Oh, she just cried and said that I was dishonoring my father by not wanting to have everything just as it ought to be for his funeral. I had to stop."

"Of course you did, Dorrie! She's a selfish pig. She could understand if she wanted to. She doesn't want to see things as they are. Daddy has kept things smooth and comfortable for her all these years and now she thinks we ought to. But I'm not going—"

Doris stopped the words by laying a soft hand over her sister's lips:

"Don't, dear! I can't bear any more to-night. Come, let's go to bed. You come over into my room and then you can't hear Florence so clearly. I wonder why Ned doesn't come? He might have stayed at home to-night!"

"I should think so!" said Rose indignantly. "He's another! He wants his way almost smoothed before him. Have you told Ned?"

"Yes, I tried to tell him a little before dinner to-night while Florence was upstairs, but he just had time to whistle and say, 'Hard luck Kid,' and that was all. Then Florence came in and began to fuss about dinner not being ready on time, and after dinner he went out."

"Yes, that's the way Ned always does, just acts as if everything ought to go on right without his doing anything. Just shirks all responsibility no matter what comes. He makes me tired. I don't see why we have to have all this trouble." And Rose caught her breath in a sob again.

"Hush, dear! You'll wake the children. They must be asleep."

"Oh, yes, I heard John talking in his sleep. He kept the radio going till I thought I would go wild, some man telling how to make an aeroplane or something. I went in and turned it off and then I heard him calling out in his sleep something the man had said. He's an awful kid. Florence just hates him. I heard her say he'd simply got to go away to school now Dad was gone, she couldn't have him around."

Doris' round chin set firmly:

"Well, he *won't* go off to school," she said decidedly. "Not if Florence has to go herself."

"How'll you help it?" asked Rose, nestling down comfortably in her sister's bed. "When Florence sets her mind on anything she's an awful bore till it's accomplished. By the way, Jean has a sore throat," Rose roused to say. "I made her gargle with salt and water when she went to bed, but I guess somebody ought to do something if we don't want her to get tonsillitis again."

"Of course!" said Doris in a weary voice. "I wonder what I did with that medicine. Oh, here it is. I'll go in and give her some. You go to sleep, Rose, I'll be back in a minute."

Rose, comforted, nestled down once more among the pillows and was soon asleep, a tear still glistening on her round smooth cheek. Only sixteen and so eager for life. Tears did not seem to belong on the velvet of her radiant skin. One longed to shelter and defend her. There was a sweet petted droop to her rosebud mouth as she slept, one rounded arm thrown back over her head on the pillow, the soft rippling lock of hair straying over her white forehead boyishly, the breath coming gently between the parted lips. Rose was beautiful to look at as a bud just opening. Beautiful, and like something made to be taken care of, not for use.

Doris sighed as she returned from caring for the little ten-year-old sister, and stood for a moment looking at Rose, with a sudden sickening conviction that while she might sympathize more than Ned had done, there was little more to be expected of her than of her brother in the way of real help in this time of crisis.

Doris took her braids down and brushed them slowly, mechanically, trying not to hear the low monotonous moaning from the front room, not realizing that a tear had stolen out and was making its slow course down her cheek. She was inexpressibly tired and downhearted. The future looked unbearably black. If only Ned were older, or would rouse to the necessity of doing something about things!

She was just turning out the light when she heard the front door latch, and throwing her kimono about her went to the hall to speak to her brother. Somehow she longed inexpressibly for a word, or even just a look of comfort and assurance.

But Ned came stumbling up the stairs without apparently having waited to lock the door or turn out the light, his overcoat still on, his hat on the back of his head.

She leaned over the railing and spoke to him in a low tone, but he came straight on not seeming to notice her till he reached the landing and was face to face with her. Then he gave her a bleared vague stare with eyes that were bloodshot and wild, and pressed past her rudely:

"Get outta my way—," he grumbled thickly, "always some women around in the way wherever a man steps."

She stepped back sharply and watched him with startled eyes. There had been an unmistakable odor of liquor as he passed. Had Ned been drinking? Was there to be no end to the horrors of this day? He was not himself! She had never seen her brother like that before, nor thought it possible for him to get into that condition!

She stood for a moment looking down the dark hall toward his door, but no sound came save a dull thud as if he had fallen fully dressed upon his bed and lain as he had fallen.

It seemed as if each moment passed like a century while she stood and felt the foundations of her life quiver under her. She did not cry out as she longed to do. She stood perfectly still till her strength began to come back, and then she went into her room and got into her bed. She felt heavy all over like lead. She thought she would never be able to sleep again. She could not even think. She was like one stunned.

But outraged Nature will have revenge, and sleep

presently stole upon the poor burdened child and erased her troubles for a little while.

Sometime before the first dawning of the morning she was brought sharply back to consciousness by a terrific scream piercing through her oblivion, shattering the darkness and peace, and precipitating her spirit into turmoil and terror once more.

She roused and sat up staring about her trying to remember what had happened, and to identify the sound which had roused her.

And now she knew it was her stepmother sobbing aloud and calling out hysterical plaints of self-pity; a self-centred woman giving way utterly to her nerves, unable or perhaps unwilling, to take command of herself and behave in a womanly way.

There was something terrifying, almost repulsive, in the sound of that grown woman giving way to her feelings without thought or care of those who suffered with her. She who should have been their stay and comfort now in the loss of their beloved father had turned baby and forsaken them.

And now the remembrance came of the little sick sister sleeping alone in the room adjoining the step-mother's. She would waken and be frightened. She must go to her! She must do something to stop those horrible sounds! The servant would hear! Her cheeks burned with shame. She would talk about it outside the house. Why, the neighbors would hear. They could hardly help it. It was like the cry of a lost soul, a voice from the tomb. It must be stopped.

Doris sprang from her bed and, catching up her kimono, went with swift steps toward her stepmother's door.

It was open and Mrs. Dunbar lay with her arms spread

out across her bed crying and sobbing in a most blood-curdling tone:

"Oh! Oh! Oh! Ohhhhhhhhh! I'm all aloooooooooo-one! I'm all alone in the world! Oh, *why* did you leave me?"

"Florence! Stop that this minute!" Doris spoke in a calm commanding voice. But the moaning and crying only grew louder.

Doris walked swiftly over to the bed, switched on the light and bent over her stepmother, speaking quietly and pleadingly, but the voice went on louder and louder, although that had not seemed at first possible:

"What shall I dooooo? Oh-h-h! Whhhhhhat shall I do?" she inquired in a frenzied scream. Doris saw that she was quite beside herself, and that pleadings and commands were alike useless.

With set lips she hurried across the room and shut the window. Then she went swiftly to the bathroom and returned with a pitcher of cold water.

She stood over her stepmother holding the pitcher and essayed once more to reach her reason.

"Mother!"

Her voice was husky.

It was the first time she had ever called her "Mother." It had been Mrs. Dunbar's wish when she was married that the children should call her Florence. She said they would feel more as if she were one of them if they did. Now it seemed to Doris that she was forcing the very stronghold of her own soul to speak that sacred word to this wild weak child of a woman. But she forced herself to speak it again, more clearly this time:

"Mother—please—!"

She was interrupted by a piercing scream from the frenzied woman.

"No! No! I *won't* be called that!" she sobbed and then screamed again in rising crescendo.

Doris in her panic remembered an article she had once read on hysteria and catching up the ice pitcher she flung its contents straight into her stepmother's face; then drew back frightened at what she had done.

Mrs. Dunbar gasping and spluttering came upright at once in her bed, her screams for the instant quenched, but her anger rising swiftly:

"You—wicked—girl!" she gasped, springing from her bed and shaking her long drenched hair out of her blinded eyes:

"You wicked, wicked—girl! What would your father say to your treating his wife this way? Oh-h-h! I've no one to protect me," she wailed with an angry sob.

Doris stood against the wall, the pitcher still in her hand, the other hand pressed against her wildly beating heart, watching her angry stepmother, realizing that she had done an unpardonable act, and wondering if after all she had been justified. She was half ready to fall on her knees and beg her stepmother's pardon, till the high plaintive tone rose into a hysterical scream once more:

"I'm *nobody, nothing* in this house any more! You, who ought to be my support and stay, your father's eldest daughter,—*you* are trying to *drown me!*—You—"

But her eloquence was suddenly interrupted by a hysterical giggle, and looking up startled Doris saw John in his pajamas, his hair ruffled into a tousle, standing in the doorway, a broad grin on his impish young face.

The stepmother heard the giggle and looked at the doorway. While she looked there came the others, Rose in her pink kimono, eyes dewy with sleep, little Jean trailing a blanket around her, her eyes full of fright; and back of them all, his overcoat and hat still on, a strange dull look in his glassy eyes, tottered Ned uncertainly.

There was an instant of utter silence as they faced each other, and then Mrs. Dunbar, still gasping and spluttering, roused to a full sense of her predicament:

"Get out of my room this minute," she shouted furiously, stamping her bare foot with as much dignity as was possible in her drenched condition. "Get out! Every one of you! I shall never forget this. Oh, you wicked, wicked girl! GET OUT!"

They melted precipitately before her violence and stood in a huddled group in the hall, a kind of hysterical misery upon them, while the echo of her slammed door reverberated through the house.

John recovered first.

"Gee, but she looked funny!" he burbled. "You caught her right in the middle of a scream, Dorrie!"

Doris shivered.

"Oh, I ought not to have done it," she said pathetically, "but I didn't know what else to do."

"Good work, Doris!" muttered Ned thickly. "Time the old girl had a ducking! Wisht I'd been here to he'p you," and he stumbled back down the hall to his room. The others looked after him with startled, questioning eyes. They had never seen their brother like this before.

Doris suddenly roused to the fact that slim little Jean was shivering:

"Get back to bed, quick, Kiddie. You'll get an awful cold. Your feet are bare. Here, pull that blanket around you, and hurry. I'll bring you a hot-water bottle."

It was a half hour before Jean was soothed, quieted, warm, and Doris crept back chilled and sorrowful to the bed where Rose had already fallen asleep again.

Doris buried her face in the pillow and felt that life was more than she could bear. She was borne down by a sense of shame over what she had dared to do. She felt degraded and humiliated, and the morrow loomed grim and portentous. What further revelations and trials did it hold? What was to become of them all?

EIGHTEEN miles away on the other side of the city from the Dunbar house, and quite on the outer rim of the most charming suburb, is a beautiful estate. At night the house seems like a castle against the deep, starred blue of the midnight sky. Half-hidden from view among the trees of the hillside, terraces lead down to velvet lawns, which stretch away to wildness and sweet woods again before emerging to the public road, as if the owner thought to make within, a retreat as near to heaven as this world may hope to come. The windows look away in one direction to a far river winding silverly along for many miles in daytime, and at night, a pathway for the boats with twinkling lights that ply back and forth to the shadowy purple distant hills, or to the glimmering city in the distance.

It is still in this great house, and very restful, and the air of the mountain is good to breathe. One wonders that so near the city there is still left all this vast loveliness belonging to one man.

There is a stately room of fine proportion, formally furnished with marvellous treasures from the four quarters of the earth, for formal occasions; a lordly dining hall where many of the great of the day have dined in their time, and where not a few of the questions of the day have been discussed, settled, and wires pulled that brought about nationwide crises.

But there is a living-room, long and wide and home-like, with a great fireplace and deep chairs; where the flickering flames are reflected in ancestral fenders and tongs and andirons of heavy brass, and the deep rugs hush the footfalls of the well-trained servants, who see that everything is at hand when needed. There the deep rich glow from shaded lamps brings out the gleam of rare books in hand-tooled bindings, books lining the walls half-way around. There a grand piano stands with lifted lid like a beloved friend, and the windows look out at night into the many stars.

In this room, that same night, long after midnight, sat Angus Macdonald, facing a problem that perplexed him as truly as if he had the weight of the whole Dunbar family on his shoulders.

Angus Macdonald's paternal ancestors had made their money in gingham, and there were no piles of unpaid bills on the great Renaissance table just behind him, which held the costly lamp of carved jade. The price of some of the trifling ornaments on the cabinet across the room, or even the worth of a single one of some of those rare old volumes in the bookcase would have cleared all Doris' bills away and left her something over, to live on. So his trouble was not financial.

But Angus Macdonald's maternal ancestors had made their brains living on oatmeal porridge in attics while they carved their brilliant sturdy way through the University; and they had left him a heritage of wisdom and common sense, and worst of all a conscience, which is a hard thing to have to carry around in these modern days.

Angus could not go the way of all the earth and be satisfied. He had to measure and mark his going by the old rule of right and wrong, by the rule of love and the fear of God.

And there was a girl—there has always been a woman, since the days of Eve, who lends herself to the devil's use—a girl, beautiful as the morning, who might have been a daughter of Lucifer himself so fair she was, so sparkling, so daring, so full of symmetry both of mind and body, she was like a wonderful magnet drawing all men to her side and holding them. She had drawn him.

Why did she want him? He was not her kind. There was not in her the fear of God nor the knowledge of right and wrong. They were to her but ancient traditions, lingering remnants of a time when the world was in its infancy. She laughed his traditions and sanctities to scorn with a voice like a silver ribbon and a smile like the light of a star, and bade him race with her down a long green sward of joyous fancy. She said there was no such thing as right and wrong. Right was your own will. Wrong was to be subservient to any one or anything. She had teeth like perfect pearls that caught the lustre of the day when she smiled. Her lips were ruby red. The kind of red he knew was unnatural. Theoretically he hated it. Yet he found himself fascinated by the curl of those same vivid lips, so perfectly formed, so emphasizing the natural charm of the flesh as to call attention to their perfectness. Her sinuous slim body clothed in exquisite films of garments that revealed her grace of motion was adorable. Her costumes did not seem reprehensible, as they would have done if worn by some more awkward sister. They were a part of her, as if they were born with her, as if she were clothed in a garment of light. So subtly had she led him on that his very disapproval openly voiced toward the abbreviated garments of other fashionable women, refused to come and stand as witness against her when his conscience called. What was there about Tamar Engadine that always made him excuse whatever she did? He knew her ways were not his ways, her habits of life all wrong according to his standards. Yet more and more she was coming to seem the one altogether desirable in the whole world for him, and he was beginning already to plan how he might induct her into his ways of thinking, mould and fashion her into the strong true woman he desired for his mate. It all seemed perfectly possible, when he looked at her; and yet he had made little headway so far in moulding her. In fact when he was with her she almost seemed to have moulded him, sturdy Scotch stock though he came from. What did it mean? Would it always be so? Would she mould and lead him, not he her, if their ways led together?

It had been weeks since any such thoughts had come into his mind. He had been led hither and yon in her golden wake. She had said come, and he had gone. From one to another of her habitual frivolities he had been her attendant, well pleased to be doing her will; humoring her whim of the moment while he watched her and thought what it would be to have her for his very own, that loveliness made sacred for him, his to care for and cherish. She would not want to flit from one man's arms to another when she was his and had a home of her own. Now she was like a sparkling iridescent bubble mirroring the rainbow, floating in the sunshine. Then she would be like a perfect flower blooming always in his garden, blooming especially for him, the complete fulfillment of which the rainbow bubble was but the promise. That was how he had explained it all in his mind as he went from place to place with her, waiting while she toyed with life, as one attends a lovely child in her games and smiles indulgently, knowing that she will presently grow up and be as eager about real things.

But to-night he had had a sudden jar which had brought him to consciousness, the immediate cause of this vigil by his own fireside. To-night, for the first time in many weeks, he had not been her attendant. An important business visitor from abroad, passing through the city for a few hours, and to sail for home to-morrow morning, made it necessary for him to call off his engagement for at least part of the evening with the promise that he would drop in later if the guest left in time. When the guest departed earlier than he had expected, and he sought Tamar's home expecting to make more elaborate apologies than he had had time for over the telephone, earlier in the day, and hoping he would find her alone for once that they might have a cosy talk together—hoping many things from this, his heart beating high—he had found only a cool little note.

> Have gone with Bobbins to the Pine Tree Inn. Come if you get back in time.
>
> *Tam.*

He had frowned as he read it and felt almost vexed with her. Then she had not cared to wait for him, although he had suggested that he would get away as early as possible. There had been no vision of a quiet evening hour together in the firelight in her scheme of things. She had gone with another man as lightly as a butterfly. And such a man! Colonel Robertson. Why should she persist in calling that ass "Bobbins"? So ridiculous! And the Pine Tree Inn! Did she not remember what he had told her about the place being common? He had been almost vexed with her.

But he had followed; and before he reached the end of his long chilly drive he was hugging it to his heart that she had asked him to come. She had not been satisfied with the colonel. Child that she was she had gone where any fun was offering, but she had wanted him to follow. He saw himself rescuing her from the commonness of the Pine Tree Inn and whirling her away to the cosy fireside of his dreams after all.

He had reached the place at last, secluded enough for the most unscrupulous, and found his way to a gallery where he might look down on the gay company and get his bearings.

He found her almost at once, the centre of all eyes as usual. But she wore a more daring costume than any he had ever seen her wear before. He rubbed his eyes in a daze and looked again before he would believe it. Her cheeks were brighter, and her lips too, than he had ever seen them; and as he watched her dance with the obnoxious colonel the scales, as it were, fell from his eyes. A hot wrath burned within him as he saw her yield herself to the intimacy of her companion, caught a look that passed between them, not the look of the innocent child with the rainbow bubble as he had imagined, and then they disappeared beneath the gallery.

He had heard them coming up the stairs and had withdrawn behind a heavy curtain as they passed. Almost he could have reached out and touched the lovely bare arm. The breath of perfume that she wore was wafted subtly in his face. A careless sentence, unguarded as never before in his presence, dropped on the air beside him and entered his soul like a knife. Somehow he saw her in a new light, and his soul turned sick within him. The impulse that had seized him to reach out and draw her away from her companion, run with her to the ends of the earth and never stop until she was safe, rescue her from a situation that he had thought by this time would have become unbearable, passed. He knew now that she did not want to be rescued; that she had come here because she wanted to come; that she liked common things because she was common herself. At least he thought he knew that.

He thought so until he had come at racing speed several miles away from the place without having been seen by the lady at all, thought so till the fires of wrath and jealousy and hurt pride had burned themselves out, and something within suggested that he should have stayed and seen it through, rescued her if need be, and that he had misjudged her. He tried to conjure up his former thought of her, but in spite of all, the vision of the jazzy little rag of a frock she wore, the look in her eyes, the words on her lips, remained, and here he was sitting the hours through and having it out with himself.

The question was, had he discovered his mistake in time or was he bound by ties he could not break? And if so—he faced the question frankly for the first time— was he prepared to marry her and bring her here? Would she ever fit with his mother, his delicate, fragile, fine little mother, who would be wrecked for life if her son brought home a bride unfit for his traditions.

He tried to think that he could change her, even if she was not all that he had at first fancied her. He revisioned the gleam of her sparkling laughter, the flash of the pearly teeth between the red lips, and tried to place her in the chair opposite him with his mother sitting where he was. He got up and paced back and forth through the length of the beautiful apartment, and fancied them all three spending an evening together. Tamar would go to the piano and play and sing as she often did, in a wild sweet voice, some foolish little song. But what would his mother think of the songs that Tamar sang? She would call them "wicked" or "vulgar"—Tamar wasn't vulgar, was she? Just modern. He had heretofore thought of it in that way, "modern!" Or stay. He remembered that he had been startled, almost shocked, the first time he heard her sing her daring songs, and turned away displeased— gone home without speaking to her again—that was the first night he had met her. Well—he had met her again, and the songs had become familiar, so that now he could even laugh with the others at the unholy ending. He had ceased to feel that she realized the import of the words she was using. He had excused her, called her "un-moral," that new word behind which modern frankness hides and masquerades as harmless.

But here, to-night, in his home, with all its traditions and habits of thought, with his saintly lady mother asleep upstairs in her peaceful room, he looked the truth in the face and wondered that he had been deceived so long.

Sometime in the course of his perambulations he paused beside the table long enough to notice a pile of mail that lay under the light of the carved jade lamp awaiting his notice. The postmark on the top letter began a digression in his mind and he picked it up and opened it.

It was a most flattering invitation from an influential business connection offering to put into the hands of his firm a difficult and extensive piece of research and investigation abroad, and suggesting that if possible he undertake the supervision of the work personally. It was both an honor and an opportunity for him to make a name for himself not only in the business world, in which he moved, but in the wider field of science, and a line which interested him exceedingly. His ambition leaped to respond to the opportunity. He read the letter again and then began to pace back and forth in the room once more, coming to a halt at the bay window that overlooked the brow of the hill and afforded a wide view of sky and city in the distance. To the observer there was scarcely a dividing line where stars ceased and lights began. It was all starred alike, a wonderful world of dark mysterious blue, jewelled from end to end.

He flung the casement window open and stood drawing in deep breaths of the cold night air, expanding his lungs to the full and finding a growing calm upon him. He felt as if he had stepped into another, wider world, a universe indeed, filled with opportunities and infinities. A place vastly different from the little giddy round in which he had been lately circling with Tamar.

Tamar! How far away she suddenly seemed. And if he should accept this offer of the letter how kindly that would solve his problem. To go abroad for a number of weeks, or even months perhaps if it took so long to complete his mission, would tend to clarify the situation and also his mind. He would be among new surroundings and other people. He would get a wider viewpoint. And when he returned if Tamar was the real Tamar he would know. If she were what she had seemed to-night it would be plain after an absence. Did he not owe this to himself, to his mother, to the traditions of his ancestors—yes, even to Tamar? There must be no delusions when he married. He came of fine clean stock where integrity and true worth counted more than show. He had no right to ignore those things, even if he desired to do so. If Tamar really cared for him, if she were ready to be the woman who would be his true mate, the absence could not make any difference. True, she might be in danger of being led into foolishness without his steadying presence, but if he could not trust her before marriage how could he hope for happiness afterward? And had he any right to save her from foolishness at the expense of wrecking life's happiness for both of them?

These were the thoughts that came to him as he stood under the stars, and let his well-trained conscience ask him questions as it had not had a chance to do for many a dazzling week.

The stars were beginning to pale when at last he turned and closed the window and went up to his room. He had fully decided now to accept the offer and go abroad at once, if the matter worked out satisfactorily with his partners when he went to his office in the morning. There was just one point about it all that troubled him—and that was his mother. Since his father's death some two years before she had not been at all well, and it seemed to him that she grew frailer, week by week. If she would go with him, the difficulty would be solved. It would probably do her good to have a sea voyage and visit some of their relatives in Scotland. But he lay down at last to snatch a few hours' sleep with a dubious sense that he was basing his plans on an exceedingly frail possibility. He knew his mother, and he knew she hated to leave home. Particularly since his father's death had she withdrawn within herself, refusing to go out among her acquaintances, or to invite much company to the house. She was not hard nor morose nor crabbed, just sad and sweet and tired most of the time. He knew that her only remaining pleasure now was to have him come and chat with her. It made the only bright spot of her day. It would be next to impossible for him to go and leave her alone with servants. It seemed an impassable barrier unless she would consent to go. He must find a way to get her to accompany him.

But when the morning came and he went to her room for his regular morning call he broached the matter and found her firm. She would not take a sea voyage. She could never go back to the old places where she had once gone with his father. She did not feel up to the journey.

But when she heard of the invitation she brightened perceptibly over the honor, and urged him quite eagerly to go, saying she would not mind staying alone a few months. He would write to her, and she would think up a way to make the time go rapidly. She seemed to be more interested in the proposition than in anything that had happened since his father's death. There was a feverish eagerness in her eyes as if she really were anxious to hasten his departure. It perplexed him.

He arose at last to go, for it was getting late, but his mother put out a detaining hand and looked at him wistfully as if there were something more behind her words than just their casual question:

"Is there—does anyone else—I mean are any of your—social—acquaintances going over at the same time?"

He looked at her keenly, noted the wistful anxiety in her eyes, and it flashed upon him that perhaps someone had told her about Tamar. Poor little mother, she would not understand Tamar—not as she was. With a sudden tenderness he stooped and kissed her soft rose-leaf cheek:

"No, Mother," he answered, "not that I know of. I haven't time for society this trip. I want to work hard on the way over, if I go at all, to have the subject well in hand so that I shall not waste any time when I get to work."

He stooped and kissed her tenderly and pressed her hand as if to reassure her, and her answer made him doubly certain that she must have had some such idea as he had thought, for she sighed happily, with a flash of her old-time smile, and answered:

"Then I'm glad to have you go. There are no people nowadays that belong with my son. Perhaps you will find some over in the old country. I sometimes feel lonesome for you, my dear. You are fine and I want you to stay so."

He thought of her words tenderly on his way in town. Dear little mother; she was fine! And she understood so many things about his soul. She always had. Strange he had expected to hide this matter of Tamar from her till he was sure what he meant to do.

But what about his mother? If he went he must make some plan to fill her days with brightness while he was gone. He could not do good work and feel that she was lonely and sad without him. Over and over he reviewed the list of their acquaintances and kinfolks and rejected each one. There was not one who was free to come to his mother, whom he felt would be the right one to cheer her loneliness, or whom she would like to have.

When he reached the office he had almost made up his mind to give up the whole matter and send someone else in his place, but when he laid the matter before his partners they were most insistent that he was just the one for the work and went on making their plans so persistently that he began once more to think about what to do for his mother.

But when he admitted reluctantly that he would be glad to go if it were not for leaving his mother in loneliness, and put the situation to his partners, they swept his objections aside with a wave of their hands and uttered the cryptic words:

"Advertise, man, advertise! You can get anything in this world if you advertise in the right way for it."

So Angus Macdonald sat down at his desk, while they busily plied him with suggestions about his journey, and wrote an advertisement. He sent it by his office boy to the newspaper, and then whirled about with this remark and a set of his firm Scotch jaw they knew meant business:

"Now, go ahead with your suggestions, but if I don't get a satisfactory answer to that before to-morrow night I don't go! Just put that down for a fact. I *mean* it!"

3

MRS. DUNBAR did not come down to breakfast the next morning after the excitement, and haughtily declined the dainty tray which Doris brought up to her door.

Rose was still in bed and Doris carried the tray to her.

"You were a fool to take all that trouble for her, Dorrie," averred Rose, stretching her pretty arms above her head and yawning. "You just spoil her. That's what makes her so babyish. If I were you I'd just let her alone and let her come to her senses."

But Rose ate the appetizing breakfast gratefully with never a thought that it might be spoiling *her,* and Doris went down for a few moments more wrestling with those awful bills in the desk before the lawyer should arrive.

Mrs. Dunbar did not make her appearance until they were all seated in the living-room, and Mr. Hamilton was unstrapping his brief-case and taking out formidable looking papers.

She came in like a small black wraith, in deep mourning, with a heavily black-bordered handkerchief pressed to her eyes, and dropped into the big upholstered chair which had been left vacant for her.

Doris was seated on the davenport with little Jean nestled close to her, her hand in hers; and John, his hair in unwonted slickness, at the other end looking uncomfortable and unconcerned. It seemed wholly unnecessary to John that he should attend this function. What was law business to him?

Ned was sitting by the front window, his back to the room, a sulky unhappy look on his lean, young face. He had not breakfasted nor spoken to any of them. His greeting to the lawyer had been abrupt and embarrassed, almost as if he were ashamed of being there. Doris watched him sadly and wondered whether she would dare say anything about last night when she had a chance to speak to him alone. Then the lawyer rustled his paper, cleared his throat, and began to read the will, and she turned to listen. There was a tense stillness in the room while the stilted old phrases rolled on monotonously: "I, John Edward Dunbar, being of sound mind . . . do will and bequeath," etc., on down to the details of a modest fortune: five shares in this railroad, ten shares of stock in a prosperous manufacturing plant, a number of United States bonds, several real estate mortgages, a row of city houses well leased, twenty shares in a silver mine, as many more in an oil well, and interest in a heating and lighting plant,—quite a proud array. Doris began to take new heart of hope. Perhaps after all her fears had been groundless. Perhaps their affairs would not be hopelessly involved after all. Perhaps she had misunderstood Mr. Hamilton yesterday when he had warned her that things were in bad shape. He might only have meant to prepare her for some of these bills that she had found, and possibly other creditors. But surely, surely all that long list of property could not be tied up so that they would be in straitened circumstances. Oh, it would be so much easier if they were going to have money enough to get along comfortably! Then she would have leisure to give to the consideration of her other problems, and her eyes wandered to Ned's back again.

At the first casual reading the property seemed to be pretty evenly divided between the widow and the children. Doris felt relieved, for now no one need feel hurt or jealous—Doris hated to have any of the family sulky about anything like that—feeling that they had not been treated as well as the others. It always somehow fell to her to smooth out their ruffled feelings. But surely everything was adjusted perfectly fairly, and no one of them could complain, not even Florence.

The house was mentioned last in the list, and it appeared that Mr. Dunbar had only had a life interest in it, and that it belonged to the children, it having been built as a wedding present for their own mother by her father and left to their father in trust for them.

When this clause of the will was read there was a perceptible stiffening of the little black figure in the big upholstered chair, and a tightening of the white fingers that held the black-bordered handkerchief to her eyes. She held herself tense during the kindly clause in which the father requested that his children give their stepmother welcome in their house during her lifetime, and then she uncovered her angry eyes, drew herself up scornfully, and said in a haughty voice:

"Mr. Hamilton, I wish to give notice right here that I intend to contest that will."

"Mrs. Dunbar," the lawyer said gently, "just a minute—"

But the lady went on angrily:

"It is an outrageous will," she declared, looking around with blazing eyes on them all, "and it is perfectly plain to me that there was pressure brought to bear on my husband while he was too ill to know what he was doing." She fixed her furious gaze on Doris who had been his faithful nurse during his last illness.

"Mrs. Dunbar, that is impossible!" broke in the lawyer. "Did you not hear me read the date? This will was made over five years ago when your husband was in perfect health."

"That doesn't make any difference!" said the angry lady. "You can't argue me out of my intention. I shall contest this will. The property should all have been left to me. The children are too young to look after business. My husband always trusted me."

"Mrs. Dunbar, I have not finished yet. Will you be good enough to let me explain the whole matter fully? I am sure you will see that what I have to say changes the whole matter."

Mrs. Dunbar had half risen from her seat as if the matter were fully settled so far as she was concerned. Now she subsided reluctantly into her chair with a resigned look on her face:

"I will listen of course," she said with set lips, "but it will make no difference with me. I intend to contest the will."

The lawyer looked about on the children with a perturbed expression, as if to apologize for what he was about to say. One could see that he did not care for his job.

"I am very sorry to have to tell you that things are in bad shape," he said and hesitated with an appeal to each one mutely before he went on. "I, as Mr. Dunbar's attorney, of course necessarily knew more or less of his moves. Mr. Dunbar had for the past two years been interested in a scheme which if it had proved the financial success he believed that it would, would have more than doubled or perhaps trebled the property he had to leave. I must say, in justification of myself, that I did not have the strong belief that he had in the men whom he trusted, and I feared greatly and urged a more conservative move; but in his great anxiety to put his family in luxurious circumstances before he died he went into the transaction with everything he had."

He paused and looked about on them to see if they were prepared for the blow he was about to deal them. There was breathless silence in the room. The widow had her handkerchief to her eyes again, but otherwise sat rigid. Ned had not turned around from his miserable gaze out of the window. Doris' heart began to palpitate with a wild fear, and little Jean feeling the impending catastrophe in the atmosphere began to cry softly. Rose's eyes were wide with consternation. Only John appeared indifferent, as he tied a cat's cradle out of a handy piece of string from his pocket. John might be understanding but he had no intention that anyone present should know it.

The lawyer resumed his unpleasant task:

"It distresses me beyond measure to have to tell you that your father's scheme fell through and carried with it everything he owned."

He paused again and looked to see if they understood, or if he must be still more explicit, but no one answered him. They sat appalled—aghast.

"Even this house," said the lawyer, gathering breath once more. "Even this house, which your father held in trust, had been mortgaged up to its full value."

The silence in the room was like something tangible, as if one could reach out and touch it.

Then when no one was noticing her, Mrs. Dunbar suddenly arose with a grand air of severity, and holding her head high, loftily announced:

"Nevertheless, I intend to contest that will." And so saying, she swept from the room and they could hear her go down the hall and up the stairs to her own room.

They all sat and looked at the door where she had gone, except Ned who had not turned around yet. The lawyer, a simple literal soul, stated the obvious fact: "She doesn't understand," in a tone of deep wonder, and suddenly Rose buried her face in her hands and broke forth in a clear hysterical laugh.

"She *never* understands anything, 'nless she *wantsta*," unexpectedly contributed John. "Don't mind her."

There was another pause while the little company gathered its senses and adjusted itself:

"Do you mean," asked Doris in a small anxious voice, "do you mean there won't be *anything*? Not even enough to pay the bills? There are a lot of bills—" She made a helpless gesture toward the library where the old desk stood.

The lawyer cleared his throat with a relieved air:

"Oh, there may be enough to clear those off," he said hopefully. "There are a few little odd matters, not more than five thousand—if there is that—I'm not sure yet till I see how much some of these little odds and ends are rated at."

"Then nothing else matters," said Doris in a dull monotonous tone. "How soon will you know? There are at least three thousand dollars worth of bills, and the people are very insistent."

"Suppose you let me have those bills, Miss Doris, and I'll attend to them at once," said the lawyer briskly, grateful at her practical way of taking things.

Doris rose and went across the hall to the desk, returning with a great sheaf of papers neatly separated into bundles and fastened with rubber bands. The others sat still waiting for the end, as if it were some sort of a service. Rose had quieted her laughter and was looking white and drawn now.

"Won't we have anything to buy food with?" she asked, her eyes wide with horror.

The lawyer flushed and put his hand to his pocket:

"Oh, Miss Rose, it isn't so bad as that, not yet," he said embarrassedly, drawing out a roll of bills. "Here is a little money, a matter of three hundred I'll be glad to advance to help you out till you can look around."

Rose felt tempted to laugh again as her quick perception saw them all going forth and looking around to locate more money. She was strained almost to the breaking point, poor, pretty, spoiled Rose, and it seemed to her that the bottom had fallen out of her world completely. Yet she would laugh with the pain in her heart. That was Rose. Laugh in an ecstasy of pain.

Doris took the money and thanked him:

"You are sure that there will be this much over the bills?" she asked anxiously.

"Oh, yes, yes, surely, surely," coughed the lawyer, "of course, it's perfectly all right."

"Because if it isn't, I will pay you back when I get something to do."

"Oh, no, no! Don't speak of it!" he said eagerly. "I'm sure there'll be a little more perhaps. But," and he looked after the roll of bills anxiously, "I wouldn't speak of this to Mrs. Dunbar if I could help it—She might not—might not *understand*."

Doris flushed.

"She would not!" she said. "I shall not tell her. She would want to buy a mourning ring with it."

The lawyer looked at her a moment and a shadow of a smile quivered around his conventional lips. He was not quite sure from Doris' grave expression whether she knew or not that she had said something witty.

Doris went to the front door with the lawyer and as he was about to leave he put out a kindly hand:

"I think you are a brave girl, Miss Doris," he said. "Your father would be proud of you."

The kindly tone brought a sudden rush of emotion which Doris with difficulty conquered. She lifted her head and tried to smile as she thanked him. He hesitated an instant and then said:

"Don't blame your father, Miss Doris, he really thought he was doing the best thing for you all. I was so nearly persuaded myself that I had decided to put in all my savings too, but the crash came before I had fully completed the arrangements. I might have lost everything but for your father. He grew anxious and told me to keep out. It was too late for him to get out. It wouldn't have been honorable, but I owe him a great deal. If there is anything I can do—"

Then Doris gave him one of her rare smiles:

"Thank you for that," she said. "I'm so glad you don't blame Father. He was a dear father!"

"He was that," said the lawyer heartily, "and remember I'm at your service if you need any help."

"Thank you so much!" she said. "It is good to know we have one friend. But I hope I shall not have to bother you. After we get these bills paid the worst anxiety will be over. Do you know how soon we have to get out of this house?"

A shade of worry came over the lawyer's face:

"The man wants to foreclose at once," he said annoyedly. "I've tried to put him off, but he wants his money. He's building a house himself, and he wants to sell this one. He says he has a purchaser. I'll hold him off as long as possible. It really isn't decent of him. But he had been hounding your father for several months, and we just held him off, hoping—"

"Poor Father!" said Doris wistfully. "I'm afraid this was what killed him, not the pneumonia."

When the lawyer was gone Doris turned back into the hall and looked at the familiar walls with a strange feeling. So they were no longer her home. Others would walk and talk and exist here. How strange and sad life was. How terrible!

She went back into the living-room but Rose and Jean and John were gone. Only Ned was left there still staring out of the window, his shoulders hunched over like an old man. Something in his attitude touched his sister. She came over and stood beside him laying her hand on his shoulder.

He dropped his head upon the window-sill and groaned aloud. She put her hand on his rough gold hair that had a way of rumpling into curls wherever he would let it. She had always been proud of her brother's handsome head. Everybody admired him. Among his mates he was known as a "looker." She knew she was weakening now as always at sight of him. No wonder he was spoiled. His personality was most attractive even at his worst. And now as he sat there in dust and ashes as it were she longed to put her arms around him and comfort him. Yet she knew she ought not.

"What is it, Ned?" She tried to speak gravely but there was more than a tinge of tenderness in her voice.

The young man lifted a haggard face and looked at her:

"I'm in an awful hole, Doris!" he said in a hoarse voice that sounded quite unlike his usual cheery care-free tones.

Doris felt her heartbeats quicken with alarm. Then he was going to tell her about last night. It would be good to have it out in the open at least. But what had happened? Had he been getting into a scrape, arrested or something? And on the night of his father's funeral!

"Yes?" she wavered out trying to make her voice seem casual, but finding herself trembling in every fibre.

He looked furtively toward the door and then whispered huskily:

"I've got to have some money right away!"

"Money! Oh, Ned! And we have lost everything! Why should you need money now?"

"I need three hundred dollars right away. I've *got* to have it. Dorrie, didn't old Ham give you some money just now? Can't you loan it to me?" he said desperately, "I swear I'll get a job to-morrow and begin to pay it back."

Doris' face blanched. This must be something desperate. What had Ned been doing? But she couldn't give up that money that Mr. Hamilton had advanced to her. It would be needed for their daily necessities.

While she hesitated he went on:

"This comes first, Kid, it really does. You'd give it to me if you knew." There was pleading and desperation in his tone. She saw that his face was chalky white and perspiration stood in beads on his upper lip and forehead. He was in deep distress.

"What is it, Ned?" she said earnestly. "You must tell me everything or I can't possibly help you. This money means our daily bread."

"I can't tell you," he said sullenly drooping his head once more in anguish, "I *can't!* You'll *have* to let me have the money though or we'll all be in disgrace!"

"Disgrace? How could that be possible? Have you been gambling, Ned Dunbar?" Her eyes flashed a weary contempt.

"No, I haven't been gambling," growled the desperate youth with a hunted look.

"Well, you haven't been stealing, or broken up some-body's automobile, or—"

"No!" said Ned sharply. "It's none of those!"

"Then what is it? You'll have to tell me if you want any help."

There was a long long wait during which Doris began to feel as if the room was swimming round her and everything was going black. But she stood her ground quietly waiting. At last when it seemed that he was not going to speak she turned to leave the room. Then he raised his head and gave her a desperate look like one about to drown, who sees a possible rescuer turning away:

"Well, then. I'll tell you. *I got married last night!*"

He flung the words like bombs into what seemed to be a great vault of stillness, in which not even a heart dared to beat. They echoed around and up and down and rang deep in the souls of the two. They seemed like an idle tale that had nothing to do with these two, and yet they beat upon the two young hearts and insisted on admission as a fact, those awful words.

It seemed to Doris that it must have been several minutes before she gathered voice to echo that word incredulously:

"Married!"

And then again some space later:

"Oh, Ned! And we in all this trouble?"

The boy dropped his face upon his arms and sobbed aloud, writhing as if she had struck him:

"That's right! Rub it in!" he snarled like a wounded animal. "As if I couldn't think of that myself!"

"But— Ned, why did you? How could you have done such a thing?"

"I don't know!" moaned the frantic boy, "I was a fool,

I guess. We had something to drink and then they dared me to do it. I didn't realize—"

Doris in spite of herself gave a little moan, and dropped her face into her hands trying to steady herself for this new blow:

"Oh, Ned!"

The boy got up furiously and strode to the door:

"Well if that's the way you're going to take it I better put myself off the map."

"Ned!" she sprang and caught his arm. "Sit down!" she said sternly. "It is bad enough to do a thing like this without being a coward and running off to leave the whole thing for us to bear. At least be a man and face what you have done. *I* certainly didn't do it."

Her biting words were like a dash of cold water in his face, bringing him to his senses. He had been so used to having his follies and mistakes condoned. He half expected Doris to find a way out of this uncomfortable mess for him. To have her take it this way, was worse than he had expected. What he wanted her to do was to pity him, and blame the girl, and then give him what he wanted.

But he had not calculated on the overstrained nerves of Doris, nor the horror that would seize her at the form of torture he had brought upon the household. Married! That seemed the culmination of all troubles. What was there to do now but bear it?

After a moment she lifted sad eyes and looked at him as he sat miserably waiting, trying to think of some excuse that would bring him back her pity:

"I don't understand," she said in a voice full of pain and bewilderment, "what has this to do with your wanting money? And how did you come to get into a place like this? Who is the girl? Have you known her a long time? How could a decent girl do a thing like that? Do I know her?"

"No!" said Ned sharply, his face stern and pinched looking, his tone as one who has resolved to make known the worst. "She isn't your kind. You *wouldn't* know her. There's nothing so bad about her. But she's not your kind. Her name is Zoe Bullard. I've known her a few weeks. We'd talked about getting married, but I didn't take it seriously. I thought it was more a joke than anything else. But she took it in earnest. They all did. They got that preacher from the little shingle church down on Phillips Street and it was all sprung on me.

"And then her mother—*her mother!* appeared on the scene and she said if I didn't get her a diamond ring and take her to a good home she'd have the *whole* story published in all the papers. Doris! I'll have to get her a ring, and go hire a furnished apartment or something. Her brother is a pretty well-known prize-fighter and he'll be coming around pretty soon to see where I am. He's a brute if there ever was one and—"

The door-bell suddenly pealed through the house, and apparently John had been on hand and opened it at once, for Doris heard the voice of Milton Page, the young man to whom she had been engaged for the past year. With staggering heart Doris looked toward her brother:

"Go upstairs, Ned, quick! and stay in your room till I come," she said in a low tone. "Milt is out there, and we've got to think before we let anyone know about this."

Ned rose as if he had been shot. He glared at his sister for a passing instant:

"If you let that monkey know anything about me and my affairs I'll cut my throat and his too. I swear I will. It's none of his business."

"Go! Quick!" whispered Doris motioning toward the door at the back of the room that opened into the back hall.

But Ned was already gone, and the door was opening on Milton Page.

4

MILTON PAGE was tall and spare, with cold blue eyes and a calculating mouth. He was chief accountant for the city Electric Company, and highly valued as an expert in his line. He had the kind of mind which knew at once what was the most economical move to make in any given direction, and it hurt him abominably to see anyone move in any other way than economically.

He was a handsome man, meticulously clothed and always in condition. Not a hair out of place. He expected such perfection in others. Yet he was a good man, a successful man, and with a somewhat pleasing personality.

As he advanced into the room Doris became suddenly aware that she was wearing her oldest pair of slippers, and that her hair was awry. She tried to pull herself together, to forget the terrors that were pressing upon her soul, and to greet him with proper interest.

His lips felt cold upon her hot cheek, and it seemed as if she was almost too tired to summon the quiet smile which she felt he would expect. She knew that he admired her for her self-control. He was not an emotional man. She had always believed that he felt deeply himself but kept himself well in hand so that others did not look beneath his always pleasant mask of personality. She had been thoroughly convinced that he cared for her before she permitted an engagement; but just at this point somehow the engagement did not seem to fit into the picture. It seemed the last straw to have him come just now. How was she possibly to pull herself back into life and be properly glad to see a fiancé when her whole world had collapsed into shame and sorrow, and the future loomed dark with problems and perplexities?

It never even occurred to her to tell Milton her troubles, to lay her head on his strong shoulder to rest for a little while, sure of his sympathy and help. Milton was one from whom one hid all troubles and perplexities. His mind was so constructed that he simply had to lay his finger at once on the spot that was to blame and blame it with all his might. One felt guilty in his presence if anything was awry.

Doris' one thought was whether Ned had really gone upstairs as she had begged him to do. She listened for his step overhead with painful intentness and to the exclusion of Milton Page's cool studied tones:

"My poor child!" he said graciously, drawing her unresisting to the davenport and sitting down beside her with a casual arm about her: "This has been a heavy strain on you. I wish I could have relieved you of some of the burden, but I knew it was useless, so I kept away that you might have less to take your attention. I am glad it is over now. I hope you had a good sleep last night. You must have been worn out. It seemed to me both foolish and wasteful to carry your father away off into another state just to bury him."

"It was Father's wish, Milton. He wanted to lie beside our mother," Doris explained gently.

"Yes, you told me that the day before yesterday." Milton Page was most exact. "But I repeat, it was both foolish and wasteful. What difference can it make where a man's dust lies? And he could not know what you did with his remains after he was gone."

Doris shrank away from him involuntarily with a little shiver:

"Oh, *don't!*" she breathed sharply as if his words had hurt her.

"Why, Doris! What nonsense! You're not sentimental! That's one thing I always liked about you, you were always so sensible."

"That isn't sentiment," said Doris, struggling with an ache in her throat. "It is right and fitting that people should be buried where they request if it is at all possible. I *liked* my father and mother to lie together."

"It just shows," said the young man didactically, "that you are overstrained, that you should make so much of a little thing. It is high time you got away from it all, and I'm glad to say that things are shaping up so you can. I got the letter this morning from the West. The position is mine, and they want me to come in two weeks. They suggested a week but I wired them it would be impossible to get there under two weeks. Of course we'll take the trip West slowly. I do not see being hurried about anything. Can you be ready by Thursday of next week?"

"Ready?" Doris lifted uncomprehending eyes. She had just decided that she heard a footstep overhead, and was relieved that Ned had not gone out again. He had looked desperate enough for almost anything. There were tragedies enough in the house without any more. But what was this? *"Ready?"*

"Yes, ready. You don't look as if you had been listening, Doris. I suppose you are tired, but you've had a whole night to rest, and, really, you know this is important. We can't very well wait. You can't begin your preparations too soon. There'll be little details that will be forgotten if you put it off. It's always well to get at a thing at once. I thought we'd have the wedding in the morning, just ourselves. Your sisters and brothers if you care to have them, and my brother will stand up with us. You won't want to have a fuss so soon after a funeral. We can go to Dr. Hillock's study, and then we'll go in town for lunch and start off that evening. If that suits you I'll secure the reservations at once. You can't be too forehanded this time of year, there is so much westward travel now—"

But suddenly Doris interrupted him, a startled look in her eyes:

"Milton! You don't mean— You're not talking about our getting married! *Now?* Why, can't you see how utterly impossible that would be?"

There was distress in her voice. She had not been wont to cross him. It seemed as if she was too tired to explain it all out. He ought to understand it himself without that. There were some things she could not explain—even to him—things that would take time— and would they *ever* get straight, she wondered sorrowfully? But he smiled complacently:

"I know," he said, "I supposed it would seem a little sudden to you, but you're a sensible girl, and you can readily see that we cannot hold up a big corporation just for a whim. As for the actual work there is to be done beforehand, I believe I've reduced it to a minimum. I've thought it all out in detail. I feared you would be appalled at first, but when I explain I'm sure you will see that I'm right, and you'll see that it will really relieve you of a lot of useless fuss and ceremony. In the first place you won't need any new clothes. You can perfectly well be married in whatever you wear on the street. You always look nice, and I never did believe in a woman buying up and making a lot of things more than she really needs. So all you'll really have to do is pack your trunk. And I wouldn't advise you to take a lot of truck along either. Let's go free. We'll probably board for the first year, and we can look around and see what we want in the way of a home, and then you can send back for whatever you want that belongs to you."

"Wait!" said Doris almost breathlessly. "Wait! It isn't for any such reasons I said I couldn't go. I don't care about clothes and trunks. I *can't go* now! I can't *leave* here! Why don't you see that? Why don't you understand that things are all mixed up and there's a lot to do, and I couldn't be spared!"

The young man's face hardened perceptibly:

"Certainly I see that. I see that you are about to be made a pack horse of, as usual, to carry this spoiled and babied family into ease and idleness somehow. And *it isn't going to be!* You're engaged to *me,* aren't you? Your first duty is to me, isn't it? Well, and *I* say *you shan't!* I say a time has come to call a halt on what has been going on for years. You and your precious father have gone on spoiling and petting that lazy stepmother, and those idle good-for-nothing brothers and sisters of yours, until they can't lift a finger for themselves; and now the time has come when I step in and assert my rights. I've waited a year and a half for you since we were engaged, and now I have the offer of a good position with a salary that will make us more than comfortable, and I don't intend to wait any longer. If our engagement means anything it means that I have a right to demand that you go with me now. Besides, if you're to be my wife I don't want you to be all used up and your beauty all gone before we're married. I want you now while you are well and strong and have your good looks."

Doris suddenly rose from the circling arm and stood out away from him:

"Milton, I never heard you talk like this before. You don't seem like yourself. It seems terrible, the things you are saying."

"I'm sorry, dear, but they've got to be said. I've thought it all out and I made up my mind that we might as well understand things now in the beginning. I'm not going to have your family hung around your neck all the rest of your life. They can come and visit you of course at reasonable intervals—all but Mrs. Dunbar. I draw the line at her. And I'm not very anxious for John to come. He's a rude boy. Perhaps he'll grow up some day. I have my doubts. But you're not going to stay here and work for them. They're all old enough to look out for themselves, except perhaps Jean, and your stepmother ought to be gracious enough to look out for her for the next six or seven years. If she doesn't there are good schools, and I'd be willing to have her come to us for vacations, sometimes, if that would please you."

"Milt! Stop!" said Doris her eyes angry now, her face white and strained. "I don't like the way you are talking. You are saying things I never can forget!"

"I don't want you to forget them, Doris," said Milton quite kindly. "It is best to have these things settled finally, and I am saying them all for your good. You will be happier to understand them, and when you are calmer you will thank me for making you see the truth."

"Perhaps I shall," said Doris with a strange calmness in her voice. "At least I think you have said enough for this time. But you must understand this. I cannot possibly think of getting married at this time. It does not seem decent in you to think I could desert them now when everything has gone wrong."

"Now look here, Doris," broke in Milton with a tone

of annoyance, "I've explained my position perfectly frankly to you. There isn't the slightest need for you to take that attitude. You understand entirely that I want to save you, and I intend to save you. You are my responsibility, and the rest of this family are not. I have felt for a long time that if they had to look after themselves they might amount to something, but they never will as long as you are their willing slave."

A sudden noise overhead of a chair falling and a window raised made Doris start and look around nervously.

"There!" said the young man triumphantly. "See how nervous you are. I really must assert my authority and insist that you come out with me and take a ride. Then we can talk this thing over more at our leisure and perhaps stop and get a few things out of the way that have to be done before we leave. You must remember that the time is short."

But Doris had drawn back, her mouth a firm little line of intention, her chin just the least bit haughty:

"Milton, you have no authority over me," she said earnestly. "I must do what I think is right. It is my own conscience that I must follow, and if you really love me you will not hurt me by talking this way."

The young man's face hardened stubbornly:

"Doesn't that ring you wear give me the right of authority?" he asked sternly.

Doris looked down at the diamond that glittered on the third finger of her left hand. The ring which had given her so much pleasure when he first placed it there, and then looked up at Milton half frightened, half questioning:

"No," she said, "I never felt that it gave you authority. If I did I would take it off and give it back to you. Nobody has the right of authority over another human being who is grown and of sane mind. Especially where a matter of right and wrong is concerned."

"But this is not right," asserted the hard, thin lips.

She looked him steadily in the eye:

"And you think if I differ from you that I must do as you think even if I know you are wrong?"

"That isn't possible, Doris, because I am not wrong. When you gave yourself to me—"

"I have not given myself to you yet, Milt. We are not married. But even if I had, if I thought you would insist on my doing what I feel to be wrong I should not do it."

"But it would be your duty—"

"Then I will never put myself in a position where that will be the case," said Doris firmly, her eyes meeting his steadily.

"Why Doris! I thought that you professed to love me. I never heard you talk in this insane fashion before. You certainly need rest badly. Come, get your hat and coat and we will go out for a ride. The cool air will do you good and you will be able to see things more rationally."

Doris felt as if the floor were reeling under her tired feet, but she knew she must control her nerves. If he would only go now and let her get up to Ned, and find out what to do. But he was waiting, urging her gently but firmly toward the door. He would call Rose to get her hat and in a moment more she would find herself whirling away in his car in spite of herself. It had always been so that he could persuade her into doing his will. It had not seemed to matter before. She had rather enjoyed it to be overpowered and carried away to something pleasant that he wanted to do. But now all seemed changed. She had a great responsibility and every moment was precious. No knowing how many more calamities were brewing in her family. She could not cut loose from them all and go her way. She loved them. She had not known till she heard him talk how beloved they all were, how part of the fibre of her very soul. Leave them? Never! Not while they needed her.

She halted in the middle of the room and faced about to his urging hand:

"Wait!" she said, "I will tell you. You do not understand or I am sure you would not wish to seem so utterly without heart. We are in great perplexity here. We have to move out of this house. We do not own it as we supposed, and we have no money, except just barely enough to pay the bills. We have got to find a place in which to live, and to find work for those of us who are able to earn, in order to support the family. Now, do you see how impossible any of your plans are? Even though as you say you are doing this out of kindness toward me, do you not see how utterly impossible it is for me to leave here at this time?"

"Certainly not," he said dryly. "I practically knew all this before. Your father went on in his foolish senseless way getting involved more and more. I knew the end had to come sometime, and it was just like him to slip out of it all and leave it for others to shoulder. And it was just for this reason that I have said what I did. I don't intend you shall pay the piper, and what is more I don't intend to shoulder his family for the rest of my lifetime. I take it that job belongs to your stepmother. She married him, didn't she? You gave your promise to marry me, didn't you? Well, then! Your responsibility for your father's family ceases. *You* belong *to me!*"

Doris was white with amazement and repulsion. She opened her mouth to answer him and closed it again. Was it worth while answering anyone who could talk that way? He blamed her dead father to her face? Well if he were to blame, that was no way to speak of it, and no time. Could anyone love her and yet dare to speak that way of her father the very day after his funeral? She looked at him and his face suddenly seemed to have changed from the man she knew and thought she loved into a cold formal mask. Avarice and selfishness seemed to gleam in his eyes, in the hard lines around his perfect mouth, in the very set of his chin. He was professing to be saying all this for her sake, but could that be? Could one love a person and not love at all those they loved? Or did he just love her because he had chosen her for his own? He was really loving himself, then, not her!

This was an impression, not a distinct thought, but her soul recoiled from it as if it had been a tangible thing.

Then she roused herself to speak:

"I do not belong to you. I gave my promise to the man I thought you were, not to the one you have appeared to be this morning. You have forfeited your right to consideration by what you have said about my father. Whether it be true or not is another question which I do not care to discuss with you now or at any other time. If he was foolish and senseless as you say, it was at least because he loved us, but you certainly cannot claim to love me when you can talk so at a time like this. If you have no tenderness for me now, how can I ever hope to have it from you? What is the use in talking any more? You and I could never forget this."

She spread her hands in a kind of final gesture, a gray weary look overspreading her face. It was as if she had got beyond feeling emotion, because the tempest that swayed about her was so great that it meant nothing to her numbed little soul.

Milton Page stood watching her in disapproving surprise. He had not anticipated a scene with Doris, she had always been so tractable:

"You certainly must be more overstrained than I even imagined," he said at last in a cold disapproving tone.

"Come, you are not fit to talk now. Get your hat and we will go somewhere for a bite of lunch and you will feel better." There was still command in his voice. He evidently expected to be obeyed.

But Doris was slipping off the ring from her slender finger:

"No," she said with finality in her tone, "I haven't time to go and ride, and there isn't any use anyway. You have shown me that you and I do not belong together. *Not possibly!*"

She held out the ring but as he did not offer to take it she laid it down on the table, and with a quick step walked out of the room.

As soon as the door closed behind her she flew up the stairs, silently, on feet that had been practising quietness during her father's illness, and arrived quite suddenly in her brother's room where he stood sullenly, despairingly, looking out of the window. She stood there some seconds before he turned questioningly to look at her, wondering at the strange mingled expression on her face:

"Well, what's the matter?" he asked at last in a sneering voice. "What did that monkey have to say about my affairs?"

"He has gone," said Doris in a queer little far-away voice. "He knows nothing about your affairs."

She was surprised to find she had said the words, it seemed such an effort to speak, yet there was a terrible calm upon her. It was as if she were made strong for this awful crisis that was come upon her.

Ned had turned and was looking at her keenly now, a good look in his eyes. It seemed somehow to warm her little cold heart.

"Doris, you're a *peach!*" he said almost solemnly, "I always knew you were a peach!"

5

DOWNSTAIRS Milton Page was by no means gone. He stood dumbfounded, displeased, staring at the door through which his fiancée had just passed with such finality. He could not quite understand. Doris, of all the girls that he knew. She had always seemed completely under his will. His slightest wish had brought her smiling acquiescence. What had got into her?

He turned his head and caught the blaze of the diamond lying on the table. He frowned. How careless of her to go off and leave it there. Three hundred and fifty dollars worth of diamond! He had explained its price carefully to her soon after giving it to her. He said it was best to know the value of one's property. He himself always thought of that engagement ring in terms of dollars and cents. Perhaps he was not to blame. He had been a poor young man and had made his way through college and into a business position under the hardest circumstances. He felt himself fairly successful now, but he could not forget the struggle it had been. He appreciated everything in terms of dollars and cents. Not in any sordid sense, merely practical. He considered that a man was not well balanced who was not thoroughly practical. In which of course he was right so far as he went.

"Careless of her! Most careless!" he murmured half aloud, and after considering the ring for a moment he reached out and took it in his hand. It caught the light and shot it into his eyes. How little it was. How very tiny. Such a little finger she had. He recalled that the ring had had to be made smaller, which had annoyed him at the time as it seemed a waste of material, but it had been necessary on account of the danger of losing it.

As he held the ring in the palm of his hand and watched the scintillating colors flash from azure to ruby through clear amber and deepest emerald with touches of violet, the satisfaction returned that he had felt when first he held it thus and knew that he had bought it, that it was his. That he was able to give his promised wife a ring so worthy of his position. So small a thing and yet it had cost so much! And he had been able to buy it. The time was when it would have seemed as unattainable as a kingdom and a crown. Something of its intrinsic worth had come over him, of course, as he looked at it in his first wonder over its rare beauty; a vague question as to why such a useless lovely thing was created; and there had been a tinge of romance too; quite unnecessary, but present. That had been a satisfaction, too. All these reactions to the stone came back and reacted once more, quite surprising him now in his preoccupied and annoyed state. He took note of his emotion as one who finds he is more virtuous than he had known.

The little ring in his hand had a further appeal. He could not quite understand it. That *little* ring! She was so small and so frail who had worn it—and cast it aside so carelessly at the end of a passing quarrel. He must speak to her about that. It wouldn't be safe for her to wear it regularly if she couldn't count on controlling herself whenever she was out of sorts. She might fling it away in wrath and lose it utterly sometime.

But she certainly must be ill to have behaved as she had done. Perhaps he had not realized what a strain she had been under. Perhaps she should have been treated as a sick child and soothed for a few hours until she got herself in hand once more before he began to talk business. It would be as well perhaps for her to lie down and rest that morning. He could do some other necessary errands and not waste much time. Then he would return later and they could make their plans. It was disappointing of course to find that she could be childish on occasion, but she had been strong so long, and shown herself superior to other girls in many ways. He must not hold this up against her. It really was not strange when one came to consider it that she should break down after all the days and nights of nursing. It was ridiculous of any parent to allow it, even if he did intend to die at the end of it. And the rest of the family preyed upon her continually. He was not sure but he ought just to pick her up and run away with her right off without waiting for her to get ready. Every minute she lingered in this house was unfitting her more and more for her life with him.

He frowned.

Yes, perhaps they could be married on Wednesday— or even Tuesday. Of course it would be more expensive for he would have to take a room at the hotel for a few days before they could start, but perhaps in the long run it might be cheaper. The next thing there would be doctor's bills.

Well, he would give her a chance to rest and meanwhile he would think out a less offensive way of approach. Perhaps it was a little raw to let her know right off how he felt about her father, but then it would have come out sooner or later of course, and it was always best to be frank. Well, he would try to be more soothing. Perhaps—he never had wasted money on flowers—but perhaps a few flowers—half a dozen rosebuds ought not to be high so near to summer. Well, he would see. Meanwhile, what should he do with the ring? Keep it and let her be anxious about it awhile? That might bring her to her senses quickest.

But no, he did not care to make even such a concession to her action. She must not think for an instant that he gave a thought to her giving the ring back. Of course that was nonsense. One did not undo solemn things. It was blasphemy to even hint at such a thing. He must find a way to make her see that.

There were pens and paper on a small desk in the corner. He sat down at the desk and wrote:

> *Doris,*
>
> *I am sending up your ring. It was not like you to stage a childish scene like that and leave your ring in a perilous position. But we will not say anything more about that. I am sure you will not try to be dramatic again. I know you are very weary, so I am going away that you may lie down and take a good sleep. Sometime this afternoon I will return and then I am sure you will feel better and we shall be able to discuss the future more amicably.*
>
> *As ever,*
> *Milton.*

He selected an envelope, addressed it to Doris, looked about for a bit of string, and finding none took a rubber band from his bank book, knotted it through the ring and then through a neat cut in the writing paper, sealed it into the envelope, put the pen and paper tidily away in their respective places, and then went to the hall door to reconnoitre.

Jean was just coming from the dining-room to go upstairs. He put on what he thought was a very pleasant smile and called her:

"Jean, will you kindly take this note up to your sister Doris? I think she has gone to her room to lie down."

Jean came promptly and took the note, a little surprised.

"Here's five cents, Jean, for running the errand."

He was smiling and trying really to make his voice sound pleasant. He noticed for the first time that she had brown eyes like Doris.

"Oh, no thanks!" said Jean with a faint color in her fair cheeks. "I'll take it without that," and she fluttered off upstairs with the note before he could recover his astonishment and press it upon her. He frowned perplexedly. Somehow he could not understand a child doing a thing like that.

He lingered a bit getting his overcoat on, half hoping Doris would repent her little temper and return after getting his note. He considered that note quite a concession. But Doris did not come down, and he reluctantly took his way out the front door, unattended. Even Jean did not come down. She might have sent Jean down. He did not like her holding a grudge so long. He did not know she had that kind of a nature. He had always thought she had a sunny disposition. But perhaps she would be all right when she got rested. He must watch in future any tendency to hold tempers and grudges and nip them in the bud. There was nothing so trying as a woman around the house always having a grievance. He had an aunt once who had them. Well, he would get a thousand little matters attended to this morning and go late in the afternoon, not too late, to take Doris for a short drive and freshen her up. She would doubtless be deeply repentant by that time. The prospect of a reconciliation was rather thrilling. They had never quarrelled before. But he would show her how magnanimous he could be—after he had shown her her mistakes of course. Anyway, it was good that Doris could get a little rest. On the whole it gave him deep satisfaction to think of her as lying quietly in her bed resting. She was doubtless thinking over all he had told her, and by this time she was planning what kind of curtains she would have in her new home in the West. Women were that way, he had often read. They made a great fuss about a thing when you first told them, but on the whole they rather liked a surprise and soon came around. Well, he would get half a dozen roses when he came back in the afternoon. It would probably please her, and a little drop of oil often made machinery move faster. It really was important that there be no delays about their preparations. If she put off deciding what she was going to do she would say she needed more time afterward to get ready. But if she began at once everything could easily be managed without hurry or excitement. Milton Page hated excitement. He claimed it was disorder, and only an indication of an undisciplined mind, like a cluttered living-room. He had a neat little talk on this subject that he sometimes delivered on occasion.

But Doris was not resting on her bed planning curtains for her new Western home. She was in Ned's room questioning him, trying to find a way out of the trouble, when Jean came to her door with the note. Fifteen minutes later she hurried to her own room to prepare for going out, but she did not notice the envelope lying on the bureau. She dressed mechanically.

She scarcely saw her own reflection in the mirror as her slim fingers disposed the shining bands of hair symmetrically about her head, and fitted on the close dark hat of fine imported felt.

Doris was accustomed to being well dressed. It did not seem a matter of great moment to her. She was not making any special effort now to appear well, only to be neatly and fittingly clad for the occasion.

She slipped into a slim dark coat edged with becoming fur, whose well cut lines marked it as coming from an exclusive shop, and while she put on her gloves she took a hasty survey of herself. She did not know how lovely she was and what an air of distinction she carried about her, from tip of dainty suède shoe to crown of becoming tailored hat. Even the dark shadows under the sorrowful brown eyes, and the pallor of her wistful face only added to her charm.

Satisfied from her hurried glance that she was all right, she went into the hall, paused a moment at the head of the stairs listening down the hall toward Ned's room, then finally went swiftly to his room and opened the door.

Ned turned with a start, a ready frown leaping into his face, then surveyed her with gradual relief. There was something reassuring about her quiet self-control, her ladylike appearance. Distinguished, that was the word that came to him as he looked at his sister.

"You're sure you don't want to go with me, Ned?" she asked wistfully. "It would seem as if that were the right thing for you to do."

The frown returned.

"No!"

Ned sprang up and began to walk the floor frantically like a caged creature, as if her words had touched some vital agony.

"No! Oh, no! I *couldn't!* It'll be much better for you to go alone! I don't *want* you to go at all, you know. But

I suppose you've got to see before you'll understand. Oh, if I only had some money!" and he began to prance frantically back and forth again.

"Listen, Ned! Now don't begin that again. Florence will hear you. Oh, why can't you act like a man?"

"There you go!" Ned made a desperate motion of his hands to his head. "I didn't ask you to go, did I? I just asked you for the loan of a few trifling dollars, and you made all this fuss. If you would just let me manage my affairs—"

"Ned, you weren't managing them. You were asking me to give up the money—all the money we have in the world with which to purchase food and shelter. If I had been the only one it wouldn't have mattered. But it wouldn't be honest to take it from the rest and buy a ring for a girl we never saw."

"She's my—" Ned began and finished with a groan, sinking down in the chair by the window again with his head on the window-seat.

"Yes, Ned, I know. But that is no reason why you should forget your sisters and your brother whom you have known and loved all your life. Oh, come now, Ned—" as he gave signs of further desperation. "This is hard enough without your acting crazy. Get up and shave and comb your hair, and go out and hunt a job while I'm gone. Then something real will be accomplished. We haven't any of us any time to waste. We've all got to begin earning or we'll presently find ourselves on the street begging."

Ned raised a haggard, scornful face.

"A job! Where would I get a job?" he asked contemptuously. "I'm only half through college, remember. You can't pick jobs off telegraph poles!"

"You don't find them moping in your bedroom either," said his sister coldly. "You should have thought of all that before you married her. But since you did not, since you have chosen to get married right in the midst of all our trouble, I think it's up to you to get busy and find a job before night. That will give you some self-respect. Come, get up and get ready! I'll tell her you've gone out to get a position. That will be a good excuse for my coming instead of you."

Ned suddenly drooped again.

"She won't think any job's worth anything unless I can give her all she wants. You don't know her. She's had a lot of swell guys running around with her. She wants a car of her own and all that. She—"

Doris turned with a kind of sick disgust in her face:

"Well, I'm afraid I can't provide her with one," she said with a faint gleam of sarcasm. "I might give her mine but I have discovered it isn't paid for, so I shall probably have to give it up. Ned, if you really haven't any sense at all, what is the use in my trying to help you?"

Ned was stung into silence for a moment, then he lifted miserable eyes and looked her over:

"Doris, I know I'm crazy. I wish I'd never seen her, I swear I do. I know you're ashamed of me."

"Yes," said Doris candidly, "I am. But that's no reason why you shouldn't pull yourself together and do the right thing, is it? Anyhow you've got to. People can't take obligations on themselves and then walk out from under them and leave their responsibilities for others to shoulder. I'm going to see her this once and make everything plain to her, and then it's up to you. But if I were you I'd have a job found before I went to her. Then you've got something solid to talk about."

"Well, tell me, where am I going to go? Shall I just stand out in the street with a placard 'Job Wanted' around my neck? *Where* am I going to go? I ask you?"

"Go anywhere! Everywhere! Go to Father's friends

and ask them. Go to Mr. Hamilton, he'll likely know of something."

"No sir! Not to old Ham. Not a step! Don't you remember how he treated me the summer I was working in his office to get my radio? Turned me down cold, too, when I apologized. And all because I forgot for a coupla days to mail a measly old letter of his that he said was so important. He told me then I had no sense of responsibility and nobody could trust me. Work for him again? I rather guess not. I guess I've got a little pride left. I'd rather starve."

"You can't let your wife starve," said Doris dryly, "and you won't find that pride will get you very far. Besides, wasn't he right? You haven't any sense of responsibility, have you? Would a person with a sense of responsibility have gone and got married in the midst of family trouble, when he knew there was no money to be left to him, and that he wasn't through college and would likely have a hard time getting a job? I ask you, would he?"

Ned's answer was to collapse into his chair again and groan.

"Well, then if you're ever going to have, get up!" said Doris coldly. "Get up and go tell Mr. Hamilton you're grown up now and want to get something to do to help. If I know anything about him he'll help you now. But for pity's sake don't take the high hat with him or he'll be disgusted with you. I sometimes think you didn't learn anything at college but nonsense. Perhaps it's just as well you can't finish. Hurry, Ned. It's almost two o'clock. Hustle and get ready and then make up your mind you're going to get something even if it's only distributing newspapers. And don't for pity's sake get an idea you're going to get a big salary to start with.

Remember even five dollars a week is better than nothing."

"Five dollars!" Ned wheeled on his sister and towered above her in scorn. "As if I'd work for five dollars a week!"

"You may be thankful to get four before you're done, Ned Dunbar. Remember you don't know how to do anything, and you aren't through college yet. You've got to make a beginning even if you pay to learn how. So don't try to begin at the top or you'll never get anywhere. I'm going now. See how quick you can come home with good news. Good-bye buddy!" She suddenly changed her tone and reaching up kissed the tip of his ear. "It's pretty awfully dark now, but there must be some light ahead somewhere. Hold on and do what you can till we find it."

She was gone.

The boy stood still for an instant looking after her, a sudden, tender, shamed look upon his face. Then he quickly brushed the back of his hand across his eyes and began to charge around his room and get ready to go out.

Ten minutes later, clothed in his finest, clean-shaven and with a new look of purpose in his unformed handsome face, he dashed out the front door and made off toward the business section of the city.

A moment later a taxi drew up to the door and Mrs. Dunbar who had evidently been watching for it at her window, sailed downstairs fully swathed in a black veil, got into it, and drove away.

Almost immediately John appeared in the upper hall, reconnoitred a moment, then stole back to his room for a bundle of wire and some tools and stealthily entered his stepmother's room. This was the long anticipated hour for which he had waited, when she should be out and away and he might step forth from her window to the ledge of the bathroom roof, the only available entrance to the roof in general without a ladder. He had been waiting to put up a new aerial for his radio for some time, but had not dared try it as he knew she would complain, but now the coast was clear and he set forth from the window joyfully. A few minutes' work and he could return the same way and close the window, and she none the wiser.

He had scarcely got safely out of sight when Rose came down dressed for the street, and charming as her name. Jean, who was curled up in a big living-room chair reading "Under the Lilacs" for the seventh time, looked up and admired her.

"Where are you going, sister, couldn't I go too?" she asked eagerly.

"No, dear, I'm going to hunt for a job, and people don't look for jobs in couples."

"A job? What kind of a job?" asked Jean puzzled.

"Just a job. Anything to earn money. We've all got to work now you know, since our money is all gone."

"Oh," said Jean, "was that what Mr. Hamilton meant? Will I have to work too?"

"No, Kittie," said Rose stooping to kiss her little sister. "You aren't old enough. You have to go to school yet."

Jean sat and thought about it for some time after her sister left until she heard the door-bell peal through the empty house, for Hannah the maid had also gone out that afternoon to look for another job.

Jean laid down her book and glanced out of the window. She saw a car standing at the door, and Milton Page was on the front steps with something in his hand tied up in green tissue paper. It looked like flowers. Was Milton bringing some flowers to Doris? How nice!

But just as she was turning to go and open the door for him she saw a shadow of something like a great bird descending swiftly from up somewhere in the sky, and it shot down heavily and struck the frail bundle that Milton carried dashing it from his hand to the stone step and completely covering it with a great lump of slime and leaves.

The little girl stood aghast and looked at the young man who seemed for the moment petrified, contemplating with consternation the wreck of the costly half-dozen, a small fragment of green wax paper held tightly in his gloved hand, his immaculate shoes spattered with the oozy black stuff, and spatters of the same inklike spots down the front of his new gray overcoat. It was very funny to see the serious Milton Page looking so helpless. But then the serious look came back to his eyes again, he glanced above toward the eaves, but there was no sign of how the dark object had started. He looked down again as if to identify its origin, and by this time he was wholly himself, and beginning to put his finger on the reason for the accident. In a moment more he would be blaming someone. Jean began to be frightened, as if she somehow were to blame, and she hurried to the door to let him in.

"Something seems to have fallen," he said almost embarrassedly as she swung the door open. "There are some quite expensive flowers under that rubbish, which I was bringing to your sister Doris." His voice was severe now, and he was stamping the mud and leaves from his shoes.

"Is anyone cleaning out your gutters?" he asked severely.

"Oh, I don't think so," said Jean.

"Where is John?" asked Milton, beginning to get back

to normal rapidly now. "He is quite capable of a thing like that."

A white look of comprehension like a fleeting ghost crossed the little girl's delicate face. John was her idol:

"Oh, I think he's gone out," she said quickly. "They've all gone out to look for jobs. We've all got to work now you know," she said with an air of entertaining him. "I'm sure John went too. Yes, a long while ago. Won't you come in and sit down till they come back? I'm all alone."

6

DORIS had taken a trolley to the address that Ned had
given her. Her own little runabout would have taken her
there more quickly, but she had a feeling that she had no
right to use it any more. More than anything on this
expedition she wished to be genuine.

She got out of her trolley a little bewildered by the
neighborhood in which she found herself; an old district
of tenements lately patched up into cheap apartments.
They reeked of various cooking dinners as she made her
way up three courses of seemingly interminable stairs
and finally knocked at a door. Her heart was beating
wildly. She began to wonder why she had come. It was
as if the whole thing were suddenly a bad dream and she
was going to bring it into reality by making this move.
Why had she not let the girl alone, let her do her worst?
What difference did it make? And yet of course it did
make a difference.

There was a sudden cessation of clatter in what must
be a kitchenette behind one of the doors down the hall,
and presently a door opened just a crack. She had a
feeling of being inspected. Then the tiny jar of the

closing door again, whispered voices, soft steppings, and finally the door before which she stood opened formally, half-grudgingly it seemed, and a woman stood there; a woman of about forty with a red face, and the appearance of a hasty apparelling. She was stout and coarse and her gray hair straggled out from under the transformation which had been adjusted to hurriedly and was awry. She looked Doris over belligerently and did not invite her in.

Doris caught her breath softly. It was going to be worse than she had feared. Then she opened her lips and spoke in a low musical voice that did not show the agitation she was feeling:

"I would like to see Miss Bullard if you please. Will you tell her I am Miss Dunbar."

The woman opened the door, still grudgingly, and admitted her, but did not offer her a chair. Doris went in, however, and sat down.

The woman gave her another cool glance, still belligerently, and walked heavily away through striped chenille portières into a room which evidently was a dining-room. Doris could see a table piled with soiled dishes, and a tall bottle half-full of some dark amber liquid. Then the curtain fell and she was left alone for a long time.

There were soft steppings about in a room beyond the dining-room, low half-whispered words which she could not understand, and she was left sitting with her heart beating wildly.

She glanced about timidly at first. The room was cheaply furnished with showy furniture, and there were a number of photographs of men in ornate frames about the room. A pile of moving-picture magazines was on the floor by a big chair as if the reader had hastily deserted them. A soiled pack of cards lay on the table, and an elaborate picture hat of coral velvet trimmed with a large silver rose lay on the top of the cheap upright piano. There was not much else in the room save a pair of silver slippers lying one in one corner of the room, the other under the centre table, as if they had been carelessly kicked off.

It was impossible now not to try to conjure up a vision of this new sister-in-law, who was presently to appear between those striped portières, and Doris thought she was prepared for the worst.

She would be dumpy, perhaps a little stout, with black hair and coarse features like the woman. The hair would likely be bobbed in the most mannish and obnoxious style, and she would wear cheap finery and many rings, perhaps long earrings and strings of beads. Her hands, if her hands would only be clean and well-cared for! Oh, how could Ned have done this! How could he fall in love with a common girl and think to fix her for life on his family? Think of Rose having to go about with a girl like that. A girl who perhaps chewed gum and bit her finger-nails, and talked loudly in public places.

She was going on adding to the possibilities ad infinitum, when suddenly without sound of any steps, the curtains parted and the girl stood before her smiling.

It was not a pleasant smile. It was set, and wooden, like a stage smile, and there was a glittering light of hidden triumph in the blue cold eyes above the smile. But she was not dumpy and stout, with straight black hair, nor any of the other things that Doris had imagined. She was tall and lithe as a willow, standing straight between the portières in a brief sheathlike frock of vivid blue satin which set off the supple figure startlingly. Her arms were bare and white as milk, graceful as a feather, and she had exquisitely moulded hands, pink and manicured to the last degree. She wore nude-colored silk stockings and patent leather pumps with cut steel buckles, and around her neck was a choker of rock crystals, which glowed and glittered almost like diamonds. Above this was a face of startling prettiness, cheeks of flaming roses on a skin of rare loveliness, features like a beautiful wax dolly of the old-fashioned type, painted vivid mouth with cupid's sharp corners, delicate black eyebrows arched just enough, big, blue, staring eyes with long curling heavy lashes generously darkened. The whole was surmounted by a lovely head of real flaxen hair, the kind the best dolls used to wear, every hair curled just so, and every hair polished to a burnished beaten gold.

Doris sat startled looking at her, unable to speak for the moment, she was so like a tall doll just out of the box. It almost seemed as if you could pull a string and she would say "Mamma!" Doris had an impulse to go to her and try to lay her down to see if her eyes would shut and open. She had to jerk her mind back to facts and remind herself that this was probably her new sister-in-law.

The dolly did not try to help her any. She just stood there, poised on her dainty high heels with that silly wax smile on her face, and that expressionless stare in her china-blue eyes, her hands grasping lightly the folds of the striped chenille curtain as toy hands would do, and for all the world as if she were a puppet just appeared on the stage. It was difficult for Doris to realize that she was not at a show where she had to sit still and watch would happen next.

But she suddenly came to herself and rose:

"Are you—?" she hesitated whether to say "Miss Bullard" again or not. Perhaps a girl just married would resent that, and yet she could not bring herself to call her Mrs. Dunbar. It seemed perfectly absurd. Perfectly terrible! This Ned's wife! How impossible!

"I'm Zephyr," said the dolly-faced girl graciously, as if she were reciting a piece, "I presume that's who you mean."

"Zephyr?" enquired Doris, with a half hope that this was not Ned's wife after all.

"Yes, didn't Ned tell you? I'm Zephyr, down at the theatre where I dance. You have heard of me of course. You're Ned's sister, I suppose?"

Zephyr! Dance! The theatre! So there were more complications! Why didn't Ned tell her?

"Oh," said Doris simply, "I didn't know. I thought Ned gave you another name. Yes, I'm his sister."

"Zoe," said the girl with a toss of her golden fleece. "Yes, that's my name, but I go by the other name almost entirely now. It's my dancing name you know." And she stared at her visitor, still with that same unmoved smile. Doris had a feeling that the smile was painted on to hide her real feelings and would continue no matter what the girl felt. It was like a pretty pink and white mask. It made her feel at a disadvantage.

"I have come," said Doris sitting quietly down in her chair again, for she felt as if she would sink down on the floor if she tried to talk standing, "I came to have a little talk with you. Have you time to sit down a few minutes and explain the situation to me?"

"Oh, surely!" said the dolly-faced girl graciously with the air of granting a great favor. She moved gracefully to a chair and sat down in the latest approved slouch with one knee flung as mannishly above the other as the narrow confines of her slim frock allowed, thus revealing a dainty garter of astonishing workmanship. "Of course I'm pretty busy just now for we have an extra rehearsal late this afternoon, a special stunt with Barri du Mille they are putting on to-night for the first you know—you ought to come and see it, it's awfully darling. And as I haven't tried it before I shall have to practise some. But then I've always a few minutes for the family you know."

She paused and lifted her china eyes and her painted smile for Doris to view again.

Doris tried to keep from wincing as she took in the thrust. She gathered voice and went quickly on with what she had to say. She had not tried to plan this interview. It had been impossible. There was nothing for it but to be straightforward:

"I'm not here to find fault with you and Ned for having gotten married this way without having told anybody," she said gently, "nor to remind you that Ned is only nineteen and not through college yet, he probably has told you all that. I just came to tell you the whole situation. I thought perhaps I could make it plainer than Ned could, he is so terribly cut up about it all."

She paused and Zephyr gave her a startled stare and lifted her rosy chin a trifle enquiringly, much as a young colt would do when it was about to take alarm.

"You know of course that our father has just died."

Zephyr's china eyes simply stared giving neither assent nor dissent.

"You probably do not know, because Ned did not know himself when he last saw you, that my father's business affairs were deeply involved before he died, and that we have lost everything, even the house that we live in."

The striped chenille portières quivered a little at this as if something had touched them.

Zephyr's smile seemed a little frozen but her eyes were smiling with the same china-blue stare. Doris hurried on.

"I am sorry that I had to be the one to bring you this news, and that it had to come this way before we knew you at all. But my brother was obliged to go out and look for a position, and he was so distressed about everything that I undertook to come and make things plain to you."

Here the chenille curtains billowed out impatiently, but Doris continued:

"My brother felt that there were things that you would expect of him."

Zephyr nodded and smiled more warmly.

"But I felt sure when you understood how things were with us—"

At this the chenille curtains parted and showed the red-faced woman with an angry frown:

"You can't put anything like that over on us," she said in a loud tone. "I wasn't born last year, and I've seen more slim, tricky hypocrites among the aristocrats than I ever did among the honest hard-workin' poor. I know your kind. You're one of them mealy-mouthed stuck-ups that don't want yer brother to marry out o' yer *class*. I've heard 'em talk, an' I know their line. I thought when you come in with them so-plain-yeh-cost-a-for-tune coats on an' that high an' mighty way o' speakin' that you was just pussy-footin' to get yer darling brother away from my girl. But ya shan't do it. I'm too smart fer yer tricks. This time he's caught, an' he'll have a nasty time ef he tries to get away fer I don't stop at nothing— I—"

But Doris arose suddenly. Strength and poise had come to her in the knowledge of this woman's weakness. If breeding and education meant anything it surely meant that she ought to dominate a situation like this, terrible though it was:

"Mrs. Bullard," she said in a low tone that arrested the attention of the angry mother, "my brother has no intention of trying to get away from promises that he has made. I have simply come to explain the situation that we are all in. I have come to say that we are about to move, that is, if they allow us to keep anything to move. But I presume in the course of a few weeks we shall find a place to live somewhere, and that then if it is at all possible we will try to make room for my brother and his wife to live with us, for I scarcely see how Ned will be able at present to set up a separate establishment.

"No you don't!" said the angry woman wheeling on Doris once more. "My darlin' child isn't going to be under the jealous eyes of any family-in-laws. She's goin' to have her own home."

"Very well, Mrs. Bullard. Your daughter and my brother can settle that matter as they think best when Ned gets a job. I am merely offering, as his sister, to do all I can. If Ned were in a position to give his wife a home I am sure that would be the best solution all around. But I have done what I could. I have no money to give or to lend to my brother, and I am not at all sure that the home I could offer him would be anywhere near as good as the one your daughter has now, for we have all got to go to work, and I do not know what we can afford. But I am ready to stand by my brother far enough to offer to share what I have with him and his wife until he can do better."

The red-faced mother stood with folded arms much like a prize-fighter about to begin another round. Her lips were pursed, her brows drawn to the lowering point and she looked Doris in the eye with a wicked glare. Behind her Zephyr sat in her chair composedly, the fixed smile shimmering over her face as if it could not help itself, almost as if this were a matter in which she were not herself in the least concerned, like a doll set aside to stare unseeingly till needed again.

As Doris glanced back to the belligerent mother, a sneering smile overspread the woman's face like the sudden lightning in a thunder cloud, and when she spoke her voice had a rumble of menace like distant thunder:

"That might be all O.K., Miss, if it was true. Very decent of you an' all that. But it *ain't!* I know yer kind, as I said before, an' I know yer lying."

Doris caught her breath angrily.

"Yes, that gets on yer nerve, don't it? But I'm plain spoken. I like to say what I mean. I say it's lyin'. I took pains ta find out what kinda young man my angel child was goin' with when he first started to trail around after her, an' take her to midnight suppers, an' joy rides an' things. It's all printed in a book how much people in this city is worth, an' anybody can find out if they try, an' *I tried!* You can put that in yer pipe an' smoke it! You say yer pa lost his money. Well, ef he did I know he's good an' got some salted down fer his family. Rich folks don't fail that way nowadays. They fix it in somebody's name, an' you got it all right, an' my daughter's goin' ta have her share ur you all 'll smart fer it. I told that brother of yours that ef he didn't come to time within the week Zoe Bullard was goin' to sue him fer divorce an' publish all his doin's in the daily papers. They won't be purty readin' neither, I can tell you. He was in some real shady places oncet or twicet, an' the p'lice 'll be only too glad ta get hold of his name you can bet. Then I guess you'll be sorry you didn't shut up and fork over."

Doris stood frozen to the spot. Every particle of strength seemed to have suddenly flowed out of her body mysteriously. She felt as if she were a mere ghost made of lace paper and would presently blow over with the breath of this awful woman's words. Her very lips felt cold as she tried to open them. She wondered vaguely why she had come, and whether they would ever find her, provided she did not succeed in getting out of this place before she was spiritually consumed.

She remembered in a kind of meaningless way that she had eaten no lunch and that breakfast too had been rather sketchy. Then to her own surprise, she heard herself saying in quite a cool little voice:

"Well, Mrs. Bullard, I suppose that people have lived through things like that before. They probably can again. If we can't, we can always die!"

And then she knew that her feet were carrying her out the door, shakily, like the tissue-paper feet that they were, but still doing it. Good little feet, she commended them, for carrying on when she was unable to direct them.

She heard the breezy voice of Zephyr calling down the stairs after her:

"If you think you'd like to go to my show to-night I could send you over tickets. I'd like you to see me dance."

And then she was out in the street walking along she knew not how, headed in what direction she had not thought, only walking, almost flying.

Often as a child she had dreamed that she was hurrying somewhere and suddenly her feet were lifted from the ground a foot or two and she went on in the air, like flying, the only danger being that she would grow lighter and lighter and rise so high she could never come down again. It was like that now. Her over-wrought nerves imagined that her feet were no longer on the solid earth, but speeding along in the air somewhere, and if nobody stopped her she would never get back to earth again. And almost she was glad.

But gradually as she walked she came out into the open spaces where houses were few and far between, and where bare trees lifted lacy brown fingers against a sky which had clouded over during the afternoon and now was piling powder-blue clouds against a leaden West.

There was more room to breathe out here, and time to think. Her feet seemed to be going more slowly now, and to touch earth again and feel more firm. The throbbing in her head had almost stopped and her cheeks had ceased to sting and burn from the shame of the words the woman had flung after her.

She came suddenly to the end of the paving, though the road stretched away over the brow of a little brown hill firm with last year's meadow grass, and dimly outlined by wheel tracks months old. There was a soft fringe of fine brush against the horizon and a faint pink tint in a lifting crevice of the powder-blue clouds. She kept on aimlessly, stumbling over the uneven ground and thinking that life was like this, all full of uneven places, and hers had come to the unpaved place. It would probably go on the rest of the way without paving. She had had her easy time while Father lived. Now it would all be hardships and how was she to bear it?

Then suddenly, as she looked up again at the place that had been pink, there burst forth a great red ball of glory, startling her with its very nearness and wonder, as if it had eyes of light that were looking into her soul; calling to her from out the universe; getting her attention for some very special message. She felt that as a conviction as she hurried on to the very top of the little hillock and stood looking across the darkening brown meadow straight into the ruby light of the setting sun. It must be God!

Just like that the thought came. There was a God. He had made her. And perhaps He was trying to signal her for something now. She was very desperate. Why would it not be reasonable to expect a great and good Creator to do something about it when one had reached the very limit? Her soul leaped to the thought.

Of course people prayed, and some professed to have answers. She knew that. She could remember her mother praying and teaching her to pray when she was a little, little girl. But that was not like this.

She had not been praying. She had not prayed in many a long year. She might be foolish and fanciful, but what if it were true that God was trying to signal her through the sun? What harm to try and understand the message? God must have created the sun. It was His instrument. How gloriously it was hung there in the atmosphere like a living fire, a jewel. No wonder those barbarous peoples worshipped the sun of old. It must have filled them with great awe.

And to think of its having burst forth there in the midst of the storm clouds and gathering darkness. Ah! Was that her message? She was in the midst of awful thick darkness, and storms rumbling, peril promising on every hand. Did God mean He was there behind the cloud? Ready to show the light when needed? Why, down below her in the little valley, where all had been gray and brown with the evening shadows, a bright reflection shone now from the breast of a tiny stream, widening into a little pond. It lay as still as the earth about it and caught the ruby reflection. It seemed to tell her she was standing at the very gates of God.

She glanced about her hurriedly—not a soul in sight. The nearest house at least two blocks away. Before her the fringe of bare brush and trees pencilled against the sky, and the great fire jewel rapidly sinking now, slipping with its edge just below the rim of the opposite hill. She must be quick or it would be gone.

Then out of her desperate need she spoke aloud:

"O God!" she said very softly, "I think you must be

here. You are very wonderful and great, and I am only one of the smallest that you have made. But I keep thinking you care. Is that what you meant this sight to tell me? If it is, if you really care, won't you please help me when I get home? Won't you show me the way through all this darkness?"

She stood silent in awe and watched the last glowing rim of the sun slip out into darkness, and then she bowed her head and closed her eyes for a moment.

When she lifted it again, a rosy glow seemed to be over everything and looking up, the whole top of the heavens had burst into coral glory of rosy feathery clouds, which touched even the leaden horizon into beauty, and glowed and paled and glowed again into golden, and emerald, then faded softly into amber and pale gold.

Long after, when she had walked back to civilization again and was climbing into a car that would take her home, she looked back and saw the pale gold opening in the dark clouds, where the sun had been, as if the peril of the storm promise had been broken by that glowing ball of fire, and riding away into the East she kept saying softly in her heart, "He answered!" in wonder, "I think He meant that for an answer," and, "I shall believe that anyway."

7

WHEN John Dunbar had attained the height of the roof and set up his aerial with elaborate care and satisfaction, he looked about him with delight. Seldom before since he had been old enough to climb had he been able to attain this position, because his stepmother in her room had always prevented, or there had been somebody about to stop him. His father had forbidden him to make the attempt.

But John figured now that his father was gone there was no one who cared enough or had the right to stop him unless it was his stepmother and he did not intend that she should have the opportunity to object. It would be sometime before she returned. He argued that she would not have gone in a taxi if she had not been going quite a distance. Besides, he was in a sightly place. He was keeping an eagle eye out for yellow taxis, and why not enjoy himself for once now that he was here? He would not soon get up here again.

He took a bird's-eye view of the neighborhood, identifying all the boys' houses, and studying their aerials carefully, deciding his was better than any of them. Then he wandered over to the front of the roof to get a cursory glance of the street from above. It was almost like going in an aeroplane, he fancied.

But after a few minutes even this new view of the world grew monotonous and he began to cast about in his mind for something more active to do. As he turned reluctantly from the parapet that was built across the front of the house like a wall, he realized that his feet were wet, for he had taken off his shoes and was in his stocking feet. He glanced down and saw that the leaves in which he was standing which had blown into a heap next to the parapet, were overlying a layer of black slime. Looking along to the corner where the gutter-pipe carried the rain-water down, he discovered that the opening was entirely covered with leaves. Ah! That was why the water came over in such sheets whenever there was a big storm, and made gullies in the little scrap of a side yard. He would clean it out. It ought to be cleaned out. He would *love* to clean it out. For once his desires and his duty were one.

With a stick, which he had brought with him in the bundle strapped to his shoulders when he climbed up, he set to work.

He started in at the opening of the gutter-pipe in the corner and pushed the refuse away little by little until he had the opening all clear, and the little wire protector set in place again as it ought to be. Then he shoved the rapidly increasing pile of leaves and slime ahead of him up toward the other front corner of the parapet. But when he reached what was approximately the middle of the wall the pile got cumbersome for the stick, so abandoning it he stooped and gathered up a great armful, as much as he could manage, taking care to tuck the leaves around the slime at the bottom, and gather up as much of that as he could get—boylike, not stopping to think where he was throwing it—he reached over the parapet and flung it with all his might.

It had not left his arms before he realized that he had flung it directly over the steps. Leaning over he took in the whole disaster with consternation, and instantly ducked back out of sight.

"Gee! Golly!" he said below his breath. "I've done it now," and streaked it across the roof like a bird, down a gutter-pipe, in at his stepmother's window, taking the treacherous leap from the pantry roof without hesitation. It was necessary that he be elsewhere almost at once or all his precautions would have been useless and dire displeasure would descend upon him.

He almost forgot to shut the window and gather up his shoes from the bed where he had thoughtfully left them when he went up, but remembered them just in time. He fled down the back stairs, pausing at the dining-room door to listen an instant, and thanking his lucky stars that Hannah was out and would not question.

He was just in time to hear Milton Page ask for him, and to hear his little sister's reply:

"They've all gone out to look for jobs. We've all got to work now you know. I'm sure John went, too. Yes, a long while ago."

Long years afterward John remembered that kindness of his little sister, treasured it in his heart, and many a time went out of his way to do her a kindness in memory of it, though he never told her why.

But he registered the whole thing, as he poised there between kitchen and dining-room, his head on one side, his weather eye out, his shoes still clutched under his arm.

Then when he heard them sit down he let the swing door go noiselessly shut, slid out the back door without a sound and over the back fence. Crouched down beside the ash can, he put on his shoes and did a bit of chain-lightning thinking.

So it was true then! They were very poor. They were all going to have to go to work. Well, then, it was up to him to get a job too, wasn't it? He wouldn't mind a bit. He wouldn't have to go to school any more. That would get it back on that teacher that said he had to stay in every day for three weeks to make up for putting the bee in his desk. Better make sure of the job right away before anyone was foolish enough to think he was too young to work and had to keep on at school for a while. He wasn't a baby. Doris would be sure to want to hold him back. Of course he had always wanted to go to college to be in Ned's frat, and to play football. But they had football other places besides college. He might work in a foundry. They had a team there, crackerjack players, too. Besides he must help support the family. It wouldn't be right for women to be working, supporting him, a great big boy. When he got older he would study by himself evenings and make up. They did that sometimes. Of course it must be awful dry getting things alone that way, but he'd do it if he wanted to bad enough and enter college without their old prep school. He'd read of fellas that did that. Sam Bazeley's cousin did that and got to be an awful grind. He could if he liked. He wasn't so sure he cared about college since he'd thought of the outside teams. He could be a professional, mebbe, if Doris didn't find it out. She wouldn't like that. Of course there was the frat, but then frats weren't everything. There were clubs and things.

He tied the last knot and looked about him surreptitiously. He must get away from the neighborhood as soon as possible. Well, he'd better begin to look for that job at once.

He tramped off down the alley at a good pace, and lost

no time in putting several blocks between himself and home. He looked dubiously down at himself when he considered trying for a job. Boys ought to look neat when they went for jobs.

Owing to the fact that he had been ordered by Rose to put on his good suit that morning for Mr. Hamilton's visit, he still had it on. No one had thought to tell him to take it off, and he was not accustomed to taking off good things himself to save them. He always wore them when he got the chance.

But the suit was rather crummy. It hadn't been improved by his climb up the waterspout and his armful of slime and leaves. He stopped behind a tree, moistened his handkerchief in his mouth and scrubbed away at one lapel where a mud stain was particularly noticeable. His shoes needed polishing too. His necktie and his hair—well, he could wash his hands and face at the fireplug downtown, and his handkerchief was almost clean. He could wipe on that. If he found Ted anywhere around he could borrow Ted's comb. Ted's mother always made him carry one, and besides, Ted had a sort of girl, and combed his hair a lot. They got that way when they got girls, even young girls. John regretted that he must pay attention to his hair; it seemed effeminate, but a job was a big thing, much more important than girls, and one couldn't be called a sissy for combing up for that. So he made his way to Ted's usual after-school haunt and borrowed the comb. Of course Ted wanted to know why this unwonted fineness. John explained that he was going to leave school and get a job. Ted at once made suggestions.

"Whyn't ya get a job at Lyman's department store? It's peachy there! I know a kid—he's my cousin—an' he works there. Ya get yer pay raised every six months, and ya get time off fer studies and ta play in the band, and they have a baseball team, and running, and my cousin he got sent up to New York to run in the races, and he got a gold medal. Whyn't ya go there an' ask fer a job? I guess they always want fellas."

"Mebbe I will," said John loftily. "I got two er three things up my sleeve. I gotta look round. Well, so long Ted! Thanks fer the comb. I'll have ta get me one myself now I'm a business man. Sorry I can't be with ya Saturday at the game. Goo-by!" and John sauntered down a block or two with his hands in his pockets whistling.

At another group of boys he paused, borrowed a bicycle of one with the promise of coming over some evening to fix up his radio by way of pay, and mounting rode away in the direction of the department stores.

Descending upon Lyman's he found a little difficulty in parking his borrowed bicycle, but presently discovered an obliging guard at the employees' entrance, who agreed to look after it for him when he heard John had a special message for Mr. Lyman and couldn't send it up but must "see him in person."

Bold because of his utter ignorance, John presently found himself in Mr. Lyman's outer office, seated in a long row of chairs with other applicants for the great business man's favor. John had not told what he wanted. He had only said he had a message for Mr. Lyman. John's philosophy was that whatever had worked once was liable to work again, so he tried the same method he had used with the doorkeeper.

It worked again. John was told to sit down and await his turn.

There were boys in that office about his own age. He had lifted his chin and told them loftily whom he wanted to see, and they treated him respectfully as if he were a man, as if they were men. He saw that was a part of their business. He watched them awhile as they came and went respectfully with messages, and sat over in one corner waiting a call, and he decided that it was a great life. He wanted to be one of those boys. He had read or heard somewhere that a boy always ought to know what he wanted to be. Well, he would decide right then and there that he would like to get to be owner of this store.

Across from the seat where he was placed, on the wall, hung an immense painting of the Lyman store. It filled him with awe and joy. To be a part of that great system! Gee! He guessed his stepmother wouldn't dare order him around if he was employed in a great store like that.

So it came his turn at last to give his name to one of the secretaries at the desk, who wrote his name and address on the typewriter and sent it in to Mr. Lyman by one of the boys. John stood waiting with very red cheeks and determined mouth. He meant to get to be one of them before he came out of that office. And presently he was summoned to the inner sanctum.

John had no sense of his own temerity in thus invading the chief's office without a bidding. He did not know that when boys wanted a job they had to go to the employment offices downstairs and bring references, and go through days and sometimes weeks of waiting while a lot of red tape was unwound, and then perhaps get turned down. John walked into the Lyman office with his head up and an eye to conquer. The same boy that climbed the waterspout, cleaned the roof, and smashed Milton Page's roses beyond recognition, the boy that put the bee in the new teacher's desk, was out to get a job!

"Well, sir! What can I do for you?" asked the merchant, eyeing the boy keenly, noting his frank merry smile, his clear complexion, his straightforward bearing.

"I want a job and I thought this was the best place to come," answered John without hesitation.

"Um! Who sent you?" asked the keen student of human nature.

"Nobody," said John, "I just came."

"Haven't you any references?"

John looked sober.

"No, do you have to have references?"

John couldn't think of a single living soul, except perhaps Ted, who might give him a reference, and Ted would hardly count. Doris might on a pinch, but Doris was not to be thought of.

"We generally have to have references," said Lyman severely. Someone was evidently to blame for letting this boy in without knowing his business.

"Don't you know this isn't the place to apply for jobs anyway?" asked the great head of the store.

"Oh," said John more hopefully, "isn't it?" Perhaps they weren't so particular about references in the right place. Then he gleamed trustfully up into the man's face. "How'd it be if you'd take me there then and give um a good reference for me?"

It wasn't impudence, it was just pure good will and comradeship in John's smile as he showed his fine white teeth between his healthy red lips and twinkled his merry eyes. But most men would not have taken it that way. Most business men would have called it impudence and sent John flying. Lyman eyed him a minute and broke out laughing:

"Sit down you young rascal, who are you anyway?"

John sat down.

"Mebbe you know my dad," he hazarded. "He was quite a little well known."

"H'm! Who was your dad?" He referred to the type-written slip in his hand. "Dunbar. What's his first name?"

"John Edward. I'm John and my brother Ned is Edward."

"Not John E. Dunbar of Dunbar, Reed and Co."

"Yes. That's my dad," said John with a gleam lighting his eyes.

"So you're his son? And you want to come into my store?"

John nodded.

"Well, what does your father say to that? Have you told him? Did he send you?"

"Dad's dead, sir!" said John huskily, his eyes drooping embarrassedly as he fumbled with a button on his coat.

"Oh," said Lyman, "I didn't know. I'm sorry. So that's it. But surely, surely—You are young yet. Wouldn't your father have wanted you to stay in school a while first?"

John shook his head.

"I can't," he said firmly, "I've got to help support the family."

"Oh," said the head of the big store again. "Well, that's a different story. Well, I guess we'll have to give you a job. What do you think you'd like to do?"

John straightened up and motioned with his thumb toward the outer office:

"First I'd like to be one of those fellas out there," he said.

"And afterward?" queried the head of the store.

"Oh, bimeby I'd like to own the store."

"You don't say!" said Lyman interestedly. "Well, perhaps you will, who knows? But meantime there's no reason why you shouldn't begin as one of my special messenger boys. Two are being promoted today, and I haven't yet picked their successors."

He reached forward and touched a bell, and one of the secretaries appeared at the door:

"This is John Dunbar, Mr. Landon. I wish you would take him down to Bergen and see that he is properly registered and has his instructions. He is to take Merryweather's place. John you may report tomorrow morning at half past eight, and if you are faithful there is no reason why you won't succeed. It all depends on whether you can hold down the job. We can't have any nonsense here, John."

"All right, sir. Thank you. And could I stick around up here after I get through down at the office and get the hang of things so I'll be of some use in the morning?"

"Sure! Stick around all you like only don't get in anybody's way. Good-bye John. Good luck!"

John went away with an impression of hearty good will, and a big warm handclasp. Already he felt that he would protect his new employer with his life if it were necessary.

John "stuck around" till the store closed and possessed himself of much knowledge. He knew about lockers, and entrances, and the code of the office. He knew exactly what he had to do in the morning, and which door to come in. He knew all of the boys in the office by name and what each thought of the boss, and he knew the different secretaries. As he went down to retrieve his borrowed bicycle from a much disgusted guard, who was about to leave it with the night police, he reflected that in spite of accidents he had done a good day's work.

Then he rode to the house of the owner of the bicycle, and paid for the use of it by working on the other boy's radio for a couple of hours. He did not go home to supper, but accepted a portion in the privacy of his friend's bedroom, professing not to have time to go home for it. So the day drew toward an end, and John arrived at last at his own door, suddenly realizing that he would be expected to account for himself and wondering if after all the family would appreciate his efforts in their behalf. He began to wonder if Milton Page had gone home yet.

8

MRS. DUNBAR reached home before anyone else. She paid her taxi, sailed up the steps with the grand air of a conqueror, opened the door stealthily with her own latch-key, and stood poised like an old purple grackle with her head cocked on one side listening.

The house was absolutely silent. She stole to the door of the living-room. Even Jean had disappeared from her chair leaving her book open at the place where she had left off reading. There was a strange sweet perfume in the air, probably remaining from the funeral flowers, and yet— She glanced hurriedly around with her small sharp eyes, bird's eyes, and spied three drooping rosebuds hanging dejectedly from a bud vase which stood on the mantel. Now, where did they come from? Had some of the children dared to extract flowers from their father's wreaths? With a petulant frown she stepped over to the mantel, pulled the flowers from the vase, glided to the front door, opened it and flung them far out across the curb, watching a passing automobile grind them to powder. Then she shut the front door and hurried down the hall to the kitchen, opening the door a crack to see if Hannah was there. Hannah was not. Hannah believed in making the most of a day off. Hannah did not return until after midnight.

With a quick glance around to make sure she was alone she stepped over to the gas stove and made a cup of tea. While the tea-kettle was boiling she rummaged in the refrigerator, and gathered quite a tempting lunch on a tray. When the tea was ready she took the tray up to her own room locking her door ostentatiously. If Rose was at home in her room as she probably was, lying on her bed reading a novel, she wished her to know that the door was locked, and locked hostilely. Mrs. Dunbar was always dramatic in whatever she did. She would like the family to think that she was starving herself. She wanted to make it apparent that she was punishing them for their disrespect to her the night before.

She took off her wraps and put them away. Then she settled comfortably and ate her supper, enjoying it with the keen relish of one who has fasted for a number of hours.

But the continued stillness of the house began to be alarming. She was a very scary person always, and doubly so since her husband's death. She began to imagine that perhaps they had all gone off and left her, and having thought of such a possibility she could stand it no longer without investigation. Moreover, if they were all out this was the very time to search for any papers that might be useful in her protest of the will. Not that Mrs. Dunbar had the slightest idea what kind of papers they would be in order to help her cause. She did not have a legal mind, she had merely gathered up a heterogeneous mass of ideas from the novels and magazines she had read. And one very strong impression was that stepdaughters and sons usually did something with their father to influence him against leaving his property to their stepmother. She had always been jealous of the children from the moment she entered the house, though she had never dared show it before her husband. He always had some good explanation for anything the children did, and a few experiments in this line at the beginning of her career as a stepmother had convinced her that it was useless to attempt to turn her husband against his children. He was prejudiced in their favor and thought they could do nothing wrong. Being of a sleek and comfort-loving disposition, she saw that her easiest path lay in humoring his whims, and taking it out on the children in such a way that they could not retaliate.

But she had always harbored a secret fear that sometime they would get it back on her in one grand coup, and for years she had been trying to entrench herself so firmly that if it did come she would be safe. And now it had come. Her husband had died, and in spite of her best efforts, and his repeated promise that she should be well looked after, he had only given her her sixth. And even that did not include the house.

She had always planned when she got that house to send the children all away to school or somewhere else, and live as she pleased. She had even picked out an old friend to come and live with her and do her work; a friend who was penniless and would therefore be glad of a home. She had always been able to work on this friend, a widow of many years, with a painful sense of her own life failure. And now to have this plan upset by a mere statement that the house belonged to the children was maddening. As if anything could belong to children before they were of age. Why, even Doris was not quite twenty-one. Surely that ought to put everything in her hands. Of course she would see that the children were taken care of till they could get work, or get married; but it could be done with far less money or annoyance if they were sent away. Now, there was Doris! And Rose, too! They were both able to take positions somewhere. They could be librarians and board where they liked, or teachers, which was better still and might perhaps take them quite out of the city or even the state. John and Jean could be sent to cheap boarding schools of course. She knew one for boys where they could work so many hours a day for part payment of board and tuition. Ned of course being a young man would have to look out for himself. What if he was only nineteen? Plenty of young men of that age joined the Navy or went off to South America to take a position. The farther the better. She had suffered enough with those children all these years, and intended to be free from them. It was high time too, when they had reached the point where one of them would dare to throw water on her in her grief, and the rest would stand by and giggle. *Giggle!* The very day of their father's funeral! It was scandalous!

To the statement of the lawyer that there was no property left anyway, she gave not the slightest heed. There had been property, and it was put in the will, therefore it was somewhere now. It could not just melt away. She was suing to recover it. If her husband had been cheated out of it she would require Court to search it out and restore it to her. That was her notion of what it meant to go to Court. In her secret heart she felt sure that this was all a cooked-up story, the joint product of the children who were trying to cheat her out of her rights, and the lawyer who probably was expecting to get a rake-off himself out of it. They probably knew well enough where all those bonds and things were hidden.

But meanwhile, since they were all out and she had the house to herself, why not make a thorough investigation? She might not have another good opportunity.

So stealing forth cautiously, and peering into each

door, tapping before she opened it softly to make sure no one was inside, she went from bedroom to bedroom swiftly, then straight to Doris' room when she found she was alone. Doris was the oldest and would be the most likely one to take charge of any papers. Also Doris would be the one who would most resent having her room ransacked if she happened to arrive while it was going on. She would get it over first.

So she locked the door and went swiftly to the closet, dragging up a chair to stand upon that she might reach the shelf.

After she had mounted the chair it occurred to her that she might not hear if one of the children came in, and if it happened to be Doris it would be most awkward to be caught in there with the door locked. If the door were open she could hear anyone and get out before they discovered her.

So she got down and unlocked the door setting it wide open. Then she mounted her chair again and began hastily to go through her stepdaughter's boxes. She found nothing more interesting than a collection of mementos of Doris' school days, valentines, Christmas cards, programmes, notes, a few photographs, some dried rosebuds tied with a faded ribbon, a broken necklace, a white kid glove, a soiled satin slipper, the kind of things that every girl has left over from the gay romantic age and cherishes because she thinks they represent the dearest things in life, until she finds something really dear and then she flings them out as rubbish or puts them away with a smile to show to her own children some day.

Doris would have been very angry if she could have known that these pleasant little tokens were being over-hauled by the ruthless hand of this shallow woman, who was acting with no more sense than an angry child would in search of some means of revenge.

She crushed the dried flowers between scornful fingers, and scattered the dust in the air. She jumbled the whole collection back into the box and jabbed the cover on in her haste till it broke, and then she poked into every hat box and shoe box in the closet and left them all uncovered. There was just one box that defied her, a large tin one fastened with a small brass padlock. She pulled it to the front of the shelf and strained at the lock, her ear alert, meanwhile, to the front door, and to every step that passed by on the sidewalk, but the lock was strong and would not give. She must look for the key.

She climbed down leaving the box on the shelf and went on a rummage through the desk and bureau for a key that would fit that lock.

Doris' desk was always in careful order. The envelopes and paper in their proper places. Unanswered letters in one compartment; answered ones which she wished to keep in a little drawer by themselves, herded with rubber bands.

With excited fingers the determined woman shuffled through these letters, looking for possible papers.

There was one small package of letters addressed to Doris in her husband's handwriting. Ah! If there was incriminating evidence against Doris it would be here if anywhere. She stuffed the letters in her pocket quickly, swept the other papers back in a mass, and moved to the bureau.

She went through each drawer swiftly, but it did not take long for Doris kept her clothing in neat piles and it was easy to see at a glance that there was no hiding place here for what she wanted. Her eyes travelled over the top of the immaculate bureau. Nothing there but an envelope addressed to Doris and apparently not opened.

Ah! Here might be the very thing she needed. She put out her hand and took it. There was something small and hard inside, and there was no address but Doris' name. Was that Milton Page's writing? It looked like it. Could he be in the plot against her? Why surely. He would be the very one to carry the whole thing out. He was a thrifty business man, and of course if he was going to marry Doris he would want to get as much money with her as possible. She hesitated, about to open the envelope. But a noise in the street made her pause and listen. Was that someone on the steps?

She slipped the envelope in her pocket along with the first packet. It would be better to get through her search first and examine these at her leisure. She must find that key and see what was in that tin box before anybody arrived.

When she was quite sure that no one had come in, she opened Doris' little jewel box on her dressing bureau, and there she found a tiny key.

She quickly possessed herself of it and closing the jewel box she climbed upon the chair and fitted the key into the padlock. Yes, it was the right key. In a moment more the lid of the box was open and the contents were before her excited view. And there on the top was a photograph of Doris' own mother. Her hated rival!

It was as if that other woman had come and found her snooping through her child's property, as if she stood there with her perfect features, and her great dark sweet eyes searching her soul and condemning her. She stood for an instant holding the hated picture in her hand, her anger rising, her face strained and white, then her other hand went into the box again investigating, and touched a long soft brown curl of hair!

She caught her breath and started back, every nerve on edge. It seemed like a dead hand. It was a dead thing, a part of the dead woman whose place she held. She wanted to scream, but dared not. She tried to draw away her hand from the dead strand of hair, but it had somehow curled itself about her finger, and a long creeping hair clung, and sent shivers over her. She shook her hand to shake it free, and her foot, with its sharp little heel, suddenly went down through the cane seat!

She caught at the shelf to save herself, but only gripped the edge of the tin box, and down they went together, chair, woman, box, and picture in a strangely mingled heap; letters, keepsakes, a tiny Bible with its leaves fluttering open, some bits of quaint jewellery, another bunch of dried flowers tied with a white ribbon, some bits of silk and muslin, samples of dear old dresses, a pen, a gold thimble, all fell around in a shower, and on the top of the fallen woman lay her dead rival's picture, sweet, serene, gentle, earnest, strong, above the confusion.

And there in the doorway stood Rose Dunbar, horror, amusement, scornful delight, and a kind of undertone of anxiety in her tired pretty face:

"Florence!" she blamed in her fierce young condemnation. "What on earth are you doing in here?"

The startled lady tried to rise, her hair fallen to the side of her head, her face excited and angry. So she was caught! She was angry at being caught.

"I was hunting for something of mine on that shelf," she said sharply. "Have you any objection? Since when was I forbidden any room in the house? I am your father's wife, am I not?"

Rose came nearer and gave a significant glance at the contents of the box which was scattered all about, and back to the face of the prone woman:

"I don't see that that gives you a right to go through Doris' closet, and examine the things that belonged to our mother!" she said in a tone with two edges. "I think you had better get out of here before Doris comes home."

There was something ominous in the tone of the girl as she looked down with contempt on her stepmother, and Mrs. Dunbar felt that her situation was intolerable. Also she realized that she did not care to be caught in this predicament by Doris. But when she essayed to scramble to her feet her ankle gave way, and she sank back again with a groan and leaned her head against the door.

"I've hurt my ankle," she moaned.

Rose stood regarding her for one contemptuous second:

"Well, I should say you pretty much deserve it," she flung back in her clear young voice of scorn. "Here, put your arms around my neck and we'll get you out, unless you want them all to come back and find you here."

The baffled woman looked at the girl with hate, but saw the logic of her words, and obediently clasping her hands about the lithe young shoulder, was lifted to her feet. Then Rose looked around:

"You'd better sit down in that rocking chair and I'll drag you to your own room," she said unsympathetically. "If you're really sure you can't walk," she added.

The older woman flashed her another angry look which she did not see, for she was stooping and tenderly moving out of the way several of the letters which had fallen across the path which they must take. She led her stepmother to the rocker which was but a yard away from where they were standing, helping her to sit down and draw up her foot so that it would not drag. More gently than her real inclination would have prompted she dragged the rocker out of the door, stopping to change the key from the inside to the outside and lock the door, putting the key in her own pocket. Then she dragged the chair across the hall to Mrs. Dunbar's room, saying significantly:

"We'll leave that room just as it is until its owner comes back. Perhaps she will be able to find your lost property for you."

Mrs. Dunbar dropped upon her bed with an angry groan and hid her face in the pillow:

"Go away!" she said. "You're a wicked girl, too! Oh, if your father knew how you are treating me!" and she burst into a wail, which had an ominous reminder of the night before in its quavering tones.

"Now look here, Florence!" said Rose standing over her fiercely. "You can stop that right there. I'm going downstairs to telephone the doctor to come and look at your ankle, and if you go into hysterics again the way you did last night I'll take him into Doris' room and show him what you were doing. I'll tell him just what happened. And I'll tell Mr. Hamilton, too, and *all* the lawyers. You've got to behave and not try any of your tricks or we'll just tell the *world* what you are."

"Go out of my room!" said Mrs. Dunbar stopping her weeping. "I don't want the doctor! I've only twisted my ankle a little and it'll be all right by tomorrow. If you send for the doctor I'll tell him what a wicked girl you are. I'll tell him how all of you have treated me!"

"Very well," said Rose retreating. "Just as you say. If you want the doctor I'll phone for him. But if you carry on any more high strikes believe me, you'll be sorry. Here's the arnica and I'll get you a pitcher of water. If you need me to help you you've only to say so."

Rose filled a pitcher at the bathroom faucet, brought the bottle of arnica, and stood awaiting further orders:

"Go out!" said Mrs. Dunbar ungraciously, "I wouldn't take your help if I was dying. Go out and shut the door!"

Rose went out and closed the door firmly behind her,

and as soon as her footsteps had crossed to her own room Mrs. Dunbar rose cautiously from the side of the bed, limped to the door, and locked it. Then she limped back, sat down again on her bed, reached in her pocket and brought out Milton Page's note to Doris with the diamond ring fastened carefully inside.

ROSE was in the kitchen getting supper when Doris at last walked in. She had made fudge for a beginning. That was her specialty. She was enveloped in a long apron, and had a streak of chocolate on her cheek. She met her sister in the hall:

"Where on earth have you been?" she greeted her. "The mischief has been to pay. Where's Hannah? Did you know she was going out?"

"Why yes, I told her we probably couldn't keep her more than another week, and she asked if she might go out for an hour and leave her name at an employment office. Isn't she back yet?"

"Not a sign of her. Nobody home but Florence when I came in, and she wasn't exactly at home. Come on upstairs till I show you."

Rose ran upstairs lightly, fishing in her pocket for Doris' key. Doris followed more slowly, suddenly realizing that she was very weary. What new form of torture had now appeared? She must not forget her sunset.

Rose fitted the key in the lock and swung the door wide as Doris reached the top step:

"But why was my door locked?" she asked surprised.

For answer Rose pointed to the overturned chair and the confusion on the floor. "That's where I found Florence!" she said with eloquent tone. "Now what do you suppose was the big idea?"

"I don't know," said Doris, wearily dropping down on the bed and beginning to laugh hysterically. "I'm glad it's nothing worse. I'm getting used to expecting tragedies."

"Well, I'm glad you can take it that way. I'm sure I shouldn't. It made me furious. Look at Mother's picture, all rumpled on the edge."

Doris reached out a gentle hand and gathered the picture to her.

"I know," she said sadly. "It's hard. But there are harder things. Florence has always been like this about Mother you know. I remember the time she snatched this very picture away from me and made me sit in a chair for an hour because I was hugging it in my arms and crying. She said I just did it to show her I hated her. But after all, she's no new proposition. We've always had to put up with what she did."

"Well, believe me, I wouldn't put up with it another minute. Isn't this house ours, at least until it is sold? Can't you tell her to get out? Right now? I wouldn't let the old snoop stay around another night. Give her a little taste of what she's always given us. Send her to a hotel, or off to some of her precious friends that are always purring and drinking tea around here. Dad never liked them."

"But Daddy asked us to give her a home here the rest of her life," reminded Doris gently. "He wouldn't like it if we turned her out. Neither would our mother. Look at her smooth straight brows and that lovely mouth and see, there's nothing vindictive about her. And it somehow seems ill-bred to be vindictive, Rose. We must stick to our traditions or everything will be gone. Come, let's forget it and go down and get dinner. I'll change my dress and come right down. What is there in the refrigerator?"

"Hardly anything. There are a few scraps of chicken stuffing and one wing left from last night. That won't go far. There's a big lump of raw meat but it looks as if it would take forever to cook. There isn't even a cooked potato to fry. We'll just have to have eggs. There isn't but one slice of bread left either. I thought Jean might run to the bakery. Why, where *is* Jean? I thought she came in with you?"

"No, I haven't seen her. When did she go out?"

"I'm sure I don't know. There wasn't a soul in the house when I got home but Florence as I tell you, and none of them have come in yet. I thought you had Jean with you?"

"Why, no," said Doris. "She ought not to be out this time of night in the damp air after her sore throat. We must hunt her up right away. Where do you suppose she is?"

"Oh, perhaps over at Mayfair's with Elsie, or down at Eberleys' with Lisa. I'll go telephone her to come right away and bring bread on her way. We can charge it to-night if she hasn't any money, can't we?"

But frantic telephoning in every direction they could think of failed to bring any trace of Jean, and for the time being dinner was forgotten and the fudge left to cool itself as best it could while the sisters put on sweaters and searched the neighborhood excitedly.

"We'd better ask Florence," said Doris at last as they met again at the house. "She maybe told her."

Rose shook her head:

"Jean wouldn't open her lips to tell Florence anything if she could help it."

But Doris was already on her way to her stepmother's door.

She tapped lightly but received no answer. Then she tried the door and found it locked.

"Florence!" she called imperatively, "Florence! Do you know where Jean is? We can't find her anywhere."

There was an impressive pause and then Mrs. Dunbar's severe voice replied:

"I do *not!*"

In vain did she try to get more information or arouse some interest in the child's disappearance.

"She was gone when I returned from an errand. I have not seen her since I went out. You will have to stay at home and look after her if you think she isn't old enough to look out for herself. I cannot be responsible for her any longer. *I'm done!*"

"What a lovely spirit!" ejaculated the furious Rose from the top step where she stood listening. "My! I'm glad Daddy didn't know what he left us to."

Doris followed her slowly, thoughtfully, down the stairs: "Sometimes," she said sorrowfully, "sometimes I'm afraid he did, and that was half what killed him. Well, what shall we do next? Do you think we've got to report it to the police? Mercy!" She shivered as she opened the front door again and looked out in the street.

It was just at that moment that John appeared, approaching his home with misgivings:

"Oh, here's John!" ejaculated Doris, suddenly realizing that she had not yet had time to take in his absence and be anxious over it. "John, have you seen Jean?"

John was quick to unfold to the warmth of his sister's welcome. He had rather expected to be blamed for staying out so late, and was meditating an entrance via the back porch and the bathroom window when that front door opened.

"No," he answered with zeal. "Isn't she home? Gee! It's getting late, isn't it? Wonder where I better go after her? She wouldn't 'a' gone off with Milt Page anywhere, would she?"

"Mercy, no!" said Rose quickly. "She can't bear him!" Then she cast an apologetic look at Doris, who seemed not to have even noticed it.

"What put that in your head, John?"

"Oh, I dunno," said John warily, suddenly aware that he was revealing more than was necessary. "He was here—just before—I mean just after I left. That is, I think I saw him—in the—*distance*—I—"

"No, she never would have gone with Milton," said Doris thoughtfully, "because I—" she stopped and began again—"she—*he* would never have asked her," she finished embarrassedly. "He is not fond of children." This last as if she was stating a sad and suddenly realized fact.

Rose gave her a quick curious look and chanted softly under her breath: "Whom children shun and dogs love not, beware!"

Then she dashed into the kitchen and brought out the pan of fudge.

"Here, take a handful of this as you go. I'm starved, aren't you? Now, who will go where? There isn't any place left is there?"

"Where you been already?" asked John with his mouthful of candy.

They recited the rounds in chorus:

"Guess I'll try Hetty Brown's," he said thoughtfully.

"Hetty Brown's! That old woman! Why she never goes there! What on earth would she go there for?"

"She's got a whole batch of kittens ain't got their eyes open yet. Jean's just crazy about 'em. Hetty gave her one, a yellow and white, and she brought it home, but Florence wouldn't let her keep it. She made her take it right back the same day without waiting to even get her hat and coat on, just held the door open and ordered her outta the living-room where she found her holding the kitten."

"That's where she got her sore throat!" moaned Doris. "Go quick, John! I'm terribly worried about her, and come back and tell us. If she's not there we must all go out and hunt her. Why, it's after nine o'clock!"

But the house of Hetty Brown was closed and dark, and no answer came to the thud of the ancient knocker, though John tried it several times.

John stood for several seconds on the dark stoop peering down the street and trying to think where his little sister could have gone. Then a bright idea occurred to him. Perhaps she had gone to the movies. She loved pictures and was always coaxing to go. What was more natural? That was likely where the kid had gone when she was left alone. She ought to have had more sense than to stay so late of course, but he better go after her first before he went home. The girls would be scared stiff.

So he hustled off to the neighborhood movie theatre which was three quarters of a mile away, realizing as he went that he was tired, and that the pangs of hunger were beginning to be felt even in spite of the liberal supply of fudge which Rose had bestowed upon him.

As he approached the Picture Palace and noted the man in the ticket booth he thought he somehow looked curiously familiar. Who was it? Not his brother Ned? Of course not, but— He hurried nearer to get a better view but the man had ducked under the little trap door at the back and disappeared somewhere, so John paid his quarter grudgingly and passed inside, with a fleeting pang that he had to pay for a show he had not the time to see. He hurried in and went systematically down one aisle and up another looking at every person in the dark congregation, but nowhere could he find his little sister.

Discouraged he came out again, and as he passed through the swinging doors he was sure he heard Ned's voice snarl out with his familiar accent: "I tell you I did. What's the matter with you? Are you deaf?" But when he looked in the ticket booth there was only a middle-aged man with a gray moustache and a grim tired look on his face. He must have been mistaken. So many things were happening he was getting all balled up. John hurried out in the direction of his home, thoroughly alarmed now as he heard a distant clock ring out ten o'clock.

Back at the house Doris had lighted the gas oven and put some potatoes in to bake. They would get themselves done without watching, and would be warm and filling if they ever got to the place again where they could think of eating.

Rose was foraging in the ice box:

"There's some boiled ham, Doris, and plenty of butter and milk but there isn't a speck of fruit."

"We could make some pop-overs," said Doris turning troubled eyes upon her sister, "but we can't give attention to that now. We must find Jean. Every minute counts when someone is lost. Time enough to bake pop-overs and think about eating when we find her. Rose, have you looked thoroughly everywhere in the house?"

"Why no," said Rose. "It never occurred to me."

"You know she might have curled up and gone to sleep somewhere. Maybe she's up in the attic by her old doll house or in Daddy's den. She's a queer little grown-up thing you know, and she was all alone and sorrowful.

We oughtn't to have left her. No knowing what notion she got."

"Mercy!" said Rose full of compunction. "I never thought of it. Everybody was here when I left, John and Florence—and Ned— Where is Ned? He ought to be home by this time. He could help hunt."

"Well, we can't wait for him to come," said Doris with a smothered sigh. "You look everywhere down here, the cellar too, and I'll go upstairs and make a thorough search. By that time John ought to be back, and if she isn't found we'll *have* to call in the police I guess. If I don't find her I'm going to *make* Florence open her door and tell what she knows."

So the girls separated and began their search, Doris taking her pocket flashlight with her to penetrate into closets and under the eaves in the attic. But no trace of little Jean was visible anywhere, not even a book or doll lying about to show she had been there. The much-thumbed *Under the Lilacs* lying on the window-seat told no tales. The only thing that Rose found to puzzle over was a bud vase on the mantel half-filled with water, and a little yellow bud broken from its stem and lying on the hearth almost out of sight behind the fire shovel.

Rose came to the foot of the stairs and listened when she heard Doris' imperative knock on Mrs. Dunbar's door:

"Florence, you must open the door quickly! I must ask you something. Jean is lost and we are about to call the police to help us find her. It isn't wise for you to be found locked in here. They will be sure to break open the door and ask you questions, and it will look bad for you. Won't you come out now and tell us all that you know about it, and whether you have seen Hannah this afternoon? Hannah is gone too. It is quite important that we know everything that has been going on here before the policemen arrive."

There was a sound of instant feet upon the floor, and the door was unlocked. Mrs. Dunbar wearing a pink negligé and her hair down in long braids came out. There was a pink spot on either cheek and her eyes were brilliant with excitement:

"I haven't the least idea what has become of your precious sister," she said angrily, "and if you think you are going to try to put that on me you are mistaken. I have employed a lawyer to look after my interests, and no hatched-up plot is going to be put over on me. You have probably hidden her somewhere and you think you can arouse sympathy for your cause and turn people against me, but I have friends as well as you, and I don't intend to let you tell any lies about me."

"Florence! As if we had any such idea!" said Doris almost in despair. "I simply want to know when you saw Jean last, and what she was doing, and whether she told you where she was going when you left? What time did you leave the house and where was Jean when you went out? Did Hannah speak to you about going out? Was she here when you left?"

"Mercy! What a string of questions! A regular cate-chism! What right have you to catechise me I'd like to know? But of course I've got to answer or you'll threaten me with the police. Well, then, *No!* I haven't seen or heard Jean to-day. She's such a sly little mouse you never know what she's up to anyway. I wouldn't put it past her to hide and try to get me into trouble herself. No, I didn't speak to Hannah either. She was gone when I got back. There wasn't a soul in the house. I looked in every room—I—wanted to find some of you—I—"

At this Doris exchanged quick glances with Rose who had come half-way up the stairs.

"I was rather nervous to be left alone in a house where a death has been—"

"What time did you go out? Where did you go?" asked Doris interrupting her.

"That is none of your business. I went out when I got ready and went where I pleased. I did not see Jean nor Hannah. Now! Are you done with your questions?"

"No," said Doris suddenly flaming into spirit. "What were you looking for in my room among my private papers?"

"That you will learn soon enough," said the step-mother mysteriously. "I was looking for something I had a perfect right to have. That is all I shall tell you. If your policemen come and want to see me I'll come down, but until then have the goodness to let me alone. I've got one of my sick headaches. You aren't the only one that has something to tell the police. I found my window unfastened that I locked this morning with my own hands, and there was mud on my clean white bed spread."

"Let me see!" said Doris moving to enter the room. But Mrs. Dunbar slid quickly inside the door with her shoulder against it.

"I shall not let you see. Isn't it enough that I tell you? You doubt my word, I suppose. Well, I don't have to deal with you. I shall deal straight with the law."

With a grand flourish she finished her speech and shut the door, locking it vindictively.

Doris stood for an instant staring at the door, then turned, with outspread hands:

"That's that!" she said to Rose. "Oh, Rose! I'm so *tired!*" and she sank down on the upper step with her face in her hands, pressing her hot eyeballs with her cold finger-tips.

Then out of the blackness that surrounded her despairing heart there came a vision, as if printed on the retina of her eyes, and brought into visibility by the touch of her fingers. A great ruby glow of glory rising out of the blackness of a valley dark and dreary, with a sketchy fringe of branches picked out against its brightness. Ah! Her sunset! She must not forget!

She lifted her head and smiled at Rose wistfully: "It's coming out right somehow, dear," she said.

"You're wonderful, Doris," said her sister admiringly, "I wish I was like you. I just hate her. I can't see how you can take everything so sweetly."

"Oh, she doesn't matter," said Doris with a little gesture of dismissal for the unfortunate Florence. "If Jean would just come back I wouldn't care what she said. I oughtn't to have gone off and left her alone to-day. The poor little soul. She was just all wrapped up in our father, and she must miss him bitterly."

And just then they heard a key rattling in the lock of the front door, and both girls stood still on the stairs, staring eagerly at the door.

IT was Ned who opened the front door. He stood for an instant looking at them, the collar of his thin spring overcoat turned up about his haggard young face, his hat pulled low over desperate eyes. Doris' heart sank. It seemed to her that he had aged ten years since she saw him a few hours before.

He shivered as he took his hat off and started to unbutton his overcoat. "I'm all in," he growled. "Been all over creation hunting a position. There isn't one fit for a pig to take within a radius of a hundred miles. I guess I better go drown myself."

"Don't!" said Doris sharply. "We're in trouble here, Ned. Jean is lost. I'm sorry you don't feel well, but I guess you'll have to help us. Nobody knows when or where she went, and it's getting very late. It's after ten o'clock!"

"Oh Time!" said Ned impatiently. "You girls are always getting in a stew about something. She can't be far off. She's likely having a good time at the neighbors' somewhere."

"Do you suppose we are complete idiots, Ned Dunbar? We've been to every neighbor and friend we can think of and nobody has seen her to-day, I tell you. And Doris has telephoned to everybody we ever heard of, I think. Now John has gone one more place. If he doesn't find her we're going to telephone for the police and have it broadcasted."

"Stuff and nonsense!" said Ned. "A little thing like that! You'll have everybody laughing at you. Here!" He seized his hat again. "I'll go out and find her in no time. She deserves a good spanking for making all this trouble, and when I find her, believe me I'll give it to her. She won't do it again in a hurry. You all have spoiled her, that's what's the matter with her. It's time somebody told her a thing or two. But say! Haven't you got some coffee or something? I'm all in, I tell you. I didn't eat any lunch and I had no chance for any dinner."

"I've got some coffee in the percolator," said Rose efficiently, "it won't take a second to heat it. It must be warm yet."

"I'll make him a sandwich," said Doris, and both girls flew at their tasks.

"It's all tomfoolery," growled Ned as he took great bites at the sandwich. "You ought to let her stay till she gets ready to come home. It would teach her a lesson."

Ned didn't say what kind of a lesson it would teach. His sisters eyed him anxiously.

"But Ned, she may have been kidnapped," said Doris, voicing an awful fear that had been creeping upon her and which she had kept in abeyance till now.

"Yer Granny!" said Ned with the superiority of the male. "Folks don't do that nowadays. Whaddaya think anybody'd want of a little kid like that? More trouble than she's worth?"

"Stop Ned! You shan't talk so about your sister," blazed Rose.

"There Rose, he doesn't mean it," said Doris, trying to control the trembling of her hands as she refilled his cup.

"Well, I ask you. Why would they do it? We haven't got any money for a ransom have we?"

Doris' sad eyes met her brother's:

"People don't know that, Ned. Hurry please. I'm nearly crazy!"

"Oh yes, crazy! Crazy! That's what you are. So am I, but it doesn't make any difference does it? I've got to go out on a fool errand haven't I? Where'm I to go I ask you? If you've been everywhere? What is there left for me to do?"

Doris turned with a despairing look and went toward the telephone.

Just then the front door rattled noisily and John burst in:

"Has she come yet?" he asked eagerly.

His usually bright color was pale with anxiety, and his round boy eyes were grave with trouble. The night was beginning to seem full of terrors for a little sister to be out in.

"I went clear down as far as the movie place," he said. "Guess I better beat it out again. Why'n'tchoo go too, Ned?"

"I'm going," said Ned briskly. "I just got in."

And at that the door-bell pealed through the house.

For an instant they stood looking startled at one another. Then John turned with a business-like air and opened the door.

There stood Jean, pale and sleepy looking, but with shining eyes. She was holding her little blue sweater together with one hand around her thin little shivering shoulders, but the other hand grasped three shining quarters.

"Oh, Dorrie, I've got a job!" she cried rushing past the rest and holding out the money to her startled sister.

"I've got three of them, and I guess there's another next week—and it's fifteen cents an hour, or twenty-five cents if I stay two hours at a time!"

But Doris had gathered the little girl in her arms and was crying softly on her neck. The strain had been so great, and she was so tired and so glad to have the child safe again.

"Why Dorrie!" exclaimed the little girl astonished. "Why Dorrie! You are crying! Has anything happened? They are all here—" looking around quickly from brothers to sisters— "Aren't you *glad* I've got a job?"

"You darling child!" said Doris brushing away the tears and smiling. "We've been so frightened about you. Where have you been?"

"I've been just around the corner at Mrs. Bryan's taking care of her baby," explained the little girl eagerly, "I—"

But Ned interrupted her angrily:

"What business have you got running around the neighborhood all hours of the night playing with people's babies? Let them look after their own brats. You ought to be whipped, you ought, and I've a good mind to do it myself! Going off without telling anybody and frightening your sisters half to death. They were just about to call out the police and get us all in the papers, and it would have served you right if they had! Aren't you old enough to behave yourself? What do you think you are anyway? A two-year-old? Guess we'll have to get a nurse for you. Why didn't you telephone, you little goose?"

Jean's large blue eyes grew wide with grief and astonishment. The joy that had sat upon her thin little face so beautifully when she came in faded as if she had been struck. She stood swaying away from her brother with a little piteous gesture that went to the heart of Doris:

"Ned! Aren't you ashamed of yourself? You oughtn't to scold her that way when she thought she was doing something to help. Let her explain. Why didn't you telephone, Jean?"

"There you go! Spoiling her again," muttered Ned. "That's what's the matter."

"They didn't have any phone, Sister. Mrs. Bryan lives on that little brick street down below Claremont. And I didn't know she was going to stay so long. She said she'd just be gone a little, *little* while. She said not more'n about three quarters of an hour, she guessed, she just wanted to see her sick sister. And then she stayed, and stayed—" Jean's lips began to quiver— "and *stayed*. And I couldn't go out and leave that baby *all alone,* could I? Not when I was getting paid for taking care of it. And oh—I didn't have any—*sup-per*—!" Jean dissolved into tears at last and dropped into a chair.

John shoved Ned aside with a gruff:

"Aw, get out you big boob!" and went over to her, his awkward hand stroking her little bowed head:

"Say, don't mind him," he said jovially. "He was scared. I saw it in his eye. You're a little duck, you are, Kid, an' no mistake! Don' cry, Kid. You're the stuff! Come on, wash up an' let's get some food. I ain't had any dinner either."

Doris and Rose had come close to comfort the little girl, kissing her and rejoicing over her, and Ned, his miserable eyes on the group, sank down into the other hall chair, his elbow on his knees, his aching head supported on his hands. Nobody was noticing him.

But when John spoke about the lack of dinner both girls sprang up, no longer feeling their weariness, and went to work:

"Come on," cried Doris, "I'm going to make some pop-overs. They won't take long. The potatoes are baked to a crisp but they'll be nice with lots of butter, and you can eat the skins. Jean, you and John set the table quick. Ned, you open a can of peaches or anything you want. I'll make the pop-overs, and Rose will get the milk and butter and some jam. Come on everybody!"

She cast a winning glance at Ned, but he did not look up. His whole attitude was utter dejection.

The others hurried into the kitchen and there was presently a pleasant clatter of dishes and tongues, as they went from pantry to dining-room, from refrigerator to kitchen.

Doris had the flour all measured out, and the eggs opened. Even the pans were greased and ready, and she had only to beat her mixture together and put it in the pans. Soon everything was ready.

"Have we got to call Florence?" asked Rose with a troubled frown. "We're having such a nice time, just us together."

"Gee! I wish Florence didn't belong!" contributed John.

"Hush!" said Doris anxiously. "She might be listening. It would be terrible if she heard you. It certainly wouldn't make things any pleasanter. Wait! I'll run up and see. At least she must not have it to say that we didn't ask her to come down to meals. Perhaps she's gone to bed."

"Here's hoping!" said John fervently.

Doris ran silently up stairs on her tired feet, but found it all dark and still at her stepmother's door. As she came down the stairs she paused by her elder brother's chair and laid her hand on his hair.

"Come on, Ned, you'll feel better when you have something more to eat."

For answer he caught her hand:

"What happened, Sister?" he asked anxiously in a low tone.

"Well,—" Doris hesitated, "I gave the invitation."

"What did she say?" his voice was feverish with excitement.

"She didn't say much. Her mother did the saying. She didn't seem to care for it. But—Ned,—I must go—the children will be asking what we are talking about. Come! Come out and eat and I'll talk with you after they've gone to bed. If you don't come they'll know there's something the matter. You don't want them to know—yet—do you?"

"Absolutely not!"

Ned pulled himself up sulkily, and went to the dining-room. He wouldn't take his overcoat off. He said he was cold. He complained that nothing tasted right, and he drank numerous cups of coffee, and sat heavy-eyed and listless at the table.

They were all engrossed in Jean's account of her afternoon and no one but Doris noticed him. She cast a troubled glance at him now and then and wondered how she should tell him the story of her visit without hurting him more than was necessary. Or would it be better to tell the whole thing without attempting to soften it? Perhaps the plain unvarnished truth was the only thing that would ever set Ned straight. But then how was he ever to get straight anyway, with a wife like that tied to him for life! Poor Ned! Her heart ached for him. He and she had been very close to one another during their motherless years. They both remembered their own mother well. But Ned certainly was not behaving in a very manly way now in their crisis. Was it possible that she had helped to spoil her handsome brother?

"Aw come, Ned, don't be a grouch any longer!" said John at last as he noticed Doris' frequent anxious glances in his brother's direction.

Ned lifted heavy eyes and gave a vindictive glance at his brother:

"Aw, shut up!" said Ned bitterly. "I guess if you felt the way I do you'd be a grouch too. Shut that kitchen door, Rose. What've you got out there anyway? It feels like the North Pole! Great Scott! Has the fire gone out or what's the matter? I don't think I'll ever get warm again. My feet are like icicles, and my throat feels as if there was a sharp knife in it. It hurts me to breathe, too."

"Aw get out! You've got the grippe that's all. I've felt like that plenty of times, and never got on a grouch like you do either. It won't hurt any more if you grin an' bear it—"

"John!" spoke Doris sharply. "That isn't kind. Ned is really sick." She laid her cool little hand on his hot forehead. "Why! He has a high fever. Ned, you've got to go to bed this minute! Rose, put the tea-kettle going again and fill two hot-water bags. He needs to go to bed or he'll be down sick, and that won't pay."

"No," growled Ned, "that won't pay. If it would I'd stay in bed. Stay in bed and get a salary for it. Anybody ever get a job like that? Aw what's the use? I feel rotten."

His head fell down on his folded arms on the dining-room table. The children suddenly sobered and looked at one another with the foreshadowing of a new disaster in the offing.

John penitently shoved back his chair:

"Aw well, I'll go down an' look at the furnace, I 'spose." He yawned and disappeared down the cellar stairs.

Doris urged her brother up to bed, and went up herself and found extra blankets, turned down his bed, and plumped up his pillows. She went to the medicine closet for the usual remedies, and finally ventured to suggest sending for the doctor.

But at this the patient blazed out so vociferously and threatened such dire rebellion that she had to be satisfied with tucking him up with hot-water bottles and giving him her own home remedies.

She dreaded lest he would ask her again for an account of her afternoon's visit, but now that he was comfortable in bed, and warm at last, the shivering stopped, he seemed to want nothing but to be left alone. And so at last the excited household settled to sleep, worn out with the efforts of the day.

Doris as she sank into oblivion seemed once more to see the bright sunset amid its dark setting, and had the feeling that she must hold on to that picture and not let it go, because it somehow had the power to brighten a path for her through the darkness that was about her.

Little Jean had not told half of her experiences that afternoon as she went from door to door where she knew they had children and offered her services, but then there were more days coming, and to-morrow she would settle down with Doris for a whole hour when she could get her alone and tell her all about it. Doris would understand and enjoy it. The others were always too much engaged with their own affairs to listen to her. But Doris was dear.

John reflected with satisfaction as he closed his eyes for the night, that he had managed to say nothing whatever about his new job, and had got away with it without any trouble. Now in the morning he would just slip off early for school, and go to the store instead. He would do that for several days, maybe a whole week or so, until he got things going pretty well, and then if they tried to put anything like boarding school over on him they would see. The truth was he feared Doris would put a quietus on his business aspirations until he was older and had more schooling. But he hoped to make himself so necessary in that store that he could appeal to Mr. Lyman for his influence in the matter if it really came to a showdown in the family.

So quiet settled at last upon the household, and a deep sleep came upon the young things who had been through so much in the past few days.

It must have been about two o'clock when Doris was roused suddenly by a strange, wild voice calling hoarsely, and groaning.

She sat up in bed and tried to open her eyes and remember what had been happening. For the moment she thought it was her father calling her, and she was back in the midst of his severe illness again, rousing at any moment to meet a crisis.

The cold air from the window struck her thinly clad shoulders and brought her to her senses, and she suddenly remembered. Ned was sick. That must be Ned! He was talking in his sleep. He sounded as if he were in a delirium.

Doris sprang from her bed and hurried out into the hall.

Yes, the sound came from Ned's room:

"Kid!" he was calling. "I tell you I haven't got it! I'd get you the earth with a gold chain around it if I had it. But I'll earn it! I *will*. Just give me a little time, and I'll show you. I'll put it all over those rotters that follow you around all the time. I'll show you a good time, better than any they give you, if you'll only give me a chance! Oh, Zephyr!"

The last was an agonizing cry. The heart of the sister standing by sank with a dull thud of agony. Did he really feel like that about that painted dolly-face? Could it be her brother who was enchained like that?

She laid a cold trembling hand on her brother's hot forehead. It almost seemed to scorch her, it was so hot.

"Zephyr! Is that you, Zephyr? Have you really come to me, darling? Oh, it is too good to believe." And he grasped her hand feverishly and drew it to his hot, hot lips, kissing it wildly.

Doris shrank inwardly from those kisses that told her brother's story so plainly. Poor foolish boy! His life ruined forever! For it was not thinkable that the girl she had seen in the afternoon could ever bring him happiness and peace. How was it possible that he had fallen in love with such a girl as that? He with his good education, his fine ancestry, his respectable heritage!

And yet he was only nineteen. Scarcely more than a boy yet. Oh why had not somebody seen this danger and saved him from it? Why had she not been more to him? Ah—she had been engaged in pursuits of her own, a love affair with a refrigerator plant, that was what her engagement to Milton Page now seemed as she looked back on it in that swift instant of self-condemnation. Poor unformed Ned! Well, he had not had a pleasant home! No wonder he had wandered out to seek amusements elsewhere! If she had only thought of this before!

But all this went through her mind like a flash while she was feeling his pulse and realizing that he was very sick, was really quite delirious, and that she must send for the doctor at once.

While she was rousing Rose and telephoning the doctor, suddenly there appeared a horror before her mind. If Ned was going to be very sick, and it looked as if he was, would she have to go and ask that Zephyr to come to him? Would she have to humble herself and bring that awful girl here to their home, with her dear brother, and have them all know that she was Ned's wife? Have her take first place beside his bed and nurse him, and likely not know how? Have her shut them all out of their own brother's room if she liked, and take the initiative in everything? Maybe send away their old doctor whom they had known since they were born, and have some less skillful physician who did not know Ned's constitution. Would Ned want that? Did he really love her like that? Would it maybe be the only thing that would save his life?

And if all that were so— *Would Zephyr come?* Would she maybe just laugh, and blow him a kiss with her rosy-tipped fingers and go on with her dance?

NED was in a serious condition. Doris knew it as soon as she looked at him. Her worst fears were confirmed by the doctor when he arrived.

The patient had gone from one chill to another followed by a burning fever. He no longer knew any of them and lay moaning and breathing heavily.

Doris ran hither and thither, bringing ice, bringing hot water, finding blankets and pillows, telephoning the drug store for a new ice bag; running down cellar to see why the house was so cold, wrestling with the furnace which proved to be just going out; answering the telephone and the front door-bell when the messenger boy came from the drug store with the things; making coffee for the doctor, who had got out of bed to come at her call. She ached from head to foot with weariness.

"Now look here!" said the doctor eyeing her keenly, between swallows of coffee. "You can't stand another bout of nursing. Don't get that in your head. You're all in now. You've got to have a nurse!"

"Oh, no, Doctor, that's impossible!" cried Doris. "We simply can't afford it. It's quite out of the question. And you know I can do it. You said I took care of father as well as if I had had training."

"The very reason why you can't start in again now," said the doctor firmly. "Human flesh can't stand everything, and you've stood an awful lot for one little girl. I ought not to have let you do it, but your father seemed so anxious for you to be with him every minute. We've got to look out or you'll be down sick next. That's all nonsense about affording. I'll see that it doesn't cost you anything. You've got to have a nurse or else send Ned to the hospital, and frankly, I don't like the idea of moving him. He's a pretty sick boy, I suppose you know. These double pneumonia cases are treacherous things to deal with. You couldn't expect Rose to help much. She's only a child, and she looks as white and frightened as one now, sitting up there beside him. As for Mrs. Dunbar, you might as well expect help from a white lily. No, Doris, there's nothing for it but a nurse. If I can just get Miss Smith she'll take the burden all off your shoulders. She's great! She's just come off a case yesterday. I'll go telephone at once. Perhaps I can get her."

He hurried off to the telephone and Doris stood staring blankly out of the dining-room window at the sunshine on the brick wall of the next house, wondering how ever she was to make both ends meet.

The doctor came back in a moment with satisfaction in face and voice.

"She's coming. She'll be here in half an hour. I'll stay till she arrives. Now, what I want you to do is to get off your clothes and get into bed just as soon as she comes. And you're to sleep till she calls you to lunch. Understand? I don't want two patients at once. It's expensive, you know."

He tried to be jocular and Doris smiled wanly. Another pall seemed to have descended upon the house.

Had her sunset promise failed after all? How was she to bear up under it, and how where they to pay all these new bills? A nurse! No maid! For Hannah had not yet returned. Oh, it was terrible! She felt like sinking down and giving up.

The nurse arrived and was installed. The doctor left promising to return early in the afternoon, and adjuring Doris to go to bed at once:

"Don't be discouraged, little girl," he said tenderly as he was leaving. "We're going to pull your brother through I'm sure, and there'll be brighter days again by and by."

He had known Doris since she was a baby.

Doris stood for a moment dazed in the dim hallway, the morning sun sifting down over her bronze hair and tired young face, and as she stood there the immediate problem of life stalked up to her and made his bow: "I am Necessity. How are you going to take care of me?"

Ah! She must get to work at once. This was not a matter to wait while she lay down and slept. She cast a hasty, frightened glance over the aspect of the intruder in the home where Plenty had always reigned, and found it was not good to look upon. She must do something at once.

On the hall console lay the neglected morning paper. No one had read the papers since her father died. It was Daddy's paper. The children never paid much attention to it, except for the sporting page and the funnies now and then. Florence's only interest in it was confined to the advertisements of bargain sales. Florence was great on bargain sales. She often bought things for which she had no earthly use, simply because they were bargains.

Doris' first quick reflection as her eye fell upon the paper was that here at least was an expense which could be curtailed at once without discomfort to the family.

Then suddenly she realized that there were "Want" advertisements in the paper. Strange she had not thought of that before!

She seized upon the paper eagerly and carried it to her own room, taking the precaution to close and lock the door. That prying nurse would likely be poking her nose in to see if she had obeyed the doctor's orders.

She spread the paper out on her bed and began to search for the advertising columns. There they were! Great lengths of them. Help Wanted! Female! And there right at the top of the column staring at her as if crying to her from afar was Angus Macdonald's advertisement:

> *WANTED: A young woman of refinement, education, common sense, and a sense of humor, who is willing to give at least a part of every day to making a good time for an elderly woman invalid. Good Salary. Call 577 Ridgeway Building after ten o'clock.*

Doris read it over again carefully, weighing the possibilities of each word. It looked good. Too good. The salary was probably a mere pittance. A play job like that of course could not be expected to bring in much money. It might be worth looking into, however. Perhaps it would be a good thing for Rose. Dear restless pretty Rose! How was Rose ever to earn a living? She dreaded to think of her having to go in an office.

Doris read on down the column, through appeals for mothers' helpers, and cooks, and nursemaids, and housekeepers and stenographers, and alluring descriptions of articles for sale which the world was fairly crowding to purchase.

With a sigh she marked a few, but came back to the first again and read it thoughtfully. Then raised her eyes to the clock. Call after ten o'clock. It was now half past ten, and suddenly in her mind's eye she saw a long line of competent refined young women making their way to the Ridgeway Building. In a panic she arose, and moved stealthily about her room making a hasty toilet. She washed her face in hot water to take the weary look away, and then dashed cold upon it until she coaxed a faint color into her cheeks. In a very short time she was ready.

She opened the door softly and listened. She could hear the nurse running the water in the bathroom. No one else seemed to be about. She slid quickly down the stairs and opened the front door quietly. She did not wish to be challenged by the nurse, nor to have to explain her errand to anyone. If there was nothing to this then nobody need know anything about it.

As she walked down the street in the crisp early spring sunshine she realized that she was all of a tremble. She wondered if Rose would know how to look out for anything the nurse might want. Perhaps she ought to go back and tell her she was leaving the house for a little while. Yet if she did there might be complications that would detain her, and she might lose this chance—if indeed it was a chance. Well, Rose had gone to lie down, and surely the nurse would ask her if anything was wanted. The children had presumably gone to school—at least Jean had asked her if it was all right for her to go, and of course John must have gone too. It was hard for a boy to hang around a house where there was sickness. But that was good, for there would be no noise unless Florence made it.

Doris hurried on to her destination, and after a short ride in the trolley arrived at the Ridgeway Building and entered the outer room of a handsome office suite.

There were other girls in the room, nine of them, waiting. There was an oppressive odor of garments worn

too long without cleansing, mingled with several varie-
ties of perfume. Doris hesitated as she glanced at the row
of chairs already filled. Now that she was here she had
an inherent shrinking from contact with an employer.
She had come too suddenly. She should have waited
until she found something more conventional, a position
with one of her father's friends—and yet—

As she stood hesitantly ready to flee, a secretary came
up to her:

"Will you write your name and address on this card
please? Mr. Macdonald will see you in your turn. I will
get you a chair."

Doris accepted the card and pencil half doubtfully:

"The—position is not filled yet?"

"Not yet," said the secretary crisply, eyeing her with
a trained glance and noting the trim tailoring of her
outfit approvingly. "You may write names and addresses
of those whom you wish to give as references, below
your own, if you like," she added.

Doris filled out the card, giving Mr. Hamilton, her
father's lawyer, as a reference. There were many others
she might have used, but she shrank from having anyone
know her position until she had worked a way out of it.

It seemed somehow a slight to her father that his
daughter had need thus to go out answering advertisements. Yet that was silly of course. She must face life as
she found it.

She settled down into the chair that the secretary
brought and began to study her competitors.

They were stylish little flappers for the most part, three
of them chewing gum and conversing in ill-suppressed
titters giving an account of their last evening's escapade.
One made her think of her new sister-in-law with a
sudden start, whom oddly enough she had forgotten
during the events of the early morning. One was openly

using lipstick with the help of a tiny, pocket mirror. At the far end sat a shabby girl with wild hunted eyes and a hungry look.

Just beyond her on the ground glass of the mahogany door that separated them from the inner office was the name "ANGUS MACDONALD" in clear black letters. Doris liked the name. It sounded like a story book. She wondered if it was his wife he wanted amused. But then, what was the use in getting interested in this? Here were all these girls, nine of them, ahead of her, and another one just entering the door, a girl with flat heels and shell-rimmed glasses, who looked thoroughly competent to supervise anyone's happiness. She would probably get the place.

The inner door opened at that moment and a stout girl in a sleeveless black satin with large pink roses painted about her waist came sullenly out. Her hair was shingled unbecomingly and she wore a large, black hat. She sadly put on a shabby coat that lay over the secretary's desk. She did not look like a prize winner.

As she strode past Doris her unfastened goloshes clanked and clattered like a cowboy's spurs, and presented a humorous vacancy of nude-colored stocking between boot and abbreviated skirt.

The hungry looking girl had sprung to the doorway as soon as the other girl had come out. Doris could see her shadow against the ground glass as she moved away from the door into the room. Then almost at once she came out again, a disappointed look upon her face, her eyes more hunted looking than ever. Of course Doris did not know that in spite of her brief stay she bore with her a card which would give her food and a chance to work off her board till she could find a position. Macdonald was that way.

But the next three girls in succession that went in,

with their gum, their lipsticks and their rolled stockings, did not remain even long enough for a card to be written. They came out suddenly, and scaredly, and waited around for one another with embarrassed giggles. As they passed out together into the hall one was heard to say in an arrogant tone flung back as of a purpose: "Old Shrimp! I wonder who crowned him!"

Pondering on this remark while the remainder of her predecessors made hasty trips into the inner office, remained briefly, and retired precipitately with downcast countenances, Doris began to wish that she had not come. This Angus Macdonald was probably some old crab and she was likely only wasting her time staying here. She was meditating flight when the secretary touched her arm and smiled:

"Will you come in now, Miss Dunbar?"

Doris was ushered into Angus Macdonald's presence.

He gave her one quick glance and arose, offering her a chair and greeting her with deference and a kind of relief in his manner. She was almost bewildered to find him a good-looking young man with the ease and grace of one accustomed to the best society. He did not look in the least like an old shrimp. His face was grave and pleasant and his eyes met hers with a direct business-like gaze that she liked.

She took the chair offered her and found her misgivings vanishing. The dignified office with its rich deep-toned rugs, its handsome mahogany furniture, and its general air of refinement and solidity gave her instant confidence. She could answer the clear-cut questions without palpitating, and she could meet the clear eyes of her interlocutor with a gaze as clear.

"You live in this city, Miss Dunbar?" he asked by way of introduction. "I wonder if you belong to any of the Dunbars I have met?"

"My father was John E. Dunbar of Dunbar, Reed and Co."

"Indeed? I think I may have met him—at a boardmeeting once, perhaps. But you say, 'was,' is he not living?"

"He was buried yesterday," said Doris, trying to keep her voice steady and her lips from trembling. This was business. She must not let her feelings be seen.

"I beg your pardon," said the young man penitently, "I had not heard. I am afraid my questions seem impertinent to you, but—would you mind telling me why you answered this advertisement?"

She lifted her eyes to his scrutiny once more:

"Certainly not," she said. "It was necessary for me to get something to do. This appealed to me as something I could do at once without training, and which would be at the same time interesting."

There came a sudden light in his eyes at that.

"I was only afraid," she went on, and hesitated.

"Yes?" he helped her a little anxiously.

She lifted courageous eyes to his serious ones. He could see that she did not like to say what she had in mind, but she went bravely on:

"I was afraid that as it would require but half time the salary would not be sufficient for my needs. I shall have others dependent upon me you see."

"I see," he said pleasantly, "but I do not think we need to worry about that. If I decide that you are the one for my needs I shall expect to pay you a sufficient salary to retain your whole time, so that when you are not employed your time will be your own. Now, suppose we waive that matter for a few minutes and get down to business. I hope you will not consider me abrupt. You see I have but a short time in which to arrange this matter, and I have already interviewed a great many people. Our acquaintance must progress rapidly if I am to be able to judge whether you will suit my needs. The case is this. I am suddenly called abroad on business matters, it may be for only a few weeks, it may be for several months. I want someone to play with my mother while I am gone and keep her from being lonely. There is no such person among my kindred or immediate friends that I care to ask to fill that position, therefore I am forced to search for the right one among strangers. Now, will you kindly tell me about yourself, what qualifications you feel you have for the job?"

A faint deprecating smile quivered about Doris' lips:

"I've had a good education," she said gravely, and named a noted woman's college at which he nodded assent, interestedly.

"I have read a great deal, not very deep things perhaps, but I love to read. I can play a little and sing a little. I love to get out of doors. And I love people," she finished almost desperately. "I'm afraid I haven't very many qualifications perhaps—but I think I could work out some pleasant playtimes."

He had a sudden thought, quite irrelevant at that time, that her eyes were very sweet with that shy wistful look in them.

"I should say you had a good many qualifications," he said interestedly. "Would you mind telling me some of the things you would do to amuse a lonely mother?"

Doris looked at him speculatively:

"I have not had very long to think about it," she said deprecatingly. "I just saw your advertisement about an hour ago. And I don't know that I could tell very definitely until I knew the lady. I should have to adapt myself to her pleasure. But there are a great many pleasant things to do. First of all I should say there was reading aloud—but perhaps she does not like that? I know some people do not."

"You like to read aloud?" he asked.

"I love it," she said enthusiastically. "It is twice as pleasant as reading alone because you are enjoying it with someone else, and you often get the other's viewpoint."

Macdonald's eyes kindled.

He opened a drawer at the right of his desk and took out a clipping:

"Would you mind reading that for me?" he asked. "It's just a little thing I came across last evening. I would like to enjoy it with you."

She took the bit of paper with a vague curiosity as to his selection. She knew of course that her reading ability was being tested, yet he had put the thing so delicately that she had a sense of personal interest, as if he were making her a friend and not putting her on the level of a girl about to be hired to read aloud by the hour. It helped her to put aside self-consciousness and read naturally:

> *"I think that I shall never see*
> *A poem lovely as a tree.*
>
> *A tree whose hungry mouth is prest*
> *Against the earth's sweet flowing breast;*
>
> *A tree that looks at God all day,*
> *And lifts her leafy arms to pray;*
>
> *A tree that may in summer wear*
> *A nest of robins in her hair;*
>
> *Upon whose bosom snow has lain;*
> *Who intimately lives with rain.*

Poems are made by fools like me,
But only God can make a tree."

"You know it," he said as she handed it back to him with a look in her eyes as if it were an old friend.

"Yes, I'm very fond of Joyce Kilmer," she answered.

"I never happened to come across him before," he said thoughtfully. "Life keeps me busy in other directions. I must look up his other writings."

"They are worth it," she said. And then they both came back to the business in hand.

"You read it well," he acknowledged gravely. "But this is a digression. You were telling me how you would amuse a lonely person."

"There is music," said Doris thoughtfully. "Sometimes it is pleasant to just run over the fine things together with someone who loves them too."

Macdonald nodded thoughtfully.

"There are lots of new pretty things two people can make together too," she went on, "either for ourselves, or for someone who needs them. We could hunt up people who needed pretty things, or useful things. And then there is always the great out of doors. Is she able to go out much?"

"She is able, but I have not been able to persuade her to go much since my father's death. Do you drive a car?"

"Yes," said Doris, a shade coming over her face. "But—I'm not sure I can keep my car now."

"We have cars," said Macdonald. "I would like her to get out. She used to love it. She loved the woods and the garden."

"Oh, we could find woods and gardens, I'm sure," said Doris with a growing enthusiasm. "We might start a garden for ourselves, just in a small way."

He smiled appreciatively, but did not tell her of the lovely gardens that surrounded his house, and the two professional gardeners who presided over them.

"I have always wanted to have a garden," mused Doris forgetting herself for an instant. "There has never been a place in town."

"There would be a place I am sure," responded the man.

"And then," went on Doris, "we might have little parties once in a while, just one or two people she loved to be with. I could make a cup of tea and some cinnamon toast."

Then suddenly the soft color mantled Doris' pale face:

"Excuse me," she said, "I'm letting my imagination run wild, and it must seem very childish to you. I was simply trying to think of things I might like myself if I were lonely. They will perhaps seem very crude and unsuitable to you. I really could not tell very well what I would think of to do for a person that I have never met. People are all quite different you know, and I would try to study her and find out her likes and dislikes. I would try to adapt myself to her pleasure."

"You seem most versatile, Miss Dunbar, and your ideas are certainly interesting. I think I should enjoy doing some of those things myself. Of course I cannot tell what Mother's reaction may be to all of them. And before we make definite arrangements I shall want you two to meet."

"Will you tell me what she is like?" Doris raised earnest eyes to meet his glance. "She and I might not fit at all of course. I would not like to undertake something I could not carry out."

A tender look came into Macdonald's eyes:

"She is like—what shall I say?—Dresden china? A delicate old-fashioned cameo? She does not wear short skirts nor bob her hair nor paint her face. She is a lady of the old type with fine ideals. Since my father's death two years ago, she has drawn within herself and shrinks from going anywhere. She does not seem to care to see even old friends much, and she will not entertain at all. She is not really ill, just frail, and without her old-time interest in life. Now, does that interest you? Or does it sound dull to you? If it does say so frankly, for this is a job which one would have to come at cheerfully to be of service."

"It interests me," said Doris simply. "I should like to try to make her happy. That is, if I can please her."

"Yes, that is something that I shall have to work out. She does not know of this plan of mine as yet, and I shall have to think of a way to approach her with it which she will not veto. A good deal will depend upon your first meeting. Can you go out to our home with me to-morrow afternoon at, say, four o'clock? I will see that you are safely taken back to the city again by half past six, if that will be convenient to you."

It was all over in a moment more. Doris found herself agreeing to meet him at the office at half past three the next day, he touched a bell on his desk and she felt herself dismissed. The pleasant secretary entered with a sheaf of letters for Angus Macdonald to sign, and a message from one of his partners that a man was waiting to see him in the inner office.

Doris walked out past a constantly growing line of applicants, the flat-heeled one staring insolently at her through the shell-rimmed glasses, as if resenting the fact that she had stayed in the office so long. Suddenly Doris' heart sank. After all, she was not hired yet, only engaged to ride out and be looked over. Doubtless there were numerous others to be put through their paces also. Her mind carried the mental picture of a quiet elderly woman with a cheery smile, and a trimly tailored younger one with a certain charm and a daintiness about her. They were not all gum chewers, and he might find several he liked better than herself. He would probably take them all home, the ones that he judged at all possible, and let his lady mother chose. It was foolish for her to suppose she could jump right into velvet like that, at least it had seemed velvet but after all he had not named the salary. His idea of what was adequate and hers might differ widely. She had better put the thing out of her mind and be looking about for something else. Of course she would keep her appointment, that is, if Ned was well enough for her to leave the house for that length of time. If he was not she would simply telephone she could not come.

Then her heart flew back to its home anxieties, and it seemed to her that the car fairly crawled, so anxious was she to know how her brother had fared in her absence. She had entirely forgotten the nice long nap she was to have taken. She had an appalling undertone of worry about Ned's wife. If he did not get better pretty soon there would be the question of whether she ought to be sent for or not. What should she do? If there were only someone in whom she could confide, someone to advise her.

In this state of mind she finally arrived at home, and as she mounted her own steps the front door was flung open and Rose appeared in the doorway tragically:

"Well, Florence has gone and done it now!" she announced tragically. "Where on earth have you been? I've ransacked the whole house for you. *Everything's* to pay!"

12

DORIS stepped into the hall and shut the door. Her face was very white. She realized that all at once she was very tired.

"What is the matter, Rose?" she said speaking low and anxiously. "Is Ned worse? Tell me quick!"

"I don't know," said Rose dropping into a chair and mopping the tears away with the back of her slim white hand. He just moans and talks the same as ever. I don't dare ask that starched-up sphinx of a nurse. She came out and glared at me and said we must have it quieter. As if I could do anything with Florence!"

"Florence? What was Florence doing?"

"She's gone and brought a lawyer here, that old Applegate that Daddy used to dislike, the one that wears spats and needs a hair-cut. They've been making out a list of the things in every room, and she says she's going to claim everything. She says if we try to carry off things or hide anything she'll bring it all out in court! She says she's going to have her rights."

"Oh, how could she? And Daddy just gone! Bring a stranger in here and disgrace us all! What a fool she is when Mr. Hamilton explained it all carefully to her that there wasn't anything left for anybody. They didn't go upstairs, did they?"

"They certainly did. They tried to get into Ned's room. Florence said there was a set of old furniture in there that Daddy had promised should be hers. She even shook the door and called out things."

"But didn't you tell her how sick Ned is?"

"I certainly did! But I might as well have talked to the moon. She simply swept me aside, took firm hold of the door-knob and threw the door wide open. But it didn't stay open long, I can tell you! That nurse sailed down on them like a man-of-war. She simply swept them out into the hall and closed the door behind her, and then she swept them along to the head of the stairs, and told them to go down and keep still, that she was in charge here, and they would be responsible for a life if they carried on any longer; and she said she would telephone for the police if they made any more noise, that the doctor had given strict orders that it must be very quiet. But I don't know as Florence would have given up even then—you know how she is—if the man hadn't got scared, and told her it would be bad for her claims if she did anything we could complain about."

"Oh, mercy!" said Doris sinking into the other hall chair. "It seems as if there was no end to things. Where is she now?"

"Up in her room, I guess. I heard her lock the door. The lawyer went away just a few minutes ago, and I heard her promise to come to his office to-morrow morning at ten o'clock."

"Well, I guess I must tell Mr. Hamilton. It's awfully humiliating to let even him know, but he heard her yesterday, so I suppose it doesn't matter so much. But something will have to be done with her. I wish I'd been here, I would have tried to explain to that lawyer. If he has a grain of sense he won't take up her case when he knows how things stand."

"It didn't look to me as if he had half a grain of sense," said Rose dryly. "If you ask me I'd say he had a case on her."

"Oh! Rose!"

"'S the truth, Doris. You watch. The way he smirks and smiles."

"Rose, it's too disgusting for you to talk like that. Father would be—so disgraced!" There were tears in Doris' eyes.

"Forget it, Dorrie! I didn't mean to hurt you. I only think he's a fool. There's a pair of them it seems to me. Doris, why don't you tell Milt? If he's worth anything in the world to this family it seems to me he ought to come in now and do some advising. He's so fond of doing that. But I should say he's the one. He knows Florence, and he ought to deal with her for us. He called up this morning. Wanted you the worst way. Said he must speak to you at once. I promised to tell you to call him up at the office as soon as you came in. You better go call up now before I go on with my tale of woe. He'll put me through the third degree the next time he comes to find out the exact minute you arrived and see whether you obeyed his command or not. I certainly am glad it isn't me that's going to marry him. He wanted to know if you got your ring. What did he mean, Doris? He hasn't been spending money on another ring for you, has he? *Doris!* Why, *you haven't got your ring on!* Was the stone loose? Did you have to have it fixed?"

But Doris was looking at her with annoyed eyes:

"What did he mean, Rose, did I get my ring? Oh, I'm afraid he has sent it back. Rose, I might as well tell you.

I gave Milton Page his ring yesterday. I am not going to marry him."

"Good work!" cried Rose with a sudden lighting of her tempestuous eyes. "But Doris! Why? Not on account of *us*?"

Doris looked at her sister with a sudden concentrating of her gaze as if the question almost startled her:

"Why—yes, Rose, I guess it was on account of all of you. You couldn't think I would go away and leave *now*, dear."

The ready tears sprang to Rose's eyes even as she sprang to her feet vehemently:

"Did he ask you to leave us?" she cried furiously. "He was a brute to do it. I always said he had a cruel mouth, but you shan't stay here and spoil your life for us. You shan't do it, Doris Dunbar! I'm grown up! I guess I can take care of Jean and John. Ned is old enough to take care of himself. I can get a job—I've got one now if I've a mind to take it, and I can make a lot of money at it, too. You needn't give up your chance for us, Doris! I'm going to the telephone this minute and call him up and tell him so. He needn't think we'll be hangers-on either. I can take care of them all right!" and with a gasp like a sob and a toss of her fluffy forelock Rose started for the telephone.

"Stop!" cried Doris, dashing after her and catching her sleeve firmly. "We've got trouble enough, Rosie, without your going and making more. Please let me manage my own affairs, Sister. Nobody is going to make me get married till I get ready."

"But I'm not going to have you lose your last chance."

"What makes you think it's my last chance, Rose?" Doris broke into an amused smile in spite of herself. "What makes you think it's my chance at all, little Sister?"

"Oh, well, if you're putting it that way, that's different."

Rose dropped her arm to her side. "I don't think it's your last chance. But I thought you did. And you said you were doing it for us."

"But I didn't mean it that way, Sister. I meant it would kill me not to be with you now, when we—are all alone. I'd feel as if I were exiled. I wouldn't go away from you all now for anybody. I don't want to! Don't you understand?"

Rose locked glances with the honest eyes of her sister.

"Doris, I don't believe you love him!" she exclaimed with a kind of joy in her voice.

"Perhaps not, dear," said Doris gravely. "I didn't know it before. I haven't had time to think about it yet. It seems so trifling beside all we have to consider now."

"You wouldn't need time to think if you loved him," announced the young woman of no experience. "Those things are settled at once. And you wouldn't consider it trifling either if it was real. It would matter more than anything else in the world if you really cared."

"Perhaps so," said Doris slowly, watching the glowing face of her young sister admiringly. "But, chicken, how did you know that?"

"I've had time to think!" announced Miss Rose with a twinkle in her eye, "and besides I just *hate* that Milton Page. He's a selfish, superior, *stingy* man. I can't abide him! It always made me sick to think of you married to him. I felt just as though you were going to be dead when you did it."

"Why, Rose! You never said anything about it!"

"Of course not," said Rose shortly. "You didn't ask me when you got engaged. It was you that had to live with him, not me, thank fortune! If I was going to have the poor fish for a brother-in-law I didn't want to say anything I'd have to live down the rest of my life, did I? You wouldn't have turned him down just because I didn't like him, would you?"

"It might have made a difference," said Doris thoughtfully. "I couldn't think of two people I loved not loving one another. It would be awful!"

"It happens!" said Rose laconically. "There! There goes the telephone again. Perhaps that's Milt or one of the others. I'm about sick of answering them. You better go."

"What others?" asked Doris as she went over to the telephone.

"Why, there were three men wanted their bills paid right away or they'd know the reason why; and one said we couldn't have any more meat till his was paid. I tell you it was fierce! And then there was the girl that wanted Ned! She was the limit! I hung up on her!"

Doris took down the receiver with a heavy load of trouble settling down on her heart again. Would perplexities and difficulties never cease?

It was Milton. He was in his most imperious mood. He seemed to think that Doris' absence when he telephoned before had been willful impertinence on her part. His tone implied that he had been most lenient with her the day before in not insisting on her going out with him, and that now this added insult was beyond all forgiveness. He demanded with real anxiety in his voice to know if she had got her ring safely.

"Ring!" said Doris. "Why Milton, I gave it back to you. Didn't you understand?" Her voice was tired. Somehow this seemed a trivial thing to come in just now.

"Child's play!" said Page haughtily. "I supposed you were above staging such scenes, Doris. Remember you didn't *give* it to me either. You left it lying on the living-room table."

"You didn't leave it there!" said Doris, wearily. "I hadn't an idea you would do so careless a thing as that!"

"No, I didn't leave it there, fortunately. I picked it up and wrote you a note and fastened the ring firmly in it. I sealed it in an envelope and sent it up to you by Jean. Do you mean to say that she didn't give it—"

"I have scarcely seen Jean since you were here," explained Doris. "Ned has been very sick. He has double pneumonia. He is delirious. We had to get a trained nurse."

There was tragedy in Doris' voice. Now if ever was the time for the lover in Milton to come to the front. Surely, surely he would see that she had more important matters than a ring to look after!

He paused, just long enough for politeness, and then a little longer with an edge to it to show her that she had interrupted. He knew that she knew he hated to be interrupted in a topic until it was finished. He had often spoken to her about that habit of hers.

"That is most unfortunate!" he said in a cold tone. "Just *now,* especially," more frigidly, as if Ned had contrived the time on purpose.

Doris made no answer.

"But, to return to what we were saying, do I understand you to say that Jean did not give you my note containing the ring? I am sure she understood that it was important. I offered to pay her for delivering the note."

"I presume it is all right," said Doris hurriedly. "She has probably put it in a safe place. I'll ask her about it when she comes from school."

"You certainly take it coolly, Doris. Will you kindly remember that the diamond is an especially fine one, and that the price—"

"Oh, Milton, please," said Doris the weary accent stronger in her voice, "we have been through a very hard time. I tell you Ned is very sick indeed and we had to get a trained nurse."

"All the more reason why you should locate the ring immediately," broke in the inflexible voice of the man, "with a strange nurse around you cannot tell what might happen to it, and I would scarcely be able to replace it for you for sometime again. It would be very embarrassing—"

With flaming cheeks and lifted chin Doris answered:

"Milton, I cannot talk this matter over the telephone. I will attend to it the very first minute I can find. You will have to excuse me now." And Doris hung up the receiver with a click and turned around to the waiting Rose:

"What did she say, Rose?"

"What did who say?" asked Rose in amazement. "Aren't you going to hunt up that ring before you speak to anyone? Milton will be down on us with a whole police force if you don't do something about it."

"Let him come," sighed Doris sinking down into a chair again with a weary little smile of contempt. "It will be only one incident in the day. I declare I never before heard of so many things happening to people all at once. Tell me about the girl who telephoned Ned. What did she say?"

"Oh! *She!* Well, she asked after Ned as if she were queen and he were a subject, and then she wouldn't tell who she was, just demanded I get him to the phone. When I told her he was too ill to come she laughed. She said I couldn't put that over on her. She was too wise. So I hung up. The phone rang a long time after that, but I didn't answer it. Why? Do you know anything about her? You *do!* Doris, I can see by the baffled look in your eyes that that girl has done something you don't like. What is it? You might as well tell me. I'll have to know eventually."

"I suppose you will," sighed Doris sadly, and she felt her lips begin to tremble. "But Rose, I don't believe I ought to tell you until I have Ned's permission. I promised him—at least I said—"

"Bosh and nonsense! How can I intelligently answer her on the telephone until I know what her status in life is? You can tell Ned she called up and said horrid things and you had to tell me to stop me having her arrested or something. If you won't tell me things and treat me like a child I'm going away. I tell you I've got a job I can have to-morrow."

"Listen, Rose, I don't want to treat you like a child, and I suppose if she's going to make trouble you'll have to know. But don't go threatening to leave. We have trouble enough now without getting cross among ourselves. I only wanted to save you from pain, dear. But I guess it's impossible."

"Well, who is she?"

"Rose, she's Ned's wife!"

"Doris! You can't mean that!"

The quick color in Rose's cheeks had fled. Her eyes were full of horror. She stared at her sister as if she thought Doris had suddenly gone crazy.

"Tell me you are kidding, Doris," she pleaded. "You can't mean that Ned would go and do a thing like that! Why, Doris, Ned's only a kid himself. Why, I can remember when he put on long trousers." She caught her breath in a sob— "Why, Doris, it's not so very long ago! Ned couldn't do a thing like that! Why, Doris, she used some bad grammar! I forget what it was, but it was some perfectly terrible break in English!"

"Bad English isn't the worst thing in this world," sighed Doris in a heart-breaking tone.

"Why? Is there something worse? Have you seen her, Doris?"

"Yes," sadly, "I went to see her yesterday."

"Oh, Doris, is it as bad as that?"

"Yes," said Doris sadly. "It is as bad as that."

The sisters were silent for almost a whole minute looking at one another, their thoughts visualizing a possible future with this new sister-in-law. Then Rose spoke with suddenly controlled voice as if the revelation had brought new wisdom to her:

"Don't look like that, Doris. There will surely be something we can do about it. When—did it happen? When were they married?"

"Night before last!"

"Oh!" said Rose with a quick catch in her breath. "How could he? *Then?* Doris— Did you ever think that Ned maybe—drinks—sometimes—just a little? He couldn't have done a thing like that if he had been himself, could he?"

"Oh, I don't know," said Doris, leaning her tired head back against the wall and closing her eyes on sudden tears. "Rose, I don't know. I thought I smelled something on his breath that night when he came in so late—but— Rose, he seems to be crazy about her. At least he was calling her name after he became delirious!"

"That's nothing. He may have been worried. I should think he would have. Doris, Ned Dunbar knew better than to go with a girl like that ever, even when he first met her. He knew what Daddy would think about it. He's got a conscience, and probably he's ashamed. But how could he go and do a thing like that the night Papa was buried! Oh, Doris, you don't suppose——? Well, never mind. It's best not to know everything perhaps. What is she like? Tell me quick. Is she like her voice?"

"Somewhat. She's very pretty in a dolly fashion. Her complexion is painted on thick, and very vividly. Her eyes are big and blue and staring. She has hair like a bright gold cap, regularly waved as if it were made out of cloth, and she wears very extreme clothes. You have a feeling that everything is too short and too tight, and that her bare arms and neck are kind of—well, dazzling! She is really startlingly pretty in a pink and white sort of way, with a wooden smile and a stare like a doll. She looks just like Jean's biggest wax doll. She doesn't seem real. Her name is Zephyr, and she is a dancer down at the Grand."

Rose sat staring incredulously, trying to take in the situation:

"And Ned did that to us! Now! When we're all alone!" she said slowly, her face taking on an old look of disillusionment.

"Don't darling! Don't take it so hard," pleaded Doris, going over and laying her hand softly about the slim shoulders of her sister. "There'll be some way—"

"Don't say some way out of it!" crisped Rose. "There isn't! For such things! Ned's got to stand by his bargain of course. That's the way the men of our family do. They're game!"

"The men of our family do not usually marry ignorant little dancers in a cheap theatre," said Doris severely, and then remembered that the brother she was discussing was lying delirious upstairs, and that very possibly a swift way out of it all was coming for him.

"Don't let's criticize Ned, dear, he is our brother, and very likely it wasn't all his fault. He hasn't had so much help at home you know. We've all been busy with our own affairs, and Father was—busy and sick. I think this has been the cause of Ned's illness. He must know what a terrible thing he has done. In fact he said he had been a fool. I'm afraid he has been among a wild set—and under such influences—sometimes people do things they wouldn't—if they stopped to think!"

"I know what you mean," said Rose, lifting hard eyes to her sister's face. "I suppose you think he had been drinking. I've smelled it on his breath several times lately, too. I wondered if anybody else had. But he had no business to go with people like that. He knew better before he started.

"But Doris, you look tired to death. Have you had any lunch? I'll get you a cup of tea and some toast. I thought you were going to lie down. The nurse told me not to disturb you. She said the doctor said it was very necessary for you to get some sleep."

"Rose, I had to go out. I'll tell you about it later. I'll get a nap after I have something to eat. But don't you tell the nurse I haven't been asleep all the morning either. I've enough to do without fighting her."

Rose hurried into the kitchen to get the tea and toast, and Doris went to the telephone and called up Mr. Hamilton.

"That's that anyway," she said wearily as she hung up the receiver and turned to Rose who came in with a tray arranged temptingly. "Mr. Hamilton says he'll settle Florence's lawyer this afternoon. He says the man will be scared stiff when he knows there is nothing in it for him. He's coming over sometime this afternoon to talk to Florence, but he says he'll get in touch with her lawyer first, and tell him how things stand. Then he'll put it up to the lawyer to explain the case to Florence. It's the only way, I guess. She won't listen to us. Her mind seems to be thoroughly poisoned against us.

Strange she should suddenly turn around and act this way. She never was openly hateful to us before."

"Oh, she thinks now Daddy is gone we don't care what we do to her. I heard her trying to tell the lawyer that this morning. She said you nearly drowned her, and that you hated her, and we all did too. My, wouldn't it be just heaven if we didn't have to have her around any more? I wonder why Father had to be taken and Florence left. She isn't a bit of good to even herself."

"There, now, Rose, don't think such things. It doesn't do a bit of good and only makes things seem harder. Come, forget it. What delicious toast you have made. And the eggs are cooked just right. I declare I'm hungry, I didn't think I was. Rose, tell me about the job you think you can get. I'm not sure I'm going to let you go to work at anything. You're too young."

"Young your grandmother!" declared Rose looking sulky. "I'm not so many years younger than you, and I'm sure if Jean can have a job I can. But you won't like mine, and I'm not sure that I do either, only it pays five dollars a day at the start, and that sounded good to me. But I suppose that dancing sister-in-law of ours will queer me for this. Doris, it's the movies, and I know you won't like it a bit, but I've got to do something and this was right there waiting. I guess we've got to put our pride in our pocket."

But Doris had laid down her teaspoon and arisen in consternation:

"Rose! You in the movies? Never! You know what Father thought of that! You would be up against all sorts of things, and I won't stand for it. Rose, it's enough for Ned to have got us all into trouble without your going off into a thing we all know is perfectly full of perils and temptations. Why, Rose, you haven't an idea what you would be getting into."

"Haven't I though!" Rose interrupted. "One of them pinched my cheek yesterday afternoon and called me a pretty child. He also said I had adorable ankles. I *hated* him! I hate the whole thing. Of course I know there must be some nice people in the business somewhere but he wasn't one of them, and I wanted to throw his old application in his face and run home. Still, five dollars a day to begin on looks good to me, and he said he thought I had a lot in my favor."

"Rose, if you go into the movies I'll go out in the street and dig ditches!" declared Doris frantically.

"You can't do it, Sister, they don't hire women for such things."

"Well, I'll get something equally horrid unless you listen to reason. I don't care what becomes of us if you are going to throw yourself into that kind of an environment."

"Oh, rubbish! Doris. I haven't gone yet, have I? I'll promise you this much, I won't sign up for the job till you agree I ought to. I'm not keen on it myself, and now with this new sister-in-law it looks practically impossible. Come, finish your lunch and go lie down to rest. I don't see myself meeting the cold black eye of that nurse if you don't."

Doris sat down relieved:

"Rose, if I thought you'd do a thing like that—"

"Well, one in the family's enough. Since Ned has acted up I guess I'll have to be sedate. Is that Jean home from school already? Hurry, Doris, and get to your rest. I didn't know it was so late."

Jean rushed in and threw her books down on the table:

"Oh, goody, eats!" she cried. "Can I have some? I'm hungry as a bear. Say, Doris, John hasn't been at school all day. He didn't come home to lunch you know, and his teacher sent him word he was to learn this before to-morrow morning. He has a part in the school pageant and she wants him to be ready to rehearse the first period sure."

"John hasn't been at school?" said Doris in a worried voice. "Now what can he be up to? Oh dear! I didn't realize how complicated life was till Father went away!" and she rested her head on her hand wearily, her elbow on the table.

"Never mind, Dorrie," said the little sister gently. "He'll come home all right. You know I did. Mebbe he's gone after a job too, Sister, like I told Milt yesterday he had."

Doris smiled wanly at her.

"You're a dear little sister," she said tenderly, "but how did you happen to tell Milton that? And say, Jean, did Milton give you a note for me with my ring in it?"

"Sure. I laid it up on your bureau. Didn't you get it? It had a queer funny little hard lump in it. I felt it. Was that your ring?"

"There, Doris, I told you Jean would know where it is. Now you go up and put it away, then lie down and take a nap."

"I don't seem to remember any note on my bureau when I was dressing. When was it you put it there, darling?" Doris spoke anxiously. "I wonder if that was before Florence was in there, Rose? I'll go up at once. Come up, Jean, and show me just where you put it."

"It was in the morning, just before Milton went away. You had gone up to Ned's room, Sister, and I put it right by the pincushion where you would be sure to see it."

They hurried quietly upstairs, but when they entered Doris' room they found no note by the pincushion. Little Jean turned white and her eyes grew dark with trouble:

"But I put it there, Sister, I surely did!" She looked as if she was going to cry. "Was it your beautiful ring?"

"Never mind, darling, we'll find it. Don't you worry, dear," said Doris with troubled eyes. It certainly was going to be awkward if the ring could not be found. How could she possibly explain to Milton? And would she dare to go to Florence and ask if she knew anything about it? It was all a horrible mess. She dropped down on the edge of her bed to try to think what to do, and suddenly the door opened and Rose came in excitedly shutting the door behind her and speaking in a whisper:

"Doris, that girl is down there! She's got a man with her and two other girls, and she says she's going to see Ned at once or she'll know the reason why!"

13

DORIS had a sensation of weakness in her knees as if the joints were going to turn the wrong way and drop her on the floor. It seemed to be nothing with which she had to do, and for a moment she swayed and reached out her hand to catch hold of the bureau. Her eyes seemed to be darkened as if she were suddenly walking into deep gloom with a thunder-cloud overhead. She closed the lids to clear her vision, and a ray of crimson like the clear bar of light from a ruby sunset shot through the darkness. For an instant she seemed to see that brown field with the fringe of bare trees against a leaden horizon, and then the clear appearing of the great ball of fire that shot out flames of glory as it slowly sank below the hill.

It was only a flash while she closed her eyes and passed her hand across them and yet there came to her that wonderful reassurance of the presence of an Almighty Helper.

She did not stop to reason it out that it was foolish and an impossible whim of fancy. She lifted her head, her vision cleared, strong in the conviction that Another was guiding this destiny, not herself. And now it was her duty to go down to that girl. She did not know what she was to say, but she was sure that it would be given her what to say.

The trembling left her. Her weariness was forgotten. She could hear loud voices and snickering laughter in the hall below. Perhaps they would even dare to come up the stairs. The sound of laughter must be stopped at all costs. Ned must not hear that voice. There was no telling what it might do to him in his delirious condition.

Doris went down those stairs as if she had wings on her feet; and yet so softly she came that the little huddled group in the front hall did not hear her until she arrived among them.

They suddenly hushed, startled. There was something about her quiet authority as she came to them that took away their nonchalance for the moment, and made them ill at ease. Without realizing it they obeyed her motion to go into the living-room, and she followed them and closed the door. Then with the door-knob still in her hand and her back to the door, she faced them. So they looked at one another for a full second before she spoke, and then her voice was low, controlled, throbbing with earnestness. It's tone held them for the instant:

"I must ask you to be quiet," she said. "I am sure you will understand when I tell you that my brother is lying very ill upstairs and the doctor said that it was most necessary that there be no noise whatever in the house. He is quite delirious, and in a high fever. He has double pneumonia. He does not know any of us, and moans and tosses continually. It might be perhaps fatal to him if he should happen to recognize any of your voices and be excited by them. May I ask you to speak very low? And will you be seated? I shall be glad to answer any questions?" Doris looked toward Zephyr with a pleasant friendliness, far from expressing the hostility her outraged soul was feeling.

Zephyr was wearing a slim fur coat of leopard skin wrapped tightly about her willowy form, and a wicked little black hat stabbed with a single topaz, like a great bright evil eye. She looked like a stunning big cat about to pounce upon her victim. Her eyelashes were heavily beaded, and her cheeks and lips were vivid against the contrasting pallor of chin and brow. She was really a most startling apparition to arrive in that quiet conservative home for the first time in the guise of daughter-in-law of the house. Doris looked at her and felt something terrifying grip her heart.

But the big handsome cat did not sit down, instead she drew her leopard skin with its bushy fox border still closer about her slim limbs, slouched with a droopier curve to her anatomy, and stared. She did not appear to have taken in a word that Doris had said. She just stood there with her impudent smile and stared. It was the young man who spoke for her. He was an insignificant young fellow with a weak face and a tiny ineffectual moustache, but the same air of utter disregard for anything that might stand for authority or law or courtesy.

"Look a here!" he blared forth in a voice that was certainly not quiet. "You ain't puttin' none o' that over on us. *We're wise! See?* We ain't takin' any bluff like that. This here lady's here to see her husband, an' I'm here to see that she sees 'im. *See?*"

He took a step nearer to Doris and his hot breath was wafted to her, rank with spirits. It was all too evident that he had amply reinforced himself for the interview.

Doris drew back from him and went a step nearer to Zephyr.

"You understand, don't you, that Ned is too ill to know you or to understand anything that you would say to him? We haven't any of us been allowed in the room since morning when the doctor brought a trained nurse to look after him. It seems unfortunate that everything should have happened this way, but I guess it cannot be helped. We are all most anxious about my brother. The doctor says he is a very sick man."

Then suddenly the red lips opened and the dolly spoke. Her china-blue eyes had that glad doll-stare as if they could only express certain set emotions and had to use those for everything.

"Of course I don't believe all that rot!" she said sweetly while her eyes smiled. "I know you're trying to keep us apart, and of course you would make up any story to do it. I don't know how you've got the gag on him, but I mean to set him free, and take him home with me till you come across. See? If Neddie hasn't got the nerve to stand out against his precious family *I have,* and I mean to use it! Now, stand aside and point me the way to his room. I'm going up. And if you try to stop me I'll have you all out in print in the papers in the morning. I guess you'll like that, won't you? 'FAMOUS TOE DANCER SUES DEAD BROKER'S SON FOR SUPPORT.' Oh, that makes you turn white. I thought it would hit you that way. Now, get out of my way. I'm going up to find my husband."

Doris had backed off against the door and was standing at bay, her face very white, but her head up, and a calm line of control to her pale lips.

"Listen!" said Doris. "You needn't believe me. Sit down and I will send for the doctor. If he says you can go up I will not stand in your way. But it is my duty to prevent my brother from being disturbed—"

Doris' words were suddenly brought to an abrupt finish. The tall lithe cat-girl stealthily advanced, and reaching out a furry paw gripped the daughter of the house by the arm unexpectedly, giving her a quick yank which swung her completely around, and sent her spinning across the room into the arms of the dapper little man of the pointed moustache. He caught her wrists and held them in a mean little grip. Then with a taunting breath that was almost a snarl, Zephyr slid forward to the door.

But suddenly, unexpectedly, almost uncannily, the door swung inward before she had touched it, and the burly doctor stood glaring under shabby eyebrows straight into the soubrette's gaudy little face.

"What is the meaning of all this?" he asked in a rumbling voice that was terrifying, while yet it did not rise much higher than a whisper. "Don't you know that there is serious illness in this house? Don't you know that you are endangering the life of my patient?"

He took the slim furry shoulder of the leopard-girl in his big powerful hand and shook it till the pearly teeth rattled behind the red lips, and the china-blue eyes stared up at him in fright.

Silently from the other door of the living-room there entered with his brief case in his hands, the immaculate and elderly lawyer Hamilton, and advanced upon the rear flank of the enemy. For Rose had been busy on the telephone.

Before Doris had opened her lips to cry out against her captor the young man with the pointed moustache was taken in a strong white hand, by the collar, and lifted several inches from the floor, where he was suspended, wildly striking out with his shiny feet and attempting to make a landing, incidentally releasing Doris as he rose.

The two attendant flappers in giddy little costumes huddled near the window and measured the distance to the ground. They had no desire to be shaken or suspended. They had their living to make, and had not yet attained stardom. This was not their quarrel.

"Now!" said the doctor, shutting the door and stepping to the centre of the room with his clutch still painfully on the slim leopard shoulder. "Let me understand this. Young lady, what business have you and these others—" his sharp eyes swept the frightened group, "coming into a house of sickness and disturbing the peace?"

Zephyr was regaining her insolence. She gave him the benefit of her china-blue stare, and her rosy smile with the hard little glint behind it:

"I have come to see my husband, Doctor, and they won't let me in. I understood he was very ill—"

"Ooh-hh!" spoke up little Jean from the back of the room, "I heard her say she didn't *believe* it. I heard her tell Doris it was all a big bluff that Ned was sick."

The doctor looked over at Jean with a twinkle in his stern eyes. Then he singled out Doris:

"Is that so, Doris?"

Doris nodded.

"Well," said the doctor, "I think we'll deal with you later, young lady." And he put Zephyr to one side, still holding his mighty grip on her shoulder. "Now then, who are all these? You two girls? Who are you? Ned isn't married to both of you too, is he?"

The girls shrank back and answered in awed tones: "No, sir," and shook their heads.

"Well,—then you may go!" and he pointed with a big burly finger toward the door.

The girls rose in hurried unison, as it were, with a single glide, and disappeared into the hall. A moment later the soft closing of the outer door, and the echo of four little high heels clicking on the pavement outside indicated their hasty departure.

"Now *you!*" went on the doctor pointing toward the still struggling young man. "Who are you?"

"I'm—Arthur—Hig-g-g-gins!" chattered the champion between strugglings to get more than one foot at once on terra firma. The accurate Mr. Hamilton, having once measured the distance from the floor to a little above the normal height of the young man's head, was calmly, patiently endeavoring to maintain his arm at an equilibrium, which made it difficult for Arthur Higgins to seem dignified.

"You didn't happen to be the best man, did you, Mr. Higgins?" asked the doctor with a tantalizing twinkle in his eyes again.

"Y-y-yes. I *d-d-did!*" said Arthur.

"Well," said the doctor authoritatively, "you're not the best man any more. You can be excused also."

The doctor nodded to Hamilton, who lowered his victim and got out his fine white handkerchief to mop his heated brow.

"But," spluttered young Arthur, "I'm not going away till Zephyr goes too. I came here to help her see her husband. I came here to protect her."

"Well, you've protected her, haven't you? You're not needed any longer. You'll find a policeman outside, I think, and you can argue the matter with him if you like, but I advise you to walk straight on by, for if you undertake to tackle him you'll find to a certainty that you're not the best man now. Good-bye."

There was something in the doctor's eye that quelled the young man, and nervously twirling the sharp ends of his tiny moustache he possessed himself of his hat and walked out.

"Oh, Arty! You aren't leaving me all alone!" wailed Zephyr.

Arty cast one regretful cowardly glance at Zephyr, and hurried by the doctor.

"You're not alone as I understand it," growled the doctor looking into the blue eyes of the bride in his hand. "Your husband's family are all here. I'm sure you will need no protection. Now, Miss Zephyr, if you will sit down we'll just look into this matter. What was your idea in coming here! No, don't go out, Hamilton! Doris! Yes, come in Rose, I shall want you all here. It is best to understand the situation. What did you come here for?"

Zephyr looked sulkily down at her gloved hands and did not answer till the doctor had asked her the third time.

"I came to see Ned." She answered like a sulky child.

"What did you want of Ned?"

Suddenly she looked up with all the boldness of her kind.

"It's none of your business!" she said, and added words that are not to be written here.

"That'll be about all of that!" said the doctor in a tone that was like a whip lash. He was conscious of the pitiful quiver of Rose's eyelashes and Doris' lips. His face became like a great rock for sternness. "You'll answer my question straight with no embroidery, do you understand? Or you'll go out from here under escort. Now, is that plain? and no amount of blackmail is going to give you license to say what you please in the presence of these *ladies*."

There was the tiniest inflection on the word "ladies" that went deep in Zephyr's crude aspiring soul, and made her cringe under her painted smile. But there was real peril in the doctor's threat. Zephyr knew that, favorite as she was at the Grand, her position would not bear an ugly publicity. She must not anger a man with a steel-blue eye and a square jaw like that. He was proof against all her arts and he seemed to see right through her waxen mask.

"Now, will you tell me what you wanted of your husband?"

"I needed some money," said the girl sullenly. "He's my husband and he ought to support me, and besides he promised—"

"I thought that would be it," said the doctor sagely. "How long have you been married to Dunbar?"

"Since night before last!" There was defiance in the girl's eyes.

"Who supported you before that?"

"I did. I'm Zephyr at The Grand!" she answered loftily.

He looked her over thoughtfully.

"Lost your job?"

Her nostrils quivered angrily:

"Well, I guess anyhow *not!*"

"Well, then, I guess you'll have to go on supporting for a while yet. Dunbar isn't going to be in shape to do it for the present, and these young ladies are certainly not responsible for your support. What's your salary?"

Zephyr scorned to reply.

"Rose, will you just look up the number of The Grand? I want to talk to the manager a minute."

Zephyr sprang to her feet furious, with a lithe leopard-like movement, her face drawn in an angry fury that reminded Doris strongly of the girl's mother.

"You do that and I'll have a policeman onto you!" threatened the girl. "I don't believe a word of this about Ned's being sick. He's just hiding away from me and you all are helping him. I knew he didn't mean to get me that ring when he promised, but he can't get out of it. I'll have it in all the papers by night. There won't one of his friends look at him any more after I get through with him. I'll—"

"Got the number, yet, Rose?" asked the doctor ignoring the angry girl. "Here, give me the phone—want to talk to that theatre manager."

Zephyr sprang at him more catlike than ever, and grasped his arm:

"You ain't going to do that!" she screamed. "Now *doncha!*" she began to plead as he took down the receiver. But he ignored her and called a number, at which she suddenly became frantic and abject together.

"I'll go away!" she pleaded. "I'll wait awhile," she urged eagerly. "'Cause you see they don't know I got married. They might put me out of a job entirely for that. They say it ain't good publicity to have a girl known to be married, especially a dancer."

The doctor covered the mouthpiece with a large hand and paused:

"Well," he said looking at her doubtfully. "Of course if you're willing to be reasonable till Dunbar gets well—"

"Oh yes, I will," said Zephyr eagerly, and then as the doctor hung up the receiver she hastened toward the door.

At the threshold some of her courage seemed to have returned:

"How do I know Ned is sick?" she asked sullenly. "You haven't given me any proof. I don't know any of you."

The doctor turned with an elaborate flourish:

"Let me introduce Miss Dunbar—" waving his hand toward Doris, "and Miss Rose Dunbar, Miss Jean Dunbar. This gentleman is Mr. Hamilton, the family lawyer, and I am Doctor Wright, the family physician. Now, young woman, if you can keep your mouth shut while you are upstairs I will take you up to the door and let you have a look at your husband. That is all. You must not stay in the room. It might be fatal to him, to have a stranger—that is to have you unexpectedly— Unless, indeed, you would like to give up your job at the theatre and come and nurse him? How about that? Could you get off?"

Doris and Rose caught their breath and looked at one another in horror, but Zephyr withdrew hastily toward the door:

"Oh, no!" she said anxiously. "I couldn't get off. And just now seeing he's sick I wouldn't dare risk losing my job. Someone has got to earn money of course." She cast a direful glance at her two sisters-in-law— "And I guess I won't go upstairs. It might disturb him. I guess I oughtta be hurrying. It's getting late."

She grasped the door-knob hurriedly.

"Just as you please of course. You're entirely satisfied now that it is true that your husband is sick?"

"Oh yes!" She opened the door.

"Of course it would be quite appropriate for a wife to nurse her husband," observed the doctor affably. "It would really be your place you know—"

"Oh, it wouldn't be *possible!*" said Zephyr looking nervously at her wrist-watch. "It's much later than I thought. I must go. I have an extra rehearsal, and they'll fire me if I'm not there on time."

She vanished as a young leopard might have disappeared into the forest. Doris and Rose stood staring after her with faces drawn and gray. When they heard the last click of her little heels down the street Rose suddenly dropped her face into her hands and burst into tears. Doris turned with white lips toward the doctor:

"How can I ever thank you!"

"Oh, nonsense, little girl. She's just a big bluff. You don't need to be afraid of her. Cheer up Rosy-Posy! This isn't the worst thing you may have to face in life. Ned isn't the only boy that ever made a mess of his life at nineteen. He ought to be walloped of course, and he'll probably have some hard going ahead of him, but there'll be a way somehow for him to come out on top if he wants to take it. It'll be hard maybe, and uphill, but there's always a chance to get straight if one wants to try. Now you two girls stop baring the burdens of the nation, and run off and rest. This isn't your burden anyway, only in a secondary sort of way. Of course you'll have some mortification coming to you, and it's too bad, but mortification isn't the worst thing in the world. Ned's the one that's got to bear this, and when he gets well don't you girls try to bear it for him, and make it easy. You've spoiled him that way since he was a little shaver. Let him take his medicine now. He'll be a better man for it. Don't be too easy on him."

"But will he get well?" asked Doris anxiously.

"I certainly hope so," asserted the doctor energetically. "He's a pretty sick boy of course, but there is everything in his favor. He's young and strong and got a good nurse. Now, Doris, you run back to bed. You look like a sick kitten. How long did you sleep this morning?"

The telltale color flamed softly in Doris' cheek.

"I thought so. You didn't sleep at all. Now positively, my orders must be kept! Rose, you take your sister up to her room at once and tuck her into bed. Lock her in if necessary, and see that she sleeps. No coming down till she has slept at least two hours."

"But I can't go just yet. I must see Mr. Hamilton."

"I can tell Mr. Hamilton everything," said Rose. "You weren't even here when it happened."

So, protesting, they hustled her off to her bed much against her will. Tucked in softly under Rose's coral, silk down quilt, with the shades drawn and the air blowing in below them, she sank into wonderful oblivion for a while, forgetting all her troubles.

Downstairs Rose gave a detailed account of her step-mother's actions that morning, and the lawyer was most comforting in his kindly formal way.

"My dear child!" he said. "I am so sorry that you and your sister have had this to bear in addition to all your other troubles. I am afraid it is my fault. I should have insisted on further talk with Mrs. Dunbar yesterday and saved you all this. Of course she does not understand that there is no property, and that therefore she has no case. I will see her at once and make matters plain to her. As for this shyster Applegate, I know him well. He'll not touch the case when he finds there's no property back of it. I only hope he has not already extracted a retaining fee from the poor foolish woman. He is great on retaining fees. Could I see Mrs. Dunbar at once?"

"She went out about an hour ago," said Rose. "But I don't think she had any money. She had to borrow some from Doris to get gloves for the funeral. She never keeps money."

"Well, it will be a good thing if she hasn't already wasted any on Applegate. Then I'll just run downtown and hunt him up. I'll let him know how things stand, and then suppose I return about five? Mrs. Dunbar will likely be back by that time don't you think? And I'll try to talk her into some sense."

As soon as the door closed on the kindly lawyer Rose went in search of her little sister, who was just preparing to go out and hunt up a job for the afternoon.

"Jeanie, you can't go away now," said Rose. "It's up to you and me to find Doris' ring before she wakes up. Milton Page is coming this evening, and Doris has simply *got* to have it by then. You know how the note looks and may be able to find it more easily than I. Let's go to Florence's room first, before she gets back. Don't make a noise. Doris mustn't hear us."

And the two crept silently upstairs to their step-mother's room.

14

"SISTER, I don't understand why we go to Florence's room," whispered Jean, when the door was finally unlocked by a key from another room. "I know I put that note on Doris' bureau. Why don't we look more in Doris' room?"

"Because Florence was snooping around in Doris' room yesterday, dear. I caught her at it," Rose whispered back. "She thinks we want to get the property away, and she is trying to find papers, I guess, something to prove her rights perhaps, I don't know. Now we mustn't talk, Jeanie, the nurse might hear us, and we must work fast for Florence might come any minute. Keep your ears open, and get to work."

Rose made quick work of the bureau drawers, rummaging swiftly through jewel boxes, and under lace collars, everywhere that a letter might be hidden, or a ring stowed away. She went through the desk and the closet, and even looked beneath the pillows on the bed, but no ring did she find. She did come upon the packet of letters belonging to Doris, however, which Mrs. Dunbar had taken from Doris' desk the day before, and stowed them quickly in her pocket for further examination, recognizing her father's handwriting, and knowing that her stepmother could have no possible right to them.

Suddenly Jean exclaimed softly: "Oh, Rose, I've found a piece of it. Yes, I'm sure. It's 'Miss Do—' and it looks like Milton Page's writing."

She was going through the waste basket carefully, bit by bit, and the basket was rather full of torn papers. But before Rose could answer they both heard a key click in the front door.

"Hurry! Bring the whole basket along!" whispered Rose, hastily closing the little drawer of the desk from which she had just extracted Doris' letters. "Go into my room just as softly as you can and lock the door till I knock. Quick! She's coming! I must lock this door!"

Jean made a silent escape with her waste basket and Rose had just accomplished the locking of the door and vanished down the back stairs as her stepmother came into the lower hall. Her cheeks were flushed with excitement and her heart was beating wildly. If worst came to worst she would face her stepmother with the truth, but it was not best that she should be brought to bay till she had more evidence concerning the ring. Florence might get frightened and not tell, if she thought they were trying to catch her.

Rose went to the sink and began to rattle the dishes to cover her escape.

Suddenly she heard a voice in the hall. It was Florence's voice. She had not gone upstairs yet. She was talking over the telephone. Rose stopped breathless. Who was Florence calling?

"Is that you, Mr. Applegate? Yes? Well this is Mrs. Dunbar. I'm afraid I'm a little later than I promised to be, but I have secured a little money, and shall be able to give you something. It isn't as much as I hoped but still I hope you'll think it is enough. It is twenty-five dollars, Mr. Applegate. Will that be all right? Oh, thank you. Yes, I can *try*. And you will call? I see. Well, that will be quite all right. Just mention that you have an appointment with me. The children are so careless. I shall be expecting you. Thank you. Good-bye."

Rose could hear the soft swish of Florence's dress as she mounted the stairs, and then the key in her door. She stood still trying to think. Twenty-five dollars! Where in the world did Florence go to get twenty-five dollars? Had she been to some of Father's friends and borrowed it? Had she perhaps drawn a check somewhere, notwithstanding she knew that there was nothing in her bank account to make it good? Was there anything she could have sold? The problem was too great for Rose to solve. But the fact remained that wherever she procured it she was about to surrender it into the hands of this rascally lawyer. And with the family funds already in such a low state it certainly should be prevented. What ought she to do? Try to telephone Mr. Hamilton? No, for Florence might hear her. If only Mr. Hamilton would come first! But would Florence listen to him? And then there was the question of the ring. Had that really been Milton's note in the waste basket? And if so what had Florence done with Doris' ring? She must get upstairs and see what else Jean had discovered.

She glanced at the clock. It was half past four. Hastily wiping her hands she hurried softly upstairs, tapped with the tips of her fingers on her own door, and was let in by an excited little sister.

"It's all here, Rose, every bit. See!"

There on the bed Jean had pieced it all out and Rose read, quickly comprehending the whole story from what Doris had told her:

"And Florence must have read it!" she said without realizing she was talking to little Jean.

"Maybe she didn't. Maybe she just tore it up," said Jean. "She's so queer and 'different' sometimes," said the little girl.

"No," said Rose thoughtfully, "I think she read it. She wouldn't dare throw it away until she knew what was in it, and she must have felt the ring too. There wasn't any sign of the ring in the waste basket was there?"

"No, I've looked very carefully," said Jean.

"Well, dearie, she's done *something* with that ring! I'm sure of it! See, she knew that Doris didn't know about the note. She thought she could get away with it without anybody knowing. She maybe is just doing it to punish Doris for throwing that water on her when she was in hysterics. She wouldn't really mean to keep it of course. But it will be awful for Doris if she doesn't find it before Milton comes this evening. He talks so much about nothing!"

"I know!" said the little girl, and then with a sigh, "Oh dear! I wish Florence was more mothery, Rose. Why isn't she?"

"Just because she can't think of anybody but herself!" answered Rose. "Hark! Isn't that the door-bell? Mercy, what next! My hair is in a mess, and I ought to be getting dinner this minute."

"I'll go!" said the little sister, and sped away down the front stairs. Rose hurried down the back stairs, and stepped softly into the dining-room to see who had come. She was relieved to find it was only a boy from the drug store with a prescription the doctor had ordered.

As she stepped back from the door her eye glanced across the telephone table set just in the turn of the stairs in the hall beyond the dining-room. And there right upon the telephone book lay Florence's new gloves and her pocketbook.

Quick as a flash Rose realized her opportunity. She had but to reach out her arm and the pocketbook and gloves were in her possession. She hesitated about the gloves and finally left them lying where she had found them. The pocketbook she hid in her blouse and retired to the laundry back of the kitchen to investigate. Here if anywhere that ring would be put for safe-keeping of course. She must be quick about her investigation too, for Florence would most certainly discover her loss in a minute or two and return for her property.

Rose locked the door between kitchen and laundry and opened the pocketbook. Yes, there was a roll of bills! Five tattered five-dollar bills. Queer. Where did she get them? They smelled dirty, too."

Rose glanced over the few addresses and business cards in the purse to see if they gave any clue, but they did not. Some of them had pencilled memoranda about prices of bargains she had seen. It was in the last little flat pocket fastened with a leather flap that she found the pawn ticket, and stood staring at it with eyes filled with consternation.

A pawn ticket! She had never seen one before but she could not help knowing what it was. There was Doris' ring described. Florence had pawned Doris' ring! And for twenty-five dollars! Milton's vaunted ring to bring only that! Even in the stress of the moment a smile of amusement came to her lips at that. How insulted Milton would be to know his ring brought only twenty-five dollars at a pawn shop.

But what must she do about it? She tried to steady her pulses and think clearly. She knew that it might be only the matter of a minute or two before Florence was upon her, and she could no longer control the situation. She wished Doris were here, but yet she shrank from having Doris know. In a flash all sorts of possibilities went through her mind. The man might sell the ring, or change the stone or lose it or something before it could be recovered, and then what would Doris do? She could scarcely offer Milton three hundred and fifty dollars in place of his ring which she wanted to return. It was a terrible situation. Determinedly she forced herself to read the pawn ticket over. There were but few words on it. The street and number of the pawn shop, the date, and price for which the ring was to be redeemed. It was called a diamond solitaire.

Rose was quick-witted. It did not take her long to act. She hid the pocketbook inside her blouse again and stepped into the dining-room. She could hear a door upstairs opening. Florence would be coming down for her things perhaps. She dared not risk going up for her hat and coat. She glanced about. There on a chair was Jean's little school sweater and blue felt hat. Rose seized upon them, and slipped out to the kitchen, struggling into the little sweater that was much too small for her, and jamming on the small round child's hat. She did not stop to think how she looked. At another time she would have gladly borne torture rather than to have been seen in the street in such a rig. But Rose was not thinking of herself now. She was only thinking of Doris.

As she sped on down the street she realized that she was carrying off Florence's twenty-five dollars, and that she had so to speak killed two birds with one stone, for now Florence would be unable to give the Applegate man his retaining fee.

She dared not take a trolley and had no money to take a taxi. She remembered that the purse had contained only a little small change besides the bills, and she might need it all to get the ring back. They would likely charge interest or something. However that would not be fair of course, because they could not have had the ring many hours. Florence must just have returned from pawning it.

Arrived at the pawn shop at last, after a devious and breathless trip, she was seized with a great fear to enter. Somehow it seemed that all horror and shame were concentrated in this necessity of going into that place, that awful place with three great balls hanging over the door and the ghosts of people's old wedding rings and violins and opera cloaks displayed in the window. Yet she knew she had to do it. And now she began to consider her costume, and wonder if perhaps they might not think her a fraud appearing in such a rig and demanding the ring. Maybe they would give it to no one but Florence! How terrible! And how could she possibly make Florence go and get it? Would they have to resort to force to compel her? Would they have to get a policeman to make her do it?

With such wild thoughts rioting through her throbbing brain, Rose took a deep breath and entered.

A grimy, greasy individual with much black beard and a large nose approached her. Rose opened her lips to repeat the speech she had prepared on the way down, but she found they were trembling too much to speak. She drew another deep breath and tried again:

"I have come to reclaim the ring which my mother left here a little while ago," she said, and found her voice growing steadier as she went on. "There has been a terrible mistake made, and the ring belongs to someone else. My mother must return it at once." She held up the pawn ticket in her trembling hand.

The man looked at her keenly with his little black eyes:

"You are not de lady vot brang de ring!"

"No," said Rose. "She could not come again. I have come in her place."

"You got de money?"

"Oh yes," said Rose. "Twenty-five dollars!"

"I sharge two dollars fer my trouble!"

"Why, you haven't had any trouble!" said Rose indignantly, now losing all her fear. "And I haven't got that much money with me. I'll give you all I have!" She emptied out the silver and pennies. There was sixty-seven cents.

The man shook his head:

"Sharge two dollars fer my trouble!" he reiterated.

"Well, I haven't got it and I haven't time to wait. That ring belongs to someone else, I tell you, and must be returned at once! You don't want to be arrested for receiving stolen goods, do you?"

The man took on a change of countenance.

"Oh, vas it den schtole dot ring vos? Vy didn't you say so? I get. You put de money out. I get. You gif me de ticket."

"No," said Rose, "I keep the ticket till you give me the ring, unless you want me to go and get a policeman."

The man eyed her half frightened and trotted off to a safe at the back of the room. He fumbled a moment in the safe, and then came back with the ring.

He handed it over and gathered up the bills and ticket. Rose slid it on her finger and fled out the door, back home, two miles and a quarter on feet that almost seemed to have wings.

She slipped in the back door without meeting anyone, divested herself of her queer outfit and started upstairs just as Jean came flying down the back way:

"Rose, where have you been? I've looked everywhere for you. Florence has lost her pocketbook and she's very angry. She's got a queer man in the living-room, and he seems to be angry too. She has been running up and down stairs and calling you. She says she knows she left her purse with her gloves by the telephone."

"Hush, Jean! Don't let her know I'm here if you can help it."

"Well, she wants to wake Doris up. She says she must have her pocketbook. She has to pay a bill."

"Well, she shan't. I'll stop her if it comes to that. Jean, run in the dining-room and call up Mr. Hamilton's office quick as you can, and talk as low as you can be heard. You know his number, 2267 Granniss. Tell him they are both here, he'll understand, and for him to come *quick!* I'll run up and guard Doris' door. She didn't disturb Ned, did she?"

"No. I guess she's afraid of that nurse," smiled Jean. "Oh, Rose! There's the door-bell. Which shall I do first?"

"Go to the door. It may be Mr. Hamilton. If it is take him right into the living-room where they are, quickly before they realize who it is."

Rose waited breathless by the swinging door till she heard Mr. Hamilton's formal voice greeting Jean. Then to her surprise she saw Jean bringing him down the hall to the dining-room.

"He wanted to see you first, Rose," she whispered as she ushered him in.

"I just wanted to tell you, Miss Rose," began the lawyer, "that you need not worry any more about Applegate. I have seen him and he has agreed to refuse the case. I presume that is what he is in there for now."

"No," said Rose, "I think he is trying to get some money out of my stepmother first. Jean says she has been hunting her pocketbook, and crying about not finding it, and I heard her telephone him that she had twenty-five dollars for him now and would get more as soon as possible."

"You don't say!" said the lawyer startled out of his usual quietness. "The rascal! He promised me he would see Mrs. Dunbar and drop the case at once. Did she find her pocketbook? I'm afraid there will be no getting back anything she has given him."

"I don't think she found it, not yet!" said little Jean.

"No, she hasn't found it, I'm sure," said Rose with her hand clasped tightly over the folds of her dress where the empty pocketbook was hidden.

"I had better go in at once," said the lawyer. "Miss Rose, you might be where you can hear everything. It is often well to have a witness. Both of you come in after me."

Mr. Hamilton walked to the living-room door and flung it open.

15

ROSE felt a sudden hysterical desire to laugh. There seemed to have been so many dramatic scenes following one after another in that living-room. It would make a good play. And was the present one about to be a comedy or tragedy, she wondered?

The lawyer stood still in the doorway for an instant, the two girls just behind him. They had come so silently that they had not given warning to the two who were quite absorbed in their own affairs.

Mrs. Dunbar was weeping, softly and pleadingly:

"I'm so sorry," she said, "I can't think where that pocketbook has gone. I must have lost it on the street. I went out on purpose to get the money for you. I was sure I would be able to get three hundred and fifty as I promised you. I have always been given to understand— at least—there should have been that coming to me— and all I could get was twenty-five. But I shall sell some of my valuables and get the rest of the retaining fee at once."

"Madame, it is quite unfortunate that you should have lost your pocketbook of course, but surely you can borrow of someone. I really must insist on this retaining fee. My time is so full that I cannot afford to waste even the hour that it has taken me to come here, for nothing; and I have clients clamoring for me to take their cases in charge. Of course I have to be fair and square, and I have made the rule that whoever pays first gets first attention. Your case I take it requires instant attention, but unless you give me your fee this afternoon, at least a part of it, I shall in honor be obliged to let someone else come first and you will have to take your chances later."

"Ohhh, Mr. Applegate!" wailed Mrs. Dunbar. "Can't you possibly make an exception in case of a poor widow who is being cheated out of her livelihood? I'll gladly make the final fees double the three thousand that I promised if you will just go ahead as if I had paid you. You see I am absolutely helpless—"

Hamilton suddenly stepped into the room:

"What does this mean, Applegate?" he said in his scrupulously polite tone edged with severity.

The man Applegate turned fairly green with the surprise of it:

"Why!—I—! Oh,— Is that you, Hamilton? Yes, I was about to tell Mrs. Dunbar that I am unable to take the case—"

"It certainly did not sound like that, sir!" said Hamilton facing the shyster lawyer with a steady gaze. "It sounded very much as if you were endeavoring to get a fee out of this lady under false pretenses. Mrs. Dunbar, I hope you have not given him anything."

The lady drew herself up haughtily.

"I will thank you, Mr. Hamilton, to let my affairs alone," she said loftily. "I am done with you until we meet shortly in the court room where I expect to get full justice and my rights."

She looked very bedraggled as she stood facing the

two men, her eyes pink with weeping, a pathetic droop to her mouth, which at some time had been pretty, and might yet have been if it had not been borne down at the corners with self-pity. It occurred to Rose with sudden startling force, that perhaps her father might really have been attracted to her at one time. Perhaps he really thought he loved her when he married her. This idea somehow gave Rose a twinge of something like pity for the poor foolish woman who was making so much trouble for them all; and a kind of a sense of protection rose within her. After all, she was a part of their family. A feeble trying part, but she must be protected even against herself.

Something of this perhaps even the family lawyer felt for he faced the other man indignantly.

"Mr. Applegate," he said in his most severe tone, "I am here to protect this lady, even against herself. You understand what that means. You will now explain to her exactly why you cannot undertake her case."

Florence Dunbar drew away from him indignantly and turned to Applegate with expectation.

"My dear lady," began Applegate clearing his throat and rubbing his hands together, "as I was about to tell you before this gentleman interrupted us, I have found that it will be quite impossible for me to undertake your—" he paused for further words and Florence looked at him half-puzzled. She was not stupid if she was foolish and impulsive.

"But I don't understand, Mr. Applegate. You were just urging me to get the money together at once for the retaining fee, this afternoon, you *insisted*! If you did not feel that you could take my case why were you demanding money of me? Are you letting this man intimidate you?"

"Oh, not at all, not at all. You don't understand, my

dear lady. It was not as a retaining fee that I wanted the money. It was as a remuneration for the trouble I have already taken to look into your case. I cannot afford to make research such as I was obliged to make into your case, without remuneration, you understand. You must know that my time is valuable, and I am charging you a very small fee."

"But why are you giving up my case if you have already begun to work on it?"

"Because I find, dear lady, that you have no case at all!"

"No case! What do you mean? You told me the case was very simple and plain."

"Ah, yes, I told you that my dear lady on your representation of the matter. But when I came to investigate I find that you have no case whatever. You see there *is* no property, my dear lady."

"No property! What do you mean?" with flashing eyes. "There is this house, isn't there? You cannot discount that."

"But this house is mortgaged up to the last dollar it would bring."

"Well, I intend to pay off the mortgage of course sometime. People have their houses mortgaged for years and keep on living in them. It is ridiculous to tell me that I cannot."

"But my dear lady, you have no money. You cannot pay the interest on your mortgage, and the interest I find has been accumulating for some time."

"I don't believe it," said Florence with a toss of her head. "Mr. Dunbar did not do things that way. Mr. Hamilton, why don't you tell him that there is plenty of property, bonds and mines and all sorts of things? I heard you read a long list of them out of the will."

"Mrs. Dunbar, I am afraid that you did not hear me

also say that all those things had been given as security in a new enterprise which your husband was launching, and from which he hoped to reap great gains. But the enterprise has fallen through, or practically so, and has taken everything with it. This house, I regret to say, is no longer yours. It was taken over to-day by the mortgagee, and you are only staying here out of his courtesy on account of Ned's very critical illness. It is hard for me to have to tell you these things, and we hope that a way will somehow be found for you to be comfortable, but it is my painful duty to tell you the truth."

Florence stood looking from one man to the other, incredulous. Till at last it began to dawn upon her that there must be at least some truth in it all. Then her roving eye rested upon Rose and Jean standing in the shadow of the hall door.

"But what about them!" she said pointing excitedly to the two. "His children! They have property, don't they? The will you read said this house was theirs and they might let me stay here as long as I lived. I heard you read that. Now do you call that justice?" Her eyes were filled with tears again, infuriated tears. "Is that the way a husband would treat his wife? Mr. Dunbar never treated me with injustice. I know he did not write that will."

"Mrs. Dunbar," said Hamilton taking on a patient look, "suppose you sit down and let me tell you the whole story. Then you will understand better. Have this chair. Now, I will explain. This house did not belong to your husband at all, ever. He merely held it in trust for the children. The house was built by the first Mrs. Dunbar's father and given to her as a wedding present. At her death she gave your husband a life home here, but she willed the ownership of the house to her children. Now, do you understand how your husband had no right to will the house at all? It was not his. It merely passed by law at his death to the rightful owners who were his wife's children."

"Then how did it get mortgaged?" asked the excited little woman. "There is something very crooked about it all, I think."

"No, nothing crooked. Your husband was the trustee of his children's property, and when he found an investment which he felt would double the value of their property he mortgaged the house and put the money into it. It was not his fault that his project failed. He may have been unwise in his judgment, but that was all. There was nothing wrong about what he did, and there has been no injustice done to you or to anyone else. If your husband had lived long enough to put his project on its feet and his plans had been fulfilled, both you and his children would have inherited a very fine property. It is most unfortunate that he has left you in this situation, but it really cannot be helped, Mrs. Dunbar, and there is no good to be gained by spending more money in fruitless fighting to get possession of something that is not in existence any longer so far as you are concerned."

Suddenly the truth seemed to penetrate the widow's consciousness, and she sank down in a perfect torrent of tears, moaning and groaning, and showing herself well on the way toward one of her screaming spells.

Mr. Applegate looked about for his hat, and backed toward the hall door:

"I really think," he said, looking helplessly about on everybody present, "that I had better be going. I am just in the way here—" but no one could hear him on account of the loud weeping of the lady. He approached Hamilton and repeated his suggestion, "I think I had better be going now."

"Certainly," said the lawyer, "*do* go, and I would suggest that you never return. Miss Rose, will you close that hall door so that the invalid will not be distressed by this noise? And Jean couldn't you get some smelling salts or something, and—I would suggest—a glass of water!"

The lawyer really was most helpful. He seemed to know just what was the right thing to do. For an old bachelor of staid habits and conservative ways, he certainly showed himself adaptable. He patted Mrs. Dunbar on the shoulder.

"There, now, Mrs. Dunbar. Calm yourself. You've been under a heavy strain. Of course we all knew that if you understood you would not have taken this stand. But you do not need to worry. Not in the least. There will be a way out somehow. What you need is a good rest."

And after a minute or two of rather wild sobbing Florence actually quieted down into a pitiful little wail like a sick child that wanted to be comforted. Rose watched the phenomenon a moment and then silently slipped from the room motioning Jean to follow her.

"Let's leave them alone for a few minutes. Maybe he can do something with her. I'm going to make a cup of tea and take it in. Florence is great on afternoon tea. Isn't there some of that fruit cake left in the tin box? If not take some of those crackers and spread a little marmalade on them. Anything fancy may take Florence's mind off herself for a few minutes."

"But Rose, oughtn't we to do something about that ring while Mr. Hamilton is here? I've looked everywhere I can think of while you were gone and I can't find a sign of it."

"Hush, Jean. Don't ask me any questions. I'll tell you all about it to-night when we go up to bed. But the ring is found. I'm going to give it to Doris as soon as she wakes up. But listen! Don't mention it to a soul, not in any way, unless you should happen to see Milton and he asks you, of course. Then you can just answer: 'Yes, Doris has it.' Not any more, mind you. Now hurry and get the crackers while I make the tea. We'll put them on the little silver tray, and use the Dresden cups—two cups, and the little gold sugar and cream. Florence hates lemon you know."

They managed an inviting tray, and entered the living-room a few minutes later to find the erstwhile irate lady reclining comfortably on the davenport, her head on a blue velvet pillow, her feet covered with a silk rug, and her eyes, which were still pink from crying, half shaded by a black-bordered handkerchief of finest linen. She was listening docilely to the kindly explanations of the lawyer, who had somehow managed to soothe her pride and bring her to listen to reason.

"But—Mr. Hamilton—" she was saying with her delicate lips in a tremble like a tired child's, "you don't mean that we won't have *any*thing at all. Not literally, Mr. Hamilton. Why, how could we live? I simply *have* to have some money right away. In fact I'm obliged to. I—I—have obligations."

"Suppose you just hand all your obligations over to me, Mrs. Dunbar. That's what I'm for, to look after the obligations. I think there will be enough somehow to cover the actual bills."

"But—this is not—exactly—bills—" she murmured as she sipped her tea and tried to control an anxious look. "It is—purely a personal matter I might say, Mr. Hamilton. And—*how* are we to live if there is no money?"

"That question will have to be considered of course, Mrs. Dunbar. I would rather wait until I have thoroughly investigated all claims upon the estate before I am prepared to say whether there will be a few hundreds at your disposal or not."

Florence caught at the hope:

"How soon will that be, Mr. Hamilton?"

"I cannot be sure," he answered. "I must wait until I can hear from some creditors to whom I have written, and I must also wait until I have thoroughly investigated one or two distant pieces of property whose value is not quite established. It may be that the sale of these things will bring a little more than our first estimate, or it may be lower. But rest assured, Mrs. Dunbar, I shall do all in my power to get every cent possible for you and the children. Now, Mrs. Dunbar, you have had an exhausting afternoon. Would it not be well for you to lie down until dinner is ready? I am afraid you may have to suffer for the strain you have been through unless you rest. And these girls are going to get a good dinner and call you down pretty soon, I know. I heard Rose rattling dishes out in the kitchen."

Florence turned a languid eye on her stepdaughters and let a feeble smile trickle into the corners of her mouth, giving the appearance of a pleasant understanding between the girls and herself.

"The little old hypocrite!" murmured Rose below her breath as she slipped back into the hall and shut the door. "The smooth-faced hypocrite!"

"Don't, Sister," sighed little Jean. "I thought it was nice of her to look so pleasant. It was so nice of her to be sort of mothery."

Rose gathered the little sister into her arms and hugged her.

"Never mind, kittie, we'll mother you, Doris and I. I didn't know you felt that way kitten. I guess I've been cross sometimes too. But don't you mind. You're a darling, and we'll all look out for you. Florence isn't much but a naughty child anyway. You needn't mind her."

The little girl clung to her sister, and there were tears in her brave sweet eyes.

"You aren't cross, Rose," she said earnestly. "I'll like you real well for a mother—when—when—Doris is gone." She caught her breath in a quick little sob.

"Nonsense, child, Doris isn't going," said Rose joyously.

"Oh, yes she is!" said the little girl sorrowfully. "She's going right away. I couldn't help hearing. I was in the back hall just coming into the living-room yesterday when they were talking, and I heard Milton tell her they were going to be married next Wednesday and go West. He said—he—didn't—*want*—our family—*hanging*—around his neck—e-e-either," sobbed the child softly. "He—he-he-said—I had—to go—to—schoooooool," she wailed. "He's only going to let me come to see them vacations. *Sometimes!* Oh, Rose, what shall we do?" and the little girl clung to her sister and sobbed as if her heart would break.

Rose held her tight and tried to quiet her.

"Listen, Jeanie, Doris isn't going! She told me so!"

"Oh—y-y-y-yes she is!" came the soft wail— "Ssshe—c-c-can't help it. Milton always mamamakes her do everything—he-he—wants—!"

"Well, this time he won't," said Rose with a dark look in her wrathful young face. "You see! Doris won't leave us, and she isn't going to marry him! She told me so."

"Not at all?" The child's face was lifted with a look like a rift in a summer cloud.

"Not at all, kitten. Now, come on and let's get dinner."

"But—" said Jean, still incredulous, "how can she *help* it?"

Then both girls suddenly became aware that the doorbell had been ringing a loud peal through the house, and just as they turned to go and answer it the front door opened and Milton Page walked in.

"This latch was off," he stated condemningly. "That is a very dangerous thing to do in a city like this one. You might lose everything. Who is to blame?"

But nobody answered him for Rose suddenly vanished through the dining-room door and fled up the back stairs. Poor little Jean had to stand still and take the punishment while Milton Page stood hat in hand and delivered an address on carelessness in a loud dictatorial voice. Jean found herself trembling and feeling as if she should sink right down through the floor. Milton was so unpleasant when he got anything like that on his mind. Oh, why did Rose go and leave her?

And then suddenly relief came in the form of the nurse who walked majestically down the stairs on her rubber heels her starchy uniform flapping about her militantly, her eyes cold and steely. She came straight up to Milton Page and addressed him, in a cool, incisive voice like the blade of a sword.

"This clamor must cease!" she declared commandingly. "I won't be responsible for the case unless we can have quiet here. If you're a visitor, get out! If you're a relative for pity's sake stop your whining and get to work! I want somebody to go and get some oxygen right away, and somebody else to get the doctor here quick. That young man is sinking fast, and I don't wonder the way things are carried on. *Hurry*, young man, and get me some oxygen, or you'll be responsible for a life!"

But Milton Page stood turned to cold fury eyeing the woman who had dared speak to him in this disrespectful way. He faced her with his steel-gray eye that never failed to strike terror to the soul of his adversary. But Nurse Smith never turned a hair. She cast a brief passing glance of contempt and gave him a shove aside as she strode to the living-room door where she could hear quiet voices, and swung it wide.

"Will somebody get me the doctor quick! And run for some oxygen? That boy's in a critical condition! This man out here doesn't seem to have good sense!"

It was Doris at the top of the stairs who heard the low-voiced word of command. Doris with the sleep in her eyes, and a flush on her cheek, who waved Rose to the telephone, and herself flew down the stairs like a swift bird past the astonished and indignant lover and out the front door toward the drug store.

Mr. Hamilton arose hastily from his ministrations beside the couch and came forward rubbing his hands with an offering motion. The lawyer was most eager to be of service. But the nurse had turned to go back upstairs. Mrs. Dunbar began to wail hysterically once more.

"Oh, Mr. Hamilton! I can't bear all this excitement!" she cried out, and suddenly the starch-clad nurse wheeled back upon her with a capable pointing finger.

"Here! You!" she spoke incisively once more. "You've got to shut up! Every time the patient hears you he goes into a frenzy again. You've either got to stop your snivelling or get out of the house! You don't want him to die, do you? Well, he will if you keep this up. You're nothing but a selfish spoiled woman, and you've no right to make a racket when there's serious sickness in the house. If the family wants to stand it when they're well that's up to them, but I'm in command here and you've got to keep quiet!"

The nurse departed in grandeur leaving Mrs. Dunbar cowering in her corner of the davenport, too indignant to even cry.

Milton Page by this time, with a withering glance after

the nurse, had withdrawn from the hall and now stood on the steps looking after his recalcitrant fiancée.

He glanced back and saw Jean still standing in the hall, her little hands clasped in fright held over her wildly beating heart.

"Here! Jean!" he ordered with a motion of his head. And when she came: "Run after your sister and tell her to come back! It is not fitting that she should go rushing through the city street bareheaded that way. Tell her I will telephone for oxygen! Such madness to get excited! No one can get anywhere if he loses his head. I thought Doris had better sense!"

But Rose's voice came in a low call.

"Jean! Come here, quick!" And Jean fled from the presence of her would-be brother-in-law. Milton stood there a moment undecided, and finally fitting his hat carefully upon his head, he walked down the street, reluctantly, toward the drug store into which Doris had disappeared.

Milton Page had gone decorously, and had but just reached the drug store as Doris came out accompanied by a boy carrying oxygen tanks. They almost knocked him as they passed. "Doris!" he said in a voice intended to arrest her attention without conveying his wrath to the errand boy. But Doris did not turn her head. She was panting and rushing on ahead. He had to take great strides to catch up with her. He decided then before he reached her that he would have to discipline her in some way for this unseemly conduct when she was once thoroughly married to him. When he had reached her side he took firm hold of her shoulder and gripped her almost painfully.

"Doris! This is madness!" he said in a low, angry voice. "You are beside yourself! You are making a spectacle of yourself! I suppose you are doing this just to get it back on me for speaking plainly to you yesterday morning. But I want you to know that I will not put up—"

"Let go of my shoulder, Milton!" said Doris excited. "My brother is dying! Quick! I've no time to talk!"

She slid out of his grasp like a flash and away, leaving him to walk slowly and indignantly back to the house alone.

He went morosely, watching her lithe figure as it fairly flew along the pavement and up the steps of her home. He could scarcely remember ever to have been so vexed with anybody. Strange that she should suddenly develop these traits. He had never seen her headstrong before.

The doctor's car dashed up to the door just as she entered, and Milton walked more slowly, reflecting that Doris might have to show the doctor to Ned's room before she would be at liberty to talk with him. He never doubted even then but that she would come down at once as soon as her first anxiety was allayed. She had always seemed so docile, so utterly at liberty for any wish of his. Naturally she was overwrought after caring for her father so long; and now Ned's sickness had unduly excited her. Foolish of course, for Ned could not really be very sick. That outrageous nurse had probably exaggerated it. Why, he had seen Ned but the night before swaggering along on the street with a lot of girls. He must speak to Doris about the kind of company Ned was keeping. He did not wish the family of his wife to be in the public eye unpleasantly. He would speak to Ned himself. Perhaps sometime he would offer to sit with him and let the nurse go out. Now, while he was in bed would be a good time to talk to him when he could not very well get away. And while he was about it he would just give him a good dressing down for several other things he had noticed that needed setting right.

So meditating he reached the house, and went slowly

up the steps. But just as he was about to enter someone inside snapped the night latch on, and pushed the door shut with a click! Milton Page was shut out and would be obliged to ring the door-bell! Now, *who* was to blame for that?

16

BUT Ned Dunbar did not so easily slip out of his lightly assumed obligations into another world. The doctor arrived and a crisis was tided over for the time. The household settled once more into comparative quiet.

Mrs. Dunbar by some magic known only to Lawyer Hamilton, had been coerced into going to her room and lying down, and was soon sound asleep.

Milton Page, after brief meditation on the front door-step, had haughtily taken himself off concluding that the moment was still unripe for further controversy with his fiancée.

Rose and Jean had retired hurriedly to the kitchen to prepare dinner for an irate nurse who had hinted dire things if she were not regularly and properly fed. Doris had gone up to the sickroom to relieve the nurse for a few minutes while she took a nap.

Sitting there in the darkened, quiet room with the silent, white face on the pillow, Doris faced her life again, and seemed once more to stand looking into a bank of dark portentous clouds. Nothing but storms and darkness ahead! Could there be any possible light?

She studied the face of her brother in the shadows, and wondered what was to come through him? Would he rally to face his ruined life? And how would they all bear it? How could they help him to bear it? For after the experiences of the day before, who could doubt that the lot he had brought upon himself would soon become unbearable? She could not think her way out of the darkness. There seemed no way out. She must just wait till light came.

The experiences of the last hour passed rapidly before her, and Milton's part in it suddenly forced itself upon her. She found a singular lack of desire to excuse him for his apathy, his unkind criticism of herself. She seemed to be looking at him with new eyes, and the cold critical tone of his voice began to reecho in her mind. How could she ever have loved him? Did he ever use that tone to her before? No, probably not, for she had never crossed his wishes before, that she remembered. Now that she recalled, he had often spoken in that tone to strangers, men who got in his way when he was driving, people out in the world where they had gone together who did not instantly jump to wait upon his needs. She had not condemned him then because he had represented the others as wrongdoers. But, perhaps she had taken his word and had not thought much about it. She had never realized that Milton Page was cruel, or that he was self-centered. He had always protected her well. Now she wondered if perhaps it were only because she belonged to him that he had done it; not to save her? She did not enjoy such thoughts. She tried to shake them off. She did not wish to be unjust, and of course she knew that her action in running bareheaded down the street had been against all his formal code of etiquette. It must have tried him. He had always disliked hurry or excitement and called it unnecessary. Yet try as she would she could not make his criticism of her at such a time seem pardonable, and she found her anger rising.

That matter of the ring now. He seemed to be more interested in the safety of the ring than in how she felt about it. It began to look as if it were going to be a difficult matter to give back his ring. And where was the ring? She must find it before he came again. Perhaps he would not come again to-night and she would have opportunity to hunt for it.

Then suddenly she remembered John. Where was John? The new teacher had sent her a note by Jean in the afternoon, something about a bee in his desk. She had not had time to read it carefully, just glanced it over before she came into Ned's room. John must have been behaving badly. And now perhaps he had run away. How could he bring more trouble upon them! John, with his round kindly face and his broad grin, his ready eagerness to be of use, his continual appetite for mischief! If he did not appear presently what would they have to do to find him? Send out a message by radio perhaps and come down to the level of all the poor families whose wayward children had wandered away from home in search of amusement. Poor John! He had been having a dull time during their father's illness,—and Florence hated him! He could not help knowing it. Her heart went out fiercely to the loving mischievous boy. To think that Milton too had suggested sending him away to school! At this age that would mean weaning him from them all. He would never be theirs again! Her whole being cried out against such a course. She almost hated the thought of Milton since he had suggested it. And Jean too, darling little Jean! How terrible that Milton could think of her dear ones as burdens! She had always visioned Milton as being a kind and loving brother to all her brothers and sisters. And now this! It was a rude awakening.

These thoughts bombarded her soul while she sat in the darkened room and listened to her brother's labored breathing, administered the medicine from time to time, and found herself praying an inarticulate prayer and pleading a sunset sky as if it had been a written word.

The nurse came back rested and fed, and gave an experienced glance at the patient, assuring Doris that all was as well as could be expected and sent her down to get some dinner.

And there was John carrying dishes out to the kitchen! He looked solid and comforting. He cast her a grin of greeting and disappeared through the swing door. So that was that! She ought of course to give him a good scolding and make him understand how embarrassing it was to her and to the rest of his family, to have a note sent home complaining of him. But perhaps it would be just as well to wait until she had eaten her dinner. She felt terribly exhausted, and it would not be an easy task. John was headstrong and would not take kindly to a sister's management.

She sank down into her chair, and Rose and John brought hot food and fussed around her lovingly. It was pleasant to feel they cared. Somehow the shadow seemed almost lifted for a moment. Then, just as Rose whisked into the kitchen to get her another cup of coffee, the telephone rang.

Doris of habit sprang to answer it, and Milton's flat practical voice struck a discordant note on her moment of relaxation.

"I trust that the excitement is over and that your brother has been found to be no worse."

Doris found herself wondering how she had ever thought she loved that cold hard voice.

"The immediate danger is past, the doctor says. He had a sinking spell. The oxygen tided him over the worst till the doctor came."

Doris' voice was cool, quite impersonal, as if she were speaking to a mere acquaintance.

"I thought so," responded the incisive tones. "I have often told you that nothing is ever gained by getting wrought up. Calm action is worth twenty frenzies. In the first place, nine times out of every ten there is no real cause for alarm. That nurse made a mountain out of a molehill, I suppose, and let her love of the dramatic sway her. She seems to me to be one who magnifies her office. I would get rid of her as soon as possible. If you like I will get you another one at once. A woman like that is not fit to nurse in a family of temperamental people."

"Thank you, no," said Doris coldly. "This is the nurse the doctor wants. He thinks her unusually skilled especially in pneumonia."

"She evidently has him buffaloed also," sneered Milton. "If it were my case I should get another doctor then."

Doris did not answer. There were no words wherewith to defend the doctor who had been their friend through the years. The idea was beyond answer.

"Well, Doris, I hope you will realize that you acted very foolishly in making a spectacle of yourself in the street. I certainly was ashamed—"

"You will have to excuse me, Milton—" said Doris sharply. "I am very tired now. I—"

"Wait! Wait a minute Doris! I certainly think you owe me some consideration after all this nonsense. What about the ring?"

Doris had risen with the telephone in her hand and was about to hang up the receiver, but now a startled look sprang into her face. She had forgotten about the ring! How embarrassing! What should she do?

"Really Milton—" she began, and hesitated for a word, "I have been so overwhelmed—" She knew Milton would think it inexcusable in her to have forgotten the lost ring.

But Rose suddenly sprang through the doorway and pressed something into her sister's hand. Doris recognized the hard sharp facets of the diamond with relief.

"The ring is all right of course!" she finished in a different voice in which was no apology.

"But *is* it all right?" he urged persistently. "Have you really found it or are you trying to put me off? I am extremely anxious about this, Doris. When you come to yourself you will realize that a thing so valuable is not to be lightly put aside and forgotten."

"The ring is here in my hand, Milton. I will send it to you at once if you wish."

"In your hand? Why not *on* your hand?" caught up the persistent voice.

"Because that is not its place any longer," said Doris patiently. "Shall I send it to you by special messenger, or would you prefer to call and get it?"

There was just the least tinge of sarcasm to Doris' voice, for she was exasperated beyond her usual even sweetness, but Milton did not seem to perceive it.

"No, certainly not. Do not trust it out of your possession again. I will call this evening. Good-bye."

The receiver clicked into place and Doris sat back with the ring in her hand. She opened her palm and looked at it as it lay there catching the light and throwing prisms out into the room, a lovely heavenly drop of dew. Her ring! And she was giving it up!

But it had somehow lost its tender significance. It appeared to cast a baleful light as it lay there in her hand.

It did not seem her own any longer and as she watched the changing color she seemed to hear the echo of Milton's voice as he uttered those terrible unfeeling words about her family! Her dear family. Sudden overwhelming tears seemed imminent. She was not a girl given to weeping and this feeling of a tempest coming down upon her almost frightened her. She looked up blinking back the tears and shutting her lips firmly against her thoughts, and there was Rose standing in the kitchen doorway.

"He's not coming back again to-night is he, Doris? The old shrimp! Doesn't he know you are not fit to see him? Give me the ring. I'll give it back to him in words that will make him understand! You go up to bed, and I'll see him for you."

Her words were just what was needed to strike the balance in Doris' self-control. She looked up smiling:

"You're a peach!" she said brightly. "But this is my job and I'll see it through. Perhaps I needed all this to get my eyes open to things."

"Are your eyes open?" said Rose studying her face doubtfully. "I'm afraid Milton will be able to bring you around to his way of thinking again when he gets you under the influence of his cold, gray eye. Dorrie, he isn't the man for you. He isn't big enough. You're far too good for him. He'll hound the life out of you if he once gets you under his thumb. I read a story not long ago about a girl that married a foreign count or something and he didn't want her to have anything to do with her family in America. When he got her over in his castle he intercepted her letters and her people thought she didn't care anything about them any more; and she thought they had forgotten her; and so they never saw each other for years, and she broke her heart. When I read it, it seemed as if Milton was just like that count. I used to lie awake and cry about it. It seemed to me when you married Milton we would lose you utterly."

"You foolish child," cried Doris laughing, "as if I would let any man keep me from my family! I would run away and come to see them. How could I possibly love a man of that sort?"

"That's it, you couldn't; and you wouldn't know it till it was too late and you were married to him."

"Well, Rose, you needn't worry about it any longer for I'm not going to marry him. I don't believe I shall every marry anyone. I'm the head of this family now and that's enough for one lifetime, at least until they are all grown up and married—and—well that doesn't seem to end it with Ned, either."

"Ned isn't grown up, that's what's the matter!" said Rose wisely. "I'm going to learn a lesson from this myself, and never think of getting married till I'm quite old and ugly and my judgment is mature."

"You child! You'll never be old and ugly no matter how many years you live."

"I hope you don't think I'll never have any judgment."

"You have a lot already," said Doris thoughtfully. "I know you would never let yourself do anything that would disgrace the family."

Rose went to the window and stood gazing out into the darkness a moment, sticking a pin deep into the window-sill before she spoke.

"Well, I *hope* I wouldn't," she said at last, turning with a sigh from the window, "but I'll tell you this, I almost have thought of doing things, once or twice—"

"Yes, but you wouldn't," Doris' eyes rested on her confidently. "I'm just sure you wouldn't, dear."

"Well, I *won't* anyway. Doris, are we going to move? *Where* are we going to live?"

"That's to be settled soon, dear. I haven't been able to think about it yet. I've got to find a good job first so I'll know what we can afford to pay. I haven't an idea what things rent for. I never thought about rent. Nor how much I can earn—"

"Doris, rent costs awfully! I heard Nance Nettleton telling that they paid ninety a month for their tiny little flat, and Charlie only makes a hundred and forty. It has only a bedroom and dining-room and living-room, with bath and kitchenette. We couldn't ever stuff into it even if we had a bed in every room including the kitchenette."

"Yes, Rose, but that's in a very good location. I know those apartments are nabbed up like hot cakes for young married people. We will probably have to go into some plain unfashionable quarter. We've got to make up our minds to that."

"It's going to be horrid to live in some low-down place. I'd like to get away off from here, where we don't see the same people. I wish we could get into the country, don't you?"

"The country costs terribly, Rose; that is, any place that will be practical for me if I have a job."

"Why do you say for *me*, Doris, as if you were the only one that is going to work? Why even Jean has a job. It's going to be tough on her if we move away. She's as pleased as she can be. Don't squelch her. She's planning to work all day in the summer-time."

"She's a darling!" said Doris.

"Doris, whatever became of that house you inherited from Aunt Doris awhile ago? Did it ever get sold? Where was it? Wasn't it somewhere near the city?"

"Why, I really don't know," said Doris. "Father took charge of it. He seemed to be fond of the old place, but I shouldn't wonder if it went in with all the rest. I'll have to ask Mr. Hamilton about it, but I suppose it's gone. Yes, it was out on the Branch line. I don't know just how you get to it. I never have gone there since I was a little girl. You know she died when I was about seven years old."

"But Doris, if that was yours you wouldn't have to let it go, would you?"

"I suppose so," sighed Doris. "There'll just have to be a clean sweep of everything. I only hope it will be clean and that every debt will be wiped out. Then we can take a deep breath and begin over again. I'm not afraid but we can get along somehow, if only we don't have everlasting debts to carry on our backs. I couldn't bear that. But Rose, where did you find my ring? Was it back of that bureau? I don't believe I thought to look there."

"No, it wasn't back of the bureau, and I'm not going to tell you where I found it until after Milton Page has been here. Jean put the note on your bureau when he gave it to her and you did not notice it in your hurry. See? Afterward I'll tell you the story. And it's *some tale*, believe me! But it's not for the honorable Milton's ears, and if you know it beforehand you'll have it sitting in your eye and he'll extract it from you. Now go upstairs and put on your slim black satin, and look impressive. Let him see that he doesn't own you body and soul. Mercy, Doris, if you give in to him and keep that ring I'll kidnap you and run away to the South Sea Islands or somewhere that isn't respectable so Milton won't dare follow. Doris, I found out that Jean is breaking her heart over your getting married and going away. She heard Milton talking yesterday it seems!"

"Oh! I'm sorry!" said Doris with a quick memory of the biting sentences about her family. "Poor little kiddie. Where is she? Gone to bed?"

"I guess so. She was about worn out."

"Well, where is John? I must give him a lecture. He simply *has* to go to school to-morrow you know. We can't have him in disgrace."

But John too was gone to bed, for a wonder, lying comfortably snuggled into his pillow, his long lashes like fringes heavily dark upon his round, healthy cheek. John was wonderfully good looking when he was asleep. There was a certain nobleness about his forehead, and a maturity about his pleasant lips that gave promise of a thoughtful manhood. Doris stood looking at him a moment, half-questioning whether she would not waken him and say to him the things that ought to be said. It was very strange that John should go to bed before nine o'clock. But something in the curve of lip, the sweep of lash, the relaxed boyishness of him lying there appealed to the motherness that is in every woman, and she turned away without disturbing him and tiptoed out of the room closing the door softly. And John, lying motionless in the dark room let the corners of his nice dependable mouth curve upward just a tiny bit with mischief, and his wicked little dimple came out and laughed at the echo of Doris' retreating footsteps. John had scored another day without being questioned, and having to own up that he had a job.

Doris had barely slipped into the slim satin when Rose came to say that Milton was there. Doris, with the ring in her hand went down to face her former lover.

Milton Page had hesitated some minutes before a florist's shop thinking to purchase another half-dozen roses. In view of the fact that the ring was found and he would not have to buy another he could afford to be generous. But when he found that the roses in this shop were fifty cents more a dozen than those he had bought the day before he thought better of it and went on without an offering. By the time he presented himself in the Dunbar living-room he had decided that it would be better to give the roses later after Doris had been duly apologetic for all her foolish actions of the day before. Virtue should be rewarded, not foolishness. So he stood there in his neat business suit looking the personification of virtuous exactness.

There was something about Doris' air as she entered the room that was impressive. Something new and definite. It gave him a pleasant thrill of admiration after his annoyance of the day before. After all she was a girl among a thousand, and doubtless her slip of the day before had been due to overexertion, with a combination of emotional strain long drawn out. When she was his he did not intend to allow any such excesses in emotion or overwork. Keeping one's body in perfect trim for the maximum efficiency was as much a duty as to keep one's machine in condition, perfectly cleaned and oiled. It was to him a law of life, and never to be overstepped for sentimental reasons.

A look of satisfaction overspread his face as he watched her graceful movements about the room, throwing open a window, for the evening was warm, pulling the cord of the shaded lamp over the chair in which he always sat, and switching off the glaring overhead light. There was something exceedingly satisfying in the womanliness of her; and she seemed to have at last returned to herself after the trying weeks of her father's illness, when she had been absent-minded and always in a hurry. A certain tenseness around his mouth relaxed, and he smiled one of his old-time welcomes. He advanced to give her the usual formal kiss wherewith their meetings had heretofore been opened and closed.

But Doris evaded him, as though she had not noticed—as though she had forgotten. She went over to the couch and got a silk pillow, plumping it up as she came, and dropping into a chair opposite the one where he usually sat, she placed the pillow behind her back.

"Sit down, Milton," she said, taking the conversation into her own hands and motioning him toward the other chair. "There is something I want to tell you."

He paused annoyed, and looked at her, upset to have her begin conversation without the usual greeting. It seemed to put him at a disadvantage, to usurp as it were his rights. But somehow her manner took the initiative, and he found himself sitting reluctantly down in his usual place. He could not help thinking how well she looked in spite of the dark circles under her eyes.

"I have been thinking about our relationship and looking facts in the face," Doris began, looking at him calmly, almost as if he were a stranger. "I have come to the conclusion that I have not been fair to you!"

Milton straightened his shoulders with satisfaction. Ah! Now she was coming to herself! This was an apology! He had felt sure she would make one sooner or later, or else he must have been much mistaken in her.

"I have not intended to be unfair," she went on.

That was bad. One ought never to attempt to make excuses. It would be better for her to leave that to him. He must tell her about that after she had finished. An apology was never a full acknowledgment of wrong done if one put forth one's self surrounded by excuses.

But what was this she was saying?

"I think you first opened my eyes to the situation when you began to find fault with my father, and then finished by showing that you wished me as your wife to be utterly separate from my family. You showed me just how you looked upon each one of them, and I thought you were hard and cruel. I was very angry with you at first. But afterward I saw that you had no intention of being cruel. You were just stating facts as you understood them—"

What was this? She was *blaming* him, not apologizing? She was actually trying to excuse *him!* This was preposterous! His expression grew hard like melted wax exposed to sudden cold. It fairly congealed. His lips set in a sharp thin line. *She was attempting to excuse him!*

"You had no conception of my feelings or you would not have done it. It seemed to you that you were just saying what you call 'common-sense' facts, and speaking frankly. You had not the least idea that I would far rather you had taken a whip and stung me across my face than to have listened to you say what you did about my family. The care that I took of my father during his last illness, which I considered a precious privilege, was to you mere sentiment. You had no conception of the tender and wonderful relationship between me and my father, and you did not realize that your rough speech was like rubbing salt in a wound. At first I was appalled. I could not think. But presently I began to understand that it was because you did not really love me that you could talk that way."

She paused and he faced her sternly, offendedly, but he did not interrupt. He would allow her to see that even at a time like this he adhered closely to his principles never to interrupt. He thought he saw now that she was merely wishing him to make love to her over again, to restate a fact that had long become a matter of course. He had read that women did things like that. When they quarrelled they wished to be petted and sentimentalized over. But he would show her once for all that he was not that sort of a man. He had given her his word that he loved her, and that ought to be enough for any sensible woman. He could not go around telling her all his life. It was a thing to be taken for granted, and she had no more right to question it than she had to be continually taking off her engagement ring and flinging it at him.

It was just at this juncture that he noticed that she was not wearing her ring and the frown deepened on his stern face.

But Doris' voice was quite calm as she took up the thread of her discourse once more:

"It was then that I found out that *I* did not love *you,* Milton. I have always thought I did, but I see now that I only loved what I thought you were. I am sorry that you have wasted so much time on me, and that I did not sooner understand my own heart, but I am glad that I have found out in time. It would be a dreadful thing for us both to have found it out afterwards."

He continued to regard her with hard cold eyes for an instant silently. At last he said in his flat practical voice, which seemed flatter and more practical than ever before:

"Now, if you have completely finished with this child's play, I think I will go upstairs and talk with your brother Ned for a little while. There are some things which need to be said to him which I think would come in very well just now while he is lying still and has time to think them over."

He stepped toward the door but Doris with her eyes blazing in a white haughty face stepped before him and stood in front of the door, her hand upon the knob.

"You do not seem to understand!" she said in a tone that she had never used to him before, a tone as cold and decided as ever his had been. "This is not child's play! I never was more in earnest in my life! You may break off the conversation and be rude to me if you like, but you must not go out of this room without taking charge of this ring. If you do I shall send it to you by mail. And you cannot go and talk to my brother! He is too ill to see anyone, and would not know what you were saying to him if you did. He is quite delirious."

Doris held the ring out and tried to put it in his hand, but he refused it:

"Doris, you are beside yourself!" he said as if he were soothing an angry child. "Put that ring on and stop this nonsense. You will think better of all this when you have had a good night's rest."

Doris laid the ring on the table.

"I will never put that ring on again!" she said excitedly. "You have broken the last tie between us. You may take the ring or leave it as you please, but I will not be responsible for it any longer."

"Well, Doris, I don't believe you *are* responsible," he said severely. "That is a good diagnosis of the case. I will take the ring and keep it until you come to your senses. You really are not fit to have charge of it at present, and as for sending it by mail that would be simply crazy. A valuable ring like that!"

His fingers closed about the ring, and Doris dropped her arms by her side with a feeling of relief, and then stealthily clasped her hands behind her. She would not be inveigled into touching that ring again. She had begun suddenly to feel as if it were a badge of servitude.

"You understand, Doris, that I am merely taking charge of this until to-morrow. I am paying no attention to the wild remarks you have been making to me. A promise is a promise, you know, as binding as the marriage vow to a right-minded person, and I am sure you have always been that heretofore. One cannot change his principles overnight like this. A plighted troth is a sacred thing. As sacred as a marriage vow."

"Yes," said Doris steadily. "But two wrongs do not make a right. If I give a promise that I cannot keep, would it make it better to take vows upon my lips that were not true?"

He regarded her with cold disapproval:

"You are not in condition to talk to-night. You are illogical," he said. "I have told you before that it is impossible to talk to a person who is illogical. I will leave you to get rested and come to an understanding with yourself. You may send for me when you are ready to talk sensibly. I shall not come until you send for me this time. I have no time to waste in nonsense. But please remember that the time is short, and that we should be making our preparations. All this fol de rol is merely wasting much needed time and energy, for which you will only have to suffer in the end. My preparations are well under way. It will be you who will have to go unprepared when the time comes."

"Milton, I told you that I am not going. I mean what I say."

"Nonsense!" he said sharply. "You don't understand yourself. You would no more let me go without you than you would cut your hand off. If you will do a little unselfish thinking and look into your own heart you will find that this is all a pose in order to make me allow you to slave for your family, and take them into my lap for life. But that would be all wrong and I do not intend to do it, no matter how long you keep up this performance. If you understand that fully perhaps it will help bring you to your senses. I am not the kind of man who can be bullied into anything. I am doing this for your good and in the end you will see it. You will live to thank me for it."

Doris' face was white with anger:

"I think perhaps I shall—" said Doris and stepped aside to let him pass.

He cast her a puzzled startled look as he went out.

There seemed something sinister in her voice, but her face was quiet, almost impassive. Now, just what had she meant by that? Was she coming to her senses—or—? But of course she *would* come to her senses. She had always been such a sensible girl.

He walked slowly out the front door.

"Remember that I shall be waiting for you to send for me," he said graciously. And then the door closed behind him and he went down the street with his usual dignity.

Doris stood in the hall for a moment looking at the closed door, and then with a long-drawn breath went slowly upstairs to her room and shut and locked the door.

"So that's that!" she said aloud to herself as she stared around and caught a glimpse of Milton Page's familiar photograph facing her on the bureau.

She stepped to the bureau, tore it across twice, and threw the pieces in the waste basket, then switching out the light she lay down upon her bed and stared up into the darkness. So that was that!

17

ANGUS Macdonald had put in three solid hours that evening trying to persuade his gentle little mother to let him hire a companion to attend her during his absence. He put it on the ground of his own solicitude. He made her understand that he could not do his own work well unless he was sure that all was well with her.

She told him she would write him every day if he wished, and that the housekeeper would wire if she were in the least unwell.

He turned a new angle and told her that she must get out more and that she could not go alone. He suggested that she might do this as a benevolence.

She said she did not want to go out, that the garden was big enough for all the exercise she wished to take, and that she preferred to be alone. If it were benevolence she would be glad to write a check to cover anybody's need in that direction.

Pleasantly but firmly she foiled every attempt that he made to introduce and lead up to the girl he meant to bring to see her the next afternoon. He made no progress whatever. Not even could he move her when he declared that if she did not submit to having someone come there and stay he would not go abroad. She looked at him with all her Scotch conscience in her eye and reminded him that he was going on a mission, something that was to be for the good of humanity if his research succeeded, and that he had no right to withdraw now that he had given his word. She drew herself up with dignity and somehow managed to summon the old command to her voice that had made her dominate him always when he was a child. Nothing short of absolute force would win his point he saw. She made him understand that it was distasteful in the extreme to her to have a hired companion, that it would look as if she were an invalid or an idiot, or growing childish, and she did not want her relatives to get any such notions. She resented the idea. She was still able to order her own affairs and young enough to have the right to do so.

Angus retired to his bed vanquished at last, but not to sleep. Over and over again he turned the question trying to find some way out of the dilemma, and when he reached his office the next morning he was not any nearer to a solution. Perhaps after all he would have to give the whole trip up. For he was just as firm as his stubborn little mother and he did not intend to go off and leave her without any congenial spirit to help her bear the dreariness of the days.

He had little time, however, to consider the matter during the morning, or at the lunch hour, for his partners had in tow a distinguished scientist with whom they wished him to lunch, a man who had done much research along the very lines which Macdonald was about to pursue, and there were certain matters which they wished to discuss together. It was therefore a quarter to three before Angus Macdonald was free to remember the appointment with the young woman, and the problem of how to manage the meeting between her and his mother. Then when he had spent ten intensive minutes trying to make a plan and failed hopelessly, a representative of one of the firm's New York associates arrived and demanded immediate audience that he might catch a train in a few minutes. The man was just taking his leave when the secretary brought in Doris' name, and he realized that he had come to the moment unprepared after all and must do something at once. He told the secretary he would be ready for Miss Dunbar in two or three minutes, and as soon as she had closed the door of the outer office he rang up his mother:

"Mother, I want to bring out a young woman—a—a—a *girl!*" he finished lamely. "A girl I have met—an *acquaintance*—"

He knew that he was doing it awkwardly, and that his mother would wonder. It was not his custom to bring home girls. He was making a bad job of it, too, hesitating along this way for words. His mother would be sure to suspect something. He searched wildly around in his mind for an excuse—but could find none.

"I—want her to meet you—Mother," he ended desperately. "Can you give us a cup of tea?"

But he knew by his mother's tone as she assented that she had taken alarm. And then his mind went back to the morning before, and her question about possible fellow voyagers. Ah! She thought he was bringing Tamar! She had heard about Tamar he felt sure. Cousin Marilla would be sure to have gossiped when she was out last week. Cousin Marilla had uncanny powers of finding out about everything that one wanted to keep to one's self.

"Is she—a very *special*—friend, Angus?" the mother's voice hesitated almost tremulously. Macdonald felt condemned and ashamed. Somehow it came to him as a good thing that he was getting away from Tamar. His mother would never have been reconciled to Tamar as a daughter-in-law.

"Oh, no! Not specially so!" he tried to make his voice sound casual, "I just—wanted you to—meet her!"

It would never come easy for Angus Macdonald to lie. He had been brought up to be square and straightforward. There had never been deception between himself and his mother.

"Will I—need to make much preparation?" she asked again half-timidly, he thought.

"No, oh no!" he answered heartily. "Just a cup of tea. Don't make a fuss or have the servants around. I want her to meet you informally a few minutes. I've—been telling her about you, you know. She's just a nice girl."

But he knew that her voice held trepidation. He hung up half wishing he had given it all up and sent the applicant for the position on her way.

Doris had been busy with Mr. Hamilton all the morning.

They had sat in her father's library at his desk and gone over all the papers together.

Doris had seemed to be the natural one to undertake the matter. Mrs. Dunbar when asked to come down held up her hands deprecatingly and begged to be excused:

"Tell Mr. Hamilton I simply cannot go over those old bills. He promised to undertake them all and now let him do it. I'll come down after a while and serve luncheon if you want me to. Invite him to stay. But I really can't come now. I'm not dressed yet, and I've got to go through my bureau drawers and see if I can possibly have left my pocketbook there. You know I lost my pocketbook last night, and it had some *very* important papers in it, to say nothing of twenty-five dollars. I can't remember coming up here before I telephoned, but perhaps I did, and I must look for it *right away*, because I'm *nearly crazy* about it."

So Doris had gone down with a sigh of relief that her stepmother was not to be on hand to complicate matters. She felt a passing wonder where Mrs. Dunbar could have got twenty-five dollars, but it was only passing, and she was presently immersed in bills and lists of stocks and bonds.

Mrs. Dunbar did come down and pour the coffee at lunch as she had promised, but she looked as if she had been weeping and a worried absent-minded expression hovered about her. Her anxiety had not, however, been so great as to make her forget to make a careful toilet, and she was most gracious to the lawyer. Rose made little wicked faces to Doris behind the pantry door as she went out to get various jams and pickles and olives that her stepmother had demanded. But Doris was too worried herself to pay much attention. Rose had not as yet had time to give Doris an account of the finding of the ring.

It was just as Hamilton was about to leave, and Doris was on her way upstairs to sit with Ned for a few minutes while the nurse came down to lunch, that the lawyer called to her:

"Oh, by the way, Miss Doris, I forgot to mention it this morning, but there is a piece of property belonging to you. It seems to have been the only thing that was untouched, possibly because it was considered valueless. It is a house and lot out at Silver Ledge. I haven't been out there to see it, but I understand from some questions I have asked of real estate men who know, that Silver Ledge is absolutely dead, so far as real estate is concerned. It might possibly sell for a few hundred, but it would probably be very few. Would you like me to try to find a purchaser? Of course every little helps. Did you know about the property?"

"Why yes," said Doris, coming thoughtfully downstairs. "It is an old house belonging to my aunt, who died when I was a little girl. She left it to me because I was named after her. I have never been out there since I was a child. My father had a fondness for the place. He used to say that sometime he would like to fix it up for a summer home. But he never did. I really can't remember much about it. Would it be a place where we could live, or do you think we should sell it in order to cover father's debts?"

"There is no obligation whatever for you to give that up if you care to keep it. It is yours," said the lawyer, "and even if you sold it the money would be your own, personally, you understand. As for living there I should say it would be quite out of the question. It is a long way out of the city and I understand it is quite out of repair. You had probably better sell it if you can. But, as I say, it would likely have to go for a ridiculously small sum, and even then I should suppose that purchasers would be scarce. I will make enquiry and let you know."

"Thank you," said Doris, "perhaps I will run out and look it over some day soon."

This was all that was said and Doris hurried up to Ned and promptly forgot all about it.

She met her stepmother in the hall apparelled for the street when she came out from Ned's room an hour later. She looked distraught and said she was going out to try and find her pocketbook. She thought she must have left it at a store yesterday. Doris passed on to her room, the memory of her afternoon's engagement suddenly setting down upon her like a pall, and she began to dread it. She wondered why she had agreed to go, and the whole thing now seemed preposterous. She had half a mind to call up this Mr. Macdonald and tell him she had made other plans and would not be able to fulfill her engagement. She half-decided to ask Rose's advice and went down to the kitchen to find her. But Rose had disappeared. Everybody seemed to be gone somewhere. She remembered about John and wondered if he had gone to school, and why hadn't Jean come home for her lunch? Why hadn't John come? Oh, why were things all mixed up this way? And where were they going to live? If that Silver Ledge property were at all salable perhaps there would be a few hundreds, enough for them to dare rent a house for a few months at least and start, until she could find something to do. If only Ned were not married he and she might manage between them to support the family in decency, but how was she going to be able to do it by herself? It was out of the question for Rose to go to work. She was too young and impulsive, too pretty and rebellious against life for her to be safe out in the world.

Thinking her troubled thoughts she prepared for the afternoon.

She was going to a tea, but it would not do to wear gala dress. She was going in the capacity of service to be looked over with a view to purchase. She must dress carefully but not conspicuously.

Having decided this she took her mind from the matter and began to speculate about Silver Ledge. How many hundreds were a few? How much could she actually hope to count on, at the lowest? Would father have minded their selling?

But then of course they could not stop on that. Father would have minded the whole thing for them. Poor father! She hoped he could not see how much trouble had come to them all. They must be brave and carry on,

so that if he could know, he would presently see that all
was well with them.

As she entered Angus Macdonald's office promptly on
the minute she noticed a plain sad-eyed girl standing by
the desk, heard the secretary say: 'Yes, the position is
filled for the present.' She saw the other girl turn sadly
away. For an instant a feeling of disappointment passed
over her. Likely she would be told the same thing. She
wondered if it were the sensible girl or the one with
goggles, and stood hesitating at the door, but the secretary recognized her with a pleasant smile.

"Mr. Macdonald wishes you to sit in the inner office
for a few minutes. He is engaged in conference just now
but will not be many minutes, and will be ready to
accompany you soon."

Doris, in the inner office alone, sat palpitating again,
and looking around upon the luxurious room. Everything in it was restful and harmonious. Again there came
that reassurance.

On the desk stood a photograph in a silver frame, its
back turned toward her. She felt a sudden desire to see
what kind of picture was in that frame. It might be a key
to the family. Somehow faces always told a great deal. It
would be some girl of course. Probably nothing that
would affect her, as she was to have to do with an old
lady, but at least it would show to a certain extent what
kind of man her future employer was. Silently she arose
and took a step forward where she could see the picture,
and found to her surprise that it was of an elderly
woman, with white hair and delicate patrician face,
lovely as the cameo to which her son had likened her.
This then was the mother to whose comfort she was to
minister during the son's absence! She stood admiring,
charmed. It was true then what her son had said about
her. She felt a strong desire to please this woman, and a

passing admiration for the son, who enthroned his mother's picture alone upon his desk. He must be a man in a thousand! Not but that most men must care for their mothers, but they usually kept their sentiments well hidden; and then too, there were usually so many girls' pictures.

Then flashed the thought that perhaps this desk was thus set for her benefit, and she turned to go back to her seat again. But there he was! Standing just behind her! And she had not heard him enter.

He smiled just as if he had left her but a few moments before.

"That is my mother!" he said as if her eyes had asked a question.

"She is lovely!" said Doris spontaneously.

"Yes, she is!" said the son with a tender light in his eyes. Then, "Shall we go down to the car now, Miss Dunbar?"

The car was as luxurious as the office had been, nothing ostentatious, however. Angus Macdonald drove it himself, and while they were going through traffic he left her to sit back restfully without talking.

She watched him thread his way skillfully through the afternoon turmoil of the crowded streets, and could not but admire the quiet control he had both over himself and over his machine. There was something about his strong face that reminded her of the more delicate features of his mother, yet with a ruggedness that was not in her face. She forgot for the moment that she was going out with a possible employer to be looked over. He seemed like a pleasant friend who was taking her out for the afternoon.

When they were at last beyond the throngs of travellers, and darted out into a broad smooth highway with arching trees and far stretches of open space, he turned to her pleasantly.

"Now!" said he, "I think we can talk, and settle a few matters before we get home. I'm in rather of a hole I'm afraid."

Doris experienced another sudden sinking of the heart. He was going to tell her that he had hired someone else! But why had he not done it in the office and saved himself and her the trip? She wondered why she felt so disappointed.

"You see I've been sounding out my mother, and I have not been able to get her to consent to have anyone in the capacity of companion."

Ah! Then that was it. There was not going to be any position! And he had brought her on a ride to let her down easily! Well, she would show him that it did not matter in the least. That she was not at all sure she would have taken it if there had been a position.

"I have had to resort to a sort of subterfuge," went on Macdonald. "How good an actor are you? Can you take the part of a good friend of mine who is coming out to meet my mother just—socially—you know?"

Doris turned a puzzled face toward the young man:

"I'm afraid I don't understand," she said a trifle coolly.

"No, perhaps I have not been very clear. You see I've failed to get my mother to see things just as I want her to see them. She insists that she will be perfectly all right during my absence without anyone but the servants, but I know that she will simply stay by herself day after day and it is not good for her. I want her to get interested in somebody or something, and then the time will go faster. Now, are you willing to play up to the occasion and take the part of a friend of mine who is interested to run in and cheer her up while I'm gone? I simply couldn't work it any other way. I called her up just now and told her I was bringing a girl—a friend of mine—out to see her for a cup of tea. Have I presumed too much?"

Doris hesitated. This was different. She began to feel that she was not just sure what she was getting into.

"It isn't necessary for you to enlarge upon our acquaintance. It might easily have been that we would have met in the city. Your father was known to me. Let that stand. I shall be away and there will be no complications. It simply places you on a social footing rather than a business basis. Will that matter to you?"

"Why—no, I'm not sure that it will matter," said Doris hesitating. "I would not like to be working under false pretences."

"No," said Macdonald thoughtfully, "I fully understand. But I do not think that will be necessary. For the present, at least, you are arriving in the capacity of an acquaintance of mine coming out for a ride and a cup of tea. If you find it consistent with circumstances to be a trifle lonesome and say you would like to run over again soon to see mother, that might open a way. If you choose to accept a position later, either with or without my mother's knowledge and consent, as matters shall develop, that will be for you to decide after you have seen my mother, and I have seen how she meets you. Is that fair?"

"It seems so," said Doris.

"Very well, then, we'll call that settled for the present. Now, will you mind telling me a little about yourself please? The time is short and you and I need to understand one another if we intend to make this thing a success. I assume that you have called up the references I gave you yesterday and therefore have my credentials, as I have done with yours and found everything satisfactory. Suppose you tell me where you are going to live and how feasible it would be for you to see my mother every day if things work out that way."

The talk was crisp and businesslike. They discussed various possibilities in the coming interview and provided for different contingencies that might arise. Macdonald told her a little about his father and mother just to give her a background for the coming interview.

Once as they passed through a little quiet country village with nothing but a trolley line, a garage, a church and a little bunch of quaint old houses, the sign on the garage caught Doris' eye and she exclaimed involuntarily:

"Oh, can this be Silver Ledge, I wonder?"

"Yes," he said, slowing down. "Do you know it?"

"I came here once when I was a child to visit my aunt. The old house is here. I wonder which it is?"

Macdonald immediately stopped the car and made enquiries of a villager who was sauntering along the roadside. They found that they were almost in front of Doris' inheritance.

"That's a fine specimen of colonial architecture," said Macdonald interestedly. "Look at that fan-shaped window over the door. And those pillars! It has a sweet old mellow look like a person that has lived well and done his duty."

"I loved it when I was a child," said Doris. "I used to play dolls on those seats by the front door. Out at the side there is a big flat stone under the lilac bush where I used to have a dolls' house with bits of broken china for dishes and acorns for cups. There was a bed of velvety moss around the stone that I called my parlor carpet. This house inside is very pleasant. There is a long low room with gold-framed mirrors and a fireplace. I remember a leaf table and a spinnet that was my delight."

"Charming!" said Macdonald. "Wouldn't it be interesting to live in an old house like that surrounded by such fine old furniture! It would bring back the shades of simple days when men were less hurried, and life was less tragic. Silver Ledge is just the right setting too, for that house."

"How far is Silver Ledge from the city?" asked Doris with speculative glances on either side of the street.

Macdonald looked at the speedometer:

"Just eleven miles and a quarter," he answered. "Strange a spot so near the city has not caught the building fever yet. I suppose it is on account of that old trolley line. I understand it is slow and dilapidated, and the owners won't spend anything on it. Still that will not always be the case. The president is a stubborn old-fashioned man, but he is very old, and sick. When he is gone, new life will come in and this place will be built up in short order. The view here is wonderful! If one or two men with money would locate here there would be a speedy change. For myself, I like it better as it is. It is restful to drive past all this quietness and peace."

Doris tried to restrain her eagerness at what he was saying, but her thoughts were busy turning over the idea.

"There is a church—" said Doris interestedly. "But I don't see any school. I wonder if they have no children? They must be all old men like the one we met."

"No," said Macdonald with a quick smile, "the schoolhouse is farther on, about a quarter of a mile I think. One of those Rural Community schools that is centrally located for a number of small settlements within a certain radius. It seems to solve the problem for better schools in the rural districts. Yes, there is the school, yonder. I often drive this way. Our home is only three or four miles farther on."

A friendly group of pines in the distance sheltered the approach to a big square modern stone structure that rose amid the pastures like the spirit of to-day greeting the past. Doris studied it critically as they passed, wondering how many grades they carried and if it were at all possible they had a High School also.

The group of pines proved to be but a forerunner of other pines scattered along the way, increasing now and then into small groves, and at last they swept into the real woods with pine needles on the ground and a resinous odor filling the air, and began to wind up a gradual incline.

"Oh, how lovely!" exclaimed Doris involuntarily. "How wonderful! It rests you just to see it and smell it!"

"Doesn't it!" said Macdonald heartily, slowing down and hushing his engine as though he were entering a sanctuary.

Presently they swept around a curve and up into the sunshine again. The fine old Macdonald castle towered just above them on the hillside; with a great burst of landscape off to the left, a silver river winding in the valley below.

"Here we are!" said Macdonald. "That's the house up there. Now, here we turn and skirt around to the other side of it through this grove. Watch for the view as we come out. You can see the city off to the left on clear days."

Doris felt as if all the glories of the world were suddenly spread before her, but she had scarcely time to look and exclaim before they drew up before the wide stone steps and a butler appeared to open the car door for her.

Sudden awe descended upon Doris. She had not dreamed of anything like this! How could she possibly presume to amuse a woman who was lonesome amid all this luxury?

18

MRS. MACDONALD was sitting by the open fire in the big living-room, with the great windows into the world of hills and valley for a background; a little woman clad in soft rich silk and touches of rare lace. Her face was like the cameo to which her son had likened her, crowned with lovely silver hair in soft bands about her head.

By her side was a tea-table glittering with glass and silver, and a fine old silver teapot. She rose to meet them as they entered, an almost feverish eagerness in the look her soft dark eyes cast upon the girl. She gave Doris her hand, and it was like warm rose leaves, soft and vibrant. Doris loved her at once.

It was good for Doris that she was accustomed to meeting people, else the surroundings and peculiar situation might have embarrassed her. As it was she forgot for the moment that she was here to be inspected, and was her easy pleasant self:

"It was so good of you to let me come, Mrs. Macdonald," she said. "I—have heard about you, you know."

The mother's hands lingered on the girl's in a soft

clinging hold, while her eyes searched Doris' face; and
Angus Macdonald, watching his mother, thought he saw
a sudden relaxing of the tension about her lips and eyes.
Doris was disarming her fears.

He watched the girl's lovely expressive face, also, and
was himself relieved to see that there was evident admiration between the two whom he had brought together.
It occurred to him that his mother was certainly taking
this girl for a more intimate friend than he had intimated
in his brief telephone call, and that was good too,
perhaps, for then she would be willing to be with her
more, in order that she might find out what kind of
person her son's friend was. This seemed an innocent
deception, inasmuch as it not only furthered his own
plan to help his mother, but would allay somewhat her
anxieties concerning Tamar, if indeed she had heard of
Tamar. On the whole he was very well satisfied to
present such a girl as Doris to his mother as a sample of
his friends. Doris seemed the kind of girl any man would
be proud to know. He could not help admiring the way
she handled the situation. Not with the fire and lure and
mystery of Tamar perhaps. She was restful, inspiring,
zestful. Why had he not met her somewhere socially
before this? Her father's position must have made her a
place in the social world. But he had been busy with
Tamar of late, and Doris must have been at college,
perhaps until recently.

He watched them, seated talking eagerly, as if each
wanted quickly to get to know the other. His mother's
voice grew in confidence, as if she were feeling her way
into the heart of the girl. He began to have a curious
interest in her opinion of the girl, as if it meant more to
him than just whether she admired someone he wanted
to hire. When he realized it he wanted to shake off the
feeling. It seemed almost as if he were deceiving his

mother. He had an unpleasant foreboding of questions she might ask after the guest was gone.

As he watched Doris and listened to her sweet, cultured voice, he began more and more to feel as if he and his mother were being looked over, weighed in the balance, rather than the girl; and withal a deep satisfaction took root in him, that this girl was the very one he wanted to be with his mother.

No afternoon quiet tea could have been more pleasant and chatty. The three sat together and ate cinnamon toast, and delectable little fluffy cakes with marvellous icing, and drank the perfection of tea. They nibbled at bonbons and salted almonds, and talked about trees and stars and books and people. The shadows of the plumy hemlocks on the rolling lawn grew long, and twilight settled down, with firelight in the room, and presently a servant entered, and lit tall shaded lamps. It was all so cosy and delightful. Doris' spirit drank in the beauty of the room and the congenial atmosphere hungrily, and enjoyed every minute. She almost forgot that she was there to get a job. Then all at once she realized with a queer little sinking of heart that it was over and that she must go back to her problems and anxieties. She gave one wistful glance around on the quiet room, that seemed like a large haven of peace, and then glanced at her host, for it was host and not employer that he had seemed all the afternoon.

"You are trying to remind me of my promise to get you back to the city in time for dinner," he said glancing at his watch. "There is really no hurry. We can make it in thirty-five minutes, or even less, and I want you to see the stars coming out when we go through the woods."

Mrs. Macdonald caught the intimate tone, and smiled:

"Angus makes all sorts of record time in that car," she

said. "He is very proud of it. But I presume you have ridden in it before, Miss Dunbar?"

The color fluttered into Doris' cheek, and she cast the flicker of a glance at Macdonald, but responded gracefully:

"It is a wonderful car, isn't it? I just love to ride in it. I wonder, Mrs. Macdonald, if you will let me run out again pretty soon after your son has gone? I am rather—well—lonely, you know sometimes, and I'm crazy to get into the country."

"Why surely," said the gracious lady. "I shall be delighted! And I shall be lonely myself when my boy is gone. Come often. It is refreshing to see a real girl again in this age of flappers. How will you come? Do you live far? I could send the car for you. Angus, you arrange that with Kendrick."

"Oh, thank you!" said Doris. It was exciting to be carrying off the thing so well. Here was Mrs. Macdonald just falling right in line with their plans. It almost made her feel guilty. She could not help seeing that the lady took her for one of her son's most intimate friends. Nothing could be better for the success of her employer's schemes, but it was exceedingly embarrassing.

"I have a little car— I'm not sure whether I shall keep it— You see we are going to move soon. It is just possible I may come quite near you to live. If I do I shall be running over all the time to ask your advice."

"Why that will be beautiful!" said Mrs. Macdonald with genuine welcome in her voice. "Come often, and come soon!"

Doris rode away into the starlight with a young thread of a moon hanging straight before the car, almost resting on the tassels of the tall pines below them. She glanced back and saw the little patrician lady smiling and waving her hand to them from the great stone balcony that surrounded the house, a brilliant electric light above her shining on the silver of her hair, and making her delicate face stand out against the dusky doorway, cameo-like; and her heart thrilled with anticipation of the days she was to spend with this delightful new friend. She wondered what the son had thought of the interview, and whether perhaps he was discouraged and felt it not worth while? At least she was glad of the experience, even if nothing more came of it. And her welcome had been so genuine that she felt she might sometime keep her promise to call, even if she were not hired to go regularly.

But Angus Macdonald said nothing about it for some time. They slid down the wonderful curving drive from the hilltop, passed into the woods and there in a certain spot he came to a standstill and bade her look up.

For an instant she could not speak with the wonder of it. Little intimate stars winking and blinking at her, so close it seemed she could almost reach up and pluck them; great blue stars and red stars so large they put her in awe and seemed to be looking into her very soul, and lower, between the branches, that single threadlike crescent moon of pure silver! Like a royal boat in a sea of sapphire among the lights of smaller craft.

They talked very little as they sat and looked. Macdonald pointed out one and another star familiarly. "That's Saturn you know. Isn't he a beauty? And down lower the Evening Star. But this is my favorite, this big blue fellow over here that changes color like an opal. You know Browning's poem, 'My Star,' don't you? I've always fancied it was written about this star.

> "*All that I know*
> *Of a certain star*

Is, it can throw
(Like the angled spar)
Now a dart of red,
Now a dart of blue;
Till my friends have said
They would fain see, too,
My star that dartles the red and the blue!
Then it stops like a bird; like a flower, hangs furled:
They must solace themselves with the Saturn above it.
What matter to me if their star is a world?
Mine has opened its soul to me; therefore I love it."

"You see I know the older poems better than the late ones. I used to have more time to read when I was quite young."

They came out at last below the resinous pines and into the straight smooth road of the highway. Here Macdonald suddenly changed the subject and began to talk business.

"Now," said he, "Miss Dunbar, I think we've carried it off pretty well, don't you?"

"I suppose so, but I feel somehow as if I had won your mother's friendship under false pretences," confessed Doris. "I think she is charming, and I shall always be glad to have met her even if it goes no farther."

He waited a whole second before he answered that.

"And why do you say 'if it goes no farther'?" he asked gravely. "Did you feel that you could not undertake the commission?"

"Oh, not that!" said Doris quickly. "I would love to do it. But I was not sure you would think it wise after you saw us together. I cannot quite see how I am to hang around every day and do my duty when she merely looks upon me as a girl friend of yours. Would she not think it strange? Would she not begin to suspect after a time? She is a very clever woman."

"Yes, she is canny, I'll admit," said the Scotchman smiling, "but all the same I'm banking on you to over-come that and become such a good friend that she will coax you morning, afternoon, and evening to come to her. Of course right at the start you'll not be able to work in a visit every day or even every other day for a while, but after you get things going, I'm sure that won't be any trouble. You see I think I've picked the right person for this job and I'm putting it up to you."

"Oh, I hope I can fulfill your expectations," said Doris timorously, "but it seems most uncertain. It does not seem to me that such a thing can really be worth money to you."

"It is worth more than I can tell you," said the young man. "I've made out a check in your name, for three hundred dollars, your first month's salary. Is that going to be enough for a start, do you think? Or should I make it more?"

"Oh!" said Doris startled, "I'm sure that is too much for such a pleasant easy job. I really cannot take a check in advance. I might not be able to please you."

"Look here, Miss Dunbar, didn't I understand that you had someone else to support—a family you said?"

Doris assented.

"Well, if you went into an office or a library and gave your whole time, and got to be expert at your job you would expect to get something like that. Now, this is a job to which I want you to give your whole mind though not all your time of course, and I want you to be free from financial worries so that you can do it well. Have I offered you enough to make that possible or had you expected to try to get more?"

"Oh, no," said Doris, "I knew that if I began with

twenty-five dollars a week anywhere I would be doing
well. I think you are offering me far too much. I do not
think it would be right for me to accept it. I shall be
satisfied with—"

"Miss Dunbar, three hundred a month is the salary I
expected to offer if I found the right person to fill the
position, and I feel sure you are that person. Now, that
matter is settled, please! We will turn to another matter.
There is one point that I forgot to speak about. I should
like a weekly account of what you have done and how
you are succeeding, and also, a hint if my mother is
getting lonely or sad without me. I will keep in touch
with you from time to time, and give you an address that
will follow me in my travels, and so I shall know how
things are going. This will give me freedom from anxiety
during my work abroad, which will be rather strenuous
and requires a free mind. Will you be willing to do this?"

"Why, certainly," said Doris, "I shall be glad to do
that, and then if you are not entirely satisfied with what
I am doing you can tell me so frankly, and I can hunt for
something else to do."

"I think I am going to be satisfied," said the young
man with conviction. "Now, about details. Transporta-
tion. I can arrange with my chauffeur to come for you
whenever you telephone him. I will write the number
among other details which I will have my secretary
prepare for you. And when you move, wherever you
move, I think it would be well to make sure of a
telephone connection at once, both that I may always be
able to get in touch with you by cable or before I go by
phone, and that my mother may get into the habit of
calling for you and making a real friend of you quickly.
Of course all details like that I shall expect to cover under
the head of expenses. Also, if any time you have to take
taxis or stay at hotels, or take tea or luncheon somewhere

or buy books, or concert tickets, or any material for carrying out your plan, these things I expect to pay for. They are not to come out of your salary. I shall place a sum of money in the bank in your name which will be for your expense account. I will have all that arranged to-morrow and will get in touch with you sometime before I leave and explain any further details. Is that perfectly satisfactory?"

Doris said it was. With glowing cheeks and eyes that shone with relief, she reiterated that it was more than satisfactory, and that she would endeavor to do her best to fulfill his expectations.

And then suddenly they were in the city again, with lights flashing brilliantly on every hand and traffic madly congested. Doris felt as if she had passed from fairyland into Vanity Fair.

She begged him to set her down at a passing trolley that would easily reach her home so that he might return at once to dinner, but he would take her home, and so the beautiful car drew up before the house in due time, and Rose, anxiously watching at the window, saw her sister handed out, and watched them as they stood talking a moment before Macdonald lifted his hat, and got into his car and drove away.

Rose was at the door to meet her:

"Doris! Who is that perfectly stunning man you came home with? And where on earth have you been? And Doris, Ned is worse again. They have sent for a night nurse to relieve this one, and John hasn't been home since morning. I've been nearly crazy waiting for you to come!"

Doris felt the heavy thud of her heart as she received the news, and throwing her hat and coat aside hurried upstairs without answering her sister's questions. It seemed always when she came home now that there was some bad news awaiting her at the door.

Ned was having a sinking spell. The doctor was there, and for a time all was hurry and silent ministration again.

"The trouble is he hasn't anything to build on," said the doctor coming out of the sickroom at last with an anxious face. "I think we've tided him through this place again, and he'll be all right to-night, but he's all run down. I'm afraid he's been going a pretty hot pace. But don't you worry, little girl," as he saw Doris' anxious eyes. "We'll pull him through yet. You go to bed and to sleep. You can't do any good by fretting and you've got to save your strength for later when the long hard pull of convalescence comes. Now, what's this Rose has been telling me about John? Is he lost? He's old enough to know better than to worry you this way when you have so much other trouble. Do you think he's lost or only strayed?"

"No, sir," said John, "I'm here! What's wanted? I'll go for it."

"*You're* wanted, young man, where've you been? Your sister has been fretting her life out about you, and Doris here is ready to drop with anxiety about you. Is that the way to act when your brother is sick and you're the only man of the family to look after them all? Speak up and tell me where you've been all day? They say you didn't go to school."

"No, sir," said John with dignity and a ring of quiet innocence to his voice. "I've quit school. I've got a job!"

The doctor looked at him with lifted eyebrows, and Doris felt a thrill of pride in him, no matter what the job was, he looked so good and dirty and lovable and funny just then! So sort of grown up and dependable!

"The dickens you have!" said the doctor eyeing him severely, half incredulous. "Where is it?"

"Lyman's," said John with a bit of a casual swagger. "Private office. I don't get but six bucks a week yet, but I get a raise every six months if I make good, and I'm gonta! The raise ain't but fifty cents, but it'll count up in a little while, and I am gonta be promoted as fast as I'm ready."

"H'm!" said the doctor. "That's not so bad! Who got the job for you?"

"Got it myself. Went an' ast for it! Whodaya spose?"

"John, you dear child!" exclaimed Doris, with shining eyes.

"Aw, that's nothin'. I just went an' ast. He came across. That was all there was to it."

"But why the dickens didn't you tell your sister?"

"Whaffor? Howd' I know I was gonta like it? Say, Doris, when you gonta have dinner? I'm holla clear down to my toes. I didn't have any lunch but an apple, an' I'm *starved*."

"You poor dear child!" exclaimed Doris in horror and flew to get him his dinner, while Rose and Jean hovered around him and questioned him eagerly as if he were some young king. And he answered them like a little sore bear:

"Aw get out! Can't ya lemma alone? I ain't the only fella works in an office am I? What's that? Say, got any kinda pie? Oh, boy! Custard pie. You're a peach, Rose. Didya make that fer dinner? Aw, gimme a piece now. I'll say I'm hungry. Say, that's pie awright!"

And then Florence suddenly appeared on the scene, a red spot on either cheek, and a voice of honeyed sweetness:

"Can't I help you, Doris dear? You must be tired."

Her eyes went anxiously to Doris' hand and a kind of fright filled them as she looked away quickly again. She went toward the stove moving a saucepan around and almost scalding herself with the hot steam from the teakettle.

"What's eating her?" growled John in a low voice to Jean who hung adoringly near him.

"I don't know," whispered back the little girl cautiously. "She's been out a long while, and she came back looking kind of frightened, and asked where Doris was, and she's been acting that way ever since. Rose says she knows, but she hasn't had a chance to tell me yet. Oh, dear, this house is dreadful. Something new going on every minute! Say, John, I knew you'd get a job. I told Milton Page you would!"

"Aw, that's nothing. Whyn't Milt come across with something fer Doris? Whyn't he come an' try to help a little? It gets my goat the way he treats Doris. 'F I was twenty-one I'd get him out in the meadow back o' the ball ground an' wallop him. He makes me sick! That guy!"

"Sh! John," said Jean softly. "Doris might not like it if she heard you say that."

"Aw, well, how c'n I help it? He's a mess! An' so is Flarnce! I don't see why we have to have 'em wished on us."

"Sh! Here she comes!"

Florence came through the swing door from the kitchen and passed through the dining-room without seeming to notice the two children standing by the dining-room window. She had a hunted look on her face and she went straight to the telephone alcove under the stairs in the hall and began to tug at the heavy walnut desk that held the telephone. She carried a small pocket flashlight which she snapped on.

John watched her speculatively with lowering brows, and sauntering toward the hall in his usual casual manner, stood leaning against the doorway.

"'S matter, Flarnce?"

Florence started as if she had been caught stealing:

"Why—I—say, John, couldn't you help me move this desk out? I've lost something, and this won't move. Take hold and pull, that's a dear boy. I can't think what makes it stick so."

"'S loaded," asserted John. "Dad had it loaded cause it was always tipping over when ya leaned on't phonin'. Watcha lost? Paper?"

"Why—no—I— You see I came in from the street and telephoned, and I think I dropped my pocketbook down behind this desk."

"Couldn't get muchova pocketbook down that close fit." John took hold of the desk and yanked it out from the wall. "Sure ya had yer pocketbook when ya came in?"

"Why—yes—I'm *almost* sure I had it."

"Where'dya ben?"

"Oh, a number of places," evaded Florence looking embarrassed. "But I'm *almost* certain I had it in my hand when I went to look up a number in the book."

"Wha'dya have in it? How much?"

"A little over twenty-five dollars," she said anxiously.

"An'thing else?"

"Oh, a few trifles, some cards and papers with addresses," she seemed deeply distressed.

"Write 'em out fer me an' I'll take 'em over to Pat an' have 'em broadcasted. Ef you lost it on the street or in a store it'll be returned to ya prob'ly in the morning. Get a hustle on an' I'll get it in ta-night. I gotta drag with the fella that does it, and he'll get it on the air fer me I know."

"Oh, no, no! John, thank you, no! But I really couldn't, not yet, John dear," said Florence all in a fluster. "I wouldn't want to be so prominent, and besides, John, they were private papers, and it would be so kind of common to have my affairs broadcasted."

"Aw, they don't tell yer name, just read out what was on the papers an' cards. You better offer a reward."

"Well, that's very kind of you, John dear." Florence hedged again. "But really I think I'll look a little farther first. I'm so careless, you know, and I do so hate to have people laugh at me for making a fuss about trifles. Of course twenty-five dollars is really a trifle—"

"Twenty-five bucks is twenty-five bucks!" stated John. "Suit yerself, but ef ya wantta get it on th'air you better get busy. I'm gonta go to bed. I'm a workin' man now ya know."

With honeyed voice Florence thanked him again and hurried to her room nervously.

John pushed the heavy desk back into place after giving the floor a careful scrutiny:

"Now what's she got up her sleeve?" he said to Jean. "Something, I'll bet. She never called me dear before, an' she better not keep it up er I'll leave home! Gosh, but she's a flat tire!"

"John, I think it's perfectly wonderful you got a job in Lyman's," said Jean adoringly. "Won't it be great to come in there some day and see you going around sort of inside things as if you belonged? I shall just be so proud!"

"That's no joke, kid. I'm gonta own that store some day, and don't you forget it! Some day I'll take you around and say: 'Now choose anything you want. A pearl necklace or—or—a canoe—or a camping outfit. They've got some dandy ones down in the basement—"

"Oh, John! Really?" with shining eyes. "I believe you will. Won't it be great. But how can you ever do it?"

"Oh, that's easy! Just stick, and go up! Just you wait and see!"

About that time Angus Macdonald arriving back at home found his mother waiting for him with a smile in the living-room.

"Well, how do you like that girl, mother? Does she come up to your standards in any way?" He said it in an offhand manner as if it did not matter to him in the least what she thought. His mother watched him wistfully, and thought she saw through his casual manner.

"I liked her very much!" she said heartily. "She seems utterly unspoiled and not at all like the modern girls that come here with your cousin Viva. I hope she will keep her promise and come to see me."

"I think she will," answered the son heartily. "She seems to be as much pleased with you as you are with her."

There was an instant's silence then, just long enough for each to feel unspoken questions in the atmosphere, and then the mother asked, quite casually herself, with a studied tone:

"How long have you known her, Angus? I never heard you speak of her before."

"Oh, not long!" answered the son hastily, as if it were not at all important. "I—she—not long you know! But I've known her father for years. That is—in a business way."

"Oh—she has a father—"

"Yes, she had a father whom everybody respected. He died very recently."

"Oh!" said the mother sympathetically. There was both question and tenderness in her tone.

"He was a man with a vision bigger than his pocket-book, I understand."

"What a pity!"

"But they tell me he almost accomplished its fulfillment in spite of that obstacle."

"She looks like a girl with such a background," she smiled dreamily. "I think I am going to enjoy her."

"That's good," said her son with intense satisfaction in his face. "Well, mother, is dinner served? I'm really hungry!"

19

THE next two or three days became a kind of blur rather than a period of time to Doris and Rose. Ned was obviously worse. Sinking, the nurse called it. The nurse was not a cheerful being to have around. She had no scruples about saying Ned's condition was the fault of the family. She said they hurried too much and talked too loud and had too many other people in the house. She had no use at all for Mrs. Dunbar.

Florence meanwhile had kept pretty close to her own room, crying a good deal, although she did it very quietly after the nurse went into her room one day and administered a shaking and a thorough good scolding. When she came out at meal times she was most humble and apologetic in her manner, especially to Doris, and always giving a quick furtive darting glance at Doris' left hand whenever she met her anew, as if hoping to find something there which had been missing.

But although she had become somewhat abject she was not any less of a problem. She was always darting hither and thither unexpectedly, looking behind the furniture, especially in the hall, as if she could not give up the obsession that her lost pocketbook was there somewhere. And when the girls in their hurry came upon her thus, they cast anxious glances at one another. Doris wondered if it could be possible that Florence was losing her mind. What mind she had to lose.

There was no time for the sisters to have confidences. Three days went by before Doris had opportunity to speak to Rose about the Silver Ledge house, or to think whether she should tell her about her arrangement with Angus Macdonald. She had not even had time to put her check in the bank. What things they needed were ordered by telephone. The girls were busy every moment in the house. Milton Page was utterly forgotten. The doctor was an almost hourly visitor. Only John went steadily to his job every morning. Even little Jean stayed at home from school to run errands, of which there seemed suddenly to be so many. Hannah had not come back at all. She had telephoned and sent for her trunk, which they found to their surprise was packed and strapped ready for her flitting. Hannah had been a recent importation and was not expected to be loyal to the family. Indeed Florence, during her reign, had seldom been able to keep a servant longer than six weeks. Now Florence seemed suddenly to have stepped into the background and everything devolved upon the two girls.

There came an hour when they sat down and waited, while the doctor and the nurse hovered silently in the sickroom. Doris did not dare to hope. She had not dared to pray for Ned's life. What had Ned to live for but misery if he did come back from the borderland? Yet how were they to go on and face life without this bright gay brother who had always been so much, especially to her?

At the end of what seemed a century, the doctor came out with a grim look of victory on his face.

"Well, he's passed the crisis and he's going to get well," he said almost sourly, as if it were in spite of the family.

And then things began to happen again, as if they had been held in abeyance while Ned's life hung in the balance.

There was a relieved hurry upon the girls as they cleared up the kitchen and prepared the morning meal. Doris had time to remember that she had a check for three hundred dollars that must go into the bank at once; and bright plans for the future began to take shape. It seemed good to see the sunshine and to discover a valiant daffodil in bloom under the dining-room window. At least they were passed this storm and calmer waters seemed ahead.

Only Florence seemed untouched by the good news the doctor had given them. She darted about like a gloomy shadow just as she had been doing, and seemed more restless, if possible, than ever, as if she felt that now that the tension was relieved, the eyes of the family were again upon her suspiciously.

Doris and Rose in the kitchen, bringing order out of the confusion that had necessarily reigned there for the last three days, talked in low tones:

"What are we going to do now, Doris?" asked Rose with her tired young brow all in a pucker. "Did Mr. Hamilton tell you when we have to get out of this house?"

"Yes," said Doris splashing the silver around in the hot suds. "He said the man was willing to wait till Ned was able to be moved. But we must go at once just as soon as that time comes. The man has a chance to sell at an advantage if the people can come in by the first of the month, and that's not two weeks off."

"Mercy!" said Rose aghast. "How can we ever do it?

Just go out and leave everything here but our clothes? Or don't we even get our clothes?"

"Oh, it's not as bad as that," said Doris smiling. "He thinks we can have the furniture or some of it at least. He thinks the creditors are going to be satisfied with the other property. He tried to save this house, but it was mortgaged so heavily that it did not seem worth while."

"I wouldn't want the old thing anyway," said Rose with a choke of tears in her throat. "I keep seeing Daddy in all the rooms. I'd like to get out to-day and never come back."

"I'm glad you feel that way," said Doris relieved. "I was afraid you would be terribly homesick. How would you feel about going into the country?"

"Country?" asked Rose apprehensively. "Why country? That's expensive isn't it? And we'd be simply buried alive. How could we work for our living in the country? Plant potatoes?"

"Rose, I saw Aunt Doris' house Saturday. It's out at Silver Ledge. As a house, from the outside, it isn't bad at all. The *place* is a dump! I don't know whether we could stand it. But if it isn't sold we might *have* to move there for a while, at least until we found something better. What if you and I were to take my runabout and go out there this afternoon and look it over—see if it's at all possible? I've a whole lot to tell you, but I haven't time now. I want to go to the bank before lunch, and Mr. Hamilton is coming at half past eleven." She glanced at the clock. "It's getting late. Could you finish putting away these dishes and let me go to the bank now? Then I'll be back by the time Mr. Hamilton comes?"

"But Doris—" Rose's face had gone blank with dismay, "how could we—how could you ever get a job if you went away out to Silver Ledge to live?"

"I've *got* a job, Rosie." Doris' eyes danced. "I meant

to tell you but there simply hasn't been time. It's a long story. It's quite romantic!"

"Doris! You're not going to marry Milton Page after all?"

"No, never!" said Doris. "Nothing like that. By the way, Rose, *where* did you find my ring?"

"Well, that story will wait too," laughed Rose. "I'll keep it to hold over you until you tell me all you have to tell."

"All right. I'll hurry, then," and Doris wiped her hands and took off her apron.

"But Doris," pleaded Rose, "is there a trolley line or a railroad to Silver Ledge? How could you possibly get to a job if you lived there?"

"There's a trolley, dearest, but I'm thinking of keeping my car if we should find it feasible to live there. Would you mind it so very much, Rose, to live in the country for a while at least, if we find the house is at all possible?"

"No," said Rose somewhat solemnly, "I don't know as I should, only— But Doris, how could you keep your car if it isn't paid for?"

"Pay for it," laughed Doris gaily. "In fact that's partly what I'm going to the bank for."

"Doris! You're *not* going to *borrow money?*"

"Don't be silly child! How could I borrow money without any security. No, child, I've *got* some money, advance salary, and I want to deposit it. It's all right, Rose, and I really must hurry now or Mr. Hamilton will be here before I get back. And don't you worry. We won't go to Silver Ledge unless you like it, not if there is a single thing else in life we can do. I'm not going to go against my partner, so cheer up!"

Doris was off, and Rose went about finishing the work, and preparing a salad for lunch with thoughtful face. Rose had affairs of her own that she was not telling anyone. She was trying to see how they would fit into the picture. And presently there came a telephone call:

"Yes, this is Rose. Oh, yes,—no, there's no one here now. Yes, my brother is better. The doctor thinks he's out of danger. But I can't go this afternoon. No, it's impossible. I have to go somewhere on business with my sister. No, I don't think she would. No, I really can't. Well—perhaps—to-morrow! I'm not sure. No. I couldn't possibly get off at night. Well, they *would* object. They certainly would! I'm not sure I want to anyway. A ride? Oh, well that's different. I might. Not to-day. I couldn't possibly. What? A new car? What kind is it? Oh the sporting model? I just adore that. I saw it at the automobile show. Is that the one you bought?—I certainly will. Well, I'll try. You'll have to call up. No, I won't go off if I'm needed here. Not till things straighten out. Not to ride in the best car that was ever made. What? Well, I'll try. Where? Oh, that's too conspicuous. No, I'd rather meet you where I did before. All right, but I've got to get back by five o'clock. Yes, I have. It's impossible now. There's nobody else to take my place, and we have two trained nurses to feed. I won't go at all unless I can get back in time. All right, to-morrow then at three at the fountain."

Rose hung up the receiver and went and stared out of the window at the blank wall of the next house for a long time with unseeing eyes. She had the look of one who has taken a step about which she has hesitated for a long time. Presently she gave a toss of the wavy lock over her forehead and went back to the kitchen to work twice as fast as before.

"Well, if I don't like it out there I don't need to stay," she said half aloud to herself. "There are ways to get away. There'll be plenty of ways," and she stepped into the dining-room, and looked at herself in the mirror over the sideboard soberly, appraisingly, unprejudicedly for a long second.

"Yes, there'll be ways," she said convincedly, and added as she went back to the kitchen with a toss of her head—"if I want to take them!"

The lawyer arrived just as Doris returned. He was in a hurry and did not stay long. He had a conference with the creditors at half past twelve.

He told Doris more about the house at Silver Ledge. He said it was absolutely hers and could not be touched by any of the creditors. He said that property out there was dead and there was very little hope of selling it at all. If it sold it would bring scarcely anything. He promised to send the key down by his office boy at once, but he put aside as impossible the idea of the family going out there to live. He said it was out of the world. Doris had a passing worry about the look in Rose's eyes as he said that. She felt deeply troubled about putting Rose away off there so far from all her friends: still—if there was nothing else to do.

"Rose," she said while they were preparing a hasty lunch after the lawyer had gone, "you needn't look so troubled. We don't have to go out there to live just because we're going to look at it. How would you like to look at a few places in town on our way out? Have you thought of any locality?"

Rose brightened.

"Out there by the new trolley terminal there are apartments," suggested Rose. "They are putting them up by the hundred. I heard they were charming. Susan Dabney has a sister living in one of them. She told me yesterday you pay twenty-five a month, and three hundred down. I don't suppose we could get the three hundred, could we? But that would be better than just paying out rent and having it gone. These you own after a certain number of years."

"We'll go and see them," said Doris interestedly. "And suppose you get the morning paper and look up anything else you think sounds good. We'll do as many as possible this afternoon. Florence will never get started. We must work fast and decide soon you know, because we've simply got to get out of here. Mr. Hamilton says the man is getting vicious. He went to the doctor to-day to find out if we were telling the truth about Ned."

"Old Tightwad!" said Rose making up a mouth. "I hope he gets stuck on his bargain!" and she went in search of the morning paper.

Doris took the precaution to call up the automobile company from which her car was purchased, and ask a few questions about payments. She explained that her father had been ill and had died, and that she was thinking of taking over the car, if she could manage the payments. They were most courteous and promised to send a man around to make the arrangements with her. Then she called up the garage where the car was kept and asked them to send it around by one o'clock.

Rose had quite a list of "For Rents" marked in the paper, and they started out immediately after lunch to look them up. But half a dozen of them were eliminated at once by the discovery that they were in an inaccessible neighborhood. Three others they passed by without stopping when they saw their surroundings. Another was beyond any possibility in price, and at last they came down to three. These they set themselves to consider faithfully. They parked the car and dragged hesitating feet up long steep flights of narrow stairs, glanced conscientiously into dismal bedrooms with one window apiece and ugly scarred wall-paper. With sinking hearts they heard the exorbitant prices that went with these dreary abodes, and then they went out and climbed silently into the car again and went on their way.

Only once did a gleam of hope come to them when they arrived at the operation of apartment houses that were going up by the trolley terminal.

Yes, there was the sign, too good to be true! Three hundred dollars down and twenty-five a month, paid the rent and bought the apartment.

With alacrity they got out and went into the show apartment which had been furnished by one of the big city department stores, and was a gem of its kind with nothing forgotten that could make the compact abode charming and convenient.

They entered the spacious living-room with its archway into a pleasant dining-room, and began at once in imagination placing their furniture. It all seemed so complete. They would have to do away with a good many things that were now in use in the larger house where they were living, but all that was really necessary could be got into this one. They exclaimed joyously over the tiny corner china closets, and decided that they would hold everything needed for ordinary use. They could pack the finer dishes into the lower part of their old sideboard until a more prosperous day.

They progressed to a tiny kitchenette, and paused a trifle taken back. It was complete, but it was tiny. One or at most two could work together there in safety if one stayed close by the sink and the other by the gas stove. A third would be overwhelmingly in the way.

With soberer faces they went on out into the narrow hall, exclaimed with delight over the white tiled bathroom over which the builder had expended his best energies. It was as large as the kitchenette, and quite without blemish. Their ardor arose. Perhaps the kitchen was not quite so bad. Perhaps they could get used to it.

After all, why did more than one need to be in the kitchen at once?

They proceeded down the hall and found but *one more room remaining*—a bedroom, opening onto a tiny sleeping porch, so called by courtesy, though how one could sleep there unless he arose before daylight was a mystery, as there were something like a hundred other such excrescences up and down the block over under and across, like the backs of tenements, and no pretence at shelter of any kind.

A card tacked up in the hall suggested a day bed in the living-room if more sleeping accommodation was needed. Rose and Doris turned and looked at each other blankly, and then Rose broke down laughing. Without a word they turned and went down to their car. Fancy trying to get the Dunbar family into that apartment! One bedroom and a sleeping porch!

"So that's that!" said Rose as they rode away. "Now, if the country house is any better than that, lead me to it!"

Doris smiled.

"Don't think because we failed to-day there may not be something in the city for us yet, perhaps," she said wisely, "and don't go to Silver Ledge thinking we've got to take it whether or no. There'll be something *somewhere*. If we don't like Silver Ledge we'll forget we have it. But it happens to be convenient for my job this summer, that's all. And now I've got a story to tell."

Rose listened with wide romantic eyes.

"What's the man like?" she asked with a mature look in her eyes that brought back that shade of anxiety to Doris' eyes. How Rose had grown up during Doris' last year at college! It seemed incredible.

"Oh, he's pleasant enough," said Doris. "That wouldn't matter anyway. He's to be abroad indefinitely.

It's his mother that I'm concerned with, and she's lovely. She looks like Dresden china. She's a woman out of a book!"

"I'm afraid she'd bore me awfully," yawned Rose. "Will you have to stay if you find something better?"

"Why yes, I think there'd be a moral obligation. But I wouldn't be likely to find anything better, Rose. He's paying me three hundred a month, *in advance!* That's the money I went to put into the bank this morning!"

"Great Caesar's ghost!" exclaimed Rose classically. "Doris Dunbar, are you talking in your sleep? That's more money than I can make in the movies—*yet,* anyway!"

"It is rather wonderful, isn't it?" said Doris smiling dreamily. They had passed beyond the city limits now and were riding along between suburban streets with pretty lawns just beginning to blush into fresh green. And presently green fields and open country came in sight.

"See that tree, Rose," Doris exclaimed impulsively. "Isn't it beautiful?"

"That! Beautiful! Doris, you're growing nutty. That's a dead tree."

"I know, but it's so—rugged—and wonderful! It has—character!"

"Ha, ha! Doris! Character in a tree! That's a good one. Mention that to our friend Milton the next time you see him, do! I'd love to watch his practical brow when he hears it the first time. But it wouldn't be the last time you'd hear of it. You'd hear the changes rung on it the rest of your natural life, and then some."

"Well, I shall not mention it to him," said Doris with her lips in a firm little line. "I'm done with Milton forever!"

"It may be so, but I don't know," hummed Rose

tantalizingly. "Not if I know Milton, my beloved sister. You've only just begun. You'll find you can't shake off Milton Page just by telling him so. He's thick-skinned. You'll have to throw him down again and again before he believes it. You've only made a little dent in his pride yet. Wait till you get down to the real him and then see what he does."

"Well, don't let's talk about him," said Doris. "I want to have a good time if that's possible after all we've been through."

"All right, Dorrie, but tell me quick, when did you know all this? Don't tell me you knew it when you came home that night. You couldn't have been mean enough to keep three hundred dollars to yourself for three whole days! The check must have come in the mail this morning, I suppose."

"No, he gave it to me on the way home. But I couldn't talk about it then, with Ned so sick, and everything upset. Why Rose, there wasn't a minute to talk except in the dead of night, or when we were sitting around waiting to see what the doctor would say."

The miles fairly flew away till suddenly Doris slowed down speed and announced almost solemnly:

"This is Silver Ledge."

Rose hushed her merry tongue and began to look apprehensively about.

"The sun still shines, here," she announced after a minute, "and there's plenty of good air to breathe. Are all the inhabitants dead, or gone to the city?"

"I'm sure I don't know," said Doris anxiously. "It does look dead, doesn't it?"

"Dead as a door-nail! I should call it Rip-Van-Winkleton. However there may be a new sensation here, who knows. Is this the house? It looks like a picture. But could we ever make it come alive?"

"It's better than Dawson street apartments, isn't it?"

"I should say it is! Don't remind me of that or I'll just sit down and stay here to-night."

Rose sprang out of the car and Doris after her, their eyes on the house.

The lilacs were just beginning to send out little green leaves, and faint purple buds. Rose discovered them, and went around to look at them before she would go into the house.

"Real lilacs of our own!" she exclaimed, "and my word, Doris! Is that lily of the valley by the steps there? I thought they only grew in florists' shops."

The house was a rambling affair, whose green blinds had weathered so many storms that they had taken on that soft bluish faded tint they call jade. The front porch and the fan-shaped window over the door were exquisite. There was a wide hall with a winding stair, and a long low room at the right with the tall gilt mirrors that Doris remembered. To the left of the stairs was a downstairs bedroom, and back of it a dining-room and lean-to kitchen, with a pump. Upstairs there were three bedrooms and a big linen closet with shelves and a window. Above there was a speck of an attic reached by a ladder through a hatch.

"We could do it," said Doris thoughtfully, standing in the biggest upstairs front bedroom. "But—a pump!—And no bathroom!"

"Build one!" said Rose quickly. "Dorrie, I guess we've got to give it a try. We could just stuff in. It looks good to me, summer coming on."

"Rose, you're a good sport."

But Rose turned quickly away to hide something that lurked in her eyes.

"Florence would have to have this room. She

wouldn't stand for the small one," she went on practically, "and she'd be afraid downstairs."

"The boys would have to take that together," said Doris thoughtfully.

"But what about Ned's wife?" Rose questioned anxiously.

"She would never bury herself away out here!" said Doris sharply. "Ned will have to go with her if it comes to that. But I was thinking, until Ned is real well and strong we could fix this linen closet for John. He would love those shelves for his junk."

Suddenly they discovered it was getting late and they locked the house and hurried away with a lingering look back.

"See, there's a barn back there for the car," said Rose, "and Doris, I would just love to open all those old chests of drawers and rummage, wouldn't you?"

"I don't think there's much there, perhaps," said Doris. "It seems to me they gave most of the things away when Aunt Doris died. Now, Rose, we'll have to break it to the children to-night, for we ought to begin to start moving at once, to-morrow!"

But when they arrived at home the nurse met them in the hall with a frown. She had evidently been watching from the window for their coming.

"The old lady has gone out!" she announced glaring at them as if it were their fault, "and that silly flapper wife of his is upstairs with the patient. She sent me out of the room. If this kind of thing is going on I'm not going to stay on the case. It's as much as his life is worth to have all this excitement when he's just turned the crisis."

ZEPHYR had indeed arrived!

Even while they were gazing at the nurse in consternation the door-bell sounded through the house, and there was the expressman with Zephyr's two trunks.

It developed that she was even now installed beside her husband's bed, his hand in hers, and when she was summoned by the nurse to a conference downstairs she declined to come.

"I've come to take care of my husband as the doctor suggested," she said in a low sweet voice. "Ned wants me, so I'm going to stay!"

Doris in the doorway saw Ned fix his large feverish eyes on the nurse and assent whisperingly.

Doris and Rose in the hall exchanged glances of consternation, in no wise lessened by the plaintive querulous voice of the invalid:

"Zephyr! Zephyr! You won't go away and leave me again?"

And Zephyr's triumphant voice rang tantalizingly sweet and clear:

"No, Honey Boy, I'll stick right around till you're on

the job again. And then we'll clear out! Nobody's goin' to put anything over on you! I gotta lawyer now myself, and we'll see who gets the go-by."

It seemed that there was some sort of a protest from the bed at that, and then Zephyr's voice placatingly:

"Oh, sure! Ef that's what you want. You're the cat's whiskers you know, so hurry up and get well and we'll have a howling time. I got a two weeks' vacation. We'll simply do the world! Come, don't you feel better already?"

An ecstatic murmur from the bed struck to the hearts of the two.

Rose and Doris stole away down the stairs.

"Oh, Doris, what can we do?" whispered Rose in a terrified voice.

"Call the doctor!" answered Doris. "But what can he do when Ned feels like that? It might kill him if we sent her away. I suppose we've got to stand her till he gets well."

Then they suddenly became aware of the two expressmen standing in the hall with the two trunks beside them awaiting orders.

"Go telephone the doctor!" whispered Doris, and went down to meet the men. But before she could give any directions Zephyr's voice floated sibilantly down the stairs!

"Bring those trunks right up here," she called, and the men shouldered the biggest trunk and pressed past Doris to the stairs.

She tried to think what to do, and hurried after them up the stairs again.

"You may put them at the back end of the hall under that window," she told them.

But Zephyr was breezily giving directions, flinging open the door of Ned's room.

"You may bring them right in here!" she commanded, "and you better unstrap them before you go. I want to show my husband some new things I've got."

Then the nurse, coming out in the hall and shutting the door with decision:

"You can't bring any trunks in here! This is a sick-room. You'll have to have some other room if you're going to stay. I can't have trunks around in my way while I'm nursing. Besides the room isn't large enough."

"Oh, very well," answered Zephyr airly. "But you needn't talk like that to me. You aren't the only nurse in the world, and I can easily dismiss you. I'll take this room then, it's close by—" and she flung open Mrs. Dunbar's door and motioned to the expressmen.

"Put the trunks right in there anywhere and don't forget to unstrap them."

But Doris had reached the upper landing by this time and came and stood in her stepmother's door:

"This room is occupied," she said firmly. "The trunks will have to go to the end of the hall until we can make some arrangements."

The expressmen paused, the trunk between them, and looked from one girl to the other uncertainly.

"I said put the trunks in that room," said Zephyr shrilly, stamping her foot for emphasis. "They are *my* trunks and I mean to be obeyed!"

For answer Doris reached in for the key and locked the door on the outside putting the key in her pocket.

"This is Mrs. Dunbar's room," explained Doris. "It is impossible for you to have it. Now—" turning to the expressmen—"you may put the trunks where I told you. It is the only place ready for them at present."

Zephyr made a quick rush toward her and took hold of her arm fiercely:

"If you don't do as I say I shall have my husband taken

away from here to a hospital!" Doris wondered in passing that even in her anger Zephyr's eyes still had that artificial stare. It seemed almost inhuman.

"I don't think you've taken very good care of him, anyway," Zephyr went on, "and I don't like that nurse. I'm going to dismiss her and take care of Ned myself. That's what I came here for. He needs cheering up. She keeps him all shut up here alone. No wonder he's sick!"

"You will have to talk to the doctor about that," said Doris coldly.

"The doctor! What do I care for the doctor? I'll get a new doctor. I hear this one is a regular old stick anyway. I'll have a consultation, that's what I'll do! *Then* we'll see—"

But the doctor walked up the stairs in the midst of it.

"What's all this?" he asked glaring at the two girls. "Don't you know it's all wrong for Ned to have all this noise?"

Then his practised ear caught the querulous tones from the sickroom:

"Zephyr! Zephyr! You won't go away and leave me?"

The doctor set his jaw and glared at the complacent face of the impudent young flapper.

"I've taken your advice and come to nurse my husband," said Zephyr sweetly, giving a disarming smile with her baby blue eyes.

But the old doctor was not to be cajoled. His jaw set in anything but a crestfallen manner.

"You've got to do as you're told," he growled, "or out you go!"

"Oh, certainly," drawled Zephyr. "But I'm not sure I shall keep you for doctor. I want a consultation. I don't think you've got my husband well very quick. I think we oughtta have another doctor."

She said off the words parrot-like as if from memory.

The doctor looked over his spectacles at her and drew down his bushy eyebrows till he seemed like some wild animal glaring at her from his lair, but about his mouth was a comical expression as if he wanted to laugh.

"Very well, young lady," he said, "you just go downstairs to the living-room and we'll talk about it. At least I'm in charge till another doctor comes, and I judge my patient has had enough excitement for the time. I'll just see how his pulse is and give him some medicine and I'll be with you. No, you don't need to come into the room just now. I'll explain to Ned. I've known him longer than you have—" and the doctor went into the sick-room and shut the door, turning the key quickly.

"That's all right, Ned," he said soothingly to the excited boy on the bed. "She's just gone downstairs for a few minutes to get something and if you'll quiet down and take a little nap while she's gone I'll let her come back again. But as long as you toss around like this and keep calling out, she can't come! It wouldn't be good for you."

The doctor administered a sleeping powder and sat for a few minutes beside the bed holding Ned's intermittent pulse between practised fingers, studying the delicate features of the sick boy with intent yearning tenderness on his rugged countenance. Ned was the eldest son of his dearest friend, the friendship dating back to school-boy days.

After a minute or two he rose softly and went back to the hall.

Zephyr was in an altercation with the nurse at the head of the stairs. She had ordered ice cream from the caterer's and was demanding that it be served to herself and Ned at once.

The doctor took her firmly by the elbow and propelled her into a vacant room near by.

"Now," said he, "it's time you heard a thing or two. Did it ever occur to you that Ned is not of age?"

"Oh, yes he is," said Zephyr pertly. "He's nearly twenty-two. He told me so himself the night I met him."

"Well, I happened to be present at his birth," said the doctor gravely. "He is just nineteen years and three days old to-day."

"Oh, well, I don't see that that makes any difference, anyway," said Zephyr petulantly. "His father is dead and Mrs. Dunbar is only his stepmother."

"It makes a great deal of difference," said the doctor. "Ned is not his own master. He is still under guardians. I'm one of his guardians. Mr. Hamilton whom you saw here the other day is the other. If we choose to contest your marriage we can have it set aside as illegal. As for your taking things into your own hands here and trying to manage, it can't be done! You have no right in the matter whatever, and you can tell that to your people that sent you here to make trouble. I am the family physician and they wish me to keep the case. I intend to keep it. If you wish to remain here you will have to do as I say. If I consider it wise I may let you remain and come into the room occasionally, but it will be only for a few minutes at a time and you must promise not to make any more fuss. You take your orders from that nurse! Understand? She is the best nurse in the county for a case of double pneumonia and she is going to stay! I'm not so sure that you are! It is entirely up to you. If you behave yourself and keep quiet and make no trouble anywhere, I may allow you in the room now and then. But it will be only because Ned seems to have taken the fancy for you to stay; not in any sense because you have the right, because legally you haven't. Now, do you understand? I may decide that Ned is worse off with you here than he would be if he fretted for you. In that case you go. It all depends on what the nurse tells me of your behavior. As for ice cream, eat all you like yourself, but don't mention it to Ned. When he is ready to eat ice cream or anything else I'll see that he has it and not before. Your part here is simply to come in when you are called by the nurse and look pretty and smile. If you do any more than that, out you go! Now, are you ready to stay on those conditions?"

Zephyr stood staring at him with a baffled look in her eyes, but her cherry lips had a sullen droop with no sign about them of surrender.

"I'll *stay!*" she said sulkily.

The doctor eyed her uncertainly:

"There's another thing," he added savagely. "You've got to behave like a lady to Ned's family. I'm here to protect them as well as him. There is no reason whatever why they should allow you to stay here except for their brother's sake, and if you do not treat them right you'll have to leave even if it is hard on Ned. Now, that's all. But mind you do as the nurse tells you."

Zephyr walked down the hall and back to Ned's door with her head up but there was anger and defiance in every line of her supple back. As the doctor watched her, he knew he was not done with her yet.

It was late that night when at last Doris and Rose locked the door of Doris' room and sat down on the bed together, too exhausted almost to try to get undressed.

They had moved everything from Rose's room to Doris', and made Rose's room ready for the irate sister-in-law to occupy, and now they looked at one another with white despairing faces much as if they had been taken prisoners in a camp of war and saw no way of release.

"Well," said Doris, with a weak attempt to smile, "we never know what is coming next, do we?"

"Don't!" said Rose sharply, and suddenly broke down in tears.

"There, there, Sister, don't cry!" said Doris wearily. "After all, it won't kill us. Really there's something almost funny about it all. So many things—and such queer ones. There is a funny side to it, Rose. Let's look at that and let the tragic part go."

"How can you?" exclaimed Rose furiously, dashing away her tears. "I don't see anything funny about having a sister-in-law like that! How can we ever hold up our heads again? I hate her! I hate Ned for having given her to us. I never can love him again—"

"Don't dear! Remember, Ned has been very near death! He is by no means out of danger yet! And he's our brother. *This* isn't a thing of life and death. Poor Ned. When he gets well he's going to have enough to bear, as the doctor said, without our making it harder for him. Let's just try to show her that we are ladies."

"How can we be ladies when she acts like a little beast? I'd like to scratch her eyes out! Great big blue china things! She makes me feel like doing everything wicked I ever heard of before. She makes me want to kill her!"

"Look here, Rose! That is terrible. Don't you see you are worse than she is when you feel that way! She is just a coarse little untaught child, who is trying to get somewhere she doesn't belong. Don't let her draw you lower than she ever was. She can't really affect us at all if we go on doing right. We are not to blame for her. She can't hurt us."

"Oh, can't she!" retorted Rose. "Suppose she goes and talks to that Mrs. Macdonald? How would you like to have her turn up there sometime?"

Doris' face blanched at the thought.

"Oh, she wouldn't do that!" she exclaimed. "She needn't know anything about Mrs. Macdonald. Besides it couldn't really hurt us. It might be humbling, but it couldn't hurt us!"

"Well, I feel it could," sobbed Rose. "And I don't see what's the use of trying to live and be decent if we've got to go around with things like that belonging to us. I hate it all!"

It was a long time before Doris got Rose soothed and quieted, and stillness settled on the house. But Doris lay thinking out what she had to do on the morrow. She deliberately put aside the detestable sister-in-law as if she were not, and set herself to plan the moving.

It was at the breakfast table the next morning that they broke the news to their stepmother. They were later than the rest, and Rose was hovering back and forth between kitchen and dining-room, bringing more scrambled eggs and fresh coffee. Doris had dark rings under her eyes and looked worn and tired. It was Mrs. Dunbar who began the conversation:

"Who is that person upstairs that claims to be Ned's wife? Why are we tolerating her? I supposed she was someone come to visit the nurse, but I met her in the hall this morning and asked her what she was doing here, and she said she was Ned's wife. How absurd! Why Ned isn't old enough to be married!"

"No, he isn't," assented Doris. "But he did it. And the doctor seems to think she'll have to stay for the present until Ned is out of danger. You see Ned is infatuated with her and wants her beside him, and he is too weak to be crossed just now. It might cost him his life. It will hasten his recovery if we let her stay."

"Well, he doesn't deserve to recover quickly. A boy that would marry a girl like that! She takes airs on herself! For my part I'd send Ned to the hospital where he belongs and not upset the whole household on his account. You look sick yourself this morning, Doris, or else that black dress you are wearing is most unbecoming."

For some reason Florence had decided to placate Doris. She was trying in every way to be nice to her, a thing she had never been known to do before.

But Doris was too preoccupied to wonder at it. It was Rose in the kitchen listening, who put two and two together and began to wonder why.

"Florence," said Doris making up her mind to plunge in and have the troublesome announcement over with. "You know we've got to move right away?"

"Right away? What do you mean? I don't see why we have to move."

"Mr. Hamilton told you why the other day," said Doris patiently. "This house is sold and the owner wants it at once. We've got to get out."

"But how could it be sold? We haven't signed any deed. They couldn't sell it without our consent."

"It is sold for debt. There is no use going over that again. The whole thing is we've got to get out just as soon as Ned can be moved. The doctor told me last night that if Ned gets along all right we might be able to take him away from here in a week or ten days. But we can begin to move the rest of the rooms at once. Now, Florence, had you any idea of where you wanted to go? Had you thought at all about it?"

"So you're going to try to turn me out after all," said Florence beginning to cry softly. "After what your father put in his will about letting me always live in this house, you are going to send me away!"

"No, Florence! I didn't say that. You are going with us of course. I was asking if you had thought about where we would go? You certainly have a right to make a suggestion about it."

"Oh, no, my word doesn't count for anything. My wishes are nothing! *I'm* nothing!"

Florence was getting well under way now in one of her tantrums, the tears flowing copiously down her thin, faded, little face. Doris was in despair.

"Listen, Florence!" she said sharply, putting her hand on the older woman's shoulder and giving her a little shake for emphasis. "I want to tell you something. Don't act like a fool! We have serious business to consider. I have a house out in the country. It was left to me by Aunt Doris years ago. I don't know if you ever heard much about it. Even I didn't know if it were still mine, but Mr. Hamilton says it is, and that no one can take it from us, because it wasn't included in father's property. Yesterday Rose and I went out to look at it, and we think that with some fixing we can all get into it and be fairly comfortable. I am asking if you have anything better to suggest?"

"There! I told you that my wishes were nothing! So you have gone ahead without consulting me and got it all fixed. What was the use of asking? *Your* house! So you would be the head of the house and order me around!"

"Oh, Florence!" Doris was in despair.

At that juncture the telephone rang sharply, startlingly, as if the caller were impatient. Rose appeared at the door and motioned Doris to go. Then she came swiftly and silently over to the weeping woman.

"Florence!" she said sharply. "Do you want me to tell Mr. Hamilton what you did with Doris' ring? Or will you behave yourself and act like a lady?"

Florence stopped weeping as if petrified for an instant, and then looked up with simulated indignation.

"What do you mean? What would I have to do with Doris' ring?"

"There is no use pretending," said Rose coolly. "I know that you pawned it, and I know where. You needn't bother to try and deny it. I *know*. I've known it several days. No, Doris doesn't know it yet. I haven't had time to tell her!" as she saw the wretched woman's frightened glance dart toward the telephone-table in the hall where Doris sat. "And perhaps I won't tell her— *yet*—if you behave yourself. But you've got to stop crying and act like a woman, or else I'll send for Mr. Hamilton this minute and I'll tell him *every*thing! Now, sit up quick! She's coming! And don't you dare make any more fuss while you're in this house or everybody'll know just what you are, and where you got that twenty-five dollars you say was in your pocketbook."

Doris suddenly appeared at the door with a troubled look in her eyes.

"Rose, where did you find that ring?" she asked. "I can't understand. Milton has telephoned. He insists it is not the same ring."

"Mercy!" said Rose. "What on earth do you mean? I'm sure—"

Mrs. Dunbar sat up suddenly and began to mop her eyes hastily.

"It's all right, Doris dear!" she whimpered with signs of immediate recovery in her voice. "I am foolish of course to care so much just for a house. But this is the house where your dear father brought me home as a bride you know." She gave a final sob and looked up more cheerfully. "But I'll be brave! I will really! Yes, of course, I'll do whatever you say, you dear child! You're such a wonderful courageous woman. What is it you would like me to do about it, Doris? I suppose your ideas will be best. I hadn't thought— If you really think we must go."

"We must!" said Doris shortly. "And if you're willing to help I wish you would get your things on and come with me this morning out to Silver Ledge. You shall have first choice of rooms of course, and I think we ought to take someone out and start cleaning at once. The house has been shut up a long time."

"Very well, I'll go at once and get ready," said Mrs. Dunbar, arising hastily and putting her napkin in its ring.

Doris was surprised but relieved.

"Perhaps you would be willing to stay out there and direct the woman about the cleaning this morning while I come back and attend to securing a mover," she said. "I suppose we could get Chloe Whitely if she isn't busy to-day."

Mrs. Dunbar assented eagerly:

"Why, certainly. And you'd like me to look up some cleaning cloths of course. Rose, you better get some brooms and mops together."

Doris listened to her stepmother in amazement, and almost forgot for the moment that a new trouble was looming on the horizon.

"We ought to get started at once," said Mrs. Dunbar with sudden efficiency, "if we are to accomplish anything to-day. You telephone Chloe and I'll go up and get my hat and gather together some cleaning cloths and aprons. We'd better take a lunch, hadn't we? Just a box of crackers and a bottle of milk will do; and tea for Chloe. You know she must have tea or she won't work. Is there a tea-kettle or a stove or anything out there?"

"I think there's a stove, but it's an old-fashioned wood or coal stove. I don't know whether we can get it to work or not."

"We'll need hot water for cleaning. We'll have to get

a man in to fix the stove and make a fire. Hurry, Doris. It isn't like you to waste time. You know Chloe won't work after four o'clock."

"But I can't go immediately," said Doris with a troubled frown. "There are some things I must do for the nurse first, and Milton is coming in a few minutes. I cannot go till he is gone."

"I cannot understand why Milton should hinder us," said Mrs. Dunbar with a frightened look. "I should think you would just leave a note for him and let him come after you if he wishes."

"Well, perhaps," said Doris, reflecting that perhaps she had better take her stepmother now while she was willing. "I must see Rose first. Perhaps she can talk to Milton for me."

She hurried out into the kitchen after Rose, eager questions on her lips, but Rose was not there. She had slipped up the back stairs on cautious feet, and was even now sliding noiselessly down the front stairs with her hat and coat in her hand and making for the front door. As Doris hurried up the back stairs after her, Rose closed the front door silently, ran down the steps and around the corner with great haste.

Doris met Mrs. Dunbar coming anxiously from the direction of Rose's room, her eyes furtive and frightened, and an artificial smile on her face.

"Where in the world is Rose?" she asked fretfully. "She ought to be getting the things together for us. I told her about the mops, but she might make some tea and put it in the thermos bottle." She looked nervously around the hall like a bird that was expecting the cat momently. "I do wish we could get off at once. Won't you telephone Chloe quick?"

"Just as soon as I possibly can, Florence," said Doris, wondering if perhaps after all her stepmother was not going out of her mind. Such a sudden change of tactics was inexplicable.

Then the door-bell rang and Doris exclaimed:

"There's Milton now! I'll go just as soon as I can get away. You be all ready!" and hurried down the stairs, wondering where in the world Rose had gone.

Mrs. Dunbar meanwhile went like a shot into her own room and locking the door began to pace up and down the room excitedly wringing her hands and exclaiming aloud:

"Oh, what shall I do? What *shall* I do? There is no one to help me! No one loves me! No one will believe me! What *shall* I do? Oh, *what shall I do?*"

21

MILTON had the air of a righteous man come to deal out justice when he stepped into the house. He looked at Doris coldly, piercingly. She almost shivered as she met his glance and felt a passing gratitude that she was no longer accountable to him. She had a feeling that he was a jailor whom she had barely escaped. She was ashamed that this was so. It seemed reprehensible that she could so quickly turn against one whom she had supposed she loved well enough to marry. Now she began to understand that love had taken very little part in the contract that had existed between them.

"Well, have you found it?" he asked pointedly, holding her glance with his steel one.

"Come in," she said quietly. "We do not talk in the hall if we can help it on Ned's account."

He stalked quickly ahead of her into the living-room and whirled about facing her, the question still in his eye, as if the voicing of it had been held in abeyance in the air until he arrived where it was effectual.

"I have not been able to find Rose yet," she said pleasantly. "She must have gone out."

"What on earth can Rose have to do with the question?"

"Why, Rose found the ring for me."

"Oh, she did!" he said significantly. "You were very careful not to tell me that before. Where did she find it?"

"I am sure I don't know," said Doris haughtily. "Really Milton, you are talking very strangely. Why shouldn't Rose find the ring? I suppose she found it on the bureau where Jean says she put it."

"Where Jean *says* she put it! You *suppose* she found it on the bureau! There seem to be a good many uncertainties. And why, pray, did you not *ask* Rose where she found it?"

"Because I have been too busy with serious matters to have even thought about it. I took it for granted that everything was all right. How could it possibly be otherwise? The ring was found and I had given it back to you. What else was necessary?"

"But it was not the same ring!"

"Are you sure you know the ring, Milton? It is a long time since you gave it to me. I do not suppose you have noticed it much since I have had it."

"On the contrary I have always watched it with satisfaction on your hand. Do you suppose that a man can work hard to attain anything in this world without taking note and pride in the thing he has attained?"

"Then why did you not notice that it was not the same ring when I gave it to you the other night? Why has it taken so long for you to discover what you claim as a mistake?"

"I did not look at the ring at the time because I was deeply annoyed with you," he answered coldly and concisely. "I carried it home and put it safely away without looking at it even casually that night, because I was too much annoyed to trust myself to look the thing over. Besides I had examined it only a few days before when you left it on the parlor table, and I knew it to be all right then."

"Well, then, how did you find out that it was not?"

"I took it out this morning to put it in a box that I might leave it in my safety deposit box at the bank when I go away this evening on a business trip, preparatory to leaving for the West. I looked at it carefully, and discovered to my consternation that the marking was not there! Then I examined the stone and saw that it had no brilliance. Alarmed, I took it to the jeweller from whom I purchased it, and he tells me that this thing is common glass, set in the cheapest kind of a setting. Now, I have come for an explanation. Are you playing some kind of a job upon me, or is there some double crossing going on in this house? It will probably be easy to discover the culprit. You have, as you told me, a strange nurse in the house, which is line enough for any detective to follow immediately. And then, where there are children you never know what to count upon. Either John or Jean or even Rose might have coveted so valuable a stone and thought they could get away with it!"

"Milton!"

Doris' cheeks were crimson with anger, her eyes flashing fire.

His gaze met hers like steel on steel, and only gleamed the brighter.

"There is no use going into hysterics over the suggestion that some of your family may be involved. Such things happen every day. I only say, Find the Ring! You certainly know this is not it!"

He handed her a ring, made in the similitude of her own, yet so obviously an imitation that even a child could have told it was not real.

Doris took it and exclaimed:

"That is not the ring I gave you!"

"It certainly is! Do you doubt my word?"

"I suppose," said Doris scornfully, "it is no worse for me to doubt your word, than for you to doubt mine— *ours,*" she added as an afterthought.

"I have never suggested that I doubted *your* word," he stated. "Your family is a different matter."

"My family and I are one."

"Very well, explain this ring."

"I cannot explain it," said Doris. "But if my word is not enough for you until I can make further investigation perhaps I had better give you a check for the ring. I believe you told me the value was three hundred and fifty dollars. I happen to have that much money in the bank just now fortunately. Wait here and I will get my check book."

"You will do nothing of the kind, Doris. You are going off your head as usual. I will wait until Rose returns and we can question her together. If she has not taken the ring for her own purposes she ought to be able to give us a pretty good idea of where it is. I will sit down here and wait. If you have duties to perform this early in the morning do not let me interrupt you. How soon do you expect Rose in?"

"I do not know where Rose has gone nor when she will return, and I have an engagement at once to take my stepmother to look at a house. If you trust me as you say you do you can go away and wait until I can have time to find the ring and return it to you. If you do not I will give you a check. In any case I must go at once. I see that my car is already at the door!"

Doris was cold and haughty. She laid the ring down on the rim of Milton's hat, and walked out of the room. She was more angry than she had ever remembered to have been before. And this was the man she had once expected to marry!

"But Doris!" His voice pursued her to the hall. "This is not a matter to be treated lightly. In the interest of justice this should be reported to the police at once. If you do not do something about it now I shall be obliged to see a detective immediately."

"By all means do your duty!" said Doris steadily. "Have us all arrested if you think that is the right thing to do. But don't expect me to respect you for it!"

And with that she walked up the stairs.

Milton stood still and watched her. Presently he went and sat down in a big chair by the window. He decided that he would wait until Rose returned. He felt sure there was something crooked here and he delighted to find out the crook. If Doris would not do anything in the matter it clearly devolved upon him to do it. So he sat in the shadow and watched out the window.

Ten minutes passed. He heard voices upstairs, quiet voices, and steps coming down the back stairs. Presently Mrs. Dunbar came out heavily veiled and went into the street with a furtive air. She had just told Doris that she could not possibly go and see a house that morning, that she had remembered an important business appointment and must go and attend to it.

Doris in dismay decided to take Chloe Whitely anyway and carry out the plan of beginning to clean. Chloe was perfectly capable and trustworthy. She could leave her there to work, and return later in the afternoon to bring her back. At least this was an excuse to get away from Milton until Rose returned and till she should have an opportunity to get hold of Jean and question her more closely concerning the place where she had put the ring when Milton first gave it to her. It was all very puzzling anyway. Where could that ring have gone? And what ring was this? Was it possible that the nurse—? But no! The doctor said he had known her for years, and she looked the picture of integrity. It was unthinkable that she had touched the ring. Could Florence possibly have hidden it for spite? That seemed more plausible. When Rose came back they would search her room together. But now she would go out with Chloe just to get Milton away from the house.

So Doris went out with brooms and mops and a roll of rags in a scrub bucket, and drove off in her car. And there sat Milton silently watching, listening, and only the sound of the querulous invalid calling for something now and then, or the occasional rubber thud of the nurse's tread, was heard overhead. Zephyr, having read a novel far into the night and finished a box of chocolates, was sleeping far into the day and had not yet appeared on the scene.

It must have been an hour that Milton sat persistently in that chair by the window taking note of every passer-by and every sound that went through the house, when suddenly he became aware of another presence in the room, and looking around startled he beheld a vision such as he had never seen before. A vision of golden hair and sea-blue eyes staring blandly between dark curling lashes; a vision of a cherry mouth wearing a smile of inspection, and cheeks that rivalled the roses; a vision in a shimmering negligée of palest orchid chiffon, diaphanous and dreamy, with lovely white arms moving gracefully, languorously, and white, bare ankles thrust into dainty gold slippers. She looked like some forbidden fruit, startling and luscious, and Milton Page turned his cold eyes away in horror. This in a respectable home! How did it get here?

"Are you another of them?" asked Zephyr impishly in her most daring voice. "I don't think I've ever heard of you. What makes you have such a long face? You look like a horse!"

"Indeed!" said Milton rising haughtily. "And who are you, may I ask? I don't think I have ever been favored with your name?"

"Probably not," laughed Zephyr mockingly. "The family are ashamed of me. I'm Ned's wife. I dance at The Grand."

"Oh! I see!" said Milton dryly, turning a cold shoulder toward the girl and looking earnestly out of the window again as if he were not interested. "Well, as I'm not one of the immediate family, don't you think you had better go and get more suitably dressed? I should think the family would have cause to be ashamed of you if you go around looking like that!"

Zephyr eyed his back for a moment amusedly, then with a comical face she remarked sweetly:

"Oh, you're what they call Victorian, aren't you? I didn't know there were any of those alive now. Aren't you an awful pain in the neck? You look so. Wouldn't it cheer you up to see me dance? Look!"

Zephyr gave a peculiar little fling out with one foot and set herself awhirling on the tip of one toe, until she was like a bit of thistledown in the sunshine, smooth golden head, pink face, staring baby-blue eyes, white arms and flashing, white, slim ankles, amid soft fluttering folds of orchid gossamer, all in a whirl on the dainty golden slippers.

Milton Page gazed in horror and disapproval for a full second, seeming unable to turn his eyes away. Then coldly he turned his back upon her and stared deliberately out of the window again, till with a final grimace she whirled away on her golden toes in search of coffee and rolls.

Milton stood there with wave after wave of furious

emotion marching over his irate soul. He stood, almost trembling, realizing that all his theories were unable to serve him adequately in a time like this, and that he was being swayed against his will, swayed, defied, laughed at! It was unforgivable!

He did not hear Rose come in sometime later. He had not seen her face in the street as she arrived. All the people passing were mere blurs while he tried to think how this family on whom he had relied so thoroughly, with whom he had almost allied himself, had suddenly failed him in every way and proved to be worse than worthless. It was not surprising of course that Ned would marry that sort of a girl. But it was beyond belief that Doris would harbor her in the house even for an hour.

Rose had spied him at the window and had hurried around to the back door and up the back stairs. She had made a hasty reconnoitre and found that both Doris and Florence were missing, so she smoothed her hair and went boldly down to discover how the land lay. There were times when Rose could be sweetly brazen.

She entered the living-room airily innocent. She bore no trace of the humiliation wherewith she had brought back her peace of mind. She came in breezily asking for Doris.

"Your sister has—" he paused, "gone out," he finished as if he could think of no word adequate to express what Doris had done.

"Oh!" said Rose, a bit confused. *"Why,* I wonder! Didn't she know that you were here?"

Milton Page swung around from the window and faced her challengingly.

"Sit down, Rose!" he ordered. He had always spoken to Doris' brothers and sisters as if they were somehow under his control and very young. Rose had generally resented his tone. She paused now, and hesitated by a chair, but she did not sit down.

"You want to see me?" she asked brightly.

"Yes. I want to see you, Rose." He fixed her with his cold eye, but Rose smiled pleasantly.

"*Where* did you find Doris' ring, Rose?"

"Ring?" said Rose composedly. "Oh, Jean had taken it up to Doris' bureau, and Doris was so upset with Ned's sickness that she hadn't noticed it. We had all been too busy to think about anything."

"Yes, I have been informed of that fact!" announced the cold, hard voice. "What I wish to know is *where* did *you* find it? That is, *where* did you find *the ring* which you gave to Doris and which she without looking at gave to me? Please be exact and answer my question. You will understand that I am fully aware that the ring which you gave to Doris was not her ring at all, but a cheap affair that might have come in a prize package of candy."

"What?" said Rose with a puzzled expression. "What can you mean?"

"I mean what I say. I wish to know what you have done with *Doris'* ring, and where you got the one which you gave her in its place?"

"Really!" said Rose with a toss of her front lock. "I don't think you'll find out much from me about anything as long as you take that tone and insinuate such outrageous things."

"I'm not insinuating anything. I'm merely stating facts and asking a question," stated Milton. "How do you explain this ring?" and he handed her the ring which Doris had left lying on the brim of his hat.

Rose gave it a glance and began to laugh.

"Explain it," she said. "Why, this way! Doris and I have been moving in together to make room for a new sister-in-law that Ned has brought home. This is some

278

old trinket that has been left lying around and Doris in her hurry got the wrong ring to give you. Wait, I'll go up and see if I can't find the other ring. I'm sure it's on her pincushion right where I put it when I found it."

She ran upstairs lightly, and was back in a moment with the ring, triumphantly holding it out to him.

"There it is!" she said haughtily. "Look at the initials inside if you don't believe me!"

Milton took the ring as if he saw a ghost. He examined it carefully inside and out, turned it this way and that to catch the light, and his eyes seemed to gloat over the color and lustre. Then he looked up at Rose, and his glance hardened. He cleared his throat. He seemed unable to get the words to express himself.

"You! You! You!—" he began.

"Yes, I found it," said Rose airily. "It was there on the pincushion right where I thought it was. You must excuse Doris. She has had so many burdens to bear. She is all upset, with Ned's illness, and his wife and everything. It was all so unexpected. Now, if you will excuse me, I must go and order the marketing." And Rose walked out and left him alone with the ring.

An hour later when she came back tiptoeing cautiously along the hall, and peeped carefully in at the crack of the living-room door, the room was empty. Milton and his ring had departed. But Rose stood a long time looking soberly out of the kitchen window, starting at every sound she heard, hoping it was not Doris, and wondering what she was going to tell her sister about the ring. For it was certain now that she could not tell her the truth. The thing had become most complicated. Still, Milton had the right ring at last, which was a comfort.

But Florence had not even that comfort.

In terrible trepidation she had put on her street things and hurried away to Hamilton's office, her heart throbbing wildly. It seemed her only hope now, and she could scarcely keep back the tears as she journeyed along in the trolley car, for she no longer had the price of a taxicab.

She had to wait almost an hour in Mr. Hamilton's office for he was in conference when she arrived and could not be disturbed, and when she finally reached his presence she was so distraught and incoherent that he could scarcely find out what was her errand. Gently he soothed her, and besought her to tell him her troubles, and at last, between subdued little sobs, she got it out.

"I'm so ashamed, Mr. Hamilton, to have to ask, when you've been so kind, but I must have some money! I really must. An article of value that is very dear to me is in the pawn shop. I placed it there when I expected to have plenty wherewith to redeem it, but now the time is up and I shall lose it forever if I am unable to redeem it before evening."

"Oh, is that all!" said the lawyer relieved. "Of course I'll attend to it at once. Just give me your pawn ticket and I'll have the office boy run down and bring it back. You can wait here till he comes."

"No, Mr. Hamilton," said the widow in alarm. "That is most kind of you of course, but I'm sure the man will not let anybody but myself have it. In fact I have made that arrangement. You see I have been trying for a week to get the money together. I sold several other things that were worth a little, and still I have not got quite enough. You see, it was most unfortunate. I lost my pocketbook containing the pawn ticket, and the owner of the shop refused to let me have my property without the ticket. I have searched everywhere, and even advertised, but with no results, and now he has finally agreed to let me have my property for the sum of one hundred dollars, and I have signed an agreement that I will bring the money before four o'clock this afternoon, or else give up all claim to it."

"But my dear lady, you should never put yourself in the hands of these sharpers. You should have asked me to look after the matter for you—"

"Yes, I know now," sighed Florence. "You are so kind, but you see I've always been of such a confiding and trustful nature. It never occurred to me that the man would take advantage of a poor woman all alone."

Hamilton wanted to go with her to the shop, but she finally shook him off, and went her triumphant way with one hundred dollars in new crisp ten-dollar bills folded neatly inside her silk hand-bag, and gripped like a vise to her heart.

When she wended her devious way at last to the shop which she had fairly haunted for the last few days, it was only to be told that the ring was no longer in the man's possession.

"De odder lady come got it," he said looking at her stupidly. "'Bout a hour ago! She got it!"

"But you promised me you would not sell it until after four o'clock. It is not two o'clock yet. I signed an agreement and I have the money here, one hundred dollars!" the widow shrilly pleaded.

"Yes, but de odder lady she pay two hundred fifty dollars. I couldn't affort to keeb my bromise."

That ended it. No amount of pleading or reproaches had any effect on the stolid keeper of the shop. The ring was gone. He had his money. He did not know the name of the lady that came after the ring. She had mentioned the police. That was enough for him.

"I will get a policeman, too," threatened Florence in her frenzied tone, high and shrill.

"You have only got a hundred tollars, matam. You can't do nodding mit de bolice!" He blinked at her from behind his great goggles and Florence, never famed for her logic, stumbled blindly out into the street and began to wander, where she knew not.

She sat in the park a long time trying to think a way out of her misery, and finally as the shadows grew long on the grass she got up, stiff with weariness and cold, blind with her fancied troubles, and the weight of a conscience newly roused by fear, and stumbled on, toward the centre of the city, with only a vague idea of where she was going. She had decided to try and find a position and leave the children forever. They would be glad, she was sure, and she would not have to answer questions.

But she pitied herself so violently that the tears kept streaming down her cheeks and mingling with the darkness caused by her thick veil, so that her vision was anything but clear, and more than once she held up traffic while she made an uncertain way across a street, piloted by an impatient policeman.

About six o'clock, John, pedalling away on his bicycle, threading among the evening traffic in a marvellous manner, narrowly escaping death from moment to moment, and whistling on his unconcerned way, came suddenly upon a denser crowd than usual, and finding it impenetrable, dismounted to find out the cause.

A traffic cop was shouting loud things to a truck driver, and admonishing the crowd to keep back. John forthwith came forward to see why, and worming his way between men and women, caught a glimpse of a little huddled figure in black lying still upon the ground, a small black silk bag clutched tight in a small gloved hand. It was the peculiar clasp of the bag that caught his attention in his brief glimpse. A lion's head in brass, with green glass eyes. He had been kept home from a circus once for fooling with a clasp like that, trying to pry out the eyes. There might be two bags like that in the world,—but—!

Someone drew back the veil and John caught a glimpse of a white face.

"Aw Gee!" he breathed under his breath, *"Aw Gee!"*

He waited until the ambulance came, and then he sidled up to the policeman:

"Say, where they gonta take 'er?"

"S'maritan!" muttered the policeman, waving his hand at an automobile that was trying to sneak by signals.

John mounted his bicycle and rode at the tail of the ambulance.

John arrived home very late for dinner.

Doris, weary and hectored, was beginning to worry about him.

"John, when you have to stay late at the store I wish you'd telephone," said Doris, almost crossly.

"I didn't have to stay late," said John sitting down at his place before the steaming plate of stew which Rose placed there. "I ran into an accident!"

"Well, eat your dinner and don't talk now," said Rose snappishly. "I want to get washed up."

John filled his mouth with stew, and then looked up at Doris.

"I thought you'd wantta know," he managed between chews. "Flarnce is in the S'maritan hospital! Thought you might wantta send 'er some flowers!"

"What!" exclaimed both girls in consternation. "Florence in the hospital! How do you know?"

"Took her there!" said John helping himself to butter and spreading it a quarter of an inch thick on his bread. "Got any jelly? Gee, I'm holla!"

"John! Stop eating and tell us what happened! Quick!" demanded Rose shaking his shoulder impatiently.

"Well, ya told me to eat first!" growled John. "I was gonta tell ya. Why, ya see Flarnce musta got all tangled up in traffic, and she got in the way of a truck driver. He was half-stewed I guess anyhow, an' he ran 'er down, an' she's got a busted leg, an' a fractured arm, an' her face all messed up. Oh, she ain't dangerous ef that's what ya mean. She'll pull through, the doc said. But she's gotta stay there awhile. Good thing to have her safe awhile till things get clearer here, I think. She had most a hundred dollars in her bag so I let her have a private room, an' I guess she'll be happy. Anyhow we don't havta have another nurse around waitin' on her! An' if you ast me, *I* say it's providential!"

22

DORIS wondered as she took her weary way to the hospital, how she was ever going to bear the added responsibility and anxiety of a new catastrophe. It seemed that her cup was more than full; dark cloud above dark cloud, piled higher and higher. Was there ever coming a rift in the darkness?

Mrs. Dunbar was slightly under the effects of an opiate, and suffering comparatively little pain. She seemed pleasantly aware of her prominence, and almost pleased at the attention bestowed upon her.

"I almost believe she is glad she got hurt!" said Doris to Rose when at last she reached home and laid aside her hat and coat. "Oh dear! I'm so tired I don't know but I'd be glad to lie down and be sick a while too!" and she cast herself down on the bed with a sudden rush of tears, a thing that was so unusual for Doris that Rose was appalled.

"Now, Dorrie, don't you give up or I can't stand it!" she cried out in dismay, and the sharp appeal of anguish in her tone reached Doris and brought her up smiling through her tears.

"I won't Rose," she said dashing away the bright drops from her eyes. "It's only that I'm dog-tired and can't see the way ahead."

"Well, perhaps that's just as well," mused Rose. "If we could always see ahead and know what was going to happen we wouldn't be able to go on. If anybody had told me two weeks ago that my father was going to die, my brother marry a fool, my stepmother break her leg, and our money take wings and fly away, I think I should have just given up. I don't know how I shall go on. I just can't make things come right no matter how much I try."

"Poor little girl!" soothed Doris. "I shouldn't have given way. It must be wretched for you, just coming into a good time in life to have things break down around you this way. But cheer up, dearie. It won't always be so. I'm just certain there will come a bright place later on. You know rain never lasts forever."

"Oh, well," said Rose recklessly, "I don't care. What's life anyway but a rotten old experiment? You just have to dash in and get what you can out of it or you get left behind."

"There are worse places than behind, sometimes, dear. Now, forget it and go to sleep. We are going to have a good time to-morrow getting ready to move. Let's make a game out of it. I think it will be real fun. Chloe has the living-room and dining-room all cleaned, windows and all. If we like we can begin to pick out things that are to go and send up a load in a day or so. The quicker the better."

Rose murmured some careless reply and turned over, closing her eyes, but it was long before sleep visited her. Her conscience was at work. Had she been justified in the promises she had given in order to get that money for the ring? Probably Doris would not approve, but

Doris would never need to know. She must get some money together at once somehow to repay the loan she had asked, and then she would no longer be under obligation. Oh, if she only knew somebody who would let her have it for to-morrow! She was tortured with the look that had accompanied the ready reply to her request. She hated the eyes that had been upon her. She spent hours calculating how many weeks she would have to work in the movies at five dollars a day before she could repay that money. Five times six were thirty, and sometimes they might want her to work Sundays, but she would never do that, not even to get her debt paid sooner. Besides she couldn't for Doris would find out— and then her brain would whirl back to the beginning again and she would toss and turn and berate herself for being so foolish. As if she was to be tied down for the rest of her life to going with people her father had approved. Daddy didn't like her to go with Colonel Carruthers just because he was a few years older than she was. But what difference did that make for an evening's frolic? She could take care of herself anyway. If Colonel Carruthers was willing to be kind to her and show her a good time and help her in an extremity she ought to be glad to return his kindness by giving him a pleasant evening. Of course he flattered her, saying all that stuff about how beautiful her eyes were, and her lovely smile. That was rot, and she didn't care for it. But he was nice to her and bought grand chocolates, the most expensive kind, and was always ready to take her wherever she wanted to go. Of course she had never been with him but twice before, and then Daddy had found out and forbidden it. But if Daddy knew now how she simply had to go to him to borrow that money to redeem Doris' ring, surely Daddy wouldn't mind. And anyhow, she was her own mistress now and must do what she thought right. But if only that horrid little pawn-broker hadn't been such a pig and asked all that money! And then she wept softly into her pillow and so at last fell into an uneasy sleep.

The days that followed were strenuous.

Everything seemed to fall upon Doris to decide. Rose got the meals, and worked feverishly in the kitchen, but she was crabby and nervous, and seemed to take no interest in preparing the new home. Doris, if she had not been too busy to give up, would have almost despaired at the way the whole matter fell upon her shoulders.

She must decide what furniture to sell and what to keep, what to store in the old barn at Silver Ledge, and what to set up for daily use. She must see a carpenter and arrange for various repairs to be made. She must wheedle the movers into taking a load late every day after their regular day's work was over, so that she could send a little at a time and put it in order before the coming of more. She must stand between the two nurses and Zephyr when there arose any question, and she must wait on and bear the brazen impudence of her new sister-in-law. She must go in to smile at Ned as if everything was pleasant as a May morning, and she must visit Florence every day at the hospital, taking her flowers and dainties which there was no money to buy and no time to prepare. She must even take time occasionally to read to her, for Rose flatly declined to do so, and she must look after John and Jean in the intervals. There was little time left for her to think about her new job. Indeed, two or three times she wondered if she would not be obliged to return that three hundred dollars advance salary and give up the job. How was she to get time to amuse Mrs. Macdonald with all she had on hand? How could she honestly receive money for work to which it was impossible under the circumstances to give a moment's preparation?

Then there would come the alarm of the thought, what could she do *without* that salary? How could they go on at all if she gave it up?

The days passed, and still she did not receive final word from Macdonald of the date of his going.

At last one morning it came. A long fat envelope with all the papers and final directions. She put it aside until she should go to the house later and could read it at her leisure. But a little note written in a quaint elderly hand and bearing a crest in silver on its heavy, gray envelope, she opened with a passing wonder.

It was from Angus Macdonald's mother, and it stated that the next evening was to be Angus' last dinner at home before his starting. Would she be so good as to eat it with them? It would give great pleasure both to Angus and herself. She was asking her as a little surprise for Angus. The car would call for her at half past four if quite convenient.

Doris felt a thrill of something—she thought it must be pride perhaps—she could not quite name it; and then a wave of almost shame. This dear old lady was taking her for something that she was not. It was not right to let her go on thinking that she and Macdonald were more than strangers. And yet, this was just the attitude he wanted her to take in order to carry out his beautiful wish to give his mother pleasant companionship. It was a curious situation, where right seemed on both sides. What was she to do? Under her contract there was nothing for her to do but go ahead and accept this invitation. Doubtless the son had been working things around for this very thing, and yet she could not ask him for the mother said it was to be a surprise.

Well, what harm could possibly come after all? The

son was going away. She would try to get the mother interested and happy and make her forget that she thought her a friend of her son's. If worst came to worst she could even tell her the whole arrangement, if that ever seemed necessary. She must not forget to make that stipulation to the son, that if it ever came to a matter of telling the strict truth she was to be allowed to reveal the plot.

And so Doris dropped everything and went to dinner at the Macdonalds' and the coast was unexpectedly clear for Rose to carry out her promise to Colonel Carruthers without fear of being detected. Of course she would be safely at home long before Doris arrived.

That dinner was like a little bit of heaven to weary, soul-tried Doris.

It was a simple meal, perfectly cooked and perfectly served, and the pleasant conversation made the girl forget that this was not just a friendly visit. She seemed among people whom she had known and loved a long time. Her eyes shone, and her cheeks glowed as they talked of all sorts of things out in the world where she had always longed to go. Scotland! What a charm the word had on the lips of the sweet patrician old lady. She could fairly see grim castle walls, and the billowing of the heather on the hillside! Little tales of Mrs. Macdonald's childhood in the old country! Tales of Angus' boyhood, and the tricks he used to play. Glimpses of the Scottish home of long ago where the father was the head of the household and the children feared with love and obeyed eagerly. Where "the big ha' Bible" came down every morning and evening and was read before them all, and then they knelt and prayed to a God they both loved and feared. Glimpses of the more modern American home where the father was still held in sweet and loving awe, and the Bible still had its place in the morning and evening. Not forced into the conversation, these things were merely incidental, but giving a background that Doris had never known.

And Angus Macdonald was a product of such upbringing! She found herself watching him and wondering what Ned and Rose would have been if they could have had such an environment. Poor Ned, with his coarse, pretty wife and his uncertain future! Poor Rose with her beautiful face and her eagerness for life, her hatred of the drab future that seemed now spread out for her!

And then she found herself shuddering to think what these people would think of her if they knew she had a sister-in-law like Zephyr. She made an inward resolve that she would keep her family entirely out of this relation. This was merely her business. It should be as separate from her home as a man's office usually was. Then perhaps there would be no harm about keeping her mortifications a secret.

Neither was the dinner-table lacking in merriment. Both Angus and his mother proved to have a keen sense of humor, and the conversation scintillated with bright stories and ready wit. Doris was delighted to find that her host and hostess could laugh over the things that seemed funny to her. She was at her very best, describing amusing incidents at college, retailing a grotesque conversation between a huckster and a lady of the back street, turning quaint little similes and sentences for which she had a trick, and in short being her sweet simple self.

She did not talk of herself or her family. She might have been utterly alone in the world for all this mother and son heard from her lips, yet she entered into their conversation as if she had known them always and fitted right into everything. More and more as the young man watched her he felt that he had done well in selecting for his purpose this one choice girl out of the multitude that had answered his advertisement.

And when it came time for Doris to leave, Angus Macdonald arose and declared his intention of driving her home.

But Doris protested.

"You must not think of doing that," she declared. "I can perfectly well go back with the chauffeur, and you should stay with your mother this last evening. She will want you."

There was quick appreciation in the glance the mother gave her, and her heart warmed at the look the mother and son gave one another, a long lingering clinging smile of understanding.

"Oh, Mother and I have a date together later," he explained. "We shall keep vigil all night to-night, I think. Did you ever happen to read the life of David Livingstone, how he and his mother sat up through the night before he left for the University? It's something like that, you see. An old family custom with us. I don't know if it's common in Scotland generally, but Mother and I keep it. You are not robbing her of her due! Besides, I have left a package at the office that should go in my trunk to-night, so don't feel that I am placing you under too great obligation."

The smile that passed between the mother and son was like that of lovers. Doris felt almost that she must lower her eyes, as if she had intruded unawares into a holy of holies.

Then the mother:

"Yes, go, Angus, and take the child safely home. I don't like the idea of sending her off with just a chauffeur. Now, dear, you'll come soon to see me, won't you? I shall be very lonely without my boy, you know, especially just at first. Come very soon, please. I want you."

"I certainly will!" said Doris earnestly, trying to keep the eagerness from showing too plainly in her voice, for in spite of herself this seemed a personal pleasure come to her, and not a business arrangement at all.

The way home was a pleasure too. They talked like intimate friends now, and he told her of places he expected to visit, and gave her a little idea of what his work would be abroad. It was as if he had opened a door into the rooms where he lived, where before she had only entered a sort of antechamber of his house.

To tell the truth, Angus Macdonald had carried about with him all day a note from Tamar Engadine bidding him come to her that evening.

There was a sense in which he felt great triumph that Tamar had stooped to summon him. Not since the night he left her at the road-house had he been near her or had communication with her. She had waited for him to return. She had been sure he would. They always did. It was her method to wait and be indifferent. It was most maddening.

And it would have brought him finally, Angus himself knew that. If he had been going to remain in his own country and pursue the usual tenor of his way, he could not have kept away from her long. The old lure would have reasserted itself. And so it was a triumph that she had stooped to call him. He could not help but feel exultant over it. The girl of flame whom other men had to beg for her favor. The very fragrance of her stationery as it rustled in his pocket brought a vision of her loveliness, her daring; her youth, that so easily excused her daring, so easily covered the things he did not admire. Sometimes he suspected in the back of his mind that Tamar Engadine was the very embodiment of the world, the flesh and the devil, which he had been taught to fear and avoid; yet always he had been haunted with the thought, why, oh, why might not he be the one who was heaven-appointed to win her back to all things good and beautiful and womanly? So now at the call of her note the temptation had been thrilling through him at intervals all day, till against his better judgment he had finally agreed with himself to go and say good-bye to her. He would not stay but an hour, but he would have that to remember, wherewith to compare her on his return. It was his right and hers, after the winter.

So he had brought Doris down to her home. She served as a pleasant screen to keep the knowledge of his intention from his mother. His conscience pricked him sharply at his mother's loving look and ready sacrifice of these last precious hours together. But all the way down to the city he was debating with himself, beginning to know that this call to Tamar was his weakness not his strength; that he was not being true to the best that was in him to answer it. It was true that this night belonged to his mother and must not be tarnished or discounted by any touch with a world that was alien to his mother's standards. He knew that if he went he could not look his mother straight in the eyes again before he left her, and he could not bear to leave her that way.

Doris so far had been a pleasant part of the change that was to come in his business life, but now as they rode along together under the stars something in her called to finer, higher things, and when he looked in her clear eyes at their pleasant casual parting she seemed to be more than just the fine girl he had hired to companion with his mother during his absence. She seemed to represent something of womanhood that was in his mother, a soul quality that lived for eternal things and not for self. It seemed to flame like a lamp and show him where his weakness would be.

So after all Angus Macdonald bade Doris Dunbar good-bye, almost reverently, and turned his car toward home. He did not even remember the package that should have gone in his trunk that night. He went back to the beautiful vigil with his rare mother. He was not thinking of Doris Dunbar then, so much as of the fineness that she represented, and the mother who was the embodiment of all that was fine and high and far from the world, the flesh, and the devil.

But afterward he remembered Doris.

Doris was filled with a new kind of elation as she entered her home. She had said good-bye to Angus Macdonald for an indefinite period, but she felt as if he had come into her life permanently. He was like a strong influence, a delicate perfume, sunshine, and air. Something impersonal which yet was hers to breathe and enjoy. It was pleasant to think she was to be in his employ even though he was to be far away. She hurried upstairs hoping that Rose was still awake that she might tell her a little about the beautiful home and the evening. Rose loved beautiful things and always enjoyed a joke or a bright saying.

But Rose was not in her room, and a whispered consultation with the nurse revealed that she had gone out soon after Doris had left.

Doris, worried, finally wakened Jean to inquire, but Jean only knew that Rose had left a note asking her to serve the dinner, saying that she would be back as soon as possible in the evening, but not to wait up for her.

Doris went and sat at the front window a long time waiting in the dark, her thoughts going back over the evening with pleasant remembrance, and forward over what she would do on her next visit, until the time slipped by without her realization, and only the sharp striking of the hour, one o'clock roused her to alarm. Where could Rose be? Was it possible she had gone into the movies after all, in spite of her promise, and they had kept her working late? Did movie people work at night? Her note to Jean had said she had gone for "something important." Poor impatient Rose! What had she done now? How could she stay so late and cause anxiety? And what ought she to do? At this hour of the night whom could she call upon to help! John was sound asleep and ought not to be waked on account of his work to-morrow. And what could he do anyway? He was only a child. The police? Well, of course young people of Rose's age stayed out till one o'clock to parties. The police would not think it strange. But she would not know where to set them searching. Rose would not have gone to a party so soon after her father's death. It was not like Rose to stay out and worry her. She must have known everybody would be in by this time.

The clock ticked on relentlessly and now and then a dark figure hurried past the house, or a taxi shot by. Once a cat shot across the street like a dark arrow and disappeared in a doorway. Doris was in torture.

It was not until five minutes after two when Doris was fairly frantic that a car drew up in front of the house and Rose sprang out. She did not wait for ceremonies, though a man got out evidently expecting to assist her. He came up the steps to remonstrate, but the key was already turning in the latch, and Rose made short ceremony of good-night.

"Oh Rose, where have you been? I've been so frightened!" said Doris appearing in the doorway.

"Mercy, aren't you in bed yet?" snapped Rose, her nerves evidently on edge. "I'm awfully sorry to have worried you. We had a flat tire, and miles from anywhere! I've been in torture to get home on your account of course but I couldn't do a thing! I just went out for a little ride."

Rose's eyes were averted. She was taking off her wrap and hat and running her fingers wearily through her hair. In the dim light from the upper hall her face looked flushed and excited.

"A ride?" said Doris. "Oh! And so late! I have thought of everything but that. Who did you go with, Anne Dryden's crowd?"

"Oh, a bunch! No, Anne wasn't along— Is there any coffee? I've got a splitting headache."

"You ought not to drink coffee at this time of night. Take a glass of milk. I'll get it for you. Who was the man that brought you home? It didn't look like Bert."

"It wasn't!" said Rose shortly. "He's one of the new ones. You wouldn't know him. His name is Carruthers. Eugene Carruthers."

"Carruthers," repeated Doris as she set down the glass of milk before Rose, "Where have I heard that name? It seems somehow associated with Father but—"

Rose looked up with uneasy glance:

"What kind of a time did you have? You look as glum as an oyster."

Doris told her a little of the evening, and then they went on tiptoe up to bed, but long after Rose was sleeping by her side Doris lay thinking, worrying about her young sister. Somehow there had been an unhappy excited look in her eyes that haunted her, and once Rose tossed her arms out over her head with a self-protecting motion and cried out: "Don't! I say! Don't you touch me!"

After that it was almost dawn before Doris finally dropped into an uneasy doze.

But in the morning there was no time to worry over

Rose. John was up and demanding his breakfast. Jean's school dress was soiled and another one had to be ironed. A telephone message from the hospital said that Mrs. Dunbar had passed a bad night and wanted Doris to bring a certain book and come right up to read to her as soon as possible after breakfast. The mover appeared at the door and said he could take those heavy pieces for the parlor right up this morning if they were ready at once, and the nurse wanted Doris to sit with Ned while she went downtown for something she needed and nobody else could select to please her. It was a hurried time, and Doris planned to go to Mrs. Macdonald that afternoon, and stop in the city to get a certain book she had heard of that she thought might interest her. It seemed as if everything came at once.

Zephyr, too, created a digression by calling up some of her friends and asking them to lunch with her. Doris was beside herself and Rose was furious.

"Let her get her own lunch, then," she said, "I'm not going to. I'll go to Silver Ledge and clean all day, but I won't cook for those slum friends of hers."

"Why of course," said Doris. "Let her get the lunch. Just leave something that the nurse can eat, and tell her we have to go out."

"Oh, all right," shrugged Zephyr, "I'll order in some things. Where do you have yer charge? Which caterer?"

"We have no charges now," said Doris soberly. "I'm afraid you'll have to pay for what you want. There are five dollars here on the sideboard. I guess that will have to do."

"Leave it to me," said Zephyr gaily, "I'll get 'em to charge it."

"But you mustn't!" said Doris firmly. "Mr. Hamilton has forbidden charging anything else. The estate is not settled up yet and it makes trouble."

"You should worry," said Zephyr. "All right, where's the money?"

"But you mustn't make a noise you know on Ned's account."

"Aw, rats!" said the wife charmingly. "You mustn't this, you must do that! No wonder Ned is sick! I'm almost sick myself!"

They heard her ordering pretzels and beer—root beer they supposed it was—and a whole gallon of ice cream, and cakes innumerable. Olives too, and salted almonds and mints."

"She'll never get all that for five dollars of course," said Rose. "I suppose I ought to have stayed at home and cooked for her old company."

"You couldn't, Rose. She oughtn't to have company now, anyway, while Ned is so sick. I know the doctor will think it is dreadful."

"Perhaps he will send her away then. I wish he would. Have we got to take her along with us when we move?"

"I suppose we have at least till Ned is well," sighed Doris. "I'm fixing the room up for them—the downstairs bedroom. I sounded out Florence and she said she wouldn't sleep there for the world."

"Well, if she's going to stay I think I'll find some way to get out," declared Rose sullenly. "I'm about sick of this. I don't see where we come in at all."

It was Rose's parting word as she got into the trolley to go to Silver Ledge. Doris took the trolley in the opposite direction for the hospital. Her car being at the garage for some slight repair that she might have it by afternoon.

Doris had been late in getting off. It was almost twelve when she reached the hospital. Florence was in tears and had to be petted, babied, talked to like a little child, and finally read to for an hour and a half before she would be pacified. It was half past one when the nurse at home called the hospital and asked if Doris was still there. Doris was just leaving and went to the telephone in alarm. What had happened now?

"Miss Dunbar, you better get home here quick! Them friends of Miss Zephyr are carryin' on high! They've got a lot of liquor, an' all of 'em's drinking, men *and* girls, an' smoking cigarettes, and howling like mad! They've smashed four glasses and a plate already, and they sound as if they'd just begun. If you say the word I'll call the perlice. I never saw such doin's in a decent household, and my patient is nearly goin' wild. There's some man here that he hates, and don't want his wife to speak to, an' she won't pay any attention. I've sent fer the doctor but he's away on a case an' dear knows when he'll get back. Can't you come quick?"

23

DORIS had to think hard and fast as she hurried away from the protesting Florence. In this new dilemma whom should she call upon for help? There was no possibility that a howling mob under the influence of liquor would yield to her request. The doctor was out of the question, and she shrank from bringing Mr. Hamilton again into the matter. Besides she knew that there was no way to reach him at this hour as he always went out of his office from one till nearly three.

Suddenly she recalled a former employee of her father's who was devoted to him because his family had been helped at a time of calamity. He was now on the police force, and would be glad to help her, if he were free at this hour.

She hailed a taxi and drove to the police station, and wonder of wonders, found Thomas just coming off duty. She recognized his broad back half a block down the street.

"Catch that policeman," she said to the driver. "I want to speak to him!" and in a moment more Thomas stood smiling with his hat off before her.

"Thomas, can you take a few minutes to help me?" she asked

"Shure! ma'am, a few hours if necessary," he responded heartily.

"Well, get in quick and I'll explain to you on the way."

He obeyed with alacrity.

They could hear the revellers even while Doris was fitting her key in the door. They were singing a riotous, rollicking song, with voices that were thick and coarse. Doris shuddered as she swung the door open, and hesitated on the threshold, but Thomas did not hesitate. He strode past her on feet that could walk as silently as doom. He swung wide the dining-room door, his badge at display, and stood his tallest in the doorway looming grim and forbidding.

They did not hear him till he was among them, and a sudden awful silence succeeded the ribald laughter. Zephyr had been dancing. The table was shoved to one side of the room, all in a huddle of bottles and plates of melted ice cream, and Zephyr whirled in the middle of the room. But she stopped as if frozen, her baby stare growing fixed and china-like.

"Now, you fellers clare out!" Thomas' voice was low and clear but he spoke with a tone of authority that struck terror to the revellers. With drunken defiance one slim fellow sidled up to Thomas with a rude:

"What'r you doin' here?"

Thomas took hold of his spindly shoulder with his great hand and shook him as if he had been a sick kitten.

"Now, you git out of here!" he said and sent him hurling with a great push toward the front door which was still standing open. The girls looked frightened and stole away to the other room to secure their hats and hand-bags. Two of the men slid out to the kitchen, but

Thomas with a swift stride was at their heels and covering the men with his revolver:

"Here! You two. You're wantid at the station house! Hands up! Now, stand right where yer are and don't shtir! Miss Doris, would ye mind phonin' to the station house an' askin' thim to sind Pete with the car? Tell him Tom says to bate it! And be still about it, too. This is two that was wanted in that raid they had last wake in the tenth ward."

And so the wagon of terror drew up before the Dunbar door and Pete and Tom emerged presently with two cowed and furtive prisoners. But the rest of the guests had all melted away like snow before the morning sun.

"You'd bist go lay down, Miss!" Thomas, as he departed, had advised to the still staring Zephyr as she stood amid the debris of her lunch party like an angry image.

She only stared.

But when Doris came in and looked about the dining-room aghast Zephyr came alive, roused to fury.

"You'll pay for this, you sneak!" she hissed. "You said you were going away! You just hung around to catch my boy-friends. I'll see that you get what's coming to you. The whole gang'll be down on you fer this!" and making an evil face she fled upstairs.

Doris sat down amid the wreckage of the dining-room and buried her face in her hands. It was not so much that Zephyr had defied her, or that things were in a mess. It was the terrible humiliation of belonging to a girl like that. And *her brother had done it!*

By and by she roused herself and gathered up the broken crockery, swept the floor and straightened the furniture. Then she went upstairs and dressed all over again for her visit to Mrs. Macdonald. Her heart was sick. How could she go and face that beautiful old lady coming from a home like this? It seemed as if she ought to confess that she was unfit and give up the position.

But she was under obligation of course, and must go, whether or no.

The nurse promised to see that Zephyr did no more damage that afternoon.

"She'll sleep!" she said with a knowing nod.

So Doris went off as soon as her car was brought from the garage, trying to summon a bright smile wherewith to cheer a lonely mother.

Just as she was going out the door the postman handed her a single letter, and she saw with a little flutter of pleasure that it was from Angus Macdonald. Probably some last direction, something he had forgotten, but it made a diversion from the tense strain under which she was living. Oh, if Angus Macdonald knew, if he had known, what she came from, what her brother was, what a wife he had, would he ever have selected her to help his mother? His wonderful mother! Doris tucked the letter in her pocket and got into her car, her cheeks burning with shame at the remembrance of the scene, just past, in the dining-room. It seemed to her that her soul was smirched with it, and she would never come clean again. What would their father have said to know that such a thing could have happened in their house a few short days after his death! Dear Father! He was safe from it all! But what was before the rest of the family all the long dreary days of a normal life? The outlook seemed as black as an outlook could possibly be.

In the shade of a great group of maples Doris drew her car to the side of the road and read her letter.

My dear Miss Dunbar, (it read)

It came to me on the way home last evening that I have never told you how glad I am that you are you, and that you have been willing to undertake my commission. It gives me pleasure to feel that I have left my mother in such good hands, and I thank you for having accepted the work. I trust it may prove not altogether irksome to you, also.

With all good wishes,
Angus Macdonald.

It was as if someone had suddenly poured a cooling liniment upon a burning wound. The courtesy of it, the pleasant personal word! All that made the difference between labor and joyful work! And so unnecessary, so absolutely kindly! It came upon her spirit with its healing touch just when she was sore and humiliated by the scene through which she had passed, and it lifted her beyond the valley of depression where her soul had fallen helplessly, and set her on the heights again, where she might exult in spite of sordid things.

Now she could go on her mission with a free mind!

What a man he was to have done it. In all his hurry to have taken the time! Not that it meant anything personal of course, but it was so nice of him to let her know before he left that he had confidence in her. It made her strong for what she had to do.

She started her car with a quick joyous motion, and the sunlight and gay spring atmosphere began to penetrate her soul and put new life into her. She saw a thousand beauties as she passed that had been locked from view behind dull unseeing eyes before. She heard a lark in a meadow, the lowing of a cow, the bleat of sheep, and noted the soft blending of colors in the new foliage that had crept out as it were overnight. Her thoughts bounded ahead to plan her visit, and she forgot home and all her perplexities. Somehow the humiliation of Zephyr and her companions fell away like a soiled garment that was not hers, and she knew herself to be not really bound by what anyone else, even of her own family, did. She was herself, and accountable for her own character. She would be judged thereby. The confidence that her employer had given had lifted her above her fears and given her peace. And something she did not understand, that made her glad, rang sweetly far away in her consciousness. She did not even try to analyze and name it. She rested in it and was glad.

Mrs. Macdonald was glad to see her. She knew it at once by the light that sprang into her keen bright eyes. It reminded her of the look in her son's eyes.

She knew at once that the old lady had questioned whether she would care to come now that her son was not to be there. She could see that she had been waited for almost anxiously, and that there was a relieved joyous look on the old lady's face that filled her own heart with a new kind of ecstasy. She was going to really love this old lady. It was almost as if she had been handed over a mother of her own, she who had not had a mother for so long.

They had a beautiful time together, first walking about the garden, examining the budding things, and searching for the shooting plants whose time of resurrection was come again. Then they went into the house and up in the great sunny circular room that was the old lady's special private boudoir. There were seats built in under the windows and wide views into the valley where the shrubbery had been cut away. There was a bookcase full of special choice books, and there were a few rare pictures on the walls, originals; and one of a castle in Scotland where Mrs. Macdonald had lived when she was a child.

The time was almost gone before she realized that she was not the one to be entertained, and that if she would make opportunity for a speedy return it was necessary to propose something herself.

"What wonderful books you have!" she exclaimed looking around panic-stricken for a chance to bring in some suggestion, for she knew she must presently take her leave. "I am hungry for books since I left college but it is so stupid to study all alone! How I would love to read or study something with you! You are so widely read and have such beautiful thoughts of your own about the books you read!"

Her cheeks reddened as she said it. She felt as if it must be so obvious that she was trying to drag herself into companionship.

The older woman's face brightened:

"Why, that would be charming!" she said. "What would you want to study—or read?"

"Oh anything!" said Doris eagerly. "Anything in which you were interested! It would be wonderful for me. Something to get my thoughts away from everyday perplexities and out of myself. I don't want my mind to vegetate!" she laughed half nervously like a very young girl. She felt she was managing this thing badly. She must be appearing almost forward to have asked such a thing so abruptly. It was not at all as she had planned it. She had meant to wait a week or two at least before asking anything so important.

"I think I should like it very much, my child," said Mrs. Macdonald thoughtfully. "I really have been terribly lonely since my husband left me. He and I used to read and study together a great deal. Angus has been so busy lately, and away so much. Had you anything in mind you wanted to study? I may not be up to a modern college girl. We are years apart you know, dear, and I'm afraid I might be but a stupid companion."

"Indeed! Never!" said Doris with sincerity. "I should

love to take up something that you are interested in. I've never had—at least I scarcely remember, my own mother. It would be good to get an older person's point of view. Besides, you don't seem old—"

Mrs. Macdonald smiled tenderly.

"That's very sweet of you, dear."

"Then won't you tell me what would most interest you? Isn't there some book—? Some special line of study?"

"Why yes—" said the Scotch woman pleasantly. "There is, a very special book, an old book—but I could scarcely hope that even so rare a girl as you would find interest enough in it in this modern day of skepticism as to spend time with an old woman studying it."

"Oh, try me!" exclaimed Doris eagerly. It was going to be so much easier if the old lady would choose her own subject. Then she would feel free to say when she wearied of it. Doris' job was to keep Angus Macdonald's mother interested, not to please herself.

"Very well, child, if you say so. It's just the 'auld Buik'," she said, reverting to her childhood's dialect, "'the big ha' Bible!'"

Doris' eagerness went blank, though she managed to keep a bright face. How was she to keep a woman amused reading the Bible? Would she not grow gloomy and long-faced? And what would Angus Macdonald say when she reported that the only study his mother would take up with her was the Bible? Was that keeping her contract? Well, there was nothing for it but to go ahead now. She had brought it on herself of course. But perhaps it would serve at least as an opening wedge, and she might be able to interest the mother in brighter, more cheerful subjects a little later on when their friendship had become better established.

All these thoughts flew swiftly through her mind

while she made haste to assure Mrs. Macdonald that nothing would be more unusual and delightful than to look into so great a book with a mind so wise as her new friend's to guide her.

"Of course I studied it a little in college. Everyone had to. But I didn't really get hold of the beauty of it." She spoke as if it were merely a great literary treasure.

"Yes?" answered the gentle-voiced lady, studying the girl's face wistfully. "Well, we shall see how it turns out. It is a book which must be studied in the right spirit, you know, or its wonders are sealed. You cannot take it like an ordinary book. You must have an open mind and a believing heart."

There was something in the elder woman's voice that startled the girl, as if great wisdom hung somehow upon her words. She could not get away from the feeling that she was to be the one helped and led along, not the woman she was there to amuse. Yet withal, she came away satisfied. She had at least paved the way to be often with Mrs. Macdonald, which had been the first step outlined by her son in order to fulfill his wishes.

An hour later, after promising to come to the great house on the hill sometime the next day and plan out their course of study, she drove swiftly away in the dusk to get Rose, for she had promised to take her home. Poor Rose! What would she think of her, coming so late? And how many things she had to tell her! Rose! What should she do about unhappy impatient beautiful Rose?

Rose was sitting on the front stoop in the gloaming, watching impatiently, resolved to take the next trolley home if Doris did not arrive before it did, and she climbed in beside her sister with relief.

"Well, I should say you made a day of it, Doris. What did you think I'd do in the dark all alone? I'm starved too, and I hadn't money enough to get anything to eat. I only had car fare and didn't dare spend it for anything to eat, lest you wouldn't come."

"You poor kid!" said Doris contritely. "But I really couldn't help it. If the telephone had only been finished I might have let you know. I was delayed beyond anything. You don't know. Listen!" and Doris retailed the story of Zephyr's doings and the grand finale, while Rose sat aghast with sober face. When the story was over she exclaimed earnestly:

"I say, I don't think it's fair! You so patient and good and giving up everything for us all, your diamond ring, and getting married and all, and then having to bear all these things! Doris, you must be Job's niece or something! I never heard of any one girl having to bear so much! You better get out on the ash heap and hunt for a potsherd and give us all up!"

"Why pick on me?" laughed Doris merrily. "Aren't we all bearing it together? I'm no better than the rest of you. You're all just as brave and dear as can be!"

"No, we aren't!" said Rose vehemently. "We're a mean selfish lot, and you are just carrying us all along on your shoulders. I'm the selfishest of the lot! Oh dear! I can't bear it for you!" and Rose unexpectedly broke down and cried as if her heart would break.

"Why Rose, *dear!*" said Doris in astonishment. "Don't take it to heart like that! I'm no more a relation of Job than you are. Cheer up, and let's get some fun out of it somehow. Don't let it beat us. I insist there is coming a bright place somewhere, and somehow things are coming out. I don't know *how* I know it, but the other day when I was so down I walked a long way off from houses and everything and saw a storm coming with clouds as dark as night piled up in awful threatening, and suddenly the sun burst through, and I couldn't help feeling— Oh, I don't know how to talk about such things. But I just *know* we are going to be taken care of somehow. I feel it in my heart!"

"You're *good!*" said Rose. "I'm not. I don't know as I ever could be."

The earnestness of her tone disturbed Doris, and reminded her of other fears about this beautiful eager little sister, who loved and hated so tremendously, and lived on impulse always. But they were drawing up to the door now and there was no further time for talk, so she put away anything she might have replied for a more convenient season and they hurried in to get a much belated supper.

They found Zephyr still sleeping, and the nurse inclined to be lenient with them about the lateness of the meal. She was grimly proud of Doris and the summary way in which she had handled the mob in the dining-room. She had evidently told the story to John and Jean for they had cleared up the dining-room thoroughly and done their unskilled best to help prepare a meal. There were potatoes baking in the oven and John had opened numerous cans of vegetables and fruits. The menu was varied and peculiar, but it made things much easier for the two tired girls; and the children stayed around afterwards and helped wipe dishes.

It was later, when the two sisters had gone to their room, and were preparing to drop down on the bed and rest and talk a few minutes, that the door-bell rang.

"I'll go," said Rose springing up. "You've taken your hair down. And I know you are tireder than I," and she sped swiftly away. But in two or three minutes she was back again, with a grimace on her face. She had just let in Milton Page.

"Well, you'll have to get up after all," she said glumly. "Bildad the Shuhite is down there!"

"Who?" said Doris with a puzzled frown. "I never heard of him. What does he want?"

"Oh, sure you did!" said Rose. "You studied the greatest dramatic poem in the world with Miss Mellon and the lit class same as I did. Don't you remember Bildad, one of Job's three friends? He's come to tell you why all this has come upon you. He met Thomas and Thomas thought the story was too good to keep and now Bildad has come to tell you why it happened to you. Hurry up and get your potsherd and come down and let him have his little say. Then we'll stand some chance of getting to bed to-night, but Doris, don't give in and let him think he's right, for he *isn't!* I'll *bet on you every time!*"

"Oh, Rose! You'll kill me with your ridiculous nonsense! I'm too tired to laugh! Go to bed and don't wait for me. I suppose this had to come some time as well now as any time. I hoped he was through!"

And Doris went downstairs with her most Jobine smile on her lips. She was thinking that she was glad that it did not really matter to her any more what Milton Page thought about anything that happened to her. There was someone greater than Milton Page looking after her affairs. She did not know how she knew this or why, but just the trying to tell Rose that evening had strengthened her faith.

24

ANGUS MACDONALD on shipboard in his leisure moments found his thoughts straying to his home and especially to the last few hours spent there. He found himself describing things around him on the ship to the girl whom he had so summarily called out of the unknown into his circle of acquaintances. He thought of her now not as one who was in his service, but as a friend, and one with a singularly true and interesting personality. He could not help wondering what she would say for instance if she were standing by his side on deck watching the opal-tinted sea with the last reflection of the dying sunset upon its smooth surface. He looked up to the stars later and remembered how they had stopped the car in the pine grove and looked up at those same stars a few nights before. And then he suddenly realized that for a man who was not given to having much to do with girls he was spending altogether too much thought on this new acquaintance. It was natural of course that he should try to fathom her character before he set her in so close and intimate a relation to his mother, but that was done now and the necessity passed. Let him put her aside as something with which he had no more to do. She would do her work and make her report and until he had to read it and pass upon it he need not further consider her.

And then he thought of Tamar Engadine.

It occurred to him that he should write her a brief note of apology for not appearing in answer to her call. He was grimly glad that he had been strong enough to stay away. Perhaps a bit vengefully glad too. He really must write that note at once so that it might be ready to go back on the pilot boat.

But instead he sat down and wrote that note to Doris!

He felt almost sheepish about that. He went and put it in the mail quickly to get it out of his mind. He knew that if he thought it over he would consider it both foolish and unnecessary and that he would not send it. So he mailed it.

Then he went back to his stateroom and wrote to Tamar.

My dear Miss Engadine:—

Preparations for a sudden and important business trip made it impossible for me to accept your kind invitation of last evening. I hope that your expectations of a pleasant occasion were fully realized, and that someone more fortunate than I was able to take any part I might have had.

I am sure you will pardon this hasty apology, for my time is short, and believe me,

Very sincerely,
Angus Macdonald.

That too he mailed quickly, and went back to the stars and his thoughts. His message to his mother had been longer and written soon after he came on board.

Angus Macdonald did not quite understand himself,

he found that he was so much more interested in the home that he was leaving than he had expected to be. He kept wondering if Doris Dunbar would be able to carry out her purpose with his mother, and how her ingenuity would work in with his mother's quiet purpose to order her life serenely along the lines she had always lived. Poor Mother! He knew what a wrench it was for her to give him up for these months of separation. He knew how hard it was for her reserved Scotch nature to take in a stranger and yet how graciously and charmingly she had taken in the girl whom he had brought home! His conscience pricked him that he had deceived her even so slightly, and unintentionally. It had never entered his thought that she would take the girl for more than a casual acquaintance when he first proposed to bring her home; and it had served his purpose so well in more ways than one that it seemed harmless. Now alone with the sea and himself he had opportunity to look things in the face as he had not done for months. And he began to see plainly that Doris Dunbar and not Tamar Engadine was the kind of girl that would fit in with his mother's thought of her son and his future.

Having reached this point in his mental process when he was about three days out, he suddenly decided to turn his entire attention to his work, and the plan of his procedure which must be prepared from copious notes furnished by his partners in many sessions of conference.

Meantime, back at home things were progressing rapidly.

In the Dunbar household the movers suddenly appeared on the scene one morning and announced that they could "do" the house that day as someone else had gone back on them and they wanted to fill in the time. Having that morning received a violent letter from the new owner of the house demanding his property as soon as possible, Doris decided to let them go ahead, reserving only Ned's room and a few necessary articles for the nurse's comfort until the doctor should give the word that Ned was able to be moved.

Ned seemed to have reached a discouraging stand-still so far as recovery was concerned. Day after day he lay white and still, and seldom moved or spoke or opened his eyes unless compelled to do so. They had to urge him to take nourishment, and only Zephyr in a gay mood could move him to take interest in life.

But Zephyr was not in a gay mood. Since the incident of the revelry she had been sullen and silent. Her baby stare was wide and unseeing, but now it had taken on a more insolent air. The stare of a neglected doll in the corner, tragic because it cannot understand an unfriendly world, arrogant in spite of being downtrodden.

Zephyr was not downtrodden. She had the best in the house. If it was not offered to her she took it. If it was not in sight she demanded it. But she was not in the high spirits she had been when first she arrived. Her zeal at nursing had soon departed, and she left Ned alone hour after hour while she curled in a big chair in the living-room, ate chocolates and read endless moving picture magazines. She was let alone most severely by the family, who had enough to do without paying attention to her, but they were uniformly polite to her in all the simple everyday affairs of living. The children kept entirely out of her way. It was plain that she was ill at ease with Rose, who went on her beautiful scornful way and would have none of her. But Doris she hated, perhaps because she knew she was her superior, and that never, no matter how hard she might try nor how many times she might score against her, could she hope to attain to the heights on which she moved.

It was becoming plainer every day that she did not

really love Ned, but had loved only the power she thought her position as his wife would give her. It was plain that Ned was breaking his heart over her coldness. If Doris had not been so busy that she had no time to think about it, the situation would have been most impossible. She could not go to Zephyr and beseech that she be kinder to Ned. She could not send Zephyr away because Ned wanted her so much. And every day the time was drawing nearer when the whole family must be transplanted to the country. And what would Zephyr do then? How would they bear it to live in still closer quarters with this uncongenial alien? Would Ned have to go with her and her impossible mother? Doris did not dare to think about it. When the time came perhaps there would come light.

Meantime, Doris, in addition to moving her family, and visiting her stepmother at the hospital, had also entered upon an intensive study of the Book of books.

She had gone the very next day to see her new friend, hoping that perhaps through the night new ideas might have come, and that a more cheerful topic for study might be selected. But instead she found Mrs. Macdonald alert and interested, her eyes bright and happy. She had been thinking, she said. She had a plan. She hoped Doris would be willing to cooperate with her. Doris would, of course. That was what she was there for, and for the old lady to take the initiative was even more than either she or the son who had put her there had been able to hope might come, at least so soon.

"There is a Bible School in the city. This is a leaflet that they publish every month," said the old lady handing her a small paper. "I have for years been contributing money to the work, and I have been reading this pamphlet. There are some very striking articles in it by members of the faculty of this school. I would like you to visit that school for say two or three days, and go from class to class, at least if you can spare that time. I don't know how busy you are. Perhaps I may be presuming?"

Doris assured her that she would be glad to take as much time as was necessary to serve her friend's wishes.

"Well, then, I would like you to go from class to class and listen for a day or two and select us a teacher. Perhaps two if you think best. They teach different books, different parts of the Bible, you know, and there is no reason why we shouldn't have the most interesting one, or ones, if they will come. We will pay them of course, and send the car for them. Would you like to do that?"

"Why certainly!" said Doris politely, hoping Mrs. Macdonald did not see how dull the thing seemed to her that she had been asked to do. After all, it was all in the day's work. If she was earning a salary why not earn it? And some work must necessarily be disagreeable. But would this work in with the spirit of her employer's plan? Well, time would tell, and she could always report to him and ask advice.

So the very day the movers came she had to send Rose out to Silver Ledge to do her best at settling, while she took her way to a quiet section of the city and entered the doors of the Bible School.

Doris owned a Bible. It had been her mother's. There were verses marked in it in red ink, and sometimes as a child when a sentimental spirit of longing for her mother came upon her she had opened it and read over all the verses marked in red ink, searching, yearning for a touch of her mother through those scattered, underlined statements.

Various Testaments, also, prizes for good behavior and attendance at Sunday School, had come her way through the years, and passed out of her hand leaving no trace in her life of their matchless meaning. Even her brief and superficial study of the Bible in college had not made much impression upon her. She had enjoyed the beauty of diction, and the perfection of wisdom in some of the great passages, but she had never looked on Moses or Paul or Noah as real, living men, had never dreamed that the book contained the way of life, or traced the story of the Cross from cover to cover. She was as ignorant about it as a child.

And now when someone placed a Bible in her hands and she was told to turn to a certain passage she fumbled about among the leaves helplessly, till a plain girl with spectacles had to help her. She had come into a new world of which she knew nothing.

She heard mysterious talk of dispensations. She learned for the first time that some of the Bible was written explicitly for the Jews, some for the Gentiles and some for the Church. She heard of types, and symbolism, of the significance of different numbers, and the uniformity of these things throughout the holy word. She heard references to prophecies astounding in their detail which her own knowledge of current events could not but fit to the fulfillment. Attention was called to the mathematical perfection of the smallest detail of this wondrous book, of hidden acrostics, and invariable adherence to the plan of its whole structure throughout every smallest part; of continuity and consistency of the whole from beginning to end, so perfectly connected, and so fully quoted from part to part as to leave no doubt in the mind of the true scholar who was spirit led but that it had no human origin. Recent excavations were cited which made plain certain passages heretofore obscure, or thought to be in opposition to so-called science. These strange people spoke of science, reverently, it is true, but as if it were a babe in arms to be cared for tenderly, but not to be always trusted against the wisdom of its parents.

She was amazed and shaken. It was as if she had been looking through a sudden opening of a great door into a vast room of such proportion and such grandeur that her eyes were not able to contain nor differentiate between the wonders there displayed. Each beauty shone like a dazzling separate jewel, and things she had never been able to reconcile suddenly took place and fell into reasonableness without her knowing how. Of course, if all these things could be so, it made all the difference in the world. But she had never known before that there was anybody living who took the Bible literally for fact, with no fancy in its weaving. It had heretofore been to her a lovely parable, misty and obscure in its pattern, except in places where rare and well-known truths stood out against a charming but impossible background.

She was startled into wonder.

She sat still in that one room throughout the morning, and let teachers and classes change as they would around her. She heard many lines of teaching, some of which she understood, and more of which was filled with so many references to things she knew nothing about that she could make little sense of it. But somehow through it all she was stimulated with a great desire to know what they were talking about and judge herself whether this great breathtaking idea of what they called Truth were really true. If it were it meant the answer to the hunger of her heart. If it were it was the flaming sun calling through the dark storm clouds of life, calling and showing her that she was not all alone, no, not even if the earth reeled under her tottering feet. There was a Rock somewhere upon which she might stand.

And so staying through the morning she came at last to the final session of the day, and Job. For a moment, when the topic was announced, a smile trembled faintly to her lips at the memory of how Rose had jocosely called her Job's niece. How amused Rose would be to learn that she had been to a class on Job that day.

It was not like a sermon. It was like the revealing of a great truth; the answer to a great perplexity that had troubled her ever since she could remember; and more opportune just now when she was passing through trouble after trouble, and seemingly stripped of all that had made her life bright in the past.

Doris began to realize that she had unconsciously been trusting all these years to her own morality, her uprightness, and refinement, to save her from whatever her vague idea of a future punishment would turn out to be. She found that she had been leaning on herself to save herself.

It was not until weeks later, however, when she and Mrs. Macdonald came to study the last chapter of the wonderful book of Job that she understood that even the godly are afflicted and that not for anything that they have done wrongly, but that they may learn to know and judge themselves. As she looked at herself in the light of this revelation she could utter sincerely the words of Job: "I have heard of Thee by the hearing of the ear, but now mine eye seeth Thee. Wherefore I abhor myself and repent in dust and ashes."

When the first day at the Bible School was done she went back thoughtfully to the same old muddle that had been with her since her father died, yet somehow things were not quite the same. It was as if she had been given a key that would open a door into another place where she might rest and breathe and understand.

She carried with her in memory a verse that had been painted in beautiful letters over the arch of the platform in the classroom where she had sat: "Thy Word is a lamp unto my feet and a light unto my path," and over the hall as she went out was another, "The people that sat in darkness have seen a great Light."

Was it possible that the Bible had been meant to be that to men? And if it were true why had the world never known it? She had never known that even ministers knew all these things about the Bible that she had heard to-day. Why, if they knew and believed it, did they not shout it to the multitudes from the housetops and go out and compel people to hear?

She was peculiarly unprejudiced because she had not lived in a world that was religiously biased. Religion had scarcely touched her life in any way since her mother died when she was a little girl, and prayer and the Bible and even churchgoing to any great extent had drifted out of her life.

Back in the world again she began to think she had been overwrought and that the impressions she had received during the day had been unreal and not fitted for everyday life. Yet there was something in it all that drew her back again for another day before she could go to Mrs. Macdonald and make her report about teachers.

And the second day was like the first, only more deeply impressive, because by this time she understood a little more of the language that these strange, ardent people used.

By afternoon she had picked her teachers, one a sweet-faced woman with deep, earnest, brown eyes, who taught the book of Job, the other a white-haired man giving lessons on Revelation. With each she made a temporary arrangement that they were to come out to the Macdonald home at a near date and talk with Mrs. Macdonald about teaching a Bible class in her home. And on her way back she began to feel that she was committed somehow to a strange new way of living and thinking, and could not help wondering how it was going to work out. Also she knew that now she must write to Angus Macdonald and find out whether he approved of this whim of his mother's to which she was now so fully committed. For she could see now that there was no likelihood of the old lady becoming weary of so fascinating a study as this was going to be under these two ardent, consecrated teachers.

So she set herself to fully put forth the matter in a letter to her employer, giving her impressions of her day at the Bible School, and incidentally revealing her lack of education in the things that he knew best but had not followed fully.

Angus Macdonald when he received the letter put aside the books and papers that were scattered over his desk, and sat down to read it. When he had finished he read it over again.

That night he answered it, and among other things he said:

> *You have recalled to me my early faith, and the Book which I have sadly neglected. It is a great Book! I have been so engrossed with the world, and the Book of Science lately that I have forgotten there were all those things to be remembered above everything else. I am glad you are taking that up. I know nothing in the world that could delight my mother so much, and you certainly are fulfilling my highest wish for her if you have found the thing that will make her happiest. I half wish I were there to study with you. But I shall enjoy the lessons secondhand if you will be good enough to report to me in outline, as you promised to do about all that you and Mother are doing. Perhaps I can sort of keep in touch with the study too, although I am afraid I left my Bible at home, unless Mother tucked it in my trunk somewhere. But I guess*

*there are a few copies yet to be had in Europe and I'll find
one, and look up the Book of Job. I'm wondering why
that held any special interest for you?*

Meantime, at home, events were moving rapidly.

25

THE DUNBARS were moved at last.

The doctor had finally decided that it would be well to take Ned into the country. He seemed listless and weak, and perhaps if he could lie in a hammock out in the open air he might gain strength faster.

So he was taken carefully in a comfortable car that was hired for the occasion, with Zephyr on the front seat making pert remarks to the driver; Zephyr, for the first time roused by the ride out of the sullenness that had possessed her since her lunch party had been so summarily ejected from the house.

But when they reached Silver Ledge, even while they were helping Ned from the car to his bed, she stood to one side glaring about with her china-blue stare on the house, on the street, on the people who sauntered curiously by to watch the new arrivals. She looked more like a china doll than ever, as she turned her sleek head from side to side, disapproval in every line of her dolly-face.

The truck bearing the last pieces of furniture including Zephyr's two trunks came driving up and began to unload.

Zephyr sauntered over to one of the men, taking care to keep the loaded truck between herself and the house so that none of the family could see her.

"You've got two trunks in there," she said sweetly, "the very first things you put in. Remember? Well, it's a mistake. They're to go back to the city. They're mine and I didn't want them out here. You can leave them at the Central Station to be called for. Ask for Tim Johnson and give him this card. It'll be all right."

She handed the man a card and some money, and he agreed and went on with his work of unloading. When his assistant came back for another load he said: "Don't touch them two trunks in there. The young lady wants 'em to go back to the station."

Zephyr tripped away to the taxi driver.

"You're to wait here for me till I come out. I may be going back with you," she said, "and don't say anything about it to the rest? See?" And she handed him another bill. Then she hurried into the house and looked around.

They were settling Ned, exhausted, into his bed in the downstairs bedroom which Doris and Rose had made comfortable at the expense of the others. The room was gay with new chintz, the handiwork of Rose who was salving a guilty conscience by many works of supererogation. Ned looked around pleased, and smiled weakly. Zephyr would like it perhaps, it looked so pretty here. Then he closed his eyes and dropped into a doze. He was very tired from the trip.

Zephyr, while they were arranging his pillows, peered hurriedly into the other rooms, stole upstairs and looked around, curled a contemptuous lip and hurried down again. Then she came into Ned's room and announced roughly:

"I can't stay in this dump. I'd die. *I'm done! I'm going!* If you want me you'll have to come to town and live.

You know where to find me when you get ready. Good-bye!" And out the door she went and into the taxi. Before Doris and Rose had recovered their senses they heard the taxi starting. Looking out of the window they saw Zephyr composedly sitting in the front seat with the driver.

Doris went quickly over to the bed.

Ned had half risen from the pillow, his face blanched, his eyes filled with dismay. He looked as if Zephyr had struck him in the face. Just an instant he held himself up looking after her wildly, and then he flung out his arms with a cry:

"Oh, Zephyr!" and dropped back upon the pillow, almost as if he were dead.

Doris sprang to him, while Rose found the restoratives that the nurse had brought for the journey, and Jean ran for the nurse, who was in the kitchen preparing some broth for the patient.

It was a long time before Ned rallied. He seemed to be stricken. And when he was at last asleep after taking a few spoonfuls of hot soup, the nurse went into the other room to find his sisters.

"What's happened?" she asked sharply. "Where's his wife?"

"She's *gone*," said Doris. "She came and told him she couldn't stay here, and if he wanted her he'd have to come after her!"

"Well, I say good riddance! She is a huzzy if there ever was one!"

"But it will kill Ned!" said Doris sadly.

"No!" said the nurse wisely. "It won't kill him. He'll come through. Folks don't die so easy, and he's got a good start now. It's hard on him, but it won't kill him. However—if it did, I'm not so sure but he might as well die one way as another. She's the limit, and if she stayed around I'm certain she would kill him with her carryings-on. He ain't had a minute's peace since she come. When she's out of his sight he frets for her and when she's in she's always nagging at him to get well and do things for her!"

So the home-coming was not a happy time, although both Rose and Doris felt the relief of having Zephyr gone.

Day succeeded day and still the elder brother lay listless, having to be forced to eat, urged to even answer a question.

"It's no use, I'm done for!" he said to Doris when she tried to rouse him. "What's the use of my getting well? I'm married and my wife has no use for me. I might as well die and be done with it!"

"That's foolish, Ned," urged Doris. "Have you ever thought that you could win her back again if you would get well and be your old self?"

Ned shook his head listlessly.

"It wouldn't work unless I had a lot of money."

"Make money, then!" said Doris. "You've got brains, and could get a good job. Why don't you try to get well quick and show her?"

"You don't understand, Doris, she's got an awful lot of fellows running after her. It just turns her head. She's fond of me, but they give her things and take her places, and she likes that sort of thing. I can't do it for her."

"What sort of a girl is it that will let other men take her to places without her husband?" asked Doris bitterly.

"She's only a kid, Doris. She's never had any bringing up. I'm crazy about her, Doris. I couldn't stand seeing her around other men like that, and I thought if I got her away she'd be all right."

"Oh, Ned!" said Doris, and dropped her face down on his thin white hand despairingly. "Poor child!"

When she looked up again there was a tear stealing weakly down the white cheek of the boy.

"Oh, I know, Doris!" he said bitterly. "I'm no good. I oughtn't 'ave done it, but I *did,* and what's the use?"

They sat quiet for a long time and then Doris said:

"Ned, if you'll brace up and try to get well, I'll find you a position somewhere and I'll help you to get a little home that Zephyr would like and you can try again."

It was still in the room for a long time, and finally Ned pressed her hand feebly.

"Thank you," he murmured. "You're a peach, Doris! You always were, and I'm not worth it. But I don't think it would be any use."

Nevertheless he seemed brighter the next day and took the food they brought him, finishing it all. The next time the doctor came he asked:

"Doc, when d'ya think I could go to work?"

The doctor eyed him grimly over his spectacles, and finally said: "Oh, about week after next, if you'll brace up and do as I say."

"Do you mean it, Doc?" There was a new spring to Ned's voice.

"Why, sure, boy! It's all up to you now."

The next day Ned sat up for an hour in the morning and two in the afternoon. The third day he was walking around, and the family began to take heart of hope. In a week he was doing little things about the house and Doris had a consultation with Mr. Hamilton who found a job in an office for him. This news brought new light into Ned's eyes. He was to begin work just as soon as the doctor gave permission.

That night Ned sat down and wrote a letter to Zephyr.

Meantime Doris had settled into her place with Angus Macdonald's mother, and there was no longer any question whether she was going to be able to carry out the young man's plan, for it was already a success.

Every two or three days Doris would receive some word from abroad, post-cards mostly, with just a greeting, and usually some little suggestion about her work. For instance:

"A picture of a garden I saw to-day. I have written Mother about it.

"Perhaps you and she will plant the bulbs together which I am sending."

Or:

"I found a charming book in this library this afternoon which I think you and Mother would enjoy. I bought a copy on my way back to the hotel and am mailing it to-night. Perhaps you will read it to her."

Every few days there came some little reminder that her employer was keeping the home in mind, and that he was most friendly to her. And yet it was all quite impersonal, and nothing was out of keeping with their relation to one another.

These friendly messages grew to be exceedingly pleasant to her, and life was becoming altogether cheerful once more. Ned seemed on the highroad to health. John was steady and faithful at his job. Jean liked the new community school. Rose had not yet complained of being out of the world. Florence seemed to be quite happy in the hospital as long as she was kept supplied with plenty of flowers and visitors. The new Bible studies were proving most fascinatingly interesting. A light was growing in Doris' eye and a spring in her step.

Then, one day, as Doris was reading to Mrs. Macdonald who had a slight headache, the maid brought up a card.

"Tamar Engadine," it read.

Mrs. Macdonald looked at it perplexed a moment and then handed it to Doris.

"I don't know who in the world she is," she said disinterestedly, "but would you mind going down and excusing me? My head is just beginning to quiet down, and I know if I get up and dress and talk to her it will just start up again. She is probably an agent of something, but tell her I don't want any. Or if it's a subscription she wants tell her to leave her literature and I'll mail a check if I see fit. Or, if she insists, she can call again. Would you mind?"

"Not at all," said Doris blithely, and laying down her book sped down the wide oaken staircase.

Tamar had not taken the seat the maid had motioned her to when she came in. Instead she stood in the doorway of the reception room in the glow of the late afternoon sun, tapping the polished floor impatiently with a tiny, patent-leather slipper and staring rather rudely, Doris thought, around the spacious hall and across to the luxurious living-room. It was as if she were appraising the articles, her eyes gloating over each one in turn.

It was summer, and she wore a costume of soft pink of a hue, newly from Paris. In its clinging outlines, scant of fold, it gave the effect of almost nakedness, until one looked closer and saw that it was buttoned closely almost up to the tip of the chin, and that the sleeves fitted down over the hands. She wore a little close hat which was set off by a sharp dark lock of deep reddish hair daringly venturing out over a cheek of matchless perfection. She turned and Doris saw that she was vividly beautiful with the charm that only travel and education and money could impart. There was make-up on her face, certainly, but put on with such skill, that while it startled with its unnatural hue, yet it could not be detected. She was like some super-being, Doris thought, not intended for common life, a work of consummate art—man's art, not God's—a wondrous fashion figure rare and graceful, but somehow not a human being like herself. And then, as the girl turned and looked her full in the face with a handsome insolent stare, Doris knew. This girl was another like her sister-in-law, Zephyr! Exactly the same type! Come of another walk of life, perhaps, but still the same. Classed in a social realm so far above the other that they would not walk the same world, 'tis true, but off the same stripe! A selfish, empty-headed, lovely piece of flesh like a will-o'-the-wisp, whose only function beyond pleasing herself was to lead men astray.

It is strange how a moral and spiritual portrait can come into vision in a flash at a first glimpse of some soulless being. Doris rebuked herself for hasty judgment and went forward graciously.

She had been long enough in the big house to have grown accustomed to its spaciousness and luxury. She moved among the rare and costly trifles of its furnishings as if they had been about her always, and now as she took command of the situation she was not embarrassed, she was just her simple natural self and might have been a daughter of the house, for all her manner.

This was no book agent, nor yet a collector for some charity, she could see that at a glance, yet she was on the defensive involuntarily.

"Mrs. Macdonald is not feeling well to-day," she said with simple dignity. "She is lying down and does not wish to be disturbed. She asked me to see you for her."

"Thank you. I don't care to see you," said the girl with a trill in her voice like the song of a bad angel. "I came here to see Mrs. Macdonald and I intend to see her. Just take my card up to her please, at once!"

The imperious tone was offensive. Doris stood looking at her and thinking she had been right at first. How like Zephyr, yet with cultured voice and graceful manner.

"Mrs. Macdonald had your card, Miss Engadine," said Doris.

"Oh!" said the girl wheeling and looking at her sharply. "And what did she say?"

"She—did not seem to remember you—" said Doris, softening the truth graciously.

The girl laughed, and again Doris was filled with that sense of soullessness in the laughter.

"Tell her it's about *her son* I want to see her! Then she'll remember me!"

Doris' heart stood still for an instant and then went forward in great slow thuds. She felt as if the color was draining out of her face. Yet she had no idea why. Then she sensed that here was something that belonged to her job. Here was a thing that Mrs. Macdonald needed to be protected from. Perhaps it was just things like this that her son had feared, and wanted a friend who loved her always at hand for a time of need. Instinctively she felt that there was something here that might hurt her old friend.

She drew herself up and looked the other girl in the eye pleasantly. She had failed somewhat in her first interview with Zephyr but it had taught her something. Besides, the other matter had come too close to home for her to be fairly self-controlled. But this was something that involved another. She could be bold.

"I'm sorry, Miss Engadine," she said pleasantly, "but I'm afraid you'll have to tell me about it. Mrs. Macdonald does not wish to be disturbed this afternoon. I shall be glad to serve you in any way I can."

"Who are you?" asked Tamar insolently. "Her secretary?"

"Oh, no," smiled Doris, "I'm Miss Dunbar."

"Oh. One of Angie's cousins?" pursued the visitor.

"No, just a friend of Mrs. Macdonald's. Won't you come and sit down? Perhaps you'll tell me who you are, and if there is anything I can do for you?"

Without realizing it Doris had put the tiniest bit of superiority into her voice, and it met with instant resentment. Tamar bowed to no one on this earth.

"I'm Angus Macdonald's fiancée," she said loftily, and again something struck hard across Doris' soul, and the sick feeling she had had when Ned told her he was married swept over her in a great wave.

But Doris had not been through months at the school of discipline for nothing. She had learned to rise to an occasion, and she had learned to keep her own feelings from sitting shamelessly on her face. She met Tamar's thrust without the flicker of an eyelash. She realized that it should be nothing to her if this girl was all to her employer. She had no right to care in the least.

"Yes?" she said with a pleasant upward inflection that really meant almost anything or nothing at all. She showed no surprise, no interest.

"*Now,* will you tell Mrs. Macdonald I wish to see her?"

Doris was considering.

"No," she said pleasantly, "I think not. If Mrs. Macdonald had known that you were engaged to her son she would have recognized your name at once. If she does not know it, this is no time to acquaint her with the fact. She is not well, as I told you. I should think it would be best for her son to give her the information first. I should think both he and she would prefer that. That, however, is of course none of my business. I am merely here to act for Mrs. Macdonald to-day. If there is anything that I can help you in I am at your service, but Mrs. Macdonald is not to be disturbed to-day."

Tamar studied her contemptuously, glanced up the broad stair as if she half meditated making a dash to obtain an audience by force, and then with a slight shrug of her silken shoulders said haughtily:

"Very well, then, give me Angus' address. I've lost my address book in which he wrote it, and I can't remember it. In fact I didn't look at it after he wrote it and I wish to communicate with him at once about a most important matter."

Now it happened that Angus Macdonald, the night he bade Doris adieu after he had stepped back from seeing her to the door, had turned toward her again and said:

"Oh, Miss Dunbar, by the way, you have my itinerary; kindly consider it confidential. There are reasons why I do not care to have everyone know just where I am going. Of course I don't suppose anyone will ask you, but they might, and if anyone does, just refer them to my office. It will save possible complications."

Doris had thought nothing of it at the time, but now it came back with puzzling reminder. Of course he probably did not mean this to apply to any of his real friends, and if this girl was his fiancée—? It was with sudden relief that she realized that she had no choice but to obey his request.

"I am afraid I can't do that," said Doris, "but you might telephone his office of course. They would be able to answer your questions I am sure."

Tamar eyed Doris keenly. She was not brainless if she was empty headed.

"Oh," she said contemptuously, "I can telephone Mrs. Macdonald of course. I thought it would be more considerate to come to her. But I'll hand it to you you certainly know your business, whatever position you hold in this household. I'm sure you earn your wages!"

With that fling Tamar Engadine went out to her car and rode away.

Doris went into the far end of the living-room, to the great bay window that looked down upon the road and the valley, and watched Tamar's flashy car go gliding down and disappear into the pine grove. She stood for some minutes looking out with startled eyes, as though she were arraigning herself. Then she went to the maid and gave direction that if anyone called Mrs. Macdonald on the telephone, she was to say she was not feeling well and ask for a message; and if they asked her for Mr. Angus' address she was to tell them to call the office.

She went back to her old friend, wondering how she was going to explain the caller. Perhaps after all Miss Engadine might come again when she was not there to protect her, and she ought to tell the whole truth. And yet, should she? That part about her being Angus' fiancée—Why should she have to announce a thing like that if the mother did not already know it? Surely it would be better for her to keep out of it entirely.

But the mother's voice broke into her thoughts.

"Well, who was it?" she asked, her voice almost sharp as if with a sudden anxiety. "Not an agent?"

"No," said Doris trying to make her voice sound disinterested, "just a young woman inquiring for your son's address. I thought you would not want to be bothered with it, and I referred her to his office. Was that right? Perhaps I should have come up and told you, but I had said you were lying down and could not be disturbed."

Mrs. Macdonald's eyes had a startled look.

"What sort of a person was she?"

Doris paused. Should she give her exact impression? No, for she felt instinctively it might worry the mother.

"About my age, I judge," said Doris, "slim, handsome, stylish. She had dark hair with the latest bob, and she came in a car which she drove herself. She really is extremely handsome!" she repeated again, feeling that perhaps she had not given the other girl full justice. "Strikingly so, I should say."

"Yes," said Mrs. Macdonald, "I think I know now who she must be. An acquaintance of my son's—that is—I think Angus would not— Oh, you did just right, dear, of course. Thank you so much for going down."

They finished the chapter they had been reading, and went over the outline of the Bible lesson for the next day, but Doris could see that her old friend was absent-minded, and her eyes far away as if she were troubled about something.

She slipped away as soon as she could, for somehow her own heart was ill at ease, and down in the pine grove she stopped her car for a few minutes and had it out with herself.

"Now, see here, Doris Dunbar, are you getting interested in the man you work for, like any common stenographer? A stranger too! You have only met him a couple of times. Wasn't it enough for you to be rescued from a loveless engagement, without getting into a mess like this? Get out from under and don't you dare think of that man again in any way but as your employer in whom you have no interest except for the salary he pays you. Now, go home and behave yourself. And be careful what kind of letters you write! You've got off the subject several times lately in your reports, and it's got to stop. A man that has friends like that Engadine creature isn't in your class at all, no matter how much you may think of his mother, so *look out!*"

26

THE summer drew on and the little house at Silver Ledge began to seem more like home. Rose settled into quite a little housekeeper, putting pretty touches in every room, and making it all most attractive. She even set to work to make her stepmother's room comfortable and pretty against the time when she should come back from the hospital. They did not hasten that time, feeling that Florence enjoyed the attention she got, and knowing that it could not but be trying to them all when she returned.

Jean had found a baby to care for one day a week, while its mother went to the city shopping, and was happy all day long, helping about the house, or wandering over the meadows picking daisies and weaving them into a chain and a crown for herself.

"Oh, Doris," she said, "isn't it good, with just us? Oh, why do we ever have to have Florence or that Zephyr thing again any more? Do we?"

And Doris would sigh and say:

"Oh, I don't know, dear. I am afraid so. Of course!"

Doris was not quite so light-hearted as she had been.

Rose noticed it and drew the puckers together on her white forehead trying to make it out.

"She can't be worrying over Milton Page," she said. "But there's no telling. I don't suppose he seems such a flat tire to her as he does to us."

Doris still loved her employment with Mrs. Macdonald. By this time they were fast friends, and it was an unspoken agreement between them that almost every day Doris spent about half the time in the big house on the hill. And most of the time now they devoted to Bible study. To Doris it was fast becoming the great absorbing interest of her life. Other things had failed her, but this seemed to come into the empty places and fill them and satisfy. She marvelled how it had been brought about. She looked back to the day that Mrs. Macdonald had proposed the study and saw how far she had come, and how the Book instead of being dull as she had expected, was now a never failing, constantly growing, source of delight.

And then one day she came upon the verse:

"He that believeth shall grow stronger and stronger," and she remembered Mrs. Macdonald's words about coming to the Book with a believing mind, and saw that it was true. She had been given the assurance and led on into a place where there was now no question of doubting. She *knew* it was all true. She had seen wondrous things in the law. Her eyes had been opened.

And then there began to be the thought of her dear ones, and the wish that they might know, too, the inevitable result of finding treasure one's self. Soon she began to wonder why the whole world was not eager to find what she had just discovered.

Ned had been working steadily every day since his recovery. He still had a white, hopeless look, but there was a growing line of determination around his mouth that Doris watched hopefully.

Zephyr had not been out to Silver Ledge again, and she had not answered Ned's letter. Doris knew that from Ned himself. He had taken to confiding in his sister again as he had been used to do before he met Zephyr, and Doris was tender with him in spite of her feeling about Zephyr. She knew that only Zephyr could take herself out of Ned's heart, or else heal his hurt by coming back and doing right. And for a long time that seemed a hopeless proposition.

But finally Ned told Doris one day that Zephyr had consented at last to come back to him if he would get a house that she liked and let her choose the furnishing.

By dint of much self-sacrifice on the part of both Doris and Ned, he was able at last to get together three hundred dollars wherewith to make the first payment on a tiny apartment, whose monthly payments were but twenty-five dollars, through a bewildering number of years, but whose showy appointments at last attracted the whimsical eye of Zephyr. She professed to be willing to come to Ned if he would buy that apartment and set her up in it away from his family.

So Ned brightened up and began to take heart of hope. He forthwith clothed Zephyr with all the virtues that his new standard of industry had desired to find in her and looked forward with almost feverish eagerness to the day when they could set up housekeeping together.

Doris sighed over him, but yet was relieved that his problem seemed to be near to the solving; though she trembled for him, for she had no faith in Zephyr.

About this time, too, Florence came home.

It had done Florence a lot of good to have a broken leg. She had had more attention than had been given her since Mr. Dunbar hastily wooed and married her, somewhat late in life. She had had flowers almost every day, and she had won many friends in the hospital. She was in her element when she could be pitied and petted and waited upon.

There had been another development also that both perplexed and somewhat annoyed Doris, and that was her stepmother's new devotion to herself. It seemed almost as if Mrs. Dunbar was afraid to let Doris go out of her sight, after she came home.

She bore the first glimpse of the new home better than was to have been expected. Doris had prepared her by many descriptions of the house, and really made it worse than it was, so there was nothing new for her to complain about and she settled quite peaceably into her room, even praised a pincushion that Jean had forgivingly made for her, and said she thought she could make some napkins out of some old tablecloths to fill a crying need for everyday table napery.

It developed during the first week of her return, that Mr. Hamilton had been the donor of many of the flowers she had received in the hospital and that he had frequently run in to see her. He now fell into the habit of running out to Silver Ledge every two or three days on one pretext or another. It certainly made a cheerfuller Florence and relieved the tenseness of the household to a large extent. The entire family were deeply grateful to him, and Florence began to go about the house with smiles, and now and then even a tremulous song upon her lips. She was not a singer, but even a twanging quaver with a flat note now and then is better than hysterics, as Rose remarked comically, and the children were getting quite reconciled to their stepmother.

And then one day Florence went to town and came back with her hair bobbed.

It wasn't so much that she had her hair cut off, for she hadn't a great deal of it to miss anyway, but it was that she got a regular boy bob, as near like Rose's as could be, only Rose's wave was natural and charming, and Florence's was thin and wiry and gray.

"Say! I think that's the limit!" said John after she had smilingly left the dinner table the first night to go to the door and let Hamilton in. "I don't see why you don't do something about it, Doris. It makes me sick to look at her."

"What would she do, John? We can't stick it on again," cut in Rose crabbily. "I think it's the limit the way everybody blames Doris for everything everybody else has done. She's just a pack horse for this family, as Milton Page said. John, go get a chair for her and make her rest. She looks worn to a frazzle. I'll tell you what I'm going to do about it, Brother. I'm going to let my hair *grow!*"

And then while they were talking about it in the dining-room, as they sat around Ned eating a late supper because he had been delayed by some extra work at the office, the door suddenly opened and Florence walked in, a pink spot in each cheek and her eyes shining like old stars.

"Doris," she said embarrassedly, "I thought I ought to tell you at once. Mr. Hamilton has asked me to marry him. Would you mind so very much if I said yes? Mr. Hamilton says he is lonely, and it would really give you more room here in case we went away. Although, Herbert"—she hesitated and blushed at the name— "Herbert says he is quite willing to live here in case you feel you cannot get along without me."

They stood about her speechless for an instant, scarcely knowing how to break the embarrassing silence after this astonishing announcement. Then little Jean jumped up and clapped her hands:

"Oh, Florence, I think that will be perfectly lovely!" she exclaimed joyfully. "Then you won't have to mind being our mother any more the way you did, because you *won't be,* will you? And we can be *real friends!*"

Florence looked at her youngest stepdaughter with a puzzled smile, unable to decide whether this was a congratulation or not, but concluded to take it for the best.

"Yes, dearie, and you can come down to visit me, and we will have cookies every time you come."

"Why, that will be wonderful, Florence!" smiled the little girl. "But isn't it funny that you seem more mothery now when you are stopping it than you ever did when you were!"

Doris hurried forward to prevent further compromising revelations, and put out a gracious hand.

"I'm glad, Florence!" she said heartily. "You deserve a good home. I know it's been hard for you here, and you will be much happier away. We shall get along all right, and as Jean says we'll enjoy coming down to see you often."

It was while the others were talking to their stepmother that Hamilton spoke to Doris aside:

"I thought maybe this might make it a little easier for you and the children, Miss Doris," he said, while Rose was going through a comical performance of giving her stepmother her blessing. "She's kind of restless and needs to be amused. And you know I've been a lonely old fellow since my mother died. She and I get along together famously."

Only John, of all the group of relieved children, stood scowling after the two when they finally went back to the living-room together.

"Aw, Gee!" he exclaimed. "Whaddee wanta marry a flat tire like Flarnce for? I thought he was a real good guy! I thought he had more brains!"

They were married quietly a few weeks later and went to live in a downtown apartment hotel, which maintained a splendid restaurant where they might take their meals whenever Florence did not feel like cooking. Hamilton said he meant to have his wife take things easy and have a good time. Florence was ecstatic.

But the night before the wedding the bride came to Doris' door weeping and asked her to come to her room a while, that she had something to tell her.

Doris went wondering and found her stepmother greatly agitated.

"I can't help it," she said excitedly. "Perhaps you'll put me in jail and spoil it all, but I can't go into this with anything on my conscience. I never was so happy in my life, but I can't take it and go thinking always it doesn't belong to me. Doris, I don't deserve to be happy. I stole your engagement ring! I pawned it! I never meant to steal it permanently. I thought it would only be gone about a week. And then I could redeem it and give it back to you. But that lawyer turned out to be a fraud and I found I wouldn't have a cent, and I was *almost crazy!*"

She buried her face in her hands and sobbed, and Doris with her arm around her tried to interrupt the excited flow of confession, but Florence would not be stopped.

"No, let me finish it all," she said, "I must tell the whole story before I lose my courage. I tried everything to get money when I found you were having trouble with Milton about that ring. I went to an agency and tried to get a job, and finally I went to Mr. Hamilton as a last resort, when I found how angry Milton was, and borrowed the money! But it was too late! They had sold the ring for more money than they asked me, and the man said he could not get it back. Then I went out and I thought I would drown myself I was so frightened, but I got run over instead and—and—you know the rest, Doris! You've been so good to me! And every day when you came to the hospital I thought I would confess before you left! And every night after I hadn't I lay awake and cried and prayed! I've been so ashamed and so frightened! And when I found Milton Page had broken off his engagement on that account I thought I *should die!* I saw how unhappy you were about it, and I felt like a murderer! Now, Doris, I'm willing you should tell him everything and get him back. I would rather have you happy and married to him, even if I have to go to jail for it! I really would! And I'll tell Herbert all about it too."

Doris sat down on the side of the bed beside her stepmother and drew her head upon her shoulder.

"Listen, Florence," she said gently as one soothes a little child, "Milton didn't break the engagement. I broke it myself. And I'm not unhappy. I don't want Milton back ever! As for the ring I got that back safely. You didn't steal it. Rose got it for me. I don't know how she did it, but she got it. Now don't worry any more. Milton doesn't need to know a thing about it. He has his ring safely back and he has gone away, and everything is all right. The broken engagement had nothing whatever to do with the ring. I found I didn't love him enough to marry him, that was all. Now wipe your eyes, and be happy, Florence, there isn't a thing in the world for you to worry about."

"But I've been mean to you all," sobbed Florence smiling through her tears. "I was always jealous of you—"

"Never mind," said Doris happily. "That's over now, and we've all forgotten it. It was hard for you too, I suppose, and we didn't understand each other. Let's just forget it."

It was about that time that Ned made his first payment on his apartment and moved in with some of the surplus furniture that could be spared, and some that Zephyr insisted on purchasing at an installment house, and the household at Silver Ledge dwindled to four.

Then the winter came on, and the early twilight and long evenings. Doris began to see a vista of lonely years ahead of her, when she let herself think about it at all. She missed Ned, dependent upon her as he had been. She felt desolate to think of him tied down to Zephyr. She could not help visualizing some of the things he would have to bear as the husband of a coarse, willful beauty without ballast or conscience.

The letters from abroad still came regularly, and Doris still sent in her reports of what Mrs. Macdonald and she were doing to fill the days, but now her letters had become brief and stilted, more formal and business-like than at first. Doris was winning back her self-respect that had been sadly shaken during her memorable talk with Tamar Engadine. She had not seen nor heard any more of that young woman, but she had not forgotten the lesson she had taught her, and Angus Macdonald in the intervals of his work, found himself vaguely disappointed from week to week as the American mail came in, and Doris' reports appeared promptly but somehow left him unsatisfied.

And once he wrote and asked her if she was getting tired of her job and wanted him to come home and relieve her? Or was the salary getting too small and was she not satisfied? And then the next week he sent a check of fifty dollars more, saying that his mother's letters showed that she was more than fulfilling her part of the contract and he wanted to somehow make acknowledgment of his satisfaction in the arrangement, and henceforth her checks would be three hundred and fifty. More and more his letters became friendly. He sometimes wrote several pages of description of a beautiful place he had visited, or a journey he had taken, or a rare book he had found in his browsings in the great libraries of Europe, for his reading was not all technical. And as often as Doris finished the reading of one of these letters she had much ado to keep her heart from bounding and her eyes from shining with pleasure at the friendliness of them. As she came to know him through his letters she grew more and more to respect him, and to find congenial points of interest between him and herself, and she often wondered how a girl like Tamar Engadine had ensnared him.

Of course, it had not escaped her perception that there was a possibility that the girl had not told the truth. She had looked like an unscrupulous girl. Yet even if it were true there might have been some quarrel between them which would explain why Miss Engadine did not have Macdonald's itinerary. However that may have been, Doris decided that it was probably all patched up between them by this time. Doubtless Macdonald had written her now, and she no longer needed to ask others for his address. Nevertheless Tamar served her as a salutary tonic to keep her from allowing her thoughts to stray into forbidden paths.

Not that Doris was a girl who was always looking for some prince to take an interest in her, but Macdonald was a man above most men, a friend whom any girl might desire to have, and Doris from the start had made it plain to herself that her relation was to be purely a business one and nothing more. There had never been a thought of anything else in her mind till the coming of a fiancée made her realize that there might have been danger in that way if she had not been warned in time.

The truth about Tamar Engadine was that she did call up Mrs. Macdonald late again that afternoon, after Doris had left the house, but the wise maid gave the message as Doris had told her, and Tamar was forced to betake herself to Angus Macdonald's office, where she met her equal in Macdonald's courteous but wise young secretary. The lady was told that Mr. Macdonald had left directions for all mail to be sent first to the office for redirection, as his itinerary was subject to constant change. Miss Engadine gained one startling truth, however! Angus Macdonald had gone to Europe for an indefinite stay and had not chosen either to see her or to tell her he was going. Angus Macdonald must be very angry indeed! And since visiting the Macdonald home Tamar decided that she would be most foolish to let a man of such wealth and attraction slip through her grasp. Suppose he did have some ridiculous puritanical ideas? What difference would they make after they were married? He couldn't help himself then.

So Tamar Engadine went home and announced her intention of going to Europe immediately.

Mrs. Macdonald had never asked Doris about herself. She had waited with true old-world courtesy for her to tell what she wished, and Doris had gone on from day to day, never mentioning her home or anything about her circumstances except that her father and mother were dead and she had young brothers and sisters.

It was therefore somewhat of a surprise to have the maid bring up a card late one morning bearing the name of Mrs. Edward Dunbar.

Mrs. Macdonald looked at the card a moment, told the maid she would come down, laid down a bit of knitting she had been at work on, gave a touch to her lovely silver hair and a brush to her pretty gray house-dress, and went down to meet Zephyr.

Certainly Zephyr was like nothing that she had ever seen before. She paused before the tall bold beauty and surveyed her, and Zephyr gave her the full benefit of her china blue-eyed baby stare.

Then she smiled, her dolly smile, as if someone had pulled the string that worked it, and Mrs. Macdonald stood soberly, with her cameo face and her old-world lady air, and looked at her questioningly.

"Are you Mrs. Macdonal'?" questioned Zephyr nonchalantly.

"I am Mrs. Macdonald," said the lady bringing out the syllables distinctly.

"Well, ya aren't so old as I thought you'd be, why I ast," giggled Zephyr. "My sister'n-law sent me. She wanted to know, could you please let her have this month's sal'ry 'n' advance. She's got a man come with a bill he won't wait for. He's settin' in the house now, so she didn't have th' nerve to leave. She said she knew you'd 'commodate her, an' she couldn't telephone ya 'cause the man would hear her, so I offered to come in her place."

Mrs. Macdonald looked at Zephyr steadily, a growing solemnity in her face. Her searching glance was keen and read many things in the vapidly pretty face before her.

"Sit down," said the lady. "Who did you say you were?"

"Oh, I can't siddown," said Zephyr manifesting by a furtive chew the presence of gum in her mouth that had been held in abeyance in her cheek. "I'm in an awful hurry. I gotta taxi down the road waiting for me. Why, I'm Ned's wife. I'm Mrs. Dunbar."

"I'm afraid I don't know you," said the lady. "Who is

this sister-in-law that you say is in my employ? I haven't any maid by the name of Dunbar."

"Oh, I don't guess you call her a maid," laughed Zephyr. "I don't know what she does. It's Doris I mean. She didn't give another name, did she? She comes here every day to work for you."

"Oh, you're quite mistaken," said Mrs. Macdonald almost haughtily. "Miss Doris Dunbar is merely my friend. She is not in my employ. I am not aware that she is working for anybody."

The rhythm of the lovely jaws paused, and Zephyr stared prettily:

"Gosh! Then she musta been putting it over on us all this time! She certainly told Ned she had a bigger salary now, fifty bucks more a month! Three hundred and fifty bucks a month. I said all the time I thought she had some salted down somewhere; and I'd bet anything she was just a tightwad and didn't wantta give us any more!"

Suddenly Zephyr looked up and there stood Doris, standing in the doorway!

27

"ZEPHYR! What are you doing here?"

Doris' voice was calm, cold, like a knife. How much she had heard of the conversation Zephyr could not be sure. Her airy manner suddenly left her and the sullen look came down upon her. She ignored Mrs. Macdonald as if she had not been there.

"Hello, Doris, thought you'd hang one on us, didn't ya?" she remarked contemptuously. "Ned an' I ain't so dumb as you think. I knew you had plenty of dough—"

Mrs. Macdonald arose suddenly.

"Perhaps you would like to be left alone together," she said with exquisite courtesy to Doris and glided out of the room.

"Zephyr, you may go out and get into my car," said Doris when she had gained sufficient control over her voice to speak. "I will take you home as soon as I have excused myself to Mrs. Macdonald. Go! Or I will call the butler to make you!"

Doris was not afraid of Zephyr though she was almost a head taller than herself and strong and athletic. She knew that the Macdonald force of servants were at her call. But she was ashamed. Somehow Zephyr amid these surroundings seemed more impossible than ever before, and she could not be sure how much she had said before she entered.

But Zephyr had no mind to linger:

"Oh, ya needn't trouble yerself. I gotta taxi of my own. I wouldn't ride in yer little tin can ef I hadta foot it all the way ta the city. But don't ya fool yerself. I'll get even with ya yet. You can't double cross me 'ithout payin' for it!"

Zephyr strode to the front door and went out and down the wide gravel drive with head up and a swagger. Her jaws had settled into the rhythm again. At least she was no worse off than when she came. But that three hundred and fifty bucks certainly would have made it easier to carry out her plans. She wondered if Rose were at home, and if there were any chance of finding anything hidden around the Silver Ledge house. It might be worth trying. She whistled softly and disappeared into the woods below the curve of the hill, and presently there was the sound of a motor far below on the drive.

Doris went slowly, solemnly up the stairs to Mrs. Macdonald's morning-room, where they usually worked together at this hour, and dropped into a chair with her face in her hands.

The old lady was not in the room but she entered almost immediately and came and laid her little warm rose-leaf hand on the girl's head softly.

"Don't feel so badly, dear," she said gently. "Tell me, who is she?"

"She is a terrible girl that my young brother was fool enough to marry!" said Doris, trying to keep her voice from shaking. "She is—*un-speakable!*"

"Poor boy!" said the lady thoughtfully. "Poor foolish boy!"

There was silence in the room for a moment while Doris tried to get her self-control. She felt weak as if she had been through a terrible physical strain. Mrs. Macdonald moved quietly over to her usual seat and took up her Bible and her glasses as if nothing had happened. "There is just one question I would like to ask, dear," she said, "and then we will put it aside if you like. Does my son pay you a salary for coming to see me?"

Doris felt cold chills creeping over her. Her throat seemed suddenly to be in the grip of a great hand. She saw her beautiful friendship disappearing into nothing. She saw the displeasure of her employer. But it could not be helped. She lifted honest eyes:

"Yes, Mrs. Macdonald, he does, but I long ago wished that I had never accepted it, for the friendship has been so beautiful to me that it seemed terrible to have had it marred by a business arrangement. I am afraid you will think that I have not been sincere. It would be harder than anything else for me to lose this wonderful friendship of yours. I would gladly continue without the salary if I may. I shall of course have to find something else to do, and it may take more of my time so that I cannot come so often, but I beg you will not lose confidence in me. It was not my wish to keep this matter from you. It was your son's arrangement."

The old lady smiled tenderly:

"I shall never lose my confidence in you, dear. I know you now, and love you. And I know that my son did this for my good. I knew of course long ago that it was utterly unlikely that a girl of your age and charm would voluntarily give as much time and interest to an old woman like me just for the sake of myself, although I value your devotion deeply, but I'll confess I am a bit disappointed and chagrined that the reason for your faithfulness which I had assigned turns out to be a fancy of my own. I had hoped, you see, that you were doing it if not exactly for love of me, yet for love of my son Angus."

Doris' cheeks grew suddenly rosy and she dropped her eyes, then lifted them again quickly, a warm glow still in her face.

"I shall always love you and come to see you as often as you will let me," she said. "But there is to be no more salary for it after this month. I shall write your son to-night that you know, and that now I can come to you as a friend without salary and shall get a job with hours that will also give me time for you."

"You precious child!" smiled the old lady, stooping to kiss the smooth rosy cheek. "We'll see about that later. Meantime, hadn't we better be getting the Bibles and pencils out? It's almost time for Mrs. Brooke to come, and the people will be here presently."

Rose Dunbar had been making fudge and salted almonds and other fancy bonbons for a large concern in the city. Every day for weeks as soon as Doris was out of the house and Jean was off to school she had hurried around the kitchen preparing her materials, and making up a great batch of candies. By afternoon she had a stock ready, as much as she could safely carry at a time, laid carefully in boxes among wax paper, and packed in two big suit-cases. She took the trolley to town, disposed of her wares at a pitifully small profit and hurried back again to get dinner before Doris and the children got home.

Slowly the sum in her jewel box in her bottom bureau drawer was increasing, although it seemed to her it would never reach two hundred and fifty dollars. She was hindered a good deal in her secret plans while Florence was at home before she was married, for Florence was always popping into the kitchen and asking what she was doing, so that twice she had had to give up some of her precious fudge to the family to keep her stepmother from suspecting what she was doing, and for a time, before she got to going out so much she had to give up making anything that would have an odor, unless she also cooked onions or burned some gingerbread to cover up the smell.

But since Florence was married, Jean in long sessions at school and Doris away every afternoon to Bible classes, she had made wonderful strides, and her hoard was mounting up rapidly.

On the day that Zephyr visited Mrs. Macdonald, Rose had found that she lacked only seven dollars of the amount she needed to repay her debt to Colonel Carruthers.

She worked hard and made an unusual amount of candy and sweetmeats, adding some stuffed dates to her regular products, and by five minutes of two she was packed and ready waiting for the two o'clock car, her heart beating high with hope that now soon she would be free from that hateful debt that bound her to accept the unpleasant attentions of a man she had grown both to hate and fear, and yet had not dared to rebuff.

Five minutes after the car stopped and took Rose and her suit-cases, a taxi drew up at the door of the Dunbar house. Zephyr got out and pried around until she found a window unfastened through which she climbed.

Half an hour later Zephyr came out holding a package wrapped in newspaper, got into the taxi and drove away again.

At five o'clock Rose alighted from the car, hurried into the house and went to put her money away in the jewel case. It was gone! Case and all! She looked all over the house, thinking she must have carried it out of her room and forgotten it, but it was hopelessly gone. Rose was in despair. While she was in the city she had telephoned Colonel Carruthers that she would meet him and pay him the money that evening. Now he would be at their regular rendezvous and would be very angry if she did not come. Yet she was afraid to go empty-handed lest he would compel her to ride with him. The last time he had taken her to ride they had gone to a road-house and she did not like the way he acted. The place was frequented by a vulgar class of people. Rose, though she knew very little of the world, and was not as sophisticated as she would have others believe, still had an instinctive dread of the man and his ways.

She had been only three times to ride with him since the incident of borrowing the money to redeem the ring, yet each time she had been more alarmed than before, and more resolved not to go with him again.

The rendezvous was down the road half a mile beyond Silver Ledge, at the entrance of a pine woods. Rose's plan had been to profess to be going to bed early with a headache and then to steal out the back door and into the woods. It was going to be hard, but she had thought she could manage it. But now, suddenly it seemed a terrible thing to do, without the money to produce when she got there. With tears streaming down her cheeks she caught up the telephone and called Carruthers' numbers. There was a chance that he might still be there.

He was.

In a distressed voice she explained to him that her money had been taken from its hiding place and she would be unable to give it to him that evening. She would perhaps find it to-morrow and would then bring it in to the city to his office.

But Colonel Carruthers gaily waved her plans aside.

He said if she would go to dinner with him that night she need not pay the money ever, if she didn't like. That he had a special reason for wanting her with him that night. That someone else who had promised to accompany him had been taken sick and he was left without a companion at this dinner with some very nice people and he asked it as a special favor. He said he would start at once and be at her house in half an hour. He put it in such a way, with subtle reminders of her obligation to him, that Rose in her simplicity dared not decline, and while she lingered and tried to think of a sufficient excuse he said: "I'll be with you in thirty minutes, my dear!" and hung up the receiver. The "my dear" lingered hatefully in the atmosphere and turned her sick as she hurried into her room and changed her dress to be ready when he should come. She kept looking fearfully from the window lest Jean would be coming sooner than she expected, though the neighbor whose baby she tended did not usually get home till five minutes of six. And what if Doris should come sooner than usual! What should she do?

But Doris did not come, and Jean was safe at the neighbor's and the early dusk came down and hid the great high-powered car as it drove up at the door. Rose had barely time to scribble a note to Doris.

> *I may be late to-night, but don't worry. I'm all right. Tell you about it when I get back.*
>
> *Rose.*

Then she hurried out and was swallowed up in the night beside the tall man who drove her swiftly and silently off into the darkness.

28

ANGUS MACDONALD was coming home. He tele-
graphed one morning to his cousin Duncan Macdonald
who had been planning for sometime to accompany him
back to the States, that he was leaving the next day for
New York and if he wanted to go he had better pack up
and start at once.

Duncan was younger than Angus, a young Edinburgh
University graduate with a burr still upon his tongue,
and the crisp of the heather in his voice. He was long
and lean and blue of eye, with curly hair and hands that
could strangle a bear if he chose, and handsome withal,
for a Scot. He had as they say "a way wi' him" and now
he was coming to visit his aunt and cousin, and see if he
wanted to leave the crags and moors of his native land.

It was somewhere on the mountain, near Cragsmoor,
the Macdonald home, that they heard the scream, and
Angus reached out and gripped the driver by the shoulder.

"Stop man! Listen!"

And then it came again, a piercing frightened scream!
Angus thought of Doris at once. He wondered how he
had thought any woman could drive a car in such a

lonely road at night? How had he dared suggest that she ever stay late with his mother? But Duncan was out of the car before it stopped and off through the woods out of sight.

Angus, after vainly dashing about in this direction and that, went back to the taxi and ordered the man to drive on to the house and send the servant down with lights and his own car. Then he listened and tramped about. Off in the distance he could hear sounds, a crackling of branches, heavy footsteps, something like a falling body, and then all was quiet.

The servants were so long in coming that Angus on a dead run strode up the winding path and was at the house before they fairly had his car ready to start.

His mother was at the door and he took her in his arms for one quick embrace, then held her off and asked anxiously, "Where is Doris, mother? When did she leave the house?"

"Why about five o'clock," she answered, a sudden light coming into her eyes at the name he had called the girl. "Why, my dear? You don't think? Oh, my son! Go quickly! But wait! We can telephone!"

But he did not hear her. He had jumped into his car and was off around the drive and whirling past the astonished taxi driver down into the dark of the woods.

Mrs. Macdonald went at once to the telephone, but could get no answer at first and then a childish voice came excitedly, as if the little girl had been crying:

"No, she isn't here. No, I don't think she has got back yet. I just came in and found a note from Rose. She isn't here either. John is late too. He had to stay at the store to-night for band practice. I'm all alone."

Mrs. Macdonald hung up the telephone, after telling the child to call her up as soon as Doris returned, and went and sat down weakly. It seemed to her that her strength was gone out with her son hunting for the girl she loved as dearly as if she had been her own daughter.

Angus Macdonald went tearing down the mountain without regard to anything but getting on and did not stop his high speed until he whirled down the road in sight of the Dunbar house with its one little light which Jean had set in the window. And then, suddenly he saw a slender little figure standing in the road, with a white hand on her heart, as if she were frightened, stepping aside to let him pass, peering at him to see if he were alone.

He recognized her outline through the dusk and stopped so suddenly that it almost threw him off his seat,—and he was out beside her.

"Doris, is this you? You are not hurt? Oh, my dear child! I thought it was you!" And suddenly his arms closed around her, and Doris, wondering, frightened, yet knowing her own when it came to her like that, yielded herself to his arms, crying softly:

"Oh, Angus! Is it you?"

And then his lips found hers.

"I love you! I love you!" he breathed softly between the kisses. "I ought not to have been so abrupt about it, Doris, but I think I've loved you ever since I first saw you. Can you ever love me?"

And Doris suddenly struggling back to propriety laughed and surrendered again, and signified she could.

They came to themselves presently and Doris said, "Oh, I forgot, Rose is lost! I'm worried sick. I don't know what to do!"

"Rose? And who is Rose," said the tall man with a protecting arm about her.

"My sister, Rose. She is only seventeen and such a pretty little girl. I'm so frightened!"

"We'll find her!" said Angus reassuringly, his heart

suddenly sinking at the memory of that scream upon the mountain. "How long ago did she go out? Come, we'll get into the car!"

"But my little sister is all alone at home!" cried Doris. "Oh, I don't know what to do."

"We'll go back and get her, and telephone for help. I've a cousin—must be at the house by this time, and we'll go out and scour the mountain—"

But suddenly two long bright lights shot down the road, illuminating the spot where they stood, a car dashed past them and stopped as suddenly before the Dunbar house.

Duncan Macdonald had made straight for the scream when he disappeared into the woods, and he made short work of hauling a big handsome man from a car that stood on a mountain trail with dimmed lights. Then he turned to find that the girl had fled.

He gave a twist and a thud to the gentleman on the ground that he knew would keep him safely asleep for a few minutes and followed the girl who fled like a deer ahead of him. A fallen tree brought her down in a minute and she lay like a broken lily almost at his feet. He had to catch hold of a tree not to step on her, and he picked her up and strode back to the car, put her in it, with gentle hand, jumped in and backed the car cautiously out and down the trail. He wouldn't have been a Macdonald if he couldn't have handled any strange bit of machinery well after a try or two. In a trice they were down in the open road.

Then he turned his attention to the girl, and found she was more frightened than hurt. He turned on the lights and she looked in his face and he in hers.

"Bless my soul!" he exclaimed with the pleasant Scotch burr on his tongue. "You're a beauty and sure! You've a face like a flower. Findings is keepings. Where do you live? We'll go home and ask your folks may I have you? I hope you don't love any other lad."

For Duncan Macdonald had the dare of his ancestors, who fought for a lady, and he believed in going boldly after what he wanted.

Rose stared, and smiled for she saw he was half in fun, and then she was not afraid any longer. She told him the way to go and she added:

"Oh, go quick, please! He'll be very angry, and I don't want to ever see his face again! I hate him!"

"Don't worry," said the Scotch giant, "he'll not be coming this path very soon, I'm thinking, and when he does he'll foot it for we've got his car."

"Oh, how will you get it back?" wailed Rose. "They'll arrest you!"

"Let them arrest!" roared the Scot. "There'll be more than one arrested then, I'm thinking. Now, tell me about it."

She told him. Briefly, but clearly. She told him in a word or two of her long bondage under a small debt, and her loss at the moment when she thought she had reached the end. And then she told him of the creature who had insisted that she take this ride—this one more ride—and he would never trouble her again.

And by the time she reached this point Rose was crying softly against Duncan Macdonald's coat sleeve, and he reached around and held her within his arm as he drove along through the night. And the queerness of it all was that Rose Dunbar never realized there was anything strange about it at all for her to be comforted so, because she seemed to have known Duncan Macdonald all her life.

"He'll never trouble you again, I'm thinking," said Duncan in his nicest roar. "If he tries I'll take him out on the mountain and wallop him so he'll never see out of his two eyes again. Now is this the house? And who is this getting out of another car? Blest if it isn't my cousin Angus with his arm around another girl. Were there two of you? And which have I got? Just so it's you, for I never saw another one I wanted, and it's me for the States till I can take you back with me, so you better be resigned."

Late that night or rather early in the morning, when the children were in bed and asleep, and the two cousins had been persuaded to go home up the mountain to their bed and the mother who was waiting, Rose and Doris sat down and looked at one another smiling:

"Well," said Rose, "you look as if you had seen a great light. I guess you don't belong to Job's family any longer."

"I have!" said Doris with shining eyes. "And I've found out that all Job's troubles were just to try him out for the blessings that were to come. And oh, Rose! It's going to be so wonderful! He wants you all to come and live with them up there in that beautiful home, with his precious mother! I love her as if she were my own."

"That's very nice!" mused Rose with pink cheeks flushing pinker. "But," with a toss of the long, dark lock over her eyes, "I may go to Scotland myself,—for a while—although I think we'll come back—eventually."

About the Author

Grace Livingston Hill is well known as one of the most prolific writers of romantic fiction. Her personal life was fraught with joys and sorrows not unlike those experienced by many of her fictional heroines.

Born in Wellsville, New York, Grace nearly died during the first hours of life. But her loving parents and friends turned to God in prayer. She survived miraculously, thus her thankful father named her Grace.

Grace was always close to her father, a Presbyterian minister, and her mother, a published writer. It was from them that she learned the art of storytelling. When Grace was twelve, a close aunt surprised her with a hardbound, illustrated copy of one of Grace's stories. This was the beginning of Grace's journey into being a published author.

In 1892 Grace married Fred Hill, a young minister, and they soon had two lovely young daughters. Then came 1901, a difficult year for Grace—the year when, within months of each other, both her father and husband died. Suddenly Grace had to find a new place to live (her home was owned by the church where her husband had been pastor). It was a struggle for Grace to raise her young daughters alone, but through everything she kept writing. In 1902 she produced *The Angel of His Presence, The Story of a Whim,* and *An Unwilling Guest.* In 1903 her two books *According to the Pattern* and *Because of Stephen* were published.

It wasn't long before Grace was a well-known author, but she wanted to go beyond just entertaining her readers. She soon included the message of God's salvation through Jesus Christ in each of her books. For Grace, the most important thing she did was not write books but share the message of salvation, a message she felt God wanted her to share through the abilities he had given her.

In all, Grace Livingston Hill wrote more than one hundred books, all of which have sold thousands of copies and have touched the lives of readers around the world with their message of "enduring love" and the true way to lasting happiness: a relationship with God through his Son, Jesus Christ.

In an interview shortly before her death, Grace's devotion to her Lord still shone clear. She commented that whatever she had accomplished had been God's doing. She was only his servant, one who had tried to follow his teaching in all her thoughts and writing.

Don't miss these Grace Livingston Hill
romance novels!

You can find Tyndale books at fine bookstores everywhere. If you are unable to find these titles at your local bookstore, you may write for ordering information to:

Tyndale House Publishers
Tyndale Family Products Dept.
Box 448
Wheaton, IL 60189